'Romance, danger and an intriguing legacy – an ideal holiday read'
The Lady

'Moving, gripping, heartbreaking'
Kate Williams

'Secrets and lies in a gorgeous and idyllic setting'
Prima

'Great characters, gorge house, intriguing mystery, what's not to love?!'
Lucy Diamond

Readers love
Harriet Evans

'Perfect escapism'
Sunday Mirror

'As beautiful as a butterfly wing'
Veronica Henry

'Gorgeous'
Stylist

'Exquisite and captivating family drama' Heat

'Reminiscent of Santa Montefiore with the emotional heart of Jojo Moyes. You'll frequently find yourself uttering the words: just one more page'
CultureFly

The
Wildflowers

Harriet Evans

Typeset in Garamond by Palimpsest Book Production Limited,
Falkirk, Stirlingshire

Printed and bound in Great Britain by Clays Ltd, St Ives plc

Headline's policy is to use papers that are natural, renewable and recyclable
products and made from wood grown in sustainable forests. The logging
and manufacturing processes are expected to conform to the environmental
regulations of the country of origin.

HEADLINE PUBLISHING GROUP
An Hachette UK Company

H
REVIEW

First published in Great Britain in 2018 by
HEADLINE REVIEW
An imprint of HEADLINE PUBLISHING GROUP

First published in paperback in 2018 by
HEADLINE REVIEW

1

Cataloguing in Publication Data is available from the British Library

ISBN 978 1 4722 2127 7 (B format)

Ty

P

Headline   yclable
products   ing and
manufa   ental

All Hachette UK Company
Carmelite House
50 Victoria Embankment
London EC4Y 0DZ

www.headline.co.uk
www.hachette.co.uk

For Caloo
'We're all right, Jack'

The split personality of a man who has had to overcome one powerful part of his nature in order to achieve a certain position in the world . . . I remember you saying about Brenda de B. that she 'tries to cry' on stage, whereas in real life one tries to stop crying.

Letter from Joan Plowright to Laurence Olivier
before his first performance as Othello, 1964

Golden lads and girls all must,
As chimney sweepers, come to dust.

William Shakespeare, *Cymbeline*

Prologue

I

Dorset, August 2014

The abandoned house covered in bindweed and brambles didn't look like anything much, when first glimpsed from the lane.

But after the two men had struggled through the tangled mass of wild flowers and creepers surrounding the house they came upon a porch. The steps up were blackened with rot; on the porch itself rested a long-abandoned cane chair, bleached silver-grey by the wind and the sea and chained to the decaying floorboards by the tendrils of a pink-and-sage Virginia creeper. Below came the shingling slap of gentle waves and when you turned towards the sound of the sea there was Worth Bay, curving away from you, cream-yellow sands, turquoise water, chalk-white rocks in the distance.

Dave Nichols, trainee agent at Mayhew & Fine, watched in irritation as Frank Mayhew paused on the sandy path, fiddling in his pocket for the key. It was a boiling hot day, the sun beating down remorselessly. A mother and a young girl in swimming costumes, carrying towels, passed by on their way to the beach, looking at them with curiosity. Dave felt stupid, standing there in his smartest suit in front of this rotten old building.

'I don't understand,' he said sulkily, 'why we have to value it when the old girl's not going to sell.'

Frank tutted in disapproval. 'Old girl! That's Lady Wilde to you, Dave, and she's not long for this world – have some respect. Listen. In a few months when she's gone, the family'll most likely want to sell. They don't care about the place, that's obvious. That's where we come in, see?' He turned to take in the glorious view of the bay, then glanced at his slouched, sullen trainee, the son of an old golfing buddy, and sighed very gently. 'If we play our cards right, we'll be the agents to handle the sale. Houses on Worth Bay don't come up often. There's only ten or so of 'em. The Bosky – it's prime beach-front property, this place.'

Dave shrugged. 'It's a wreck,' he said, staring at the bindweed, the algae-coated windows. 'Look at these floorboards! Rotten through, I shouldn't wonder.'

'Most buyers don't care. They'll just level it and start over again.' Frank pulled the bindweed and dead roses away, then inserted the key, pushing against the peeling door with difficulty. 'Makes me sad, seeing it like this, if I'm honest. How it must be for Lady Wilde, stuck in that old people's home up the road, looking out over it all day, I've no idea. Bugger me, this is jammed fast. Come on, you—' He threw his rotund form against the frame. Nothing happened. Frank stepped back and to the side, looking through one of the shuttered windows. 'Hmm . . .' he said, bouncing on his heels, and then suddenly he gave a loud, outraged yelp.

Dave, who'd been staring at the view, turned in alarm: Frank had sunk a foot or so into the ground, the wooden boards simply melting away, as though they were made of butter.

Trying not to laugh, he lent Frank his arm as the older man pulled himself out of the hole, with some difficulty.

'I'll explain that to Lady Wilde myself.' Frank smoothed down his ruffled hair. 'Now, you give me a hand. It'll come open with a bit of extra oomph. That's it—' Together they fell against the door: it gave way with an aching crack, and the two men tumbled inside.

As the warm, musty smell of the dark house tickled their

2

A Place for Us

Harriet Evans

Welcome to Winterfold, a home built on love and lies

'An unputdownable thrill of a novel . . . *****' *Heat*

'An emotionally intelligent, thoughtful and engaging read' *Daily Mail*

*

Available now in paperback and ebook

The
Butterfly
Summer

Harriet Evans

Locked inside the crumbling elegance of Keepsake's walls
lies the story of the Butterfly Summer, a story you've
been waiting all your life to hear.

'An epic, sweeping, romantic story told brilliantly . . . I could
practically feel the butterflies brushing against my cheeks . . .
Heart-stopping and wonderful' Sophie Kinsella

'Wonderful' *Woman & Home*

*

Available now in paperback and ebook

noses Frank turned on his torch, shining it around the hall. He pulled the yellowing tendril of some dead plant from the ceiling.

'Well,' he said quietly. 'Here we are.'

Dave sniffed the musty air. 'Perfume. I can smell perfume.'

'Don't be daft,' Frank said, but he shivered. This was air that no one else had breathed for years; it felt heavy with something.

There was a cloakroom to his immediate left, and stairs in front of him, down to the bedrooms below. Off to the right was the kitchen, and to the left was the sitting room which had French windows leading back on to the porch.

'Let's open these,' said Frank, going into the kitchen, flicking back the faded sand-coloured curtains, the original colour now long forgotten. In the corner of the room, a window seat padded with faded yellow-and-grey patterned fabric and dotted with a decade's worth of dead flies and wasps faced the porch. The galley kitchen was at the back, the windows looking out over the lane.

There was nothing on the surfaces or shelves, no sign of occupation.

Frank flicked a switch a couple of times. 'No, not a thing.' He sniffed. 'I can smell something too. Scent, or flowers, or something.' He shook himself. 'Right. Let's open some windows. Get some fresh air and light in and we can go downstairs and measure up the bedrooms.'

But the window frames were too swollen with damp to open and after struggling for a minute they both gave up and went back into the hall.

Dave said, 'The bedrooms are downstairs?'

'It's an upside-down house. All your living rooms are up here overlooking the sea. Bedrooms are for sleeping in, doesn't matter what you're looking at.' Frank ran his hand along the bannister.

'It's a good idea. I used to dream of having a place like this when I was a lad.'

Dave stared at him, quizzically. 'You knew them?'

'Everyone knew them,' Frank said. 'They was quite something, the Wildes.' He moved his torch up on to the wood-panelled wall and both men jumped, as a face leaped out at them. Frank recovered himself first. 'It's just a photo,' he said, slightly shakily.

The picture on the wall gleamed in the darkness. A middle-aged woman with a floppy hat and large nose, smiling broadly, holding a dangling crab between her forefinger and thumb.

'She looks like a witch,' Dave said.

The torch juddered suddenly in Frank's hand, lighting up a pair of faces.

'Who are they? What – what on earth is all that?' said Dave, eventually.

Frank moved the torch along, and slowly the walls were illuminated with more faces, staring out from frames. Faces laughing, gurning, smiling politely, groups clinking glasses together, children dancing – more faces, some in colour, most in black-and-white. There were theatre posters too, and newspaper cuttings.

'That's them,' said Frank, gesturing. 'Weren't they quite something?'

Dave peered at the photo next to him. A beautiful Titian-haired woman sat with two girls on her knee, one blonde, the other dark. A group of adults reclined on the porch, glasses and cigarettes in hand. A grinning pair of young children danced on a beach: a boy and girl. More groups of smiling people. The man and woman were in the newspaper articles too, always elegantly dressed. In one they were holding hands and laughing, and she was turning slightly towards a knot of onlookers, waving with the other hand. Dave scanned the photos, sliding the torch along, plunging one, then another photo into white light and then darkness, searching for her. He stared at her, transfixed. She was the most beautiful woman he'd ever seen.

'"Anthony Wilde and his wife Althea arrive at the Royal Court for the First Night of *Macbeth*",' Dave read with difficulty, holding his phone up to the text. '"Curtain call went on for ten minutes as ecstatic crowd gave Mr Wilde a standing ovation." OK then.' He turned back as Frank reached into his briefcase. 'Who the hell are they?'

'I can't believe you've never heard of Anthony Wilde,' said Frank, pointing his laser measure at the walls. 'Two point four metres. Greatest actor of his day. And that's Althea Wilde, his wife. You must have heard of her. She was in *Hartman Hall*. Lady Isabella?'

Dave shook his head. 'Nope.'

'Lordy, Lordy. How can you not know *Hartman Hall*? Bigger than *Downton*, better 'n' all.' Frank sighed. 'What about *On the Edge*? That sitcom about the older lady, talking into her mirror? That was her, too.'

'Might ring a bell, maybe.' Dave looked at her again, the long neck, the slightly too-large nose, the liquid green eyes flecked with hazel. She was staring at him, only him, in the gloom of the house. He turned his torch away from her. He didn't like it, suddenly.

'They were known as the Wildflowers, the lot of them. Spent every summer here. Oh, the people they used to have staying. The glamour of it! You'd walk past on your way back from the beach and you'd see them above you, gramophone on, drinking cocktails, women in these beautiful dresses, and their kids running up and down the steps – a boy and a girl, bit younger than I was . . .' Frank's eyes grew misty. 'What a life. I'd watch them playing, on my way back home from the beach . . . Dad'd be yelling at Mum, she'd be head down trying to pretend she weren't with him, both of them after a bottle or two too much of ale and the sun . . . And I'd think, what I wouldn't give to be up there.'

He scratched his chin with one finger. 'They lived in some huge house by the river in London, too, 'cause she liked being by water, that's what I heard. He'd do anything for her. Anything. And those kids, bloody hell. Lucky isn't the word, every summer down here, and he was the best father, Sir Tony, he really was, always fun and games . . .' Frank shrugged, and then said pettishly, 'Take your hands out your pockets. Come on, you. You do the bedrooms off to the left, I'll do the rest. Show me you know how to use that laser measure.'

Reluctantly, Dave followed Frank into the downstairs gloom. He measured the bedrooms and bathroom as fast as he could, all the while listening to the wind whistling around the outside of the house. Inside, it was muffled, warm, deadeningly quiet.

'What happened to them?' Dave asked his boss, as they were climbing back up the stairs. 'Why don't they come any more?'

Frank smoothed his ruffled hair across his pate, then fiddled with his wristwatch, as though readying himself for outside again. 'Something happened. 'Bout twenty years ago.'

'What?'

'I wasn't ever sure. A family bust-up. The daughter's a famous singer. Was, I should say. Cordelia Wilde. The son's a big director, he did them *Robot Master* films.'

For the first time Dave was impressed. 'No way! I love *Robot Master*.'

'Well, that's him. Ben Wilde. He was married . . . I don't know what happened to her.' Frank screwed up his eyes, and jotted down some figures into a little notebook. 'Anyway his sister, the singer, she don't speak to them any more. Nice kid she was, mad as a hatter but I liked her. Then Sir Anthony, he died, and after a couple of summers Lady Wilde sent someone down to clear the place out. The big house up the lane, that used to be a holiday home too, strange family as lived there. They converted it into an old people's home and she moved in. She never came again. No one does now.'

The gloom was oppressive after a while. That, and the sense that those faces on the walls in darkness were watching you, wanting the lights on so they could come alive again, to go back to living their golden summers. Dave shivered as Frank stepped carefully over the hole in the porch by the front door. He followed him, breathing in heavily.

'Fresh air,' Dave said, pulling out his phone. 'Thank God. Look, reception again.'

'It's just a bit musty. I've seen worse.' He pulled the door shut, and there was a loud clang as an object fell from the lintel above the front door, down into the hole, and hit something.

'Oh, dear.' Frank bent to pick it up, reaching in between the cracked boards. He pulled out a stone angel on a rusting hook. She had vast, spreading wings, bare breasts, huge eyes, an enigmatic smile. She stared up at him. In one hand she held a pine cone, in the other a small, unblinking owl.

'What's that?' said Dave.

'Welcome angel or something,' said Frank, gazing at the little square panel. 'Yep, that's it. The old girl who lived here before was an archaeologist.'

'What old girl?'

'The one in the floppy hat. She's his aunt. Lived here with Sir Anthony during the war. Dad remembered her, right crackers she was. Now . . .' He scratched his chin, holding the panel in his hand. 'Can't remember her name. But I remember this from when I was a lad, remember it hanging here.'

'Shouldn't it be in a museum?' said Dave. He didn't like the way the huge eyes with their uneven pupils gazed balefully at him.

'Don't be stupid.' Frank looked at it doubtfully. 'It's not real. Course not. I'll give it to Lady Wilde.' He peered into the hole again. 'There's something down there, under the porch.' Squatting with difficulty, he pulled out a tin. 'What's this, I wonder.'

It was a metal tin, so rusted away in places that it fell open easily. Inside was a square of black plastic sheeting, and inside that – Frank tugged at the strips of tape that bound it up, and then he pulled out a thick, battered book the same shape as an exercise book, with a piece of elastic over the front making it into a folder. *The Children's Book of British Wild Flowers*, it said. Someone had added an *e* after *Wild*.

'What the hell's all *that*?' said Dave.

But Frank shook his head, after staring at it for a moment, and said repressively, 'I don't know, my boy. I don't know, and I don't want to know. I'll pass it all on to Lady Wilde.' He wrapped the angel in a handkerchief, shaking his head. 'Sad. Makes me sad,' Dave heard him mutter.

As Frank slid the angel and the tin into his satchel, Dave exhaled.

'Tell you what, I don't care who they were. I got a bad feeling, being in there.'

'Like I say,' said Frank, casting one last look back at the wooden house as they descended the rickety steps, 'it wasn't like that, once.'

II

Dorset, July 1975

The Children's Book of British Wilde Flowers

Sunday, 9.15 p.m.

I have done something bad.

*The Wildflowers left the book out on the porch last year when they
went. It's a book for children. It has pictures in it of the wild flowers
you get in the countryside. And an elastic thread with a wallet inside it
and another exercise book. For drawing in. Cord has drawn in it. Then
you put the elastic round to keep the whole book shut.*

*I stole it. I am good at writing, they told me I am at school. I will write
in it things that I have Noticed about the whole family. It will be useful.*

*There is a loose floorboard on the porch of the Bosky. I found it
yesterday before they arrived. I will leave the book in a tin there at the
end of summer. I will make the tin secure so that water cannot get in. I
will wrap it in plastic sheeting & put the board back. I will go away
& they will go away & it will be safe there, all year. Then I can write
what I've Noticed about them next year.*

*They have been here a week, Althea & the 2 children. He came last
night, just for a night, he is in a play. I watched them arrive and I have
been watching them all week, last night I watched most of the night. I
don't have anything else to do.*

My stomach hurts all the time. I tried eating grass. It's disgusting but perhaps that's because a dog peed on it. I will try blackberries again only they make it hurt more. But Daddy's not back till tomorrow & I'm too scared of the ghost in the kitchen to go in there and the food is in there. I miss Aunt Jules in summer, I miss her so much it hurts my stomach even more. That's why I like thinking about other things to not think about being on my own & the ghost making noises & being hungry.

<u>Cordelia</u>: new Osh Kosh dungarees, pale orange-pink stripes. She had blue stripes last year. An apple-green T-shirt, canvas T-bar shoes, same as last year. She doesn't remember me. I want to say, I remember playing with you on the beach two years ago, don't you? She's very loud. They call her Cord.

<u>Benedick</u>: red & yellow striped towelling T-shirt, blue cotton shorts to the knee, rubber-soled plimsolls, yellow socks. Wore the shorts and socks last year. He hasn't grown as much as Cordelia. He was carrying a book on ships. SHIPS and BOATS it said across the front. They call him Ben.

<u>Mr Wilde</u> (Anthony): suit, some sort of check, pale grey-green with black squares on it, very faint. Wore it last year. 'He's very dashing,' Aunt Jules said to me once when she would still talk about him. 'Oh, Ant was very dashing.' **<u>Use this word.</u>** Brown shoes, a yellow shirt, red tie, a felt hat, yellow ribbon trim. Wore that last year. He has sunglasses. I don't ever remember seeing a man in sunglasses. He left today to go back to London to the theatre, I heard him say it this morning at 11.46 a.m. He dropped them off and now has to go back to be in Tony & Cleopatra, a play.

<u>Mrs Wilde</u> (Althea): beautiful shirt-dress, in silk, deep royal blue, rippling & sort of black when it hits the sun. Espidrilse, or some kind of shoe like that, the soles were cork. A lovely string belt. All new. She's very slim. I am very slim. Dad calls me String or String Bean. She had sunglasses on too.

Althea looks kind. Like a mother should be. Her hair is waved, but I think it's like that naturally. It is beautiful & thick, red-gold coloured & swept up into a huge bun & her eyes are dark green & hooded & sparkling. Her cheeks are like apples. She's beautiful (but she looks in the mirror too often & she shouldn't, Daddy says it is vain). They all seem so jolly. We should all be friends together. But they don't need anyone else as they are the Wildflowers and they are not lonely.

I don't really remember being a four, or at least I remember Mummy a very little bit but not the baby, as it wasn't here for long enough. So sometimes I think what it would be like to be part of a four. Or be in their family and be a five. I like the number five, even more than four. Five is a prime number.

It would be nice to all sit together when the sun goes over the cliffs & have cocoa in different coloured mugs. They have their own mugs. But I could bring my own one too if they asked me.

<u>*Mr W*</u> *– white with a message on it*
<u>*Mrs W*</u> *– blue*
<u>*B*</u> *– plastic beaker, blue*

*Last night they had a special meal but I couldn't quite see in to see what it was but it smelled delicious, crusted meat & onions & baking. I think a pie, or shepherd's pie. My tummy hurt smelling it & watching them. Then they listened to some music. They have a record player on the porch & a tape cassette player in the kitchen playing songs. **<u>Get the tape of the musical Oklahoma from the library and listen to it as it kept saying Oklahoma & I think that must be what it was.</u>** I heard the children talking in bed. I listened outside their bedroom because it's on the lane.*

<u>*Cordelia*</u>*: likes someone at school called Jane, likes Wonder Woman & ABBA.*
<u>*Benedick*</u>*: likes the Rolling Stones and Jennings. And ships.*
<u>*Both like*</u>*: the film the Jungle Book & It Ain't Half Hot Mum.*

Then it was silent & they went to sleep. I didn't realise until I looked at my watch that it was eight-thirty. At school, we're asleep at eight. In the holidays I do what I like. When I tell the girls at school they're so jealous of me staying up late. I don't tell them I really hate it or about Daddy leaving me alone.

I wonder what I could do to be part of them.

Mrs Wilde: leave her a present, some flowers perhaps. Last year she smelled some honeysuckle outside our house & told me it was lovely. **_Nothing to do as honeysuckle is already there._**

Mr Wilde: ask him a question about Shakespeare because he is an actor. He has been in Macbeth this year.

Cordelia: show my Sindy that I got from Aunt Jules. She has a tennis skirt on and sneakers and a woollen cardigan with blue and red stripes on the cuffs and the edges. The Sindy I mean.

All of a sudden I think something important as I watch them eating and the smell of good food & Althea stroking her son's head like she loves him. I am determined to go inside the house this summer. This summer will be a great summer. It will be the summer I become one of their family. Aunt Jules will be amazed when I tell her. Aunt Jules has come back from Astraylia to look after me. The summers here are my time with Daddy but I hate it because he leaves me on my own and hits me, it hurts & he is so nasty when he is cross. So if I can be friends with the Wildes I won't have to see him. I will tape this book over at the end of summer so no one reads if they find it.

These are all very well organised plans. But I do get very tired of being me sometimes & I'm glad to write it all down. I am tired now.

III

Perhaps the reckoning with her past would always have happened but when it came, it seemed quite out of the blue and it was only afterwards Cordelia Wilde realised how strange it should be that she had been singing the *Messiah* when the phone call came. She had sung it on the night of her father's death and it always reminded her of him. He had loved it as much as she did and for a long period afterwards it broke her to hear the first aria and its gentle, hesitant opening chords. *Comfort ye, my people.*

The final notes were over; the church doors had been flung open, allowing the faintest breeze of the suburban summer's night to ruffle the back of the aisle; the last audience member, arthritic and lame, had shuffled from his seat towards the exit, still blocked by elderly people dressed in cheesecloth, blowsy florals or pale linens: the summer dress code of the English middle class. While the choir retreated to the side chapel, changing and chatting, Cord busied herself with some new binding tape on her tattered score, ignoring their accusatory glances, delaying the moment when she would have to return to the vestry, take off her concert clothes, become her usual self again. She didn't want to leave, to walk through the quiet streets bathed in the light from the huge August moon, a silver-and-gold ball in the ink-blue sky. To smell the end of summer in the air. She hated this time of year.

The conductor, a thin young man named William, approached. Cord smiled up at him, gesturing to the sticking tape and the score.

He watched her for a moment and then said awkwardly:

'Ah – thank you, Cordelia.' Pity, or embarrassment, coloured the words; he was nervous, she knew, for it was clear to him now exactly why he'd been able to book the once-famous Cordelia Wilde for his small suburban choir's concert. She knew all this: it was always the same these days, after a performance. 'It – it was a lovely evening.'

Cord tore off the last piece of tape from the spine of the score. 'Oh, thanks to you too, William. Well, it's the *Messiah*, isn't it? Can't go wrong with the *Messiah*.'

'Um. Absolutely.'

'My father used to pretend to be the trumpet,' she said suddenly. 'You know, in "The Trumpet Shall Sound".' She mimed playing, as he stared blankly. 'I'd sing, you see, and he'd be the trumpet.'

Every Christmas, together on the sofa in the sitting room at River Walk where the light from the Thames flickered on the yellow walls. The crackle of the fire, the damp, sweet smell of chestnuts. Daddy made an excellent trumpet substitute: he could do most things, mend a kite, put a plaster on a bloody knee, run up a wall and flip back over . . . '*Rejoice, you men of Angers . . .!*'

Her mind was drifting – it did that a lot lately.

William smiled politely. 'Several choir members are opera buffs and remember your Countess in *Figaro*, you know. It's a real thrill to have you here.'

'That's very kind,' she said politely.

'I wish I'd seen it . . .' He stopped. 'It's such a long time ago you must be awfully bored of people asking you about it.' Behind his spectacles his eyes bulged. 'I mean . . .'

Cord laughed. 'You mean I'm old and washed up and some of your members remember me before my voice was ruined.'

William looked absolutely horrified.

'No! No, Cor-Cordelia.' He stumbled over the words, his face flushing a vibrant plum colour. 'I assure you, I didn't.'

'I'm only joking,' she broke in gently because though that was, of course, what he meant she knew it was the only way to get past moments like these, the intense, sharp pain she felt in her chest when she allowed herself to recall, even if just for a second, how it had been to open her mouth and have this godlike, glorious sound pour forth. Once, long ago, another age.

'I did enjoy singing with you all. You're a lovely choir.' There was a tiny, strained pause. 'Now, sorry to mention it but the filthy lucre. Do I send in the invoice, or—'

He coughed. 'No, no, we have your details, the secretary will pay you as soon as the box-office takings have been processed.'

'Of course. Wonderful!' She heard the censure in his tone, but these days she had no shame: you had to chase small choirs like this for the money. She'd had one booking recently where they had tried to get out of paying altogether. The choir's chairman had even left her a snooty voicemail saying she shouldn't have accepted the gig knowing the state of her voice now: Cord had called in the Musicians' Union and they'd paid up, albeit ungraciously. But she was long past the point where she could wait for payment; the triumph of Countess Almaviva had been twenty-six years ago and the most she could hope for nowadays, in addition to her teaching, was a concert every few weeks, enough to keep her in bills and food. Even then it was tight.

'Well, thank you again,' said William, his high colour fading. He gave her a tiny, rather pompous bow. 'Forgive me – I must go and join the others. We're having a little party—'

'Oh, lovely,' said Cord, smiling at him.

'Oh – oh, gosh. I'm awfully sorry, the numbers are rather tight in the pub. I fear—'

Cord patted his arm, torn between horror and wanting to laugh. 'I wasn't inviting myself along. Honestly.'

How quickly it becomes farce, she thought and she shivered, and tried to focus on shaking William's hand, nodding as he backed away in almost comical relief.

Back in her dressing room – in reality a tiny curtained area behind the vestry where the vicar robed – Cord quickly changed out of her heavy velvet dress into linen trousers and a loose top, trying to buoy herself up, still shivering slightly in the chill of the old building though the night was warm. She knew churches like this all too well, their dreadful heating systems, the odd lavatory placements, their officious churchwardens and worst of all the harsh, unforgiving acoustics that seemed to taunt her, magnifying the flaws in that once-flawless voice.

Brushing her hair, Cord stared frankly into the spotted old mirror. For some reason she felt particularly blue this evening, more than her usual post-performance comedown. She was tired, sick of that London August dry, dead feeling: she knew why, of course, it was the same every year.

'You silly girl,' she said aloud.

It was also most likely performing the *Messiah*. Cord knew herself: singing was like a drug, it affected her, it pumped adrenaline and oxygen through her body so that sometimes she could *almost* capture that feeling, the feeling of triumph, of immersion in one's art, the swell of exhilaration that made you feel you ruled the world—

Her phone rang and she jumped; it never rang. She fumbled clumsily for it in the bottom of her rucksack.

'Hello?'

At first she couldn't tell if someone was speaking or not, the background noise – like a wind tunnel – was so loud.

'Hello? Anyone there?' Cord was about to end the call and then she heard the voice.

'. . . *Cordy?*'

She felt herself stiffen. No one called her Cordy. Not any more. 'Who's this?'

'Cordy? Can you hear me now? I'm moving away from the beach huts.'

She said again, woodenly, 'Who is this, please?'

'It's me,' said the voice, clearer with every second, and Cord felt anxiety and fear envelop her, a blush of red that began on her breast bone, flooding her skin, burning her up. 'It's Ben, Cordy.'

'Who?'

'Your brother. Benedick.' He was shouting. 'Gosh, the reception's terrible here. I couldn't call you at all inside the house—' More rapid footsteps. 'I'm walking towards the lane. Can you hear me now?'

'Yes.' Her heart seemed to be in her throat. 'Aren't – aren't you in LA?'

'I'm back in England for a while. I've been trying you all day.'

'I haven't checked my phone. I had a concert. We rehearsed most of the afternoon.'

'Really?' The surprise in his voice needled her. 'Hey, that's great.'

Gazing at the reflection of her face in the clouded mirror, Cord watched the scarlet flush begin to creep up and over her jawline, saw the naked terror in her eyes and was astonished at how even now, years afterwards, it was like this. 'What do you want, Ben?' she said, struggling to stay calm. 'I have to get changed.'

'Oh, I see – oh, right.' Unlike her, Ben had not inherited his parents' ability to dissemble. 'Well – the thing is . . . it's Mumma. She's not well. I wanted to let you know—'

'What's wrong with her?'

'I'm so sorry, Cordy. She's – she's dying.'

'She's been dying for years, Ben.'

'Not like that.' He cleared his throat. 'Oh, Cordy. She's only got a few months at the most. It's a brain tumour. A butterfly glioma, it's called. So pretty-sounding, isn't it? But it's Stage Four.' His voice was faint. 'They've told us it's inoperable.'

There was silence, waves and static crackling over the line. Cord swallowed.

'I didn't – I didn't know.'

'Obviously.'

'What about chemo?'

'Lauren and I asked her that today. She doesn't want it. They've said it'd buy her some time, but only a few months, and the treatment is really rough.'

'Oh, Mumma.' Cord closed her eyes, and for a second felt the soft touch of her mother's slim white hands cupping the back of her head, the scent of her perfume, lilac and rose, the glint of her red-gold hair, and sadness pierced her heart. 'Poor Mumma.'

'She's OK, actually. Strange though it may sound. She loves that home. And they can take care of her until the end. I think she's been – well, like you say, she's been dying for years, and now she's been shown her way out it's almost a relief. Oh, Cord – I'm so sorry to—' The voice broke off for a moment. 'I didn't want to speak to you again like this, Cordy.'

Cord placed a cool hand on her spinning head. She didn't know what to say.

'The thing is, she wants to see you. She says she's got something for you. And – well, the Bosky. It's about the Bosky.'

'What about it?'

'It's – it's yours, after she's gone. Daddy left it to you.'

'Me?' Cord put one hand against the wall to steady herself. 'The – the Bosky?'

Oh, saying it, saying the name of it, the pleasure of the sounds on her tongue, when she never said it, never said phrases like 'When we're at the Bosky', or 'Last summer at the Bosky', the chart she used to keep counting down the days, the smell of the place – she remembered it still, pine and lavender, warm dry wood and sea salt . . .

'They've valued it today, so you can decide what to do when she . . .' Ben trailed off. 'But she just wants to see you, Cord. Wants to explain some things to you.'

'What things?'

'I don't know.' For the first time she could hear the exasperation in his voice. 'She says you have to come and see her, just once, so she can explain. I can handle the sale later on, if you don't want the house.'

'It's not fair, you should have a share—' she began.

'You know I don't care about any of that,' he said, furiously. 'Just come down. Come tomorrow. The girls will be there. Your nieces. You haven't seen them for ten years.' His voice was hollow. 'Good God. Cordy, come and meet Lauren – she's my wife and you've never laid eyes on each other. Come and see Mumma one last time. You have to.'

'No.'

'How can you—'

But she interrupted him. 'I can't, Ben.' She tried to sound calm. 'Don't. I really can't.'

'Can't because you're working or something, or can't because you won't?'

'Both. Neither.' She gave a sound between a laugh and a sob.

'I used to know you better than anyone, anyone in the whole world, and now I – I don't understand you at all, Cord.' The bewilderment in his tone broke her heart. The lying, the huge, dreadful web of lies spun by her over the years to hide the truth from him. 'I went there today, after the estate agents. There's nothing in the house at all except those photos all over the walls. There's one of you and Mumma and Mads after she gave her the new clothes, that first summer with her . . .' Cordelia closed her eyes, twisting herself against the cold stone like a cornered animal, her stomach stabbing with pain. 'All these memories . . . The place is in a dreadful state and still . . .' He trailed off. 'Oh, honestly. I just bloody want to see you, that's all.'

She swallowed, holding on to the dusty lectern stowed in the corner of the crowded vestry. With huge effort she said, 'I'm not coming down, Ben. Call me – call me when she's dead.'

He began to say something, something about Daddy, but Cord cut him off. She stood staring at the phone then, with shaking hands, turned it off.

She knew where he'd have been standing. At the entrance to the beach behind the house where the dark pine trees reared up like a wall, near the field with the horses, darling Claudie with the soft grey muzzle she used to love to stroke. Hedgerows which, now, right now, would be thick with the tight early blackberries of autumn, sharp as ice water, sweet as a kiss. At the top of the lane there was a telephone box and a beach shop, selling plastic balls, shrimping nets, ice lollies. Her first expedition alone had been, at eight, to go and buy some iced buns from the beach shop. The crunch of sand on the stone floor, the smell of cake and tannic tea and suntan lotion. Trotting back along the uneven path, the relief when the gate of the Bosky appeared, her father's pride in her. 'Little Cord. You are marvellous, my brave girl. All by yourself.'

Cordelia had not cried when she lost her father, or her best friend. She had not cried when she had ended it with Hamish nor later, when she realised what she had lost by giving him up. She had not cried when she woke up after the operation on her throat to find it had failed or after any of the dreams that haunted her sleeping hours, taunting her with a life she might have had.

But she cried now, pressing her hands to her cheeks, mouth wide open, like a child.

She knew she had to get back to the safety of her flat, to be alone again. As soon as she could manage it, she plucked up her bag and velvet dress with shaking hands and, dashing out into the quiet street, ran away from the church, not caring who saw her.

She was glad of the emptiness of the overground train that carried her back to West Hampstead. She could see her reflection in the darkened, grimy carriage window opposite: pale face, swollen eyes . . . a ghost, that's what she was, a ghost of another, entirely different, person. When she got home, she shut the door on the outside world, and sank to the ground, hands covering her face.

Golden lads and girls all must, / As chimney sweepers, come to dust . . .

She knew she would not sleep, not now she had looked back, down into the darkness again. Yet through that airless night as she lay with the duvet thrown off the bed, hot and restless, arms spread wide, eyes fixed unseeingly at the ceiling, Cord could only remember the good times. They had been the

Wildflowers, and they had been so blissfully, gloriously happy – hadn't they? Before she – and it was her, the fault was all hers – had deliberately dismantled it all. Bit by bit. A family's happiness. Her family.

Chapter One

Summer 1975

It was very strange that no one could agree when, and how, Madeleine Fletcher first came into their lives. Afterwards, in late autumn when the Bosky and Worth Bay seemed to be nothing but a golden memory, they could recall every little detail of the summer. But at first, it was always too painful to think about. They were emotional children; or at least, Cordelia was, her brother following in her lead. They could not mention the Bosky to one another without tears starting in their eyes, lips wobbling tragically: the wood pigeons lazily cooing in the trees, or the feeling of the fabric of the window-seat cushion worn so fine it felt like silk, or the cool sand behind the beach huts: dirty grey, mixed with pieces of bark from the pines, the brambles along the narrow path that led to the sea. The smell of the place, the sounds of the water, the huge skies above them. Silly games that Daddy or Cord invented: 'Follow My Flapjack', 'Waves' and the current favourite, 'Flowers and Stones', where you dashed into the huge patch of wild flowers beside the house with a blindfold on and picked up as many stones and flowers as you could in ten seconds. Points were added for different colours, and deducted for shells. Ben always won, though he was often sick with the excitement of it afterwards, and sometimes strayed into the brambles, scratching himself terribly.

Back in Twickenham, when the autumn rain fell in grey rods over the old house by the river, gradually giving way to winter, the children would comfort themselves, parcelling the holidays up into days, or events, cross-referencing memories to keep them clear. 'We went to the ice-cream shop together seven times.' 'Mrs Gage made us boiled eggs for tea four times.' 'I won Flowers and Stones ten times in a row.' 'We had fifteen different people to stay.' 'Daddy came down for twenty days.'

Even Althea, who swore she heartily disliked the place, could remember the colour of the kite that crashed into the porch and got entangled with the tassels on the cushion that summer of 1972. She remembered too the new kaftan tunic from Biba she had bought in 1973 the week before her annual exile to Worth Bay, Bertie's voice as he stretched out his lanky frame languorously on the porch and gave his pitch-perfect imperson-ation of Mrs Gage, who 'did' for them, until she got hiccups with laughing. And Althea could perfectly recall the sad little girl next door whose face, small and dreadfully pale, had begun to appear that summer of 1975 as she and the children were having tea every evening. But she couldn't remember exactly when she had first noticed her. Perhaps even the year before.

Benedick and Cordelia knew it all – the price of sweets in the beach shop, the times of the bus taking them into Swanage, the first lunch they had at the Bosky, laid out and left for them by Mrs Gage (cold chicken salad, tomatoes, crusty bread, cherries and clotted cream), the trouble with Mrs Gage's toes and the tide times printed in the little blue book, instantly pored over upon arrival each year. But they disagreed bitterly on when they first saw Madeleine. Ben didn't remember her at all, but Ben was in a dream world most of the time. Cord said she remembered Mads from long ago, that she'd played with her before, but when they asked, she couldn't ever remember where or when.

The truth was that the year Mads came into their lives was the summer everything began to change, when they all looked back on it. In the end, it was Tony who first properly met Madeleine, and that was when he almost killed her.

They always left for the Bosky first thing. If Tony was in a play, he insisted the bags be packed and lined up in the hall before he left for the theatre in the late afternoon so the car could be loaded at dawn and they'd be there for breakfast. This added to the staged sense of drama around their departure. Ben and Cord barely slept the night before: they'd be too excited. At five-thirty they'd be lifted into the car in their night things by Tony and would doze all the way, occasionally being woken by their own sagging heads. They would then gaze out of the window at the deep blue of the early August sky, the still, heavy trees just starting to turn a crisp dark green, the golden dawn bathing the roads out of London in warm light: nostalgic before they'd even got there. And it was always chilly, Cord's bare legs cold on the leather seats in the car, and they'd shiver, and moan, and go back to sleep, but all of them were always awake by the time they passed Wareham and drove the final few miles down the winding country road set high up against the looming chalk barrow that rose and fell away over towards the coast (and where Daddy had once told them in exasperation during a fraught teatime that a witch lived who would come for them if they didn't eat their liver and onion).

The first one to see the sea picked what they'd have for breakfast. Cord always won. She was eagle-eyed. 'There. There! The tide's out.' And she noticed every little change each year. Cord was born watchful, as her Aunt Isla used to say.

The soft crunch of the car on the sandy lane, that turn of the old key in the flimsy lock, the sound of children's feet, thundering up the stairs and along the worn parquet flooring that sagged and dipped throughout the top floor, the windows that swelled shut in the spring rain and often had to be wrenched open with a little extra force if no one had been there for a while. That beautiful first smell of salt water beneath them, the distant call of gulls and of the sea, drawing back and then crashing over the sands: these were sensations all so dear, and familiar, forgotten every year and then there again, as though kept in a box that couldn't be opened until August.

'Shall we do the call?' Cordelia said to Ben, pausing in their running through the house and examining everything carefully for any alteration. She stood rattling the French doors that opened on to the porch. 'We have to do it ourselves, since Daddy's not here.'

Her arms full of freshly ironed linen for the airing cupboard, Althea watched them from the hallway.

'Don't pull the door like that, darling. Try the key.'

'I have, it's broken—' Cord tugged viciously at the door frame. 'Ugh.'

'I said, don't, Cordy! Listen to me!'

'Mumma. Please don't be mean and horrible like we're back in London, not exactly *right* at the beginning of the holiday,' said Cord, urgently. '*Please.*'

Help me. Althea turned away towards the airing cupboard, gritting her teeth. The previous year she had returned to the stage for the first time since having the children, as a young mother of two in a daring new play at the Royal Court. She had been required to do very little other than stand there and watch while her husband threw chairs around and complained about the state of the world. The description of her character had been: 'Vicki, Harry's wife, sweet-faced, patient, nurturing, a typical young-mother type.' (Of course, as her sister Isla had grimly pointed out, the play had been written by 'a typical Angry Young Man type'.)

Every day, Althea would get up, promise herself she wouldn't shout at the children or be irritated by them, and every day by five-thirty when she had to leave for the theatre she would once again feel awful about making one of them cry for not allowing an extra biscuit, or refusing to turn on the television, or some such. Once at the theatre, she'd don Vicki's simple smock, brush blusher on to her cheeks and simper sweetly at Harry for two hours whilst hugging the two angelically behaved children who played her offspring and then a car provided by the theatre would take her home and the whole business would start again the following day. A cereal bowl thrown against the dresser at breakfast, a poem pinned to her bedroom door entitled, 'Why is Ar Mother Never Hear?'. *She* was neither patient nor nurturing, and her darling children were not angelic. By the end of it, she felt she might be going slightly mad.

And now a month on her own with them. Bloody Tony. *He* should be running through the house with the children, flinging open the doors and playing hide-and-seek. Every year, on arrival, he'd stand on the porch and call over the bay, his beautiful voice ringing out, Cord and Ben wriggling with excitement next to him. He should be here having this marvellous time with them that he was always telling her was so vital to family life, instead of . . . instead of getting up to God knew what in London. She loved the children to distraction, but they were so *loud*. Asking questions *all the time*. Wanting to play games when she wanted to sit on the porch and read a Georgette Heyer. Or chat to whatever guest was down . . .

Althea squared her shoulders and opened the cupboard door, inhaling the calm smell of fresh linen and lavender. Well, with Tony away, she'd damn well invite whom she wanted this year. If he was in London, she'd ask Bertie – he hated Bertie. And Simon – yes. She nodded. This was the year Simon ought to come. If she handled it well, it could all be arranged for the best. Rather hastily shoving the sheets into the airing cupboard, she brushed down her skirts as she always did when she was nervous or flustered, then turned back to the children.

'I don't want to do it without Daddy,' Cord was saying.

'Go on, darling,' she said. 'Daddy'll want you to.'

'You do it with me.'

'Gosh, no,' said Althea, in horror.

Ben pushed the door open for his sister and they stepped out on to the wooden porch, shaded in the late-morning sun. Althea watched them, Ben's thick golden hair that stuck out in clumps, his small square shoulders in striped towelling T-shirt, the tiny mole on the back of his neck. He held his little sister's hand tightly, though she led the way, as she always did, and she turned back to her mother with a small smile, her heart-shaped face lit up, her halo of messy dark hair a web of black through which sunshine flooded.

'Come on, Mumma,' she said.

The cool breeze and the sounds of the bay soothed Althea after the long drive. It would be all right, here without him. Damn him. She swallowed, as Cordelia put both hands on her chest and bellowed, '*HOW NOW, SPIRIT! WHITHER WANDER YOU?*'

She nudged Ben, who said, more timidly, '*Rejoice, you men of Ang– Ang—*'

'Anjeeers,' Cord interrupted him. 'Anjeers, it's a place in France, Ben. '*REJOICE, YOU MEN OF ANJEERS, RING YOUR BELLS,*' she hollered, and Ben shuffled to the side, watching her half in exasperation, half in resignation. 'What else does Daddy say to start the holiday?'

'*Look, but where he comes and—*' Ben began, but Cord interrupted him again.

'*LOOK, BUT WHERE HE COMES—*'

'Cordelia! That's far, *far* too loud.'

'*LOOK, BUT WHERE HE COMES,*' Cordelia began again,

totally ignoring Althea, her voice ringing out over the bay, and Ben joined in. '*AND YOU SHALL SEE / THE TRIPLE PILLAR OF THE WORLD TRANSFORMED INTO A TRUMPET'S FOOL.*'

They stepped back, and looked at each other, satisfied.

'Was that right?' Cord asked their mother.

'Wonderful. It's strumpet, by the way, not trumpet.'

'What's a strumpet?'

'Ask Daddy. Now, come into the kitchen, you two, that's enough noise. Cordelia, can you—' Her daughter blinked furiously. 'Cord, sorry. What's wrong?'

Cord pointed at the wall. 'Look, the picture of the boats has gone. What's that? A painting? Who is it? Who changed it?'

Althea, heaving a box of food on to the kitchen counter, paused. 'Don't know. Oh, it's Daddy's aunt. The one whose house it was.'

'Where's the picture of the boats?' Cord demanded.

'I don't know. Maybe Daddy moved it when he was down in May.'

'I hate it when things change,' said Cordelia, furiously. 'He shouldn't come down without us.'

'Yes,' said Ben. 'It's not fair.'

'You two, honestly. Go and wash your hands and then we'll have some breakfast. Ben, you saw the sea first, so you pick. Scrambled eggs or fried?'

'Scrambled, please – but oh dear, Daddy always makes the scrambled eggs – who'll do it now?' said Ben, looking worried.

'I think I can scramble some eggs, Benedick.'

'Don't call me BeneDICK. I hate it. And sorry, no, you can't, Mumma. Sorry.' Althea laughed. 'Well, you can't. You can't cook anything.'

She felt rather stung. 'That's not true.'

'Daddy can't really either,' said Cord, helpfully. 'Oh, I miss him,' she added, moodily sweeping her hand across the dining table. 'I wish he was here.'

'I know. Look, we'll try our best to eke out some scant seconds of muted enjoyment for ourselves without him,' said Althea, evenly. She glanced at the blue Bakelite clock on the wall, wondering when, whether, if the phone would ring.

'It'll be hard,' Ben sighed. 'Is Aunt Isla coming at all?' Althea's sister, a brisk, jolly headmistress who retained the accent and flavour of her own upbringing, was a great favourite with the children. They had been to Kirkcudbright to stay with her in the white Georgian terraced house in which the sisters had grown up together. It was a beautiful spot: Isla had converted their painter father's old studio at the bottom of the long rambling garden into a playhouse, below which flowed the River Dee, where the tugboats and fishing vessels slid past the glistening brown waters out to the Solway Firth.

'No, Aunt Isla's away with the school.'

'Ohhhh,' said Ben and Cord together, exaggeratedly. 'Ohhh, nooo, that's awful.'

Althea paused. 'Perhaps we'll have some other people down. Like Mummy and Daddy's old friend Simon. Do you remember Simon?' she added, carefully.

'No,' said Ben.

'He used to live with Daddy. He has blonde hair and Daddy gave him a haircut on the porch once, and we could see the goldy hair through the slats for the rest of the summer,' said Cord, pachyderm-like. 'He brought you a scarf, Mumma. And he helped you with the washing-up all the time.'

'That's him. He might come. And – Uncle Bertie.'

'Yippee!' said Cord. 'But, oh, I'm still sad about Aunt Isla. I wanted to show her my new book.'

'I wanted her to teach me to fish again,' said Ben. 'If Daddy's not going to be here to do it. She's great at catching little fish.'

'I can do that,' said Althea. 'I used to fish all the time.'

'No, Aunt Isla knows how to fish properly. Her house has a river at the bottom of the garden.'

'Oh, good grief. I grew up in that house,' said Althea, exasperatedly. 'I know how to fish. In fact,' she added, wildly, 'I was much better at fishing, and crabbing. Aunt Isla only liked playing dolls.'

The children stared at her in a politely disbelieving way; Ben rubbed his nose. 'Oh. I thought you were just pretty, Mumma,' he said. Althea closed her eyes, briefly, and then gave a huge start as Cord flung her arms around her waist.

'You can't help not being awfully good at some things,' she said, seriously. 'I'm sure we'll have a great time without Daddy and Aunt Isla, Mumma.'

Althea hugged her fiercely, and after a moment said, 'Thank you, darling. Now, for the last time, go and wash your hands. And get changed into shorts, please. You can go to the beach afterwards. No, just go, otherwise there's nothing to eat.'

Tony loved an audience: that was the great difference between them as actors. He looked forward, through them, past them, seeking to connect, to draw people along with him. At home in London he knew the names of the river boatmen, he remembered every cabbie, the rag-and-bone men who often made a special detour to see him; he leaped aboard buses and talked genially to conductors and passengers who didn't know who he was. Here, down at his beloved Bosky, he was even more in his element, greeting old friends, tickling children under the chin, scurrying up the steps of beach huts to help women down with their wicker picnic baskets, joshing with the old men sitting on the bench outside the pub – he was theirs, and they all loved him. He was very lovable.

'What a shame Mr Wilde can't get away till later,' said Mrs Gage, putting the crockery down on the table.

'Yes, very sad. Children!' Althea called, raising her voice. 'The eggs are nearly done. Come up for some food, please.' She turned to Mrs Gage. 'It's been a huge hit, and they've extended the run.'

'What play is it, then?'

'*Antony and Cleopatra.*'

'Oh.' Mrs Gage didn't seem that impressed. 'I read it at school, long time ago now. We saw a play at Christmas, I wanted to tell him about it. Ever so funny it was. *No Sex Please, We're British*, and it's about this wife, and she orders some smutty magazines by mistake, and they start—'

Althea interrupted. 'Could you get the children, please, Mrs Gage?'

'Anyway, that Cleopatra was a nasty piece of work if you ask me,' muttered Mrs Gage, moving slowly towards the door. 'I'll tell him when he comes.'

Althea nodded. She stood up and glanced into the mirror, then past her reflection at the newly positioned portrait of Aunt Dinah. She peered at the older woman's eager smiling face and long pointed noise, the disconcerting familiarity of her that she couldn't quite put her finger on. She stared at the picture.

'What's got into him, in the last year or so?' she said quietly. 'Do you know? Oh, I wish you could tell me.'

The tread of the children's feet crescendoed and they appeared, skidding into place at the table. Althea smiled at them and poured them each a glass of milk, then sat down, smoothing a napkin over her dress.

'Here we are. Eggs, bacon and fried bread.'

Ben glanced at his younger sister. 'Thanks, Mumma—' he began.

'Mother,' Cord said. 'We want to tell you something.' Ben picked up a piece of bread and crammed it into his mouth.

'Go on,' said Althea, as she seemed to pause.

'We are changing our names. Aren't we, Ben.' Cord looked at her brother, as if for reassurance. 'We don't like our names any more. It's silly having names after Shakespearean people.'

'They call me Dick at school and I hate it.'

'They call *me* Lime Cordial.'

Althea said nothing, but nodded.

Taking encouragement from this, Cord said, 'So can you please tell everyone. That . . . da-durr . . . please hear a drumroll now –' Ben tapped gently on the table – 'that our names are now Flash Gordon and Agnetha.'

Althea let out an unintended burst of laughter. 'No, I can't,' she said, and they both turned their faces towards her in astonishment.

'Well,' said Cord, solemnly, 'When we are back from the Bosky we are going to go to the Council and get a form to change them in law. You can't say no.'

'Yes, I jolly well can.'

Ben shook his sister's arm.

'Cordy, you said she would . . .' he hissed, and Cord shook it off.

'I'm not calling you Flash Gordon and Agnetha, and that's the end of it,' Althea said. 'Your names are fine. They're lovely names!'

'But we don't like them, Mumma,' Ben said, too loudly, the sign that he was getting upset. 'And we're not babies. You can't stop us.'

'I jolly well can, darling. Now, eat your food.'

'I hate you,' said Cord, suddenly. Althea's eyes snapped open.

'How dare you,' she said, her patience gone. 'Don't ever say things like that.'

'It's not rude, it's true. And you – oh!'

She gave a small sharp cry.

'What?' said Althea, sharply, swivelling her head round.

Cord had jumped up. 'Who's that? Oh – is it a ghost?'

Ben clutched his mother's hand fiercely. There came the pattering echo of footsteps, beating on the porch steps down to the beach, and Althea stood up. 'Who was it, did you see?'

Cord's face was red. 'It was a ghost. It had silvery hair. It was staring at us.' She pointed out of the window with one shaking, nail-bitten finger. 'It was Virginia, the witch like the one I saw that time in the grass. Virginia Creeper. Come back to kill us and then to haunt us.'

'Sit down, darling, it's not. It's a little girl, not a witch. I saw her running away. She's not going to kill you.'

'I'd be upset if you died,' said Ben. 'And Cord.' He slid his hand into hers. She squeezed it.

'Agnetha, you mean.'

They both gave a small smile. 'Yes, of course I meant that.' She stood up, and dropped a kiss on both their foreheads.

'Daddy's coming, isn't he?' Cord asked, almost under her breath.

Althea kissed the crown of her daughter's head fiercely, so she couldn't see her face. 'Yes, darling. Of course he is. In a few weeks. And in the meantime we'll have an absolutely glorious time, I promise.'

Chapter Two

A few weeks later, in a muggy, distempered dressing room in the bowels of St Martin's Lane, Anthony Wilde OBE let the door slam behind him. He advanced towards his companion with a smile on his face, deftly peeling off his thick, moss-like black beard as though it were a rubber mask, then threw it on the dressing-room table. 'Now, my dear –' he said, and, pulling her towards him, he kissed her neck. 'Well, well.'

She dimpled. 'Well, well,' she whispered.

'It's jolly nice of you to pay me a visit,' he said. 'Can I get you anything to drink?'

'No, thank you,' she said. 'Where's Nigel?'

'I got rid of him for the night.' Nigel was Tony's loyal dresser of many years' standing. 'So we're all alone.' His hand slid up her firm leg. 'Oh, I say – what have we here, darling?'

She gave a small, nervous giggle. 'But you told me not to wear anything underneath,' she said, whispering in his ear, pressing her young, firm body against his. 'All evening, I've been waiting. It was quite hard, in the bit when I have to fall down dead – I was worried the skirt'd fly up and leave me showing my . . . um . . . to the whole audience.'

'Naughty,' he said, kissing her creamy neck, the tendrils of hair escaping from her cap. 'Very naughty. You were wonderful tonight. I was watching. *Finish, good lady, the bright day is done / And we are for the dark* . . . just terrific.' He unfastened her cotton bodice, deft, experienced fingers sliding the buttons out of the holes like pips from a juicy lemon. 'Terrific.'

'That was Iras. I'm Charmian,' she said, slightly discouraged.

'Yes, of course,' said Tony, sharply. 'I know that. But I love that line. Favourite bit in the play actually . . .' Rosalie's head snapped up as he teased her small, plump breasts out of their bodice.

'Did you mean to ask Rosie in here instead?' she said. 'She gave me a funny look – I saw it. Well, I say. Anthony, did you?'

No, because I had her last week and she was rather a let-down. Nice girl but lank hair. Awfully moany, he wanted to say. Tony inhaled, telling himself to ignore the slight whiff of drains, and the sound of the Tube rumbling underneath their feet. *Concentrate. Come on, old boy.* Instead, he answered, 'Course not, darling.' He pulled her towards him so they were facing each other, and cupped her chin in both hands. 'You, it's you I wanted, you sweet, innocent angel. I've been watching you all night. I couldn't wait to get you in here.' He kissed her, gently. 'To touch you –' He ran his hand between her legs again, and she shivered in surprise, then blinked. 'It was agony.'

'Yes,' she said, swaying slightly. 'Oh – yes, Anthony.' She ran her hands through his hair.

'Ow,' he said, sharply, gingerly touching his forehead. 'Sorry. Don't. Got a bit of a bump there.'

'Oh!' Her brown eyes were troubled, her adorable cherry-pink lips parted. 'You poor thing. I see it, it's a real lump. How did you get that?'

'Oh, doesn't matter,' he said, hurriedly, then he smiled wolfishly at her. '*I am dying, Egypt, dying.* Now, where were we . . .?'

He supported her with one hand around the waist, and then, pushing her very gently backwards, walked her to the table that ran along one whole wall. He settled her on it, lifting up her serving maid's skirts – the production was eccentric, with Cleopatra in full Ancient Egyptian regalia, her maidservants in Elizabethan costume, and the Romans wearing business suits to a man. Tony tugged off his jacket and tie, undoing his fly button with deft haste.

'Oh, Anthony—' she said again as he tugged her dress down over her shoulders, and he rather wished she wouldn't.

'Darling, I said, call me Tony.'

She stuck her chin out. 'I couldn't. That's what *she* calls you. And Oliver.'

'"*She*"?'

'Helen.'

'Oh, her.' Tony dismissed his co-star with a murmur, and kissed her again.

She hung her arms around his neck and her hard little nipples scraped against his shirt as he struggled out of his trousers; he tried to keep calm; he felt woozy, high on the thrill of it: it was always like this for him. Beforehand, anyway.

'Oh,' she said, dismissively. 'She's so rude about you behind your back. In that American accent. I want something else to call you. My own special name.'

'It's what everyone calls me, my dear,' he said, kissing her swiftly. She was a darling, really, but – he was meeting Simon and Guy later, and he didn't have all evening . . .

She bared her little teeth at him, breasts pressed against him, nipped deliciously at his ear, and then she said softly, 'Ant.' She nipped at him again, and moved against him. 'I'll call you Ant, it'll be our special name for you.' She breathed in his ear. '*Ant—*'

'*No.*' Tony pulled away from her so roughly his fingers caught in her hair and she yelped. 'Don't – sorry. Don't ever call me that.'

'I'm – I'm sorry,' she said, flushing red. 'Tony – I didn't mean to—'

'It's nothing. Just don't. Sweetheart,' he added, caressingly, and he carried on stroking her, with increased attention, almost too much. Now he just wanted to get inside her, for it to be done with. He eased his way in, feeling sick, his head throbbing more than ever.

She clutched him, pulling him closer to her, further into her. 'Oh – oh, my God.'

Suddenly, unbidden, the image of Althea, lying sprawled on the bed, came into his head, and nausea rose sharply in his gullet. Her large creamy thighs, her auburn hair loose, covering her shoulders, the hooded eyes, her supreme indifference until the point of entry when she would become frenzied, ecstatic, possessed – her need for chocolate, or booze, or some sort of luxurious consumption afterwards . . . Jesus Christ, not now, not now . . .

The room she had made safe again . . . his sobs, the smell of a lit match in the dark . . . He touched his throbbing head. The scent of wild flowers outside, inside the gritty smell of oil lamps . . . a candlewick bedspread, bobbled and pink, that first time . . . tape criss-crossing the windows . . . sirens . . . Tony blinked, as he thrust harder inside Rosalie, and she gasped, and moaned loudly. *Don't think about it. Don't think about the room, dammit. Why now, after all this time? Dammit . . . The bedspread . . .*

He came inside her, crying out, slumping over Rosie – Rosalie? Rosalie. She cried out too, a little too loudly. In the silence afterwards, broken only by his heavy breaths and Rosalie's small, panting gulps of air, he could hear tinkling laughter and conversation, coming from Helen's dressing room. Damn her. Damn it all.

Tony sat scraping his make-up off with almost vicious haste, as the sound of his co-star's honeyed tones drifted through the paper-thin dressing-room walls. The sultry summer heat seemed to be doing half the work for him, as the greasepaint had melted and slid off in parts: Tony peered anxiously into the mirror, to assure himself that the stuff hadn't collected in his pores, and around his nose. It wasn't vain, was it, to want to go out to dinner with a few friends and not be caked in stage make-up? Especially Simon, who loved to mock. One of Helen's vacuous acolytes said something in a low voice and a silvery peal of laughter reached Tony again. He flinched, resisting the urge to bang on the wall and tell them all to shut the hell up.

He hated London in August. Why was he here, when he could be at the Bosky? Sweating away in this awful broken-down theatre on disgusting wages while Clive over at the National was absolutely packing them in with *Othello*? Because he wanted to do Antony, because it was working with Oliver Thorogood, the director of the moment, and Tony couldn't possibly have turned him down. Because he was forty-two, and convinced his looks and virility and talent were going and Antony was the perfect role to prove to himself – his worst critic – that it was otherwise. Because he'd wanted to work with Helen O'Malley, damn it. What a *fool* he'd been.

He and Althea had one rule only – no jobs that interfered with August at the Bosky. That lead part in the Thames Television mini-series Althea had been offered last year – he'd been coldly angry with her for suggesting she even take it, even though it had been the first decent TV thing she'd had come in since the children. So she'd said no and taken that awful part as the simpering halfwit mother instead and hated it, and Tony knew she was better than that, knew probably more than she did how good she was . . . It terrified him, the idea she might be better than him.

And then in March came Thorogood with his offer of *Antony and Cleopatra* at the Albery, one of his favourite theatres – he was superstitious about everything but particularly theatres – and the chance to star alongside the one and only Helen O'Malley in her first appearance on a London stage and he'd said yes, and then had to explain to Althea. She'd been utterly furious. At the memory of the fight they'd had, Tony closed his eyes, briefly. He was still taken aback at some of the things she'd said. They'd rowed before – oh, they had – but this was another level, something quite different . . . Tony leaned forwards, resting his weary head in his hands.

It felt like months since she and the children had left for the seaside and he hated being alone in the Twickenham house. He was never on his own, couldn't stand his own company. Aunt Dinah used to say he had to stand on his own two feet:

'You're all alone in the world apart from me, Ant dear. You have to learn how to jolly well get on with things if I'm not around. Life's a gamble. You hold the dice.'

His great-aunt had played dice with a Foreign Office solicitor for a place on the last boat out of Basra when she had to come back for him. She'd won, and presumably the young man hoping to return to Aldershot was abandoned by the quayside for the duration of the war. It was in Dinah's blood, gambling, and in his, too. Tony's father, an actor like Tony, used to tell his son of the time she came to his first professional engagement, as Bluebeard, on the London stage – and, having forgotten her reticule (so she claimed), bet the lady at the Alhambra box office she could keep her eyes open without blinking for a minute. She won the bet and Tony remembered his father's description of her, pushing past disgruntled theatregoers to the middle of the front row, sitting down and watching him with her eyes wide open, almost on stalks, as if she'd forgotten she was allowed to blink.

Tony blinked now himself, pushing the image of her away

– more and more he found when he closed his eyes he saw Dinah, leaning over him . . .

Did you come back? Was it really you?

He touched the bump again, gingerly. Now the glow of sex was wearing off his head felt as though it were in a vice. The previous night, at home, he'd jumped at the sound of something – a mouse? Someone crying out in the park behind the house, or on the river? He'd slipped, and banged his head on the back of the door, knocking himself clean out. Been unconscious for God only knew how long, he wasn't sure, and now he had a lump the size of a duck egg there and felt pretty strange.

As the laughter from the next room rose to a crescendo Tony looked at his watch. Time to get a move on, if he was to make dinner with Simon and Guy. He'd be all right after a stiff drink and a decent meal. On the way out, Tony paused; then, despite himself, he knocked on the neighbouring dressing room.

'Night, Helen,' he called, opening the door a fraction. 'See you Tuesday.'

One of the acolytes lounging in a chair next to the door jumped up. 'Good night, sir,' he said eagerly.

Tony waved a gracious hand. 'Tony, please.' He nodded at Helen, who did not turn from the mirror. 'I say, have a wonderful weekend, won't you, darling.'

'I will,' she said. 'Thank you, Tony.'

He stared at her coolly. She was taking off the heavy fake gold collar that he, onstage, had fastened around her neck earlier that evening. Her intoxicating scent, cloves and jasmine, reached his nostrils: early in the run he'd utterly believed she *was* Cleopatra, come to life. '*Other women cloy the appetites they feed, but she makes hungry where most she satisfies.*'

But she'd been so angered when he'd given her his usual little speech that she'd barely spoken to him since and the run had been somewhat strained. She knew about Rosie – Iras. She must soon work out about Rosalie . . . he thought of Rosalie again, her cheeks flushing as he touched her, her youth and beauty . . . the hopeful glance she'd given him as she'd left . . . if he'd been on better form it would have been a great fuck, really just what he needed. She'd definitely liked it. Hadn't she? That was the rule, the rule that let him live with himself, ridiculous as it might seem, that they had to enjoy themselves, all of them. Helen didn't seem to, any more . . . oh, what a mess it was.

It was the boy next to her who broke the silence.

'Sunday and Monday off, eh? Positive holiday in the theatre, isn't it? Why no show on Monday?'

'There's a charity revue, it was booked in long before the run was confirmed,' said Tony. 'So we have two nights without a performance, which is marvellous.'

'In that case,' said the younger man, 'I say, Helen, would you like to catch a train up to Oxford tomorrow? Or Monday? I'll take you punting.'

Briefly, Helen's eyes met Tony's. She gave a small, measured smile. 'No thanks, honey. My plans are not yet confirmed, but I think I'm busy.' She said softly, 'Tony? How about you?'

Tony tried to ignore the rushing, reeling feeling that coursed through him. He clenched his fists, just once, and looked away, then heard himself say, 'Actually, I'm driving to Dorset tonight.'

'To your cute little place by the sea?' she said, coolly. The vein on her forehead pulsed, just a little. 'What fun.'

'Yes,' he said, warming to the idea. 'Yes, I'm – I'm surprising the family.'

'How wonderful.' Her eyes met his and the look of disdain in them was so powerful he wondered why the others didn't see it. 'Well,' she said. 'We must let you go to them. It's a long drive for you – ah, thank you, Rosie.'

Tony jumped, taking a sidestep, as Rosie appeared behind him and handed Helen some cosmetic product. 'H-hello, Rosie darling,' he said, as she brushed past him.

Rosie merely nodded, and Tony shrank against the wall to let her pass. 'Right,' he said, 'I'll be off then.'

One of Helen's admirers nodded, but Helen ignored him. Alone in the dank corridor, Tony wiped his brow with something like relief and ran up the stairs. He waved to Cyril the doorman, who opened the stage door as he approached.

'Anyone waiting?' Tony said, warily.

'There were a few. Couple of keen older ladies but I think they've all gone, Mr Wilde.'

'I say, lucky me. Thanks, Cyril.'

'Off somewhere nice for the break, sir?' called Cyril, as Tony shook Cyril's hand and climbed into the shiny red car parked on the narrow back street.

'The seaside, Cyril. Off to surprise my darlings. Oh,' he added carelessly, 'could you telephone Sheekey's? Explain I've had to dash off for the weekend and won't be able to meet my companions for dinner. It's – Guy de Quetteville, Simon Chalmers or Kenneth Strong. Can't remember who made the booking. Do say how sorry I am. Domestic crisis or something. Tell them – ah, tell them my wife needs me.' He smiled ruefully, climbing into the car. 'The truth is, I damn well miss them so much I rather need to go down tonight while I can.'

'Well, isn't that nice to hear. I'll just pop round there now, when you've gone, don't you worry about a thing, Mr Wilde,' said Cyril, approvingly. 'Hold on a second, sir.' He retreated into the stage-door office. 'Hold on. Yes, I've got a message for you, come to mention it . . .' He unfolded a grubby bit of paper; Tony stared at him in irritation. 'Mr Chalmers had to cancel your dinner. He's coming back from Dorset tonight and won't be in London till later, he's afraid, but he's telephoned to say he had a lovely time with your missus and the children.' He looked at Tony over the note. 'Isn't that nice, Mr Wilde, sir. Very like Mr Chalmers, to have his fun with one. A very amusing gentleman.'

Tony gritted his teeth. 'Very amusing,' he repeated, and then he looked down at his lap and smiled. Ridiculous situation. 'Could you let Guy and Kenneth know? Make my apologies. I hope they understand. Thank you, Cyril.'

He waved at Cyril and, starting the engine, drove down St Martin's Lane, the glinting light bulbs flashing around the different theatre signs on the road. A bulb on the Garrick burst suddenly with a splintering crack and people jumped out of the way, screams shattering the air. They were nervy – no bombings in London for a while but the IRA had targeted a bar in Belfast only two days ago. Four people killed. One was always rather on edge but what could you do? Square your shoulders and get on with it, like the war. What was the alternative?

That Sondheim musical was still packing them in at the Adelphi . . . Respectable couples, in heavy wool coats, hats jammed on heads, flocking towards the Tube station . . . Tony's last dressing room had looked out on St Martin's Court and he could always tell by the gait of each passerby who'd been at the theatre, escaping into another world, who'd had their ideas challenged, their heart broken, their ears filled with song and laughter . . . He loved the brightness of the West End, the lights that never went out above each theatre, their cramped seats, warren-like structures, where you buried yourself underground to emerge as Romeo, or Ivanov, or Willy Loman. He had played them all, more than once. He'd been Hamlet in space, and he'd done Pinero in Roman togas; he'd worn a doublet and hose literally thousands of times over the years, all the way back to his first performance, a humble production of *A Midsummer Night's Dream*, performed in a golden English vicarage garden as German planes studded the evening skies and death was always a possibility, just around the corner.

As he passed the Coliseum he remembered, in this nostalgic mood, the offices of his first theatrical agent a few doors along. Above a hairdresser's; *Renée Creations*, that was it. Maurice Browne, camp and stern with a twist of pale purple hair which Tony had found odd at first and then come to secretly envy – the idea that you cared so little what others thought that you dyed your hair a delicate mauve . . .

After leaving Central he'd looked for an agent for weeks, tramping up and down St Martin's Lane like hundreds of other young actors in the wreck of post-war London knocking on doors, begging for a chance, the one piece of luck. Maurice had taken him on that very day, had him in *Hamlet* in a month, the famous, groundbreaking production of *Hamlet* that would launch Tony straight into stardom. On the last night, they'd had to draft the police in to control the crowds who'd turned up to see the young star leave his dressing room for the final time.

He'd loved it, of course . . . Tony smiled reflectively, and slowed down to let a party of nuns cross the road. They smiled at him and he smiled charmingly back, his eyes drifting up to the windows of that first agent's office again. It was part of his career, that meeting with Maurice – '52? '53? 1952, it had been. Which was how long ago now?

'Jesus,' said Tony under his breath. Twenty-three years ago. He'd been working for one whole young person's life. (He wondered queasily how old Rosalie was.) 'I'm past it,' he said under his breath, and he was even more glad to be getting out of town.

The traffic was clear. The roof was down, the midsummer's

night breeze in his hair: slowly Tony began to feel calm again. He always did when he knew he was going back there.

He hoped Rosalie understood the rules. Too often they didn't, and it became tricky. Like Helen. Or Jacqui, the cloakroom girl from White Elephant who'd written him all those letters. Or Bryan, the sweet boy he'd mentored for a while. Or . . . or any of them, any of the beautiful young things he needed who would appear at the stage door, or at the Garrick door or, for Christ's sake, once at River Walk, tear-stained face, pale, tortured look in their eyes. 'You promised me . . .' 'You said you'd tele-phone, Tony . . .' 'I love you. You can't make me switch that off, you know.' 'Twelve weeks along, the doctor said.'

The girl who'd turned up at their house a few months ago – who was she? He screwed up his eyes, trying to recall, and swerved to avoid a black cab which blared its horn at him. Tabitha? Jemima? Something like that. The nanny of those kids who played with Cordelia and Benedick. Didn't wash. Earthy smell, bushy hair everywhere, armpits, between the legs, proud of it too. He'd got that one wrong too, disastrously so. Sexual liberation didn't seem to sit with the girls as well as with the boys, he found. He'd rushed happily towards the sixties thinking it meant that at last everyone would be as into it as he was and what a mistake: they still wanted the house and garden and the children, a promise, a ring . . . they wanted *him* for ever and he was Althea's, for better for worse. Last time he'd seen her was outside the clinic on Devonshire Street first thing on a freezing May morning, putting the cash in her hand – Tabitha, yes, her name was Tabitha.

Somewhere past the New Forest Tony realised his head was worse than ever, banding his thoughts with pain. It was as though a crack was opening up in his brain and inside were constant thoughts of naked bodies, bent, twisted, glimpsed through silk or lace, mouths open, hair tumbling . . . thoughts crowded with the most arousing memories and the panic of knowing Simon had been down at the Bosky while he was up in London . . . she wouldn't, would she? The crack was tiny, he could still just close it if he tried his hardest, but it was becoming harder and harder . . .

He drove on desperately, the moon lighting his way as the roads of Dorset grew narrower and greener, the empty lanes that in the daytime filled up with day-trippers and farm machinery. Only a few more miles, and then he was home, and he'd slip into bed beside his darling wife and the next morning the children would see him and scream with pleasure, and they'd go crabbing and he'd swim and build them sandcastles, and Althea would sit on the porch with her gin and tonic and put her book down to talk to him in the evening cool, the condensation of the sweating, plump glass running over her slim, creamy fingers, slender feet propped up on the porch balustrade, the sound of her carefree laughter, the look in her eyes that said, *I know you, darling. You're safe with me.* For he was; he always felt with her that she was the only one who could save him when it all started up.

And then he saw Julia's face, appearing in front of him as if it were yesterday. *Come on*, she was saying, tossing her hair, bottom lip caught in her white teeth, the deserted beaches, the lines of barricades set up against the imminent attack. *Come over here, no one's around.* And her hands on him, and his own eager, searching hands reaching inside her dress . . . Sex, skin, the smell of summer nights and sweat and soap: Tony shook his head, jaw clenched, hands aching as he held on to the steering wheel like a drowning man to a lifebelt. *No, no. No. Not her.* Glancing at the sky, he grimaced and drove on. There were thin stripes of puffed cloud across the huge August moon, and the fields were silver with corn in the dark. All else was still. Hunched over the wheel, he sped towards the sea, as though something or someone were pursuing him. Home. He would be home soon.

He had not brought his keys, however, and so it was that when Tony drew up to the slumbering house he could not open the front door. He dared not wake Althea, much less the children, invoke her wrath and start this little surprise off on a bad footing. He pulled out a jumper from the boot of the car, shutting it as quietly as he could, then climbed into the back seat, put the jumper under his throbbing head, draped his tweed jacket over himself. His last sight was of the listing hollyhocks, bobbing black against the house in the light of the moon and, as relief washed over him, he fell unconscious and slept the sleep of the dead.

Chapter Three

Tony woke at six-thirty with a start. In London he could sleep till noon if undisturbed but at Worth Bay he always woke at the same time. Aunt Dinah had kept early hours, being used to rising at dawn before the heat of a Baghdad summer got to her.

The lump on his skull was still tender; his head ached. Gingerly craning his stiff neck, Tony looked up at the house. The curtains remained drawn. His tongue was thick and oily with sleep; his stubble itched at the place where his head had lolled on to his collarbone. He felt dirty, London-ish. He wanted to be up on the porch reading the paper in fresh-pressed trousers and shirt, the feel of the early morning breeze on his smooth, close-shaven cheek. But to wake them . . . it seemed so selfish. Tony sat still, clutching the steering wheel again.

Suddenly he knew what he ought to do. He'd drive to Wareham and pick up the paper and some buns that the old inn on the square sold fresh out of the ancient bread oven, through a hatch: Rhoda the landlady knew him of old, as it were. He'd get back and settle himself on the cane chair so he'd be on the porch reading when they emerged. What a surprise they'd get! He could picture Cordy's face now . . . Without further ado he reversed the car, almost joyously – but at that moment he heard a thud, and only then looked in the rear mirror.

It was a girl. He could see by her fair hair, streaming out like ribbons on the dirty sand path. She lay flat on her back and, as Tony leaped out and rushed to her, he saw blood trickling from her nose. For a moment he wondered if the bump on his head meant he was hallucinating. He stared at her tiny frame – she must be younger than Ben, her flat pale face lifeless, her thin arms and legs flung out as if in defeat . . . His blood froze.

'Oh, Lord. Oh, my God. No.' He reached for her, then remembered Aunt Dinah's first-aid training that you should never move someone who might have broken their neck or back. He stroked her cheek. 'My dear girl – I'm so sorry. Can you—' He felt ridiculous, sweat breaking out as the enormity of it washed over him. He stared at the small face underneath all that hair. He knew her, he was certain . . . Frantically, he patted her hand.

'Can you hear me? Hello, little one?'

And then – miraculously! – she opened one eye. He could have shouted with relief. When she saw him looming over her she shut the eye immediately again.

'Sweetheart,' said Tony, quietly. 'I've hit you with my car. Can you hear me?' He took out a handkerchief and gently wiped away the blood snaking down her cheek. Something made him say, 'It wasn't your fault, you know that? It was mine.'

He looked down and saw the little fists unclench, and noticed the grime on her dress, on her socks: the untarmacked lane threw up dust at the first invitation. He took her hand in his. 'Little one, if you can hear me, I need you to sit up. My name's Tony. If you can, will you say, "Hello, Tony"?'

And she opened her eyes, and sat straight up, and said indignantly, 'I know who you are, course I do.'

Tony laughed with relief. The little girl sat up, holding her pale silvery hair in a fist, briskly shaking the dirt from it, brushing her skirt and socks.

'Oh, you do, do you?'

'Yes, my auntie tells me about you,' she said seriously, her huge eyes on him. 'My mummy actually saw you in *Hamlet*. She abs'lee loved you.' She paused. 'She's dead,' she added. 'She was five foot seven. She died having my brother. He died too.'

He stroked her hair, involuntarily, and clutched the little fist. 'I'm so sorry to hear that.'

She shrugged, matter-of-factly. 'How well do you know Bristol?' she said, as though she were entertaining the Queen at a tea party, and he smiled again. 'I live with my daddy here in the summer but when I'm at school I live with my auntie. *She* came back from Australia to look after me. She likes you. *She* lives in Bristol.'

Tony knew too many aunts like that: they tended to press inedible home-made cakes upon you and sticky autograph books, and to want to regale you with stories of seeing *Hamlet* and they always stood too close. 'I don't know Bristol very well. Look, are you hurt in any other way? Where's your father? I think we should get you back home and—'

Instantly, she shook his hand off hers and scrambled to her feet; she was like a stork, thin and ungainly. She said abruptly, 'No. Really no need, thanks. Daddy's still asleep. He'd be furious.'

'Where's your house then? Where are you staying?' Tony put his hands on his hips and looked down at her.

'Over there. It's thirty yards. I've measured it. My father's there. I'm honestly fine. Sorry. Very sorry. See you later.' And before he could say anything else she'd scarpered, darting down the track in seconds. Tony followed her, his tired limbs aching, and though he searched down the lane and behind the empty beach huts, she had gone.

He stared down the lane where she'd disappeared, towards Beeches, Ian and Julia Fletcher's house. He hadn't seen Ian at the place for a couple of years . . . was this little thing his daughter? Julia's *niece*? *My auntie too* . . . He rubbed his eyes, pressing his fingers to his pounding head: he needed something to eat, a wash and a change. Julia – of course, it was her of whom he'd been reminded. He went back to the car and, glancing up at the house to make sure there were no new signs of life, reversed again, extremely carefully.

Driving back forty minutes later with four iced buns and a copy of the *Observer* on the seat beside him it occurred to Tony that to truly surprise them he'd better leave the car at the top and so he parked and walked down the road. The same clump of grasses in the middle of the lane, the same scent of sea salt and wild flowers, the sound of seagulls and wind . . . He hadn't been here since May. That weekend with Tilly, the dresser from *Trelawny of the 'Wells'*. No inhibitions, father in the navy, little moles all over her skin. Then, spring held the bay in thrall, swallows skidding across the fields and the sky a fresh, vivid blue. But he loved August here best, when he'd seen the place for the first time all those years ago, the bleached grasses, the dark trees, the chill in the evenings, the sense of something ending.

He'd been taught the trick of moving without noise long ago, at Central. As he approached the low wooden house Tony was pleased to see Althea's curtains drawn. He moved towards the side gate that led up to the porch at the front and the beach, so very glad that he had come, that he was here, that he would see them. Joy at the thought of their dear faces coursed through him.

He stood still for a moment, looking up at the porch. The kitchen window was open but he couldn't see inside, and then suddenly there was a thud, then a rattle on the door handle of the French windows and a figure in a pale blue felted dressing gown and with wild hair flung itself against him.

'Daddy! Daddy-daddy-daddy-daddy!' it cried, wrapping its arms around his torso. 'You surprised us! Mummy said you'd never come and I said you would, oh, Daddy!'

'Darling Cord,' Tony said, squeezing her as tightly as he could without hurting her. 'Look, but where she comes! Hello, Ben, old boy, how are you, poppet?'

'Fine, Daddy,' said Ben, hurrying towards him, hair sticking up, arms crossed in an effort, Tony knew, not to suck his thumb. 'Jolly nice to see you.'

Tony hugged the boy, as Cord clung on to him, trying to pull him back towards her. 'Been all right, you on your own with two demanding women, Ben?'

'Just about. Awfully glad you're here.'

'Oh, I love you, Daddy,' Cord was saying, kissing his ears, his cheek, his hair. 'I forgive you – I forgive you for everything! Oh—' She held her father's face, beaming at him, and then suddenly looked over his shoulder with a scowl. 'Oh, good grief. Ben, it's that spying girl. The one I told you about. What's *she* doing here?'

The little girl had reappeared, her small face sticking over the wooden rail. She stared at them all, grey-blue eyes impassive.

'What's your name, little one?' Tony said to her.

'Madeleine,' she said, folding her arms. 'Madeleine Fletcher.'

'So you're Julia's niece,' he said, nodding, and he smiled at her.

She nodded, and didn't budge, as though she were glued to the rail.

'She keeps hanging around,' said Cord, carelessly. 'Listen, buzz off, will you? He's our dad. Don't you have your own home?'

'Yes, I do, and –' Madeleine paused, and stuck her tongue out – 'I do, so there.'

'She's always here,' Ben said, crossly.

'She spies on us,' Cord added.

'Madeleine,' said Tony, turning to her and leaning over the railing. 'It's lovely to meet you properly. Maybe you'll come and play with Cordelia one day. Would you like that, Cord?'

'My name's actually Agnetha now,' said Cordelia, slithering down her father's body and landing on the floor with a thud. 'I played with her before, actually, when we invented Flowers and Stones.'

'Flowers and—' Tony stopped, remembering how much of his summer last year had been taken up playing Cord's latest enthusiasm. 'Oh. Yep.'

'We *have* to play it again, we've got really good,' said Cord, and Tony nodded; then, turning to Madeleine, he saw that she had vanished again. He wondered if she was Ian Fletcher's child – she must be, of course. Poor little sod. He couldn't help thinking being Ian's daughter might not be much fun.

'You should be friendly to Madeleine,' he said.

'She's crazy, Daddy, honest,' Cordelia told him firmly. 'Don't you remember the day I played with her, that lady found her crying on the beach? And I found that angel, you hung it up above the house.'

'Yes,' said Tony. 'Yes, I remember,' and he turned to look at the angel for the first time. He nodded greetings at her, but she simply stared impassively back, the furled wings pointing downwards, the eyes glassy and unblinking, a mystery. He'd liked adventure stories as a boy, especially ones about lost treasures and ancient gods. Aunt Dinah always said she'd found the angel in a market in Baghdad, but he never believed her. He imagined her, swooping up the steps of a ruined Mesopotamian ziggurat one night, the moonlight picking out the peacock colours of her old kimono. She'd swipe the angel and those little bird figures she used to bury around the house for good luck, taking them out of an ancient burial chamber, rescuing them before the Nazis came and took them, bringing them home to safety where they could protect him, and his family to come . . .

He blinked, realising Cord was pulling his arm.

'I'm telling you, Daddy, that girl's a spy. She remembers all these things about us like what colour my shoes were last summer. We hate her and she never washes.'

'You mustn't be so unkind, either of you. You must go and apologise to her,' Tony said. 'Ask her to play with you.'

'Only if you come with us,' said Cord, meeting her father's gaze. 'Come to Beeches with us. We're scared to go on our own. Her father is mad too.'

'Well,' said Tony, weakly. 'We'll see.'

'Yes. We will,' she said pertly, and he wanted to laugh. 'Come on, FG. Come on, Daddy.'

Tony followed his children into the house, and inhaled the scent of pine, wood, spiced cleanliness, warmth. The smell of Aunt Dinah, the smell of safety, of home. 'I'm very tired, my darlings,' he said, taking off his shoes. 'I'm going to have a wash and a shave and then I'll come back up. Here are some buns.'

'Mummy said you'd make us breakfast,' said his daughter.

'I doubt it – she didn't know I was coming,' Tony said wearily.

'She said she'd bet us fifty pee each you'd come up after the show as a surprise and you'd be here for breakfast and we were to act amazed when we saw you,' said Cord.

'Cord, I—'

'It's *Agnetha*.'

Tony laughed, he couldn't help it. He put his head in his

hands and gave way to mirth. 'Ah, darlings, it's wonderful to see you.'

'How long will you be here?' they asked, almost in unison.

'Today, tomorrow and until lunchtime on Tuesday. I've bought iced buns for breakfast. Now, please, let your poor tired father go and wash and then we'll think of all sorts of things to do.'

'Will you finish reading us *The Hobbit*? Simon tried but he gets the voices all wrong and then he had to go back to London after we'd only just got to Rivendell.'

'I – I will.'

'Will you buy more bacon for the crab lines? Mrs Gage says that's the only thing that'll work.'

'Yes, Cord.'

'It's *Agnetha*. Daddy, you've got to remember. We're changing it when we get back to London. By deepole.'

Ben nodded, then tugged his father's arm, still wrapped around his torso. 'Can we take the boat out of the beach hut?'

'Can we do Beach Races? And Follow My Flapjack? Oh, and can we show you our new way to play Flowers and Stones – I've written some new rules and they make it *even more* exciting . . .'

Tony pulled them both close again. 'Yes,' he whispered into his son's hair, gritty with sand. A lump rose in his throat. He was home, he was safe, they were here . . . he heard footsteps, looked up and there was Althea, in the doorway, sunshine forming a halo around her generous frame, encased in her periwinkle-blue silk dressing gown . . . Without her make-up she looked young, the statuesque shy girl just down from Scotland whom he had pursued across London for years, in cafés and smoky clubs, whom he wanted with an intensity that still surprised him. Her face was a mask, but she bit her lip as his eyes met hers and he knew he still had her – just.

'Hello,' he said, looking up at her.

She pulled the cord of her dressing gown a little tighter, watching him.

'Well, hello,' she said. 'This is a nice surprise.'

The children were watching them curiously.

I missed you.

You had Simon down here then.

I'm sorry about the last row.

Tony shook his head, closing his eyes briefly.

He knew it was his choice, that if he could just stop listening to the voice in his head that had, this year, started to whisper again, he could wipe out the mistakes – they weren't catastrophic, not quite yet. He knew it rested with him, the power to make them all happy. If he could just be strong enough. He gave a deep breath, exhaled.

'Yes to all of it.' He kissed his daughter. 'Oh, I'm so glad to be here, Cord.'

'For the last time, Daddy. I'm not saying it again.'

Althea shrugged. 'You have to talk to them about this names nonsense, darling. I've given up.'

'I will. So did you miss me?'

'Yes,' she said, evenly. 'You silly man. You know we did.'

'A little bird told me Simon was here.'

'He was, and it was terrific. He was great with the children.' She cleared her throat. 'But he's getting married, moving to the States for a few years. He won't be coming down for a while.'

Her eyes met his. He nodded, in gratitude.

'Uncle Bertie was here too. He brought a kite,' Cord said. 'It broke.'

'I can fix it.'

'I know you can.'

Tony stood up, and went to the bottom of the porch steps, so that the sun shone on his bare head, and he spread his arms wide. '*REJOICE, YOU MEN OF ANGERS,*' he bellowed, and the children wriggled with delight, dancing around him. '*Ring your bells!*'

Going out on stage every night, being someone else, was a very peculiar job. It got harder, not easier. He sometimes thought his brain might fully crack open at any point and these vile, amoral, crazed thoughts would leap out like evil sprites, jumping up, screaming, biting his legs, running everywhere, knocking things over: last night they almost had. People would be horrified, they'd lock him up – but then it'd be over, and so the cracking open, maybe it wouldn't be so bad . . . Tony shook his head. It was always there, the past, waiting for him, waiting to get him. But not just yet. Not today.

Chapter Four

London, July 1940

In the hospital, you could hear the sound of feet approaching from the other end of the corridor. They echoed on the red tiles, the sort that looked like they should be warm but were always cold. So even if you were pretending to sleep you knew if someone was coming.

When Ant was first taken there he'd turned over every time he heard footsteps, even though he couldn't sleep on that side, because of the raw-red skin shrinking, contracting into hundreds of scabs. Turning was agony but he still did it. He had to check, you see. Because perhaps they'd got it wrong and she'd come back for him. Perhaps she'd been taken to another place.

But it wasn't ever her.

The old Victorian hospital smelled of something sickly sweet and it was chilly, even in the height of summer, and very quiet. The other children in Ant's ward were silent, like him. Some of them couldn't speak, they were too badly hurt; some of them wouldn't speak, because of what they'd seen. Ant had talked to one little girl across the way from him. She was called Cherry. She was permanently clutching a bear that one of the Red Cross workers had given Ant, which he'd given to her. He was too old for teddies, he told her. She had bedraggled bunches, one lopsided. No one had taken the ribbons out and brushed her hair since whatever had happened to her. She was a chatterbox, not like the others. When she talked she waggled her head and powder fell in gentle clouds from her grey hair, shining like a halo round her head in the cold sunlight. It was rubble dust, from her bombed-out house. Ruby, the girl in the bed next to Ant, had whispered to him when Cherry was finally asleep that her whole family had been killed, both parents, two brothers, a newborn baby sister, her grandparents. But she didn't talk about them. She just talked about Mickey Mouse; she'd been to the flicks to see some cartoons the day before it happened. She was mad on Mickey Mouse. Had the gas mask too. Ant liked talking to her – she was sweet, and he preferred talking to girls anyway.

About two weeks after he'd arrived Ant woke up and looked across, and Cherry wasn't there. He was confused: he wasn't sleeping well, these dreams that bound him tight like chains and left him screaming and the mattress drenched in sweat and urine. But her bed was neatly remade, new sheets, scratchy blankets, waiting for someone else.

'Where's Cherry?' he'd said to Ruby.

'Didn't you see?' She was reading a comic; she looked over the top of it, pityingly.

'No. Where's she gone?'

'Little blighter bought it in the night. Didn't you hear her yelling? Till they came for her?'

Ant swallowed, and looked across. 'I – I must have been asleep.'

'You were, but even with all the racket you make I'd have thought you'd have heard her—'

'Was she that ill then?' He was staring at the window sill, high above Cherry's bed, where his teddy bear was sitting.

'Course she was. Skin turned purple. The shrapnel got in her leg.' Ruby was not a sentimentalist. 'They cut it off last night, only hope. Nurse said she died in the middle of it.' She shook her head with relish. 'Heart stopped.'

Colin, the fat, weeping boy on the other side of Ruby, blinked fast. 'Shut up, Ruby.'

'P'raps it's for the best,' said Ruby, wise beyond her years. 'Where would she have gone?'

'I said shut up, Ruby, otherwise I'll knock your bleeding block off,' said Colin, furiously. 'Just shut up.'

'Well, it's true, ain't it?' Ruby turned to Ant, as if he was her ally. 'No one come for her, did they? No one visited her.' She stopped suddenly. 'I mean—'

Ant had lain back down in bed, turning himself away from her; he was rarely rude, his mother was a great one for manners, but he couldn't listen any more.

'Sorry, Ant,' she was saying. 'Just meant it about her, 'cause she was – sorry.'

Sorry.

At the end of the long room the doors suddenly swung open, banging as they did; some of the children looked up, but for the first time Ant didn't. He heard footsteps, approaching; he felt his injured leg ache with the pain of twisting away, the scabs smarting as his broken skin stretched over the rough sheets; he felt one of the scabs break open, as the sounds grew louder. He smiled as Sister Eileen went past followed by a lady in a drab coat, clip-clopping towards a bed at the far end of the room. 'John?' Sister said in a firm voice. 'Mrs Havers is here to take you to a nice new home. Sit up, dear. No, no crying, please. Time to get dressed.'

No one was coming for him. He understood that now even if the others didn't.

Daddy had been killed only two months into the war. Because there was no fighting, no one dying, people began calling it the Phony War which Ant liked, it made him feel better – only Philip Wilde *had* died, when his plane burst into flames during training in Newquay. His father, the flight engineer and the navigator were all killed instantly. 'A hero. He wouldn't have suffered,' said the man from the RAF who came to tell them. 'He wouldn't have known what was happening.'

Mummy and he had actually laughed about that when he'd gone. 'I'd jolly well know what was happening if a fireball engulfed my plane,' Mummy had said afterwards, lighting a cigarette and pouring out the last of the gin. It sounded awful to be laughing but they did; the RAF chaplain who came the next day said it was shock.

'I'd bloody know it too!' Ant had chimed in, hugging his knees. He couldn't stop laughing, great gulping roars of it. 'I'd bloody realise if I was being burned to death!'

'Don't say bloody, darling.'

So even as he watched his mother die, even as he saw the puddle of vomit left by the squeaky-clean new ARP warden who helped drag him out of the cupboard first, leaving his mother behind, half of her blown away, clean down one side, Ant was still saying it to himself, whispering it rather as they stretchered him out of the pile of bricks and pipes and torn fabrics flapping in the summer breeze that had once been his family's home. 'I'd jolly well realise if I was being burned to death!' He thought he should keep saying it, keep joking. Mummy hated people being serious. It was only when one of the nurses slapped him, the next day, when he couldn't stop repeating it, that he realised he shouldn't say it out loud. And it was only when they came and told him he'd missed her funeral that he began to wonder if it was true, that she wasn't coming back. So Cherry's death was when it started for real:

the idea that what he'd seen that night had happened, that this was his life, not something up on the pictures, or in make-believe, nightmares.

A month after he'd arrived it was almost August and for the first time Ant dreamed of his mother and their little house with the red front door in Camden and he saw her coming in from the tiny garden, still laughing about something. And he heard a voice saying, in the dream, quite clearly, *The house is gone. She's dead. Daddy's dead. You're all on your own.* And then the scene and the people in it vanished, sliding quickly away like the pieces of the magnetic theatre his parents had bought him for Christmas last year. The front of the house, the characters on the stage, the back scenery walls of the parlour with the photographs and the radio – all of it disappeared, pulled away, cardboard and paper. Years later, when he was old, this is what he remembered as the worst time. Often he thought that everything sprang from the days following that realisation: the darkness that was always, always waiting for him. To the end of his life, he was terrified of the dark.

And then, one day, she came.

Ant was sitting in bed reading a book about lost treasure in Central Africa, picking idly at the scabs on his legs – they had threatened to bandage his hands to stop him picking at them, they didn't understand why he kept doing it, why he liked to see them grow back, again and again. A bluebottle buzzed loudly in the window above him. He could hear children playing outside, the ones who were well enough to. They were quiet, not like street games back on his road.

It was summer. He wondered what his friends were up to. He didn't know what you did in summer when a war was on. It sounded funny when you said it like that. Ant tried to smile again but he couldn't.

By now he was relieved every time the footsteps came and they weren't for him. It was better to be in this misery than contemplate anything else. So Ant arranged his face into a mask of unconcern, thinking how proud of him Mummy would be, and smiled at the woman advancing along the corridor, who was dressed head to toe in varying shades of brown and black – brown boots, high-necked blouse and a long brown rippling silk skirt – all topped off by a velvety, swirling kind of jacket in a pattern of peacock feathers.

As she bent over him, Ant wondered idly how she could bear all those clothes in the heat. Her nose twitched as he nodded at her. It was a long nose, slightly bent. She had messy hair, and thin, red-raw hands, which waved around as though unconnected to their owner. It was her eyes, though, that was what he noticed. She had dark green eyes, beautifully expressive and full of life; they sparkled as she talked, they looked at him shrewdly and made you forget the long bent nose, the odd, slightly grubby clothes. She was talking to him, saying something.

'Dear Ant, I'm so glad to have found you, and in one piece.'

She was actually clasping his hand, and Sister was nodding. Ant was too surprised to say anything. He was sure there was something about her that seemed familiar, but his addled, broken head couldn't remember what it was, and her eyes danced as she smiled at him, and it was as though they were bewitching him.

'I'm so sorry to have left you here for so long. There was some trouble getting back. In the end I had to get the train to Basra and wait for a boat going to England. It was rather tricky at times,' she said breezily, as though she were describing a fresh afternoon on the Serpentine. 'But we got here in the end!' She sat down on the bed, tucking a stray strand of chestnut hair behind one ear. 'Ah,' she said, nodding. '*Queen Sheba's Ring*. Rider Haggard, jolly good. Jolly good. Tell me, do you like adventure stories then?'

He was silent.

'Anthony's a good reader, loves his books,' said Sister. 'Now, Anthony. Say hello to your aunt.'

A throbbing ache began to beat against Ant's skull. The lady – who looked, he thought now, a bit like a pelican he'd seen in the zoo, all flappy and long arms and folded bits – just smiled. She put a package, wrapped in creased pieces of brown paper, down on the bed beside him.

'I said, say hello to your aunt,' said Sister, in a menacing tone.

'She's not my aunt. I've never seen her before.'

The woman nodded, just as Sister clicked her tongue in annoyance. 'Don't be so silly. Of course she is.'

Ant said, quite politely, 'Sister Eileen, she's not my aunt.'

'No, it's quite true, I'm not.' The strange woman looked up. 'I'm his great-aunt, Sister Eileen. Philip was my nephew. Dear Philip. In the interests of accuracy I feel one should point this out.'

'I see,' said Sister Eileen, without enthusiasm. 'Anthony, get up. Clear up your things. Miss Wilde is taking you away now.'

'But I don't –' Ant began. Panic seized him, and he flicked off one of the scabs on his arm, and moved the package out of the way to show Sister Eileen. 'Look – it's bleeding. I don't know who she is. I don't know a Miss Wilde. You can't make me go with her. Who are you?' he said, and he knew he was being rude.

Miss Wilde seemed unbothered. 'Why on earth should you know?' she said. She tapped the book. 'We do, however, have the same surname, and I do seem to recall sending you one or two carefully selected presents from time to time.'

He narrowed his eyes, drawing the book closer. 'Did you give me this?'

'Well, I did. It's rather contrived, but the adventure's jolly good. We actually don't know anything about the Queen of Sheba, but I have been to King Solomon's Mines.'

'Really?' Despite himself, Ant sat up. 'Where are they?'

'Near Jerusalem. The copper in the mines turns the sand into different colours. Red, green, blue – like a rainbow.'

'And did you find anything?'

'Many things,' she said, her eyes twinkling. 'That's my job.'

'I should like to be an adventurer,' Ant said. 'Or a tomb raider, like Belzoni.'

'Well. His methods are rather frowned on now, dear Anthony, although if it wasn't for him the British Museum would be fairly empty. But I'm very glad to hear we have a common interest.' She patted the package beside her. 'And I've brought you a present today.'

'What's your proper name?'

'It's Dinah. Dinah Wilde.'

Anthony eyed the brown-paper parcel, speculatively. 'Dinah,' he said, rolling the familiar name around on his tongue. 'I do know you. But you don't live here, you live in the desert.'

He wished he could remember more, but his brain didn't seem to work properly these days, hadn't since the night he lost Mummy. But he remembered now his father had adored his aunt Dinah, who lived far away and almost never came back to England. Philip Wilde, a great storyteller, had told his young son the tales about her, passed down by his own mother, who was much older than her younger, eccentric sister and who remembered the terrible things Dinah used to get up to. It was her, wasn't it. Naughty Aunt Dinah. 'She stole a parakeet from Regent's Park Zoo.' 'She and my grandfather bet on woodlice

66

crawling up the pews at Midnight Mass.' 'She fired a gun once out in India and blew a man's fingertip clean off.'

Mummy frowned on these stories. Aunt Dinah had stayed with them once when Ant was tiny, Ant was sure, and Mummy didn't like her. Mummy frowned on any mention of Aunt Dinah now, not to mention Dinah's father, Philip's grandfather, a colonel in the army who had Come to No Good. There was more, he was sure, but he couldn't really remember . . . Ant blinked, swamped by other memories.

Terrible Great-Aunt Dinah now took his hand and Ant didn't, for some reason, shake it away. 'I used to live in the desert, yes. I live here now, Ant dear.' She pushed the package towards him. 'Open it.'

Ant peeled back the layers of brown paper and lifted out a small stone slab. He stared at a female figure, whose arms were outstretched. She had wide eyes, full lips, huge wings – she was naked, and he felt rather funny looking at her huge breasts, but she was definitely an angel, or a fairy, not a real woman. In one hand she held a pine cone; on the other rested an unblinking owl.

Sister Eileen gave a sniff of disapproval, but Ant was interested.

'What is it?' he said, turning the smiling figure with the bulging eyes and thick, curving lips over in his sore hands. It was cool to the touch.

'It's from an ancient city thousands of years old. I bought her in a bazaar in Baghdad. I take her everywhere I go, and she keeps me safe.'

'Really?'

'Yes,' Great-Aunt Dinah said, smiling. 'I was in Nineveh excavating King Ashurbanipal's library. It may well be the greatest library there ever was. I felt funny suddenly. I'm not normally claustrophobic – you spent hours in those places, cramped, searing heat, no light, smell of gas lamps. But I suddenly felt strange. Faint. I picked her up and stepped out of the chamber for some air and there were sand lizards everywhere. Thousands of them, lined up perfectly still, watching me. I went back to my tent to lie down. A sandstorm blew up and trapped the others in the chamber. Three other tents were blown away. Five men died. I held her in my hands all through it and she gave me comfort. She kept me safe. She told me when to leave. Important to know.' Ant looked from his aunt to the small figure. 'So I thought you'd like her, too. She's very old.'

'Older than Jesus?'

She smiled, pushing her finger up the ridge of her nose, as though there were glasses there, which there weren't. 'Much, much older. You can hang her above the front door. It's to keep bad spirits out.'

'Oh, I don't have a front door,' Ant said. His voice wobbled. 'It – it got blown off.'

Sister Eileen cleared her throat, in irritation.

'You do now. You're going to come and live with me, by the sea.' Dinah's eyes shone. 'You'll be safe there. I promise.'

Chapter Five

Late August 1975

Cord wriggled in bed, her toes bent by the over-tightly tucked-in sheets. She looked across at the pale lemon wall where the slatted blinds cast light and dark shadows and knew it would be another white-hot, cloudless day.

In the bed next to her, Ben snored gently. Cord glanced at his resting face, nose peeling and covered in freckles after a summer at Worth Bay, and then hugged herself, feeling the delicious smoothness of the sheets on her bare arms. Sheets at home were never silky like this, the weather was never kind like this, food didn't taste like this at home: delicious, fresh, even if covered in sand. Leaving here every year was, she'd come to see, unbearable. Yesterday, she'd promised Ben he wouldn't have to go to the dreaded new school. And Cord never broke her promises.

They had hidden the food and the suitcases in the beach hut the previous afternoon. The suitcases wouldn't be needed until the Saturday after the August Bank Holiday, when summer was over, the house shut up and they were dragged into the car for the drive back to London. But Cord had reasoned that it was wise to hide the provisions now: it would avoid suspicion closer to the date. Daddy always said he had to get the shoes of a character right first to know how to play him. These days, it seemed to Cord as though she were wearing the right shoes all the time: she felt invincible.

They'd hatched plans before, silly plans really: the lemonade stall had hit the skids after only a day, and the sponsored sing-along last year had been cancelled after Daddy actually put masking tape over Cord's mouth when she entered her second hour of singing a combination of songs from ABBA and *The Sound of Music* on the porch. There was, too, the dog-napping plan earlier in the summer which had not ended well. This, however, was the boldest yet. Ben was still afraid but Cord knew they could pull it off.

They were going to run away.

Run away and stay here, rather contradictorily. They'd never have to leave Worth Bay again and Ben wouldn't have to go to the big boys' school in Sussex, which he was dreading and which Daddy was adamant about, even though he himself had hated it. *Antony and Cleopatra* had finally finished and so Daddy had arrived two days ago to spend the last week with them and they had tried to talk to him about it. But Daddy, normally so reasonable, wouldn't brook any discussion on the subject. 'You'll love it when you're there, Ben,' he'd say.

Ben was getting more and more desperate. He'd stopped sleeping, he was hardly eating – he'd even abandoned work on his model aeroplane. Cord thought it was utterly heartless; you only had to look at Ben to see he wasn't supposed to be sent away. He was nothing like her: small for his age, shy, diffident. He'd be eaten alive at boarding school, that or worse, Mrs Berry, their housekeeper in London, had said grimly, though Cord didn't think there was much worse than being eaten alive.

She had even discussed it with Simon, when he'd been down to stay. She'd found him sitting on the porch one afternoon while Mumma was napping, ostensibly doing the crossword, though in fact he was chewing a pencil and gazing into space.

'Can you talk to Mumma and Daddy?' she'd said. 'About Ben going to school because he really doesn't want to, and they won't listen.'

Simon was ever so good to talk to when you managed to get his attention. The rest of the time he was almost as bad as Bertie, who was great at doing silly impressions and telling the children dirty jokes, but absolutely hopeless at things like finding hair ribbons or making sandwiches – he'd looked after them for an afternoon the previous year and Cord had actually got stuck in the toilet bowl, bottom almost touching the U-bend, hands, head and legs waggling frantically, crying out for help while Bertie was on the phone to someone called Johnny for half an hour about some silly play. But Simon could at least listen, and give advice.

'Cordy, all I know is your old dad's very keen on it,' he said. 'Mind you, I can't see why.'

'He hated it! Poor Ben. It's horrid.'

'He wants what he had for himself, that's it, Cordy,' Simon had told her, lighting a cigarette. He'd blown out the smoke and stared, ruminatively, out to sea. 'He thinks he ought to fashion Ben in his own image. I'm afraid you won't change his mind.'

Cord had stuck out her chin.

'I will.'

Simon had simply laughed, and gone back to his paper. 'And woe betide anyone who gets in your way. You do what you want. That's my girl.'

This Cord took to be almost a tacit approval of their plans, which accelerated as a result of this conversation. A can here, a packet there, over the course of the summer and now there was more than enough for them to live on. Still in bed, Cord ran through the inventory, memorised in her head:

x 2 tins pineapple chunks
x 2 packets jelly (one raspberry one lime)
x 1 packet of cornflakes
x 5 tins soup (x 2 tomato x 2 minestrone x 1 scotch broth)
x 1 packet dried stuffing
x 1 bag raisins
x 1 loo roll
x 1 Cord's cassette of 'Waterloo'

She reckoned this should provide enough for them to live on for at least a week in the beach hut, by which time she hoped her parents would have stopped searching for them and gone back to London.

It had to be done very carefully, of course: Mumma was surprisingly adept at spotting mischief-making. Behind the huge paperbacks or the *Sunday Times* magazine, behind the put-on languid hand-waving 'run-along dear'-ness of her, under the great black sweep of that expertly applied eyeliner were sharp green eyes that noticed everything.

Ben was already in trouble, being rude to Simon when he stayed, then being rude to Daddy when he arrived, and then for the great dog-napping incident when he'd 'borrowed' a nice dog and taken him to the beach hut before alerting Cord to his actions. They'd called him Sandy, wittily, and played with him all afternoon and he'd been ever so friendly, wagging his tail and letting them feed him biscuits, and then the owner had gone past and seen Sandy in the open door of the beach hut and had called the police, accusing them of kidnapping his dog from up the road at Worth Farm and all hell had broken loose. He was not a kind farmer with a tweed hat and a piece of wheat hanging out of his mouth. He was thin and angry and kept saying how Sandy was a working sheepdog and a she, not a he. He pulled Sandy around a lot by the collar. And it turned out she laboured under the truly depressing name of Spam. Ben had been more furious about that than anything.

'Such an undignified name to give her. Horrible. She should be called Hermione or Larch or something. Spam is so nasty.'

After it was over Ben brooded on Spam and her depressing life working for the horrid farmer, whom they'd seen about before, once carrying a dead kitten down the lane near the farm by the scruff of its neck and throwing it away like rubbish. He mentioned it to Cord several times, how unjust it was, how foul that man was.

But it was the dog-napping which had planted the seed in Cord's head about running away. If they'd only kept the door of the beach hut shut Spam might not have been found and they could have kept her for ever. The grown-ups never went into the beach hut. Daddy was always saying they should sell it, but somehow he never seemed to get round to it.

The beach hut was the children's private world, where they could keep all their beach kit – spades, sieves, windbreakers that made excellent tents and dens. It had the legendary points system and rules for Flowers and Stones stuck to the wall. It was where she and Ben would live in their own private world when the grown-ups had finally gone back to London. They could put up posters of Wonder Woman and some cricketers, there'd be tinned tomato soup and jelly and pineapple chunks for tea, and in the winter, when it was cold, they would burn the old theatre programmes of Mummy and Daddy's which they kept in a big box under the stairs and which Cord had also secretly been transporting across to the hut. She knew how chilly it could be; they had come back in winter for Mrs Gage's mother's funeral; it was quite different here, out of season, the sand grey, the meadow dead and the branches bare, berries instead of green leaves. There were pine cones littering the lane and the fields behind; she'd never seen them there for they had always vanished by summer. Gone where? She didn't know; she had collected a handful of them and stuffed them into the pockets of her winter coat and, once back in River Walk, had lined them up on her window sill, where they rattled when the winds blew, a reminder of the Bosky in winter, its other life she knew nothing about.

Dear Mumma and Daddy,

We do not want to go back, and FG (Ben) does not want to go to Downham Hall. We have told you this lots of times. We are going to stay in Worth Bay and teach ourselves how to live by the beach. Like the children who lived in the barn. We shall be fine. Please do not come and find us, we will write to you again to let you know we are all right, also perhaps to send us money and things to help us if we need it.

Once again we shall be fine please don't look for us. See you next summer.

Love from Flash Gordon and Agchnetha.

P.S. I would still like a Ballerina Sindy with the Gingham Mix and Match Clothes Set for Christmas. Perhaps you could leave it on the porch on Christmas Eve? Thank you.

Ben had cried signing the letter – but Ben was utterly wet, so useless. Cord told herself she'd be strong and tough about it. She wouldn't miss Mumma, not even Daddy . . . She gritted her teeth.

'Cord! Ben!' Their mother's voice outside the door. 'Darlings, breakfast's ready. Get up, I've a surprise for you.'

Cord stiffened, and looked over at the slumbering Ben in alarm. She didn't like surprises and she knew from Althea's voice it wouldn't be a puppy-and-ice-cream surprise, more of a someone-awful-coming-for-tea surprise. Uncle Bertie was already here – who else? They'd had friends to lunch yesterday, Kenneth the actor and his girlfriend Lavinia who was a model. Kenneth had a beard and Lavinia drank too much fruit punch and flirted with Daddy till Mumma suddenly went inside for a nap. Their friends were *always* coming to stay at the Bosky, or motoring down for the day, bringing gin and gramophone records and keeping Mumma and Daddy up late with too much noise and stupid raucous laughter.

'Darlings! Wake up!' her mother called, still nearby. 'The surprise is in the beach hut.'

'Ben,' Cord hissed, urgently shaking her brother awake. 'Wake up. The beach hut. She's found us out.'

But upstairs in the kitchen, everything was normal, and Cord relaxed, wondering if their mother had just made a mistake. Althea had fixed them their special treat breakfast – Weetabix with golden syrup and a slight moistening of milk. Their father sat studying a script and drinking coffee. The day was fine, but blustery.

Outside on the porch, Uncle Bertie was smoking and reading *The Times*. He had been with them for a week and he got on Daddy's nerves and so was often to be found on the porch. Bertie always had something new on the go to fascinate the children. This time it was his new shoes with antique gold compasses sunk into the back of each heel which swivelled as he changed direction. He'd got them from a fellow in World's End, he'd told them, and this had impressed them mightily, though they weren't entirely sure whether World's End was real or a magical place, like Narnia.

Althea was humming to herself, tapping the children's spoons together. Her hair was twisted up on her head and she was wearing a smart green dress. Cord said suspiciously, 'Why have we got a special breakfast?'

'Do I need an *excuse* to be nice to you?' said her mother, laughing. 'Well, that's a damning indictment, isn't it, darling?' She looked over at her husband. 'Tony? I'm off now, and I'll be back tomorrow.'

'Tomorrow?' Ben's lip trembled slightly. 'Where are you going?'

'To London, for an audition, and Uncle Bertle's driving me, so I'll be safe, Ben.' Ben had taken to laboriously reading the newspaper when the adults had finished with it, and was convinced that anyone parted from him would be blown up by the IRA or die in a train, car or plane crash, depending on what was in the news that day, and despite the efforts of his parents to explain the likelihood of accidents to him.

'An audition? Why?'

'For a part in a TV series,' said Althea. 'If I get it, it'll be very exciting.'

'But you don't really act any more,' said Ben, sounding cross. 'Daddy's the famous actor.'

'Oh!' Althea looked at Tony, who shrugged his shoulders, grinning, and took a sip of coffee. 'Well, I do, darling, I just haven't done much for a while, because I've been waiting for the right part.'

'And looking after us.'

'Oh – that too, of course. But this is the right part. Bertle's convinced it's mine.'

'What's it for?'

'A drama series. And – gosh, it'd be . . . Never mind,' she trailed off, staring into space.

Ben furrowed his brow. 'Uncle Bertle drives like a maniac, Daddy said so.'

Daddy stroked Ben's soft, pink-and-cream cheek. 'Bertie's a fine driver, and your mother's going to have a wonderful night in London and make them fall in love with her at the audition so they give her the role and take her out for champagne afterwards. Don't you think they will?' Daddy was standing up now, and had wrapped his arms around Mumma, who was flushing pink.

Cord, scandalised, nudged her father. 'Daddy. You shouldn't be wanting men to take her out for champagne.'

'Oh, I should,' said Daddy, gaily. 'Everyone falls in love with your mother because she's very, very lovable.'

'That's enough, what nonsense,' Mumma said, suddenly sounding Scottish. 'I'll – Tony, you'll be all right, won't you?'

'My love, of course,' he said, and he kissed her hand, almost formally, and they stared at each other for a split second until Mumma turned aside.

'Althea,' called Bertie, appearing in the French windows, waving his cigarette behind him. He ran a speculative tongue in between his lower lip and teeth. 'I say, darling, we'll be cutting it fine if we don't leave soon.'

'I'm ready this moment.' Mumma had picked up her silk jacket and was giving forlorn-looking Ben another kiss. 'I love you, sweet boy. Cord darling, look after Ben. Yes, there's a lovely treat in the beach hut, and I want you both to be very, very good for Daddy. Are you listening to me?'

'What's the treat?' said Ben, stabbing furiously at his Weetabix, syrup clotting on his spoon.

'Well . . . Oh, there she is!' Mumma's voice rose a notch. 'She said she was too shy to come up here. I thought she wanted to wait for you both in the beach hut. Come in, darling! Tony, she's here.'

Through the door came Madeleine. She stood on the threshold, not moving, and gazed around at them all, with a strange look on her face: Cord didn't know if it was fear or excitement. Her cheeks were flushed. Her hair was in uneven bunches, ribbed and bumpy where it hadn't been brushed beforehand. She was a sort of grey-sand colour, because, as Cord was to discover, in summer no one ever told her to have a bath. She wore some tiny apple-green linen shorts, made for a child half her size. The flies were strained open in an O to reveal blue knickers. She had on a large woman's denim shirt and sandals with strange mustard-coloured socks. Her grey eyes were large and round, her small oval face pale.

Again, Cord would always remember the first proper sight of her, not obscured by doors or window frames or running away, and the feeling of falling, of struggling to remember her.

She hung off the side of her chair. 'That's not a surprise. That's Madeleine,' she said, rudely.

'Oh,' breathed Ben. 'Her.'

Their mother's tone was firm. 'Cord. That's enough. Now you two, listen.' She glanced at their father and he nodded. 'Daddy met Madeleine at the beach shop yesterday. Her daddy is . . . ah . . . away, so she's been alone.'

'All on your own! You lucky thing,' said Ben. Madeleine looked at him blankly.

Althea put her arm around her thin shoulders. 'I've asked Maddy to play with you, because she'd like some friends.'

'We don't want friends,' Cord said, folding her arms.

'No, we don't,' added Ben, emboldened.

Their mother sighed in harried frustration. 'Tony. *Tony*,' she

78

hissed into her husband's ear. 'You deal with this. She needs a bath, and some food – she was practically feral by the time I found her, just out on the lane, and she hadn't been in all night because she says she's too scared . . . I have to go, I really do . . . You talk to that man, Tony. Bloody talk to him.'

'Sweetheart,' said Daddy, smoothly to Madeleine. 'Come in and sit down, we'll give you some breakfast.' He held out his hand to Madeleine and she smiled shyly back. He clutched her fingers. 'It's all right. We don't bite, I promise. I'm your friend, aren't I?'

'Yes,' she said quietly. 'Even if you did try to run me over.' Tony put his hands over his mouth and laughed, his eyes half-moons of mirth.

'What?' said Cord, but Madeleine folded her arms again and wouldn't speak.

'Gary, if you could keep an eye on her—' Mumma was saying to Mrs Gage, using the pet name Mrs Gage hated. 'Look out some of Cord's old clothes, poor lamb—'

'Oh, of course,' Mrs Gage answered, heavy sarcasm in her tone. 'Because two of them's not enough is it, and . . .'

Althea ignored her. 'Ben! Don't kneel on your chair. And button up your shirt.'

'I wasn't kneeling, I was doing something Cord showed me. The Bay City Rollers had no shirts on, just jackets on *Top of the Pops* last week, sequinned jackets, and—'

'Don't blame me for it,' Cord bellowed, angrily. 'Don't make it sound like I'm making you behave badly at the dinner table, Flash—'

'I'm starting the car, Althea darling.' Uncle Bertie reappeared in the doorway.

'Uncle Bertie, can you do that thing when you pop your eyeball out?' Ben knelt up on the chair again.

'*Ben*—'

Suddenly, a clear voice cut through the babble.

'Excuse me. Excuse me!' They all stopped, and stared over at the small figure. She was pointing at Ben and Cord. 'I don't want to play with either of you. I'm used to playing by myself. It's much better, in fact, playing by myself. I wouldn't have come at all only your mum and dad were nice to me and there's only dried rice in our kitchen and I get scared there. I think you two are simply awful. So spoiled *and* you're so *pleased* with yourselves.'

Cord stared at her, eyes narrowing. 'Well,' she said, trying to think of a good answer. 'We – *are* pleased with ourselves, so there,' she said eventually, and then she screwed her face up in annoyance as Madeleine gave a superior smirk.

'Cord!' her mother said, sharply, and a car horn sounded at the front of the house. 'Oh, Maddy darling, I'm sorry to have to leave you. Cord and Ben are so excited to have you with them, poppet . . . I do hope you all become friends and – goodbye!'

She dashed down the stairs, slamming the front door, and was gone.

'I say, you three,' said Daddy, heartily, into the silence. 'Isn't this lovely. Now, shall I take you down to the beach? Or shall we all play Happy Families?' There was an awkward pause. 'Or any old game.'

'You don't have to look after me, Mr Wilde,' Madeleine said. 'I'm going now too. Oh, you left the beach-hut door open,' she added in a clear little voice. 'All those tins and piles of food and everything that you're keeping in there, shouldn't go to waste, Mr Wilde, could I possibly take something for my lunch?'

'The food?' said Daddy, bewildered. 'My sweet, there isn't any food in there.'

'But there is. And a pile of theatre programmes and a letter that Cord and Ben have signed about running away – is it part of a game?' She was smiling thinly at Cord now, two spots of pink burning on her grubby cheeks. She hitched the voluminous shirt up over her shoulders. 'I wasn't sure but perhaps I don't really understand about games because I prefer playing on my own.'

Daddy stood up, and without a word strode out down the porch steps and as they saw him weave between the grasses and down towards the beach huts Cord snarled at her brother, 'You *said* you'd locked the door, Ben. I'm never trusting you again. You stupid *baby*.' She shoved him, harder than she meant to, and he fell against the sideboard and banged his head and cried, and got up and tried to push Cord but missed and cut himself again, and Mrs Gage pulled them apart and called them ungrateful little horrors and actually held Cord by the ear, which hurt a lot.

All the time Madeleine Fletcher stood there watching them, arms wrapped round her tiny frame, uneven bunches and that stupid O in her too-tight shorts showing her blue pants and her seemingly not even caring. When Daddy returned, grim-faced, holding the bag of food and the note in Cord's handwriting and the spare teddy that Ben had left there, and when he saw the cut on Ben's head, he sent Cord to her room for the rest of the day.

He came down later on, before lunch, and sat on the edge of the bed, those long sensitive hands that were exactly like hers fiddling with the blancmange-pink fringed bedspread. She pretended to still be crying and he said to her, 'You must be kind, Cord. It breaks my heart when you behave like this.'

'Ben doesn't want to go to school, Daddy.'

Daddy's hair was thinning on top. His face was sad. 'I keep

telling you both, it's not till next year. He's got lots of time to get used to it. Oh, Cord. It's not the lying, or the making plans behind our backs. Sweetheart, have you any idea how upset Mumma and I would have been if you'd run away?'

Cord said in a tight voice, 'Mumma wouldn't care. She told you she never wanted children and you'd taken her whole young life away from her. I heard you both.'

Daddy looked aghast. 'When?'

'Easter. When Mumma wanted you both to go to Venice with Guy and Olivia and Simon and you said no.'

'She – er, well, she didn't mean it. It was the heat of the moment.'

'What's that?'

Daddy suddenly sounded impatient. 'Doesn't matter. Don't change the subject, monkey. I want you to be kind, Cordy. It makes me sad when you're cruel.'

Cord's throat hurt. 'I'm not cruel. But we want you to ourselves. Don't make me be nice to Madeleine what's-her-name, that's all.'

'Her father has been very unkind to her,' he said, picking at the bedspread, and his jaw was tight, so that the words hardly came out at all. 'He left her alone in the house, no food, she can't even reach the taps without standing on a chair.'

'Why?' asked Cord, too young and too securely happy to understand how badly a child can be mistreated.

'He's a sad man. Like his father was. His mummy died.' Daddy gave a big sigh. 'And the war changed a lot of people.'

'Your mummy died and it didn't change you.'

He stroked her hair. 'It did, darling, I'm afraid. Maddy's father is a damaged man. We should be kind to her, till she goes back to Bristol, then her – her aunt looks after her and she's a very nice woman.'

'Did you know her too in the war?'

'Yes.' Daddy paused. 'I loved her very much.'

'More than Mummy?'

'Not more than Mummy. No one more than Mummy.' He slapped his legs. 'Now. That's enough histories. You'll hurt yourself if you're not nice to her, Cordy.' He stroked her cheek. 'Now, you'll stay down here while we have lunch, then come up and help tidy the beach hut. Then we'll all play Flowers and Stones – and that's an end to the matter. For now. But I'm going to go over and talk to her father. I want you to like Madeleine. I owe her aunt something, and the least we can do is make sure her niece is safe with us. You're too young for this. I'm telling you because you're the same as me. And maybe one day you'll understand.'

'OK.' She nodded even though he was right and she didn't understand. 'I'll do my best, Daddy.'

He shut the door behind her and quietly, so she could hear the boards creaking gently, ascended the stairs.

Chapter Six

When Mumma returned from London the following day, without Uncle Bertie in tow, she was glowing. Normally Mumma was slightly chaotic, either dozing or smoking or in a panic, losing things, yelling, making mess wherever she went and, strange to say it, Cord never minded, so this Mary Poppins-like Mumma – joining in when Cord sang, unexpectedly blowing kisses at Mrs Gage, laughing in a trilling birdy way ('like a stupid woman in a stupid film about love,' as Ben put it, disgustedly) – was disconcerting. Cord didn't realise, until Althea jumped violently in the air and dropped a glass when the telephone rang, that her mother was nervous.

She took the phone call in the bedroom and was in there for ages. When she came out on to the porch, her cheeks were pink. She had got the part, she'd told them.

Daddy leaped up, flinging his arms wide, mouth open in a rictus of joy.

'Darling, this is marvellous!'

The children were allowed to stay up and eat nuts and have their own tonic water while their parents drank champagne. 'To Mumma,' Daddy said as they clinked glasses. 'Every actress in town went up for Isabella and she beat them all to it. She's going to be *wonderful.*' His eyes shone; he pointed at Mumma, who shook her head. 'Darling. You deserve this. It's your time, truly it is.' He leaned against the railings, spreading his arms wide and looking out to sea he roared, '"*OTHER WOMEN CLOY THE APPETITES THEY FEED UPON, BUT SHE MAKES HUNGRY WHERE MOST SHE SATISFIES!*"'

'How charming, and how flattering to all women,' said Althea, taking a hefty sip from her glass as the children clapped, rolling around with mirth.

It turned out Althea's new role was rather a big deal. It was the lead in an adaptation of *Hartman Hall*, the eponymous best-seller of the previous summer about an aristocratic Cornish family at the turn of the century. Mumma was Lady Isabella, the tempestuous heiress who wanted Hartman to pass to her, and the Australian actor Ray Harrington was the distant cousin who'd come back to claim his inheritance.

'It's very Women's Lib, really, the whole thing about her inheriting. But I still have to toss my hair a lot and weep on a strong manly shoulder,' Mumma was explaining to Daddy. 'And wear corsets, darling, that's the awful bit. I'm so fat.'

Daddy laughed. 'You! Darling, you're as thin as you were at nineteen.'

'Urgh,' Ben said. He of all of them had greeted the news of Althea's success with the least enthusiasm. 'How old were you when you met Mumma?'

'I was much older. Ten years older. A *coup de foudre*.'

Ben was silent, then he said, 'What's a coo de fooderer? Someone who loves young people?'

Mumma clicked her tongue. 'Honestly, Ben. What do they teach you all day? No, he was twenty-nine. And a *coup de foudre* is . . . Oh, when your heart is captured. That's what Daddy did to me.'

'And me to her.'

Daddy clinked his glass against Mumma's. Sitting in front of them at her father's feet with her own pile of roasted nuts, her back against his shins, her nightdress pulled over her knees, Cord gazed out at the white cliffs of Bill's Point around the bay, glowing coral pink in the evening light. The sea was perfectly still, a calm azure blue, and in the lane behind she could hear a wood pigeon, cooing lazily in the trees. Cord felt serene, utterly happy, and she wished she could bottle the feeling, of being here, the warmth on her arms, her father's bony brown legs supporting her, the faintest scent of her mother's Chanel No. 19, the light fizz of the champagne bubbles.

'When do you start filming, Mumma?'

'October. I'll be away for a while. I have to go to Cornwall for the scenes with the house. So Mrs Berry has kindly agreed to help us out.' The children groaned, and Ben made a loud disgusted noise. 'Well, Daddy can't be expected to look after you.'

'Why not?' said Ben.

'He – well, he has to prepare for *Macbeth*.' Althea looked at her husband.

'So we're just going to be left on our own,' Cord said. 'Like orphans. To fend for ourselves.'

'Don't be dramatic, Cord. Mrs Berry will take you to school and in the evenings she'll make you tea.'

Cord knelt up, eyes round. 'I can walk along the river into Richmond and catch the train by myself. I'll be ten next year.'

Her mother leaned forward and stroked her chin. 'No, you can't.'

'What about me?' said Ben. 'I can take her. I'm ten and I've been thinking, I can easily walk her on my way—'

Mumma said gently, 'No, Ben. Anyway, you'll be away at school the year after.'

'I've said before,' Ben whispered. 'I won't go to that school. I'm sorry but I just w-won't.'

Daddy said, 'Listen here, old chap, let's not talk about it now. You'll love it when you're there. Look at Jennings. You adore the Jennings books.'

'Yes, but that's when . . .' Ben's small voice trembled. 'I thought it was like *The Magic Faraway Tree* or – or *The Lion, the Witch and the Wardrobe*. Not – not real. Made up. I didn't know you could really send a child away to school in real life. Or that you'd want to . . .'

'Oh, darling,' said Mumma, shaking her head sadly.

'Anyway,' Daddy turned to Mumma as if Ben hadn't spoken. 'This is your night, darling. Wonderful.'

'I'm not going,' said Ben again, and he put his hands over his ears. Cord looked at him in disgust. She jabbed his forearm. 'Shh. I say, shh, Ben! You're ruining Mumma's night.'

Ben shrugged defiantly but he lowered his hands. Mumma slid the nuts towards them. 'Here. I shouldn't have any more. It's a strict diet for me from now on. Tony darling, take them away—'

But then Ben screamed and they jumped. 'What are you doing?' Cord said furiously, and she turned and saw Madeleine Fletcher again, standing on the stairs up to the porch. In the fading light she blocked out the sun, casting a long shadow.

The Wildes looked up at her and, instinctively, Cord felt them all huddle together a little closer.

'I came to say thank you for yesterday, Mr Wilde.' She looked at Cord. 'I did want to play with you. I was cross because you were nasty to me. I wanted to say sorry for being a sneak and sorry for fostering emnity between our two houses.'

Daddy laughed. 'No, no emnity to you, darling.'

'Sweet girl,' said Mumma, smiling at her. She came forward. 'Look, won't you stay for some supper? Oh, please do.'

'No!' said Ben.

'Yes, please,' said Madeleine, and she came up the steps, and said, shyly to Mumma, 'Thank you very much.'

'It's nothing. Hadn't you better run back and tell your father?'

'He's gone away.'

'Oh.' Cord glanced over. Her mother was shaking her head at her father. 'Tony, didn't you talk to him . . .'

'Yes,' said Daddy, under his breath. 'I thought I had.' To Madeleine he said, 'He's really left you alone again?'

'You can check the house if you want,' Madeleine said, putting her head on one side. 'I'm not lying. I don't lie. He had to go to a meeting in Birmingham. Steel rods. He's an engineer. He left me some sausages, but I don't know how to cook them.'

Something in Cord's heart was jabbing into her ribs. She didn't feel sorry for Madeleine, not even in the odd Victorian white broderie-anglaise pinafore and buckled-up shoes with no socks that she was wearing, with her bitten nails and her tired face and thick hair hanging like a cloak around her. She realised she was in awe of her. How desperately lonely, or afraid, she must have been to swallow her pride and come back over to this house with these children who'd been so mean to her.

I am going to be nice, she thought, remembering her father's words. Understanding obscurely that Madeleine wouldn't want her to feel sorry for her, Cord stood up and said offhandedly, 'I'll show you where to wash your hands for tea if you want. We were – we were just going to have some supper with our parents.'

'We've had tea,' said Ben. 'What are you talking about? She can't stay, we've had tea.'

Cord sighed. Ben never understood when the battle had moved elsewhere, when the armies were pitching their tents on another field.

'Ben,' said Mumma, whisking a tea towel off the food that

Mrs Gage had laid out ready for Tony and Althea. 'That's enough.'

'Well, I think she should go home.' Ben glanced at Cord for approval.

'Madeleine is a guest in our house,' said Daddy, finally losing his temper.

Ben shouted, 'I DON'T CARE! I live in this house and you don't take any notice of me.'

Daddy stood up, his face white. 'Get out.' He pointed towards the French windows. 'Get out. I'm sick of the sight of you, you ungrateful little coward. Complaining about every little damned thing when I try my best for you. Go to your room. We'll see you at breakfast.'

Ben gaped at his father, and Cord and Madeleine, in the doorway, stood quite still. Then he said, 'Cord—'

There was a tone in her father's voice Cord had never heard before. 'I said, go to your room. Now, otherwise I'll beat you.'

Cord felt hot, sweaty. He'd never do that, would he? Daddy, so soppy he wept loudly when Ben found the dead blackbird chicks in the nest, or when Cord sang *Ave Verum* in her school concert?

'I – sorry, sir,' said Ben softly. 'I didn't mean to be rude.'

'Yes, you did. You're the eldest child and you still behave like a baby. You let Cord lead you around like a whipped dog. Get out of my sight.'

Mumma was in the doorway, watching them both, and she beckoned Ben through, kissing his hair. 'Off you go, sweet boy,' she whispered, hugging him tight. 'I'll see you in the morning.'

'He has to grow up, Althea.' Cord heard her father hurl the words viciously at her mother as Ben went slowly downstairs. 'You spoil him.'

'I don't spoil him,' Mumma said, under her breath. 'Tony – you have to go easy on him. You know you do. It's not his fault.'

There was silence for a few moments, and they heard Ben's bedroom door bang shut.

'I'm going to make a phone call,' said Daddy, and he stamped down the stairs towards the bedroom.

'Is it really all right?' Madeleine said behind her and Cord jumped. 'If – if I stay?'

'Oh – oh, yes, of course. Come in with me.'

Madeleine seemed to hesitate. 'I wanted to go back and get something.'

'What? I can lend you some clothes. If you want. I think you look nice. And we can look at my cassettes while Mumma finishes getting supper ready.'

Madeleine shrugged. 'OK. Thank you.'

Cord shrugged too. 'S'fine. Do you want to look at my ABBA photos? They're downstairs, in our room.'

But Madeleine said no, it was best to leave Ben to himself for a while and so they should stay upstairs. Cord, wishing she'd thought of that, had to agree.

'Did you see them on the *Seaside Special* on TV last week?' Cord continued, leaning against the door frame and pushing herself away with her hands behind her back. 'They did "Waterloo", and "SOS". We're doing a show out here on the porch next week, different songs and music. You should—'

Madeleine interrupted. 'Well, I don't really know ABBA's songs. I've got a transistor radio. With an earpiece. I listen to John Peel in my dorm at school.'

'Oh.' Cord considered this for a moment. 'You should talk to Ben about boarding school, he thinks it sounds awful.'

'It *is* awful,' said Madeleine. 'But it's better than being with Daddy. I'm with Aunt Jules at the weekends and that's fun. We go to the zoo and walking across the downs. She makes cinnamon toast. And she's got a huge cat called Studland . . .' She rolled her hair around her finger, then shook it in front of her face, as though she'd said too much. 'Anyway. Aren't you all pleased about your mother's news?'

'What news?'

'Well, the big part, in that TV series,' Madeleine said.

'How do you know about that?'

'I – I overheard you. As I was coming over here. The wind's in the right direction.'

'Oh. Yes, it's great, I suppose.'

'None of you seems that excited!' said Mads. 'I'd be excited if my mum was going to be a huge TV star.'

'She won't be,' said Cord, dismissively. She could hear the low rumble of her father's voice from downstairs. 'I mean, she's always acted, but Daddy's the star.' She pointed down. 'He's the best actor of his generation. Guy told me.'

'Who's Guy?'

'One of their friends. He's a stage actor too, like Daddy.' Cord tried to explain. 'Mumma doesn't like the attention. She acts to hide away. Daddy acts to see everyone, to be loved, to feel the crowd adoring him. He's like a dog, he just wants affection. Poor Spam,' she said, inconsequentially. 'Poor girl.'

'Spam?'

'A dog Ben found.'

'I saw him with it.'

'Her. She was called Spam.' Cord was only half concentrating; through the wooden boards she could hear that Daddy's voice was raised and he was shouting.

'*I'm trying to be as reasonable as I can! How dare you. No – that's too far.*' There was an awkward silence.

Cord, who always talked too much when she was nervous, said, 'Well, that's great. We can play ABBA, the actual album called *ABBA*, on the record player. My favourite song ever is

"I've Been Waiting for You". Then, I like "I Do, I Do, I Do, I Do, I Do". Five times!' she said, breathlessly. 'Ben hates them. I want to be a singer when I'm older. Or a judge. I'm actually going to change my name to Agnetha.'

'I don't understand why you called yourself Agnetha when you like Anni-Frid's voice better.'

'How did you know that too?'

Madeleine seemed to freeze. 'Oh – I was on my way to the beach. With some friends. They heard you say it.'

Cord had made up her mind now to be nice to this strange girl, so she sat down on the sitting-room floor, and pulled over her basket of cassettes. 'Look, here's the *TV Times*, look at Anni-Frid there, she's got her yellow cat tunic on, that's the advert for the *Seaside Special*. Uncle Bertie's promised me if they do *Top of the Pops* he'll try and pull some strings so I can go and watch them. I can't remember what you said your favourite ABBA song was?'

'Don't have one,' said Madeleine. She shook her long hair so it fell around her shoulders and over her knees. 'I like Bolan, Fleetwood Mac, Bowie. Don't really know ABBA apart from "Waterloo".'

'Gosh. OK then, let me play them to you,' said Cord, pretending not to show how very shocked she was by this. 'Shall I?'

'Yes, go on then,' said Madeleine, smiling behind her sheet of hair, and Cord began hunting through her stack of albums.

How could they have known what would happen?

Fifteen minutes later Daddy returned from his telephone call and was on his most sparkling form and they sat down to supper. He apologised, held Mumma's hand and called her a genius and told them she was destined for superstardom, he drew Madeleine out of herself, got her to tell them about her school in Bristol and how she'd been Mytyl in *The Blue Bird*, looking for the blue bird of happiness. Madeleine was almost animated, propping her elbows on the table as she talked. The quiche was delicious and Daddy said, at the end of it, 'I'll take Ben down a plate. I shouldn't have been so harsh.'

'You weren't too harsh, you were sticking up for me, he was being quite rude,' Madeleine said unexpectedly, and Mumma and Cord smiled at each other, at the obviousness of Madeleine's adoration of Daddy. Over the years it would become a joke, how Madeleine worshipped Daddy, all because he'd run her over.

Now, as Daddy pushed back his chair with a plate for Ben, Mumma poured herself some more wine. 'Children do the plates at supper,' Cord told Madeleine, collecting up the dishes.

'Cord, she's a guest,' said Mumma.

'No,' said Madeleine. 'I'd love to. Please. Then I'll go. Thank you awfully.'

'You're staying the night,' said Mumma, lighting a cigarette and leaning back in her chair. 'You shouldn't be on your own, Mads.'

Madeleine said, 'I'm always on my own, I'm used to it,' and then they heard Tony, crying out into the night.

'He's gone,' he was shouting, and he appeared at the bottom of the stairs. 'Ben's gone, he's run away.'

'No, Daddy, it's a joke, we're not going to do it any more,' said Cord, smiling at him and then her expression froze, her father pushing her aside, thrusting the note at his wife.

'No. This is real.' Flecks of his spittle flew into the dark air. 'He's packed his things – he left this –' He was holding a note, which fluttered in his shaking hands. 'Ben – Ben's gone.'

Cord, looking from Daddy's agonised expression to her

mother's face frozen in horror, mouth wide open, felt a terror that never really left her. That her parents were not in control, that, in fact, they knew as little as she did.

Chapter Seven

Three years later

Sunday, 26 July 1978

When I took up the floorboard on the porch this year to remove the book I felt rather embarrassed. I know them so well now surely I don't need to keep the book there. But I am still afraid they might decide they don't like me so it is good to keep the book safe. I feel calm when I think about it in its little box, safe under the house next to the strange bird man & the old toy car & the ice-lolly sticks.

The Wildflowers are arriving today. When was the last time they were all here together? Well, I know, obviously, I know everything, it was when Ben disappeared.

I can't believe it's been a year since I saw any of them. In fact it is Three Hundred and Forty-Nine Days.

Cord is terrible at writing letters. Ben is even worse. I have so many questions but I obviously can't ask them all, they'd be scared if I did as it is rather strange to want to know as much as I do & I know that but during the rest of the year (349 days) without them sometimes I think I will burst with wanting to know what they are up to as Althea is the only one I ever see and even then that is because she is on television, and not in real life.

1. What clothes will Althea have bought? She seems to have more than ever now. Will she tell me anything about the new series of "Hartman Hall"?

2. What will Cord be into? She is always into something new,

ABBA, then when Ben was in hospital she listened to a lot of David Bowie with him, he's got a transistor radio like mine. So being Cord she is suddenly world expert on <u>him</u>. I learn all about something so we can talk about it together and she's always moved on to something else. After Bowie it was space shuttles. Everything about how they're made. Last year she was obsessed with chess and Garry Kasparov! And I've never played chess ever before so I spent all year learning it & joined the chess club. I got really good because of my strange brain liking things like chess, in fact, I am the best at chess in the whole school and represented Bristol in the Inter-School Chess Championships & then I got one letter from her, ONE LETTER this year in June and she said she hadn't played chess all year she was obsessed with Brezhnev and the Communist Party and Russia and she was a communist!!!!!

I give up!!!!

Well, I haven't learned about Communism. She can whistle for it. I understand what she's like why she's like it, Cord needs something to think about and I like that too. The thing is we don't have anything in common really, apart from laughing. We laugh all the time. She's just so funny.

3. What about Ben? How do I feel about Ben?

(((((No one knows about last summer in the beach hut and I have kept it to myself all year. Anyway there is no one to tell. I don't know much if Cord would like it. It was the last night. I was sad. Ben told me what happened when he was missing for the very first time and we were very quiet afterwards and then he leaned over & kissed me & said thank you for being my friend & not feeling sorry for me. I said, that's OK.

I hate people feeling sorry for me. Althea does a bit and it makes me feel all funny inside. I DON'T like it.

It was the nicest thing that's happened to me and I will carry that till the day I die which I hope is right here with all of them because I will never ever love anything or anyone as much as them.)))))

That is the most top secret thing I have ever written.

Gary says they are coming in time for a late lunch because Althea has an interview with a newspaper in the morning. Gary is their name for Mrs Gage. Althea likes nicknames, Mads, Bertle, Gary. Gary has made meat loaf & a salad. I am hiding behind the wild roses watching her. The hollyhocks are out, they wave in the wind, they're almost as tall as the roof. The doors on to the porch are open, I can see the checked lemon curtains flapping in the breeze and I can hear Terry Wogan on the radio and I can see into the beloved house, I can see the picture of Great-Aunt Dinah on the wall opposite, the raffia wine bottle that's the candlestick, the two wooden stools we always fight to not sit on, the huge chocolate brown teapot on the side, the old worn basket chairs, the dresser, the pile of board games all neatly packed away for once. Stuck behind the dresser on the floor I can see the paper ballgown of the Queen of the Fairies cut-out set we had two years ago which Cord lost & she was so upset about. It's funny, here we play with childish things, silly games and dolls, and it doesn't matter. The ballgown is jammed between the skirting board and the dresser, it must have fallen down there. I will creep in now and go and get it and give it to Cord when she arrives, she will be so pleased with me and I need to straighten the floorboard, I can see I didn't put it back down properly.

The looking forward is almost the worst with the Wildflowers. Because it will end one day & they will be gone. Just for one day, one day I would like to know a feeling where you are totally, utterly happy with nothing else but happiness in your heart, no worries about anything else. Just one day please.

I must go now cos Gary has gone downstairs. I will grab the doll dress and do the floorboard, like a little fairy myself, and no one will know I was there.

Chapter Eight

August 1978

The visitor at the Bosky this summer was expected daily and yet never seemed to turn up. At breakfast, in the fourth week of the heatwave, Mumma turned to Daddy and said, 'A pound says your singer doesn't turn up by the end of the week.'

'Kenneth telephoned yesterday,' said Daddy. 'She's arriving today, apparently.'

'Oh,' said Althea, and Ben saw her frown. 'You might have told me.'

Tony shrugged. 'Where will she sleep? You'll have to tell Bertie he's in the beach hut, if he's thinking of staying this weekend.'

'Bertie's not coming,' said Mumma, shortly.

'Not coming? But I saw him at Claire's the other day and he said he was.'

'He's off for a few days,' said Mumma. She started buttering a piece of toast. 'Got a better offer.'

'You're still annoyed with him about putting you on that sketch show, aren't you? Darling, I thought you were jolly funny.'

Althea spread more and more butter on to her toast. 'I don't mind having the Michael taken out of me, darling.'

'Oh,' said Daddy, with a guffaw. 'Really?'

'No, absolutely not. Not like some. If you must know, Bertie's off to Simon's fiftieth,' said Mumma, almost viciously. Daddy leaned back in his chair and folded his arms.

'*Ohhh*,' he said, a long, drawn-out sound.

'Simon who used to come here and stay with us?' said Cord. No one answered her. 'Who could make birds and things with paper and—'

'Not now, Cord,' said Mumma.

'Why doesn't he come any more?'

'Shut *up*, Cord,' said Ben, desperately.

'He's married,' said Mumma, and she drummed her fingers on the table. 'Some actress he met doing rep. Can't remember her name but she's a sweet thing. I had a drink with them, when he came to the filming. Gosh, what was her name?'

'Typical Simon.' Tony raised his eyebrows, and drank more coffee.

'Rosalie, that's it, Rosalie Byrne.' Daddy started coughing. 'She's Irish.' Daddy exhaled loudly; Ben stared at him.

'Look, I can go home, and Ben can share with Cord,' Mads broke in. Ben watched her anxious face, looking from one parent to the other, and he rubbed his missing fingers, or the stump where they had been. It throbbed most in the mornings, when he'd just woken up and hadn't eaten enough.

'No, darling, it's fine,' said Mumma. She put down her toast. 'It's absolutely fine. Listen, Tony, are you *sure* she's coming today – oh, what's she called?'

'Belinda Beauchamp,' said Daddy. Mumma gave a snort of laughter.

'What a name. Is it real, or a stage name?'

'I don't know, *Dorothy* dear,' said Daddy, shaking out the newspaper with a cracking sound. Dorothy was Mumma's real name, which she absolutely hated, Ben knew that. 'She's coming to teach me to sing this damned song, and the only reason she's staying is because she's Kenneth's god-daughter and he said she's mad about *Hartman Hall* and wants to meet you. All right? She's got pictures of you up all over her wall, apparently.

99

Pretty cracked for a twenty-three-year-old, but there you go.'

'Oh. I see. Well, it'll be lovely to have her here,' said Mumma and Cord sniggered, taking her mother's discarded piece of toast. 'Cord, don't be cheeky.'

'Sorry,' said Cord innocently.

'Darling, that's enough toast for you. You've had five slices,' Mumma said, snappily. Cord pushed the plate away. 'You won't have room for lunch and it's ham.'

'Oh, lovely ham,' said Mads, smoothing over the peace as she always did. 'Come on, Cord, let's go and change our outfits, I'm too hot already in this.'

'Yes,' said Cord. 'Then let's go to the beach shop and get an ice cream.'

'No, darling, not before lunch,' Mumma called out to her as they skipped inside.

'Cord's awfully fat,' said Ben, faux-casually, after they'd gone. 'It's good you're telling her not to eat so much.'

'Don't crawl, darling,' said Mumma. 'She's a growing girl, she needs to eat. I was the same shape when I was her age. It's just she scoffs all morning and then won't have her lunch and she's so rude about it in front of other people. And those plaits . . .'

'What about the plaits?' said Tony, mildly curious.

'Oh, they're the bane of my life. They look like stubby cigars. I wish she'd have it cut into a bob. Or grow it out. She looks like one of the worst St Trinian's girls.' Mumma looked up, and around. 'Don't glower at me, Tony. It's true.'

'Cordy's beautiful.'

'I'm not saying she's not. But facts are facts . . .' She trailed off. 'Never mind. Horrible old Mumma, eh?' She smiled at Ben. 'You, on the other hand, are perfect, my darling. Always have been.'

Ben felt distinctly uncomfortable, whether because of her

stroking his face which he wished she wouldn't do or because of Daddy's quick, contemptuous glance at them.

Daddy stood up. 'I'm going to the beach for a swim before it gets too hot,' he said. 'You chaps coming with me?' He looked at Althea, and held out his hand to her.

'Yes, absolutely,' said Mumma, meeting his gaze and taking his hand in hers. 'Let me just chat to Gary about lunch and I'll join you. I might try making potato salad to go with the ham.'

'Oh, my favourite, how wonderful,' said Daddy. He always greeted every minor effort by Mumma to do something in the kitchen as though it were an attempt on Everest. 'You are amazing, isn't she, Gary?'

'Yes, isn't she,' agreed Mrs Gage, drily, removing the breakfast plates with a clatter. 'Don't worry about the salad, Mrs Wilde, it's best I do it.'

'Oh, well,' said Althea, as though this were a great disappointment. 'Right, let's go to the beach.'

Cord was a brilliant swimmer – she loved being in the water more than anything, and could go out further than the others, and was strong enough to swim against the tide. That day they all swam together, Mumma in her deliciously silly aquamarine swimming costume covered all over in flowers that ruffled in the breeze, Madeleine falling out of one of Cord's costumes from last year, and Ben and Daddy, racing each other in the sea. Cord kept ducking under water when no one was looking and pinching people's toes – only when it was too late could you see her blue form coming towards you like a barrelling torpedo.

'Your lung capacity is astonishing,' Daddy said, wrestling her out of the water as she tried to attack him. 'You should enter one of those contests they have in Bournemouth, the underwater breathing ones.'

'I know,' said Cord, panting, and she dived down again, and tugged at Ben's shorts, suddenly, and Ben screamed in shock, and collapsed, giggling, backwards, into the sea, and they all joined in, laughing as well, and then he found he was choking because he was laughing so much. Madeleine pulled him upright and Mumma patted him on the back, and he hiccupped.

'I'm sorry,' said Cord. 'I didn't mean to—'

'I'm fine!' he said, batting his hand at her. 'I'm going to sit on the sand for a bit.' He waded back to the beach, collapsing on to his beach towel, and glanced casually down. He had thin, spindly brown hairs on his chest, eighteen or so, and he wished they were a bit darker or more visible, and also that he wasn't still so weedy-looking in his orange trunks.

It was strange, all being here again. The year after it happened Ben thought they wouldn't go – Mumma was away filming the second series of *Hartman Hall*. And Daddy was busy with rehearsals for something, he had to do a Scottish accent, and it wasn't very good. But somewhere through the summer something changed – later, much later on when he was a grown-up, Ben realised his father had probably pulled out of the play or TV commitment, whatever it was, because Daddy took them himself and though Ben wasn't sure he wanted to go back to the Bosky yet, the moment the three of them arrived it was wonderful. Mads had made it better too, she seemed to understand, she didn't fuss – Daddy and Cord both did, a bit, at first.

The second summer after, Mumma was filming the third series, and so Mrs Gage had stayed with them and Mumma came down at weekends. Daddy was away in New York doing *Macbeth* on Broadway. It had been OK too, again mostly because Mads was there to do fun things with, and three of them was a gang in the way two wasn't. She and Ben liked the same music, they all liked the same jokes and frantic games. But the great thing about Mads was, she knew when to leave you on your own. Because sometimes Ben wanted to be alone. Not before but now he did, and especially here, when he'd look around and see this beloved place where once he'd been a boy who believed nothing bad could happen to him. But it had and sometimes he wanted to shake Cord awake at night, to tell her she didn't know, didn't understand the real world was very, very different from the shimming, spinning little sphere they'd grown up in. It was a harsh place, where bad things happened.

Mumma being famous changed everything too, almost as much as the accident. Day-to-day life was different because of it, you couldn't walk down the street with her and she was always giving interviews or being on TV shows like *Parkinson*. 'Oh there's Mumma,' Cord said once, casually, turning the TV on and seeing Althea sitting on a sofa looking glamorous as usual. She'd even been in a *Morecambe and Wise* sketch, Eric got a bucket stuck on her head and she'd been so funny, which Ben and Cord liked because Mumma *was* funny.

Sometimes it was great – the viewing parties they had at River Walk, with champagne and all Mumma and Daddy's jolly friends, going to see the filming, people at school asking them about her – and sometimes it wasn't, when she was away for weeks on end and it was them on their own, trying to fill the hours in the big empty house and missing her while Mrs Berry sat in the kitchen knitting. The truth was, anyway, they were a different family now.

Ben hugged his knees. Being at the Bosky brought it all back. Cord had told him once that Mumma had scratched her face to pieces with worry while he was missing. He'd seen the raised red torn skin on her face when he'd woken up at the hospital but hadn't asked – he'd been too out of it, too confused. And then Daddy had appeared, and Ben had told him to go away.

He'd screamed at him, thrashing around and pulling out the tubes and the doctors had had to ask Tony to leave.

Mads waved from the water, and Ben waved back, remembering her lips on his, feeling the warmth on his drying salty shoulders, feeling right and safe and happy. He wished he could stop the world right now, for he hated how when he felt like this the other feelings were not far behind, as though you had to pay some sort of penance for being happy – he drew his arms tighter around him, and shook his head and then there he was, remembering it again, and once he was in it, he couldn't ever stop the reel unspooling in his mind's eye: he would have to relive the whole business, like being strapped to a chair and forced to watch a horror film you've seen many times before. Cord had stopped asking him about it because he'd told her to. But he wondered if they thought about it.

He was fine now, he told Mumma or Daddy or anyone who asked. But it sat with him all the time. Photos in his head, smells that would set it off. Pink-white dogs, like greyhounds, or the smell of tar, or the sight of the silhouette of a tall thin woman ahead on the street. There was so much else in his mind, too, sometimes it seemed there wouldn't be room for it all – how much he hated school and how he worried all the time about IRA bombs and plane crashes, or whether Cord would be knocked over on that corner turning into the station where the motorcycles went too fast, or if Mumma would die of the cancer that killed Jones's mother, or whether Daddy would leave them for another woman, someone younger who would want more children and they'd get forgotten. This had happened to a boy at school, he'd stopped getting birthday presents and eventually he'd had to leave because his mother couldn't afford the fees.

In truth he knew why he worried about these things: so he wouldn't have to think about the others, which were real, which he had heard and knew to be true.

He had heard Daddy say it on the telephone that night he'd left, heard the words float out of his mouth. What if he'd known Ben was listening? What would he have said? *Sorry, Ben, but it doesn't change anything.* Or would he have said, *You've heard the truth now about why I don't love you, Ben, and that's why I'm sending you away to school. I want you out of the house.*

It was all so clear as though it were yesterday.

He'd been minded to run out of the house after the row with Daddy about going to school. He'd decided to go to the beach, paddle in the sea for a bit to calm down. But as he'd stood in the corridor outside his parents' bedroom and he'd heard Daddy talking, he'd realised he had to run further away than that, so far away that none of them could ever find him.

In his pocket that night was a bar of chocolate he'd bought that afternoon at the village shop, as part of the running-away bounty. He'd kept it as a surprise for Cord, a treat to cheer them up on the way back to London. Next to it he slipped in some string, and in the other pocket he wedged a pair of socks, and a clean handkerchief, and two pound notes, his pocket money, saved up to see *Monty Python and the Holy Grail* which was still showing in Swanage. Into his school satchel he put a clean Aertex shirt and a pair of shorts, and *Robinson Crusoe* which he thought might be helpful.

He could still hear Tony in his room talking on the phone. He crept into the hallway, looking up at the lights from the porch, listening for the sound of his sister's voice one last time, but couldn't hear her and so, opening the front door silently, Ben left the Bosky behind and began walking down the lane.

He didn't look back. He tried to feel brave and excited but he didn't. He felt miserable.

As he'd turned on to the road he tried to hold his head up high, slinging the satchel casually to one side so it hung at a jaunty angle. He was a troubadour, a wayfarer. He didn't care if what he'd overheard was true. He didn't care about any of them. Now he wouldn't have to go to that boarding school. He'd find another family, live with them, go back to the Bosky when he was grown up. 'See?' he'd say. 'I'm all right. I turned out all right. I didn't need any of you.'

It was getting dark when he left the Bosky. For a mile or so he was fine, in fact he might almost have been cheerful but for what he had overheard and because he had had to leave Cord and Mads. He ate the chocolate bar and mused about whom he'd live with. A rich family who lived by the sea all year round who had a sports car and a whole floor for Scalextric. They would have fish and chips every Friday and a puppy.

Ben went down a lane he thought led to Bill's Point. He had the vague idea of walking to Swanage over the Downs and going to a Wimpy bar for something to eat. But the lane was the wrong turning and it carried him further up the hill inland, away from the cliffs, where the new holiday bungalows were being built, a long line of them towards the farm. There were no street lights nor any moon so it was very dark now, and when the lady appeared from one of the houses, Ben jumped half out of his skin.

'What are you doing, out this late?' she'd said. She was smoking, wearing a dressing gown, and she had slippers on. Ben felt uneasy. He looked up at the clouded, dark grey night sky.

'I'm going for a walk.'

'A little thing like you? Aren't you a bit young to be walking out by yourself?' She peered at him. 'Oh, my goodness. I know you. You're Tony Wilde's boy, aren't you? I seen you on the beach.'

She laughed and he could smell her stale cigarette smoke. There was something unpleasant about her, with her dyed blonde hair with the black roots growing out, and the thin, disconsolate face. Cord's voice came to him, her face orange and black in the shadows of the candle on the porch. *There's a witch up on the hill. I've seen her. She flew out of the sky one day and she's living here now. Her name's Virginia Creeper. She takes children away.*

He backed away from the house, towards the hedgerow opposite.

'I knew him after the war, you know that? He doesn't recognise me, of course. We were matey, your dad, he's quite the Casanova.' She peered down and stared at him. 'P'raps I shouldn't be talking like that to you. Very friendly, is what I mean to say. He used to be down here all the time after the old lady did a runner . . .' She waved her cigarette at him. 'Your father, oh, ho ho! Them parties he used to have after the war, the people he'd bring down . . . Ho, yuss!' She blinked rapidly. 'Not many left who remember it now, before he got together with your ma, she always looked like she had a poker up her jacksie. 'Scuse my French . . .'

'It's quite all right,' Ben said automatically, feeling sick.

'Strange lot that was, that woman with the scar, the old biddy, him . . . the three of them together, didn't seem right to me even though there was a war on.' She jabbed her cigarette at him. 'Mind you, she was cracked in the head, with her old bits of pottery and her chickens and all sorts. My dad always said he saw her a-stealing one of the candlesticks out of the church but he was a drinker, my dad, didn't know what was what . . .'

She stopped and stared at him, refocusing, and Ben understood then that she was drunk.

'Excuse me, I have to go now,' he said, trying to sound polite. 'Excuse me . . .'

'Oh, don't go, come in! You shouldn't be out, sweetheart.' She leaned against the low wall of her front garden, putting her hand on the bricks, trying to collect herself. 'I'll phone your dad, we'll get him to come and pick you up . . . Have a bit of a laugh, have a drink. Be fun to see him again, after all this time, me and him, we ain't caught up for years now . . .' She was smiling and she leaned forward, and he saw blackheads on her nose, her curious yellow eyes. 'I'll give him a call. Your dad!'

'He's not my dad!' Ben started running, terrified she would reach out and grab him and that he wouldn't be able to get away. He could hear her calling after him, and he kept running now, the change jangling in his pocket, his heart thudding in his throat: 'Oi! Come back, you! Come back!'

He'd run and run past the houses and at the end of the lane he stopped. There was a thin byway stacked high with early blackberries and coral-orange rambling wild roses. It led to the side entrance of the farmhouse where horrible Farmer Derek lived, Spam's owner.

Ben had hesitated, but then as he stopped, heart pounding, he could hear the woman further down the lane, and her voice was getting closer. 'Come here! I want to tell you something!'

He'd run even faster, down a tiny, overgrown lane, through the back of the farm, and hidden in the barn.

It was warm and quiet and he huddled up under some straw, which smelled of piss and sweat; cows, he hoped. But it was safer than being outside, and he stayed very still until his eyes grew heavy.

When he woke up, there was a terrible sound nearby. Ben realised he'd fallen asleep, and he grabbed his satchel, got up and crept slowly towards the door, feeling his way carefully as it was entirely dark now. He opened the latch as quietly as he could, just a few inches.

The noise was a screaming sound, though it wasn't that loud. A whimpering rough bark. As his eyes gradually began to take in shapes and he woke up a little more, Ben could see Farmer Derek, holding a wrench, hitting a dog tied up to a pole in the yard by the farmhouse. It was Spam.

She was so thin. Bones rippled under her white-pink skin, tail curled around her drooping body as if keeping herself tight from the blows she was being given, and Farmer Derek was bellowing at her, hitting her with so much force Ben didn't understand how she could still be making all that noise.

The reason for the starving dog's beating could be seen on the dirt nearby. A dead chicken lay on the ground, neck torn out.

'You fucking waste of fucking nothing, take *that* – can't even keep your own puppies alive, you stupid bitch, *that*!'

Though Spam was frail as a feather in the wind the farmer held on to the pole to give himself greater purchase and, with huge force, kicked her in the ribs. That awful, choking, agonised bark came again. Ben cried out, unable to stop himself, yet the man didn't react: it was as though he were possessed, muttering under his breath as he kicked her again. This time, Spam collapsed on to the floor, and was still.

Run, Ben's inner voice was screaming at him. *Run and stop him. You can bite him, or kick him.*

But he did nothing, rooted to the spot in terror.

With one more kick Farmer Derek gave a semi-satisfied grunt and muttered, 'Get up from that and snaffle one more of my chickens, just you try, you greedy bitch,' and left the still body of the thin dog as he went inside, slamming the door shut with his foot. Ben waited a moment, sick with guilt and disgust at himself, and crept over the shit and mud in the yard towards Spam.

He stroked her thin, warm body and whispered in her ear, but she didn't move, not at all. And he'd realised he couldn't go home, perhaps not ever, because he was a sissy who watched a dog being beaten instead of trying to stop it. Daddy was right, and he'd deserved it.

Ben stayed there for a long time, in case he could hear her breathing again. But she was heavy, and perfectly still, and he knew she was dead.

He thought he'd carry her away somewhere to try and bury her, up on the downs, and so he tried to stand up with her in his arms, but she was still chained to the pole and it made a great clanking sound, the heavy links banging against the metal.

The door of the farmhouse opened, and Farmer Derek stood in the doorway. He was small, really – Cord had remarked on this when he came to collect Spam. 'Such a titch,' she'd said, dismissively. He stared at Ben, there in the dim light – Ben still wasn't sure if it was dusk or morning.

'Oi, you,' he said. 'Who's that?' Ben put his head down. He couldn't recognise him. 'Come here,' and he started after Ben. Ben put Spam back down on the ground, as gently as he could, and then ran again, so fast he tripped once or twice. He ran out through the farmyard past the little lane and past the barn and towards the edge of the farm boundary.

'Come back! You little – who's that, is that that little git – come back you, you come here!'

Farmer Derek was short but he was fast, gaining on him with every second. Ben, swinging his satchel out of the way, climbed up and on to the fence that ran alongside the open country. The fence was wood and metal, and as he moved one foot from the bottom plank of the fence to swing his leg over the top and jump out, his other foot, carrying his weight, slipped. He jolted, and tumbled forwards, and his hand caught the metal tread that bound the fence together, where the wood had been worn or chewed away. In a split second, freeze-framed, he moved his body away and tumbled to freedom but his hand, moving from the top plank, caught the sharp metal and tore through it.

He landed with a thud, rolling over, almost pleased with himself – he remembered that bit. He was, he was pleased, he could hear the farmer's shouts, his white fury, the terror of it. And it wasn't until he'd run a couple of hundred yards or so, out of sight of the farm buildings, and suddenly fallen into the long, swaying grass that he'd looked down, almost with surprise, and seen his skin sticky with blood and this strange, odd hand, nothing about it right.

It wasn't painful. And he looked at it and wondered why.

Then everything went black, and the pain kicked in, a roaring, gnawing pain, and he tried to keep running, but he couldn't. He could see the strange woman on the path, the witch with dirty blonde hair, and the farmer, and he could hear Daddy's voice, dismissive, curt, on the phone, and feel still the sensation of Spam's rippled ribs under her soft, thin coat, the warmth of her body. Then nothing.

They found him two days after he'd run away, unconscious, in an old stone barn up on Nine Barrow Down. He didn't remember how he'd got there; he must have crawled somehow. He was lying on the ground, his copy of *Robinson Crusoe* as a pillow, and had covered himself with his coat.

'It's a miracle, really,' one of the nurses had told Althea and Tony at the Royal Bournemouth Hospital. 'The infection, the amount of blood he lost – he could have . . . He must have had an angel watching over him.'

Ben had torn three fingers away from his left hand which was infected; this was why he'd eventually lost consciousness. In a way Ben liked having some sign, a memento that reminded him it was real. He told them about the crazy lady in the bungalow and the horrible farmer, and the police went to talk to him, gave him a telling-off, nothing more. Ben wrote to *Blue Peter*, trying out writing with his right hand. 'People should do more to help animals in bad houses,' he wrote. Mumma posted the letter. They sent him a badge, and a special note from the programme's editor. He wore the badge for weeks. But he never told them the rest of it, about the reason he'd run away in the first place. They had no idea, none of them, and so they never asked.

The midday sun gave the sand on the beach a blinding glare. Sitting there, knees drawn up under his chin, Ben blinked, pushing the memories away. When his eyes were closed he could see the red of his eyeballs and when he opened them the world was momentarily black, the bodies of his family in the clear blue sea forming slowly into jumbled shapes of yellowish pink and suddenly he got up and ran into the water, the cool slicing across his hot sandy body.

'Oh, hello, darling. I'm going back up now,' said Mumma, and he reached out and grabbed her arm, suddenly frantic.

'No, don't, please, Mumma, stay in a bit longer.'

She turned and saw his pale face. 'Of course,' she said, and hugged him in the water, and he let her, let her kiss his wet head. They played sea battles, Mads on Cord's shoulders, Mumma on Daddy's, splashing each other in the cool water until one fell over with great shouts of hilarity, and they dived through each other's legs, and Daddy swam out, so far he said he could see the tank left behind in the Second World War. The day was calm, hot – not as hot as the previous years but almost. After the games were over Ben lay on his back in the water, gazing at the Bosky, perched high above the beach, towels drying on the porch, cool pine trees behind, the flowers tangling themselves around the front of the old wooden house.

Eventually Mumma and Daddy went up before the children, to wash and get ready for lunch. Cord, Ben and Mads stayed in the water until their fingers were waxy-white and they were shivering. When they got out, slightly sick through excess swallowing of seawater, the sand was almost too hot to walk on.

'Ow,' said Mads, who had no shoes. 'This is agony.'

'Even for you, who feels no pain?' said Cord.

'I know. It must be a hundred degrees today,' said Mads. She hopped from toe to toe.

'Here,' said Ben, distressed at her wincing, wet face. He scooped her up in his arms and carried her to one of the beach-hut steps, and deposited her there rather hastily. Cord watched them.

'Oh, thanks, Ben,' said Madeleine, and she smiled up at him through her hair.

'No problem,' he said, shrugging.

'Mads, you're red!' Cord yelled. 'Oh, my goodness. You love Ben!'

Ben was suddenly furious, the heat of the day getting to him at last. 'Shut up, Cord, just shut up.'

'OK!' Cord stared at him, then raised her hands.

Ben stomped on ahead of them, feeling his sister's gaze on his back as they wound through the scrubby grass back to the house, the crystal clarity of the euphoria he'd felt in the sea utterly washed away. He could hear them laughing, and could see, if he turned slightly to the right, their distorted midday shadows, heads melded together like conjoined twins. Suddenly he was annoyed with Mads, instead. Why did she *always* have to be there?

The memory of her warm, thin lips on his last summer – how they had kissed as if drawn together like magnets, then both instantly sprung apart. He shivered, confusion mixing with pleasure at the memory. He thought of her small pale face and her tiny feet hopping across the sand and how Mumma had stood at the window watching her and Cordy running down to the beach and telling him Mads's bruises were from where her father had pushed her down the stairs when he was drunk. And how the police had warned him about it but they, the Wildes, still had to make sure she was all right. He thought about how lucky he was, and yes, he was, even the secret he carried around with him now, and the running away, all of that wasn't as bad . . . He saw her sweet, solemn face, the eyes with their heavy lids shut tight, hair rustling as she moved slowly towards him, wanting to kiss him . . .

The truth was he liked thinking about her, even if it made him feel funny, hot with guilt. *Don't. It's Mads. Think about something else. Flowers. Or Stones.*

Slowly, head down, he ambled towards the porch steps. But as he threw his shoes down on them a low, lilting voice said, 'Oh, hello. I'm so glad someone's here! I was starting to wonder. The radio's on inside but no one's answering. This is Anthony Wilde's house, isn't it?'

Ben, blinking in the shade of the porch after the glare of the sun, saw a long skirt, long top, floppy hat, long hair. Ever alert to danger, he peered towards the plumpish figure, suddenly scared of the low voice and thinking it might be a man in disguise – he'd heard that's how they sometimes operated, dressing up as women – but then he shook himself. That wasn't a man.

'I'm his – I'm Ben.' He wondered where Mumma and Daddy were. Hadn't they gone back ages ago?

The woman – though really she was more of a girl, not that old – leaned forward. 'Hello, Ben. It's lovely to meet you.'

Ben felt shy, and he wished he knew what to do in this situation. Cord would have had Girl-Woman correctly evaluated and, if she deemed her trustworthy, chatting on the seat on the porch within five minutes.

'Um,' he said. 'Come in then?' He stopped. 'I mean – sorry. Who are you?'

'I'm Belinda Beauchamp.' She pulled at one strand of honey-coloured hair. 'I'm the singer who's coming to train your daddy for *Jane Eyre*.'

'Of course.'

'I nearly gave up. I'd been driving round for ages before I found the right place.' She took the floppy hat off and threw it smartly on to the basket chair, and shook out her long hair, smiling at him. She had a gap between her teeth, like Mumma. 'I was crying at one point, I was so worried. I mean, it's *Tony Wilde*!' She gave a little laugh.

'Yes,' said Ben.

'I'm being silly,' and she shrugged her shoulders with a wide, gleaming smile. The material of her top was strange. He didn't understand what was going on with it: there were lacey strings on it, up and down and he could see . . . He shuffled on his feet, wishing Cord was here, once again.

He took Belinda inside and gave her a glass of water, and they came back out on to the porch, and he offered her a seat, and all the time she talked: about her training at the Royal Academy, how she'd met Joan Sutherland once at a schools concert and it was the proudest moment of her life when she'd said, 'This girl was born to sing.' How she was a singing teacher, because she'd had problems with her voice so she was training people instead and that was wonderful, very interesting work . . . She kept on talking and Ben watched her and watched the strange top and her breasts jiggling inside it and the gap in her teeth and her slim feet, which were caramel brown, whereas he could see her legs weren't.

Then he heard thudding footsteps on the rickety stairs and he looked over to see his parents, Daddy halfway up, Mumma just emerging from the bedroom. 'Where have you been?' he demanded.

'Downstairs,' said Daddy, peering at the guest. 'We were dressing.'

'We were . . . sorting some things out,' said Mumma, who had changed into a sundress, and was patting her hair into place. 'Oh,' she said, coming forward. 'I do apologise – darling Ben, you should have told me someone was here.'

'Belinda Beauchamp,' said Belinda, and she held out her hand to Mumma. 'I'm awfully late, I should be the one apologising.'

'We thought you were coming this evening,' said Mumma, and she shook her hand. 'Oh, dear. Have you been marooned on the porch wondering where we all were?'

'No, no, I had Ben to take care of me,' she said, and she smiled at Ben. 'Hello, Mr Wilde. Belinda Beauchamp. I'm so grateful to you both for offering to put me up.'

Her blue eyes glinted briefly at Mumma, but drifted back towards Daddy and Daddy laughed. 'My pleasure, my dear,' he said, and he shook her hand. 'Kenneth tells me you had a beautiful voice. I'm so sorry about what happened.'

'Thank you,' said Belinda, and she glanced down at the wooden deck. Ben, watching her, felt a bit funny, as though his heart were full, as though he wanted to cry. He pulled surreptitiously at his shorts. *No, please not now.*

'I'm very lucky you're here to teach me a thing or two,' said Daddy, scratching his neck and gesturing to her to sit again. 'Can we get you a drink? Althea darling, you stay here and chat to Belinda Beauchamp.' He dropped a kiss on Mumma's bare shoulder and she closed her eyes, just for a second, and caught his fingers as they lightly gripped the back of her neck.

Ben guessed what they'd been doing downstairs. He shuddered. His parents were mortifying in that regard. He'd heard them once doing it on the porch, when he'd come back upstairs to get a glass of water late at night. *On the porch*, when they had a perfectly good bedroom.

Belinda Beauchamp had tucked her feet up under her and her hair behind her ears and was listening rapt to Mumma when Ben reappeared with a gin Martini for Mumma and a ginger ale – 'Oh, gosh no, I'm a little inexperienced when it comes to alcohol' – for Belinda Beauchamp. Daddy passed around the delicious little cheesy biscuits they saved for guests and they stared out at the sea, where the heat of the day seemed to shimmer in front of them, bouncing in wavy lines off the beach-hut roofs.

'The singing lessons, then,' said Daddy. 'How do you want to do it?'

Belinda Beauchamp sat up, untucking her feet. 'Of course. Well, I have a little guitar with me. I'll teach you the song and make sure you're comfortable singing it. Mr Rochester needs to sound authoritative when he's singing. Not shy. Or tentative. He's the sort of man who—'

'I know how to play my character, thank you,' said Daddy drily.

She coloured a deep raspberry red. 'I'm – I'm sorry – I only meant with regards to the song . . .'

'I'm teasing you.' Daddy smiled at her.

What had happened to her voice? Why was she a teacher? Why was her hair blonde in some places at the front, dark amber in others? Did she have a boyfriend? He stared at her, hungrily, as though she were an exotic animal that might at any time escape, fly out into the afternoon.

Luckily Cord and Madeleine arrived back that instant, having got chatting to some other children by the beach huts, and he was able to hang back and let them take over, exclaiming over Belinda Beauchamp's hair and sandals, her necklace – 'It's lovely, did you make it?' 'No, my mother brought it back from Marrakech.'

That was the sort of chatter he was hopeless at. It wasn't until they were downstairs washing their hands for lunch that he said to Cord, 'She's nice, isn't she? I hope she's nice. I don't want her ruining our holiday.'

'She's nice enough,' Cord said darkly. 'But she needs to wear a bra. It's totally inappropriate to have *them* hanging out like that, not with a top that see-through. I don't care what Women's Lib says. Mumma won't like it either.'

Chapter Nine

Belinda Beauchamp was only supposed to stay for two nights but a week later she was still there. Uncle Bertie reappeared after two years' absence, sporting a mysterious black eye he claimed was the result of an argument with a belligerent milkman blocking the road early one morning. Daddy's old friends Guy and Olivia de Quetteville were there too, for the weekend: they knew Kenneth, Belinda's godfather – in Mumma and Daddy's world everyone knew everyone. Ben found it wasn't like that in the real world.

While the de Quettevilles were staying Ben slept on the sofa and Bertie on the porch hammock, really quite happily, and Madeleine had to go back to her father's, he said, though Cord said it was jolly mean to make her. But Mumma was firm, saying Madeleine had to make an appearance there once or twice in the holidays, it wasn't fair to ignore her father completely. Cord said – with reason, Ben thought – well, why did he still bother to go to Worth Bay in the summer anyway when he obviously hated it so much?

Ian Fletcher came to fetch Mads after tea, and Cord stared at him – they never saw him. He was thin, and wiry, with a small bristly moustache, a long face with a tuft of hair at the top. 'He looks like a toothbrush,' Cord had said, and Ben had wanted to laugh out of nerves, because Mads's father barely said a word, didn't make eye contact, spoke to Mads whilst staring at the floor. Mumma invited him in for a drink, and he said no, and Ben loved her for trying, for being friendly.

'Thank you, but it's time to go back,' he'd said to Mads, and she'd trailed along behind him, head down, waving one listless arm, and Cord had squeezed Ben's hand. They hated the idea of her staying at Beeches with him now. She didn't belong to him any more: she belonged to them.

Belinda Beauchamp shared Cord's room. Cord was funny about Belinda Beauchamp, Ben could tell she was falling for her a bit and he didn't like it much. Cord was a great one for crushes, on the French mistress and Carolyn who'd starred in the play at school. That summer she was very into poetry, and songs. She was always quoting things Belinda said and had entirely stopped wearing her plaits, although instead of her hair flowing around her shoulders like rippling sunlight-ish water, as Belinda's did, it sort of stuck out at the edges, brown and dried with sun and sea.

They'd sing together in their room, Ben would hear them. It was lovely. Cord rarely sang in front of her parents. She'd only sing inside the Bosky when Mumma was sunning herself out on the little patch of sand in front that got the sun. This was in the mornings, and Belinda Beauchamp would strum her guitar softly waiting for Daddy to come out on the porch and then they'd rehearse together, he laughing, she gently encouraging. She was a good teacher, Ben could tell, having had ample experience of bad ones. Daddy *didn't* have a good singing voice, though his speaking voice was obviously fine. He made a sort of strangulated noise when he had to sing; it was something of a family joke and though when they were younger he'd sung often, and loudly, over the years he'd become self-conscious about it. He'd turned down several parts because they had singing in them. Ben wondered why he hadn't turned *Jane Eyre* down, only everyone said it was going to be the next *Hartman Hall*. They were giving it the big BBC Sunday-night slot on TV, beginning the week after the next series of *Hartman Hall* came to an end.

Guy de Quetteville had a small part in *Jane Eyre* too. His wife, Olivia, was a wonderful stage actress. Normally Ben and Cord avoided the theatre – they'd been forced to go as children and their overriding memory was usually of the too-scratchy velvet lining the boxes they were allocated that prevented them going to sleep. But Ben and Cord had actually enjoyed the one thing they'd seen Olivia in, the previous year. Althea had taken them to see Daddy, who was Bottom to her Titania in *A Midsummer Night's Dream* at Regent's Park Open Air Theatre. As the sun set, twinkling fairy lights had come on in the branches. It was completely magical, and the children had both actually laughed at the business with the chink in the wall and the Rude Mechanicals. Daddy was so funny, waving directly at them at the end of the play, calling out their names so everyone turned to look at them, blowing them kisses – Ben had hated it, but Cord had lapped it all up, the whole evening. Olivia as Titania was beautiful and terrifying and silly at the same time, with blue and green make-up and a gold headdress, and wings, her voice sharp, husky with passion. She was nothing like the elegant, rather dry Olivia whose hair was always perfect and who said very little. Afterwards, when they'd all met at the theatre bar for a drink, the children were too shy to talk to Olivia, normal again in her Breton striped top and cropped trousers.

'Wasn't she *amazing*?' Cord had whispered, in the long cab drive back to Twickenham afterwards. 'Wasn't she just like a real queen? Wasn't it *incredible*?'

On Olivia and Guy's last evening they all sat out on the porch after supper – the children were up later than usual, Madeleine having eaten with them as well. A full August moon hung low in the sky; the stars were brighter than ever, the Plough just over the roof north of the house.

It had been another heavy, hot day: no wind, no chill at night.

Daddy was downstairs, talking to his agent in America. Mumma and Bertie were flopped out in the chairs and Guy and Olivia were on the sofa. Belinda Beauchamp sat on the footstool, gently plucking at the guitar, just a few random chords here and there. The crickets chirped loudly in the hedgerow behind them; candles burned to ward off the mosquitos. It was perfectly still. The children sat huddled together on the old patterned mattress in the corner, half asleep but not wanting to move in case the grown-ups realised and made them go to bed. And suddenly, Olivia started speaking.

> *Fear no more the heat o' the sun*
> *Nor the furious winter's rages*
> *Thou thy worldly task hast done,*
> *Home art gone, and ta'en thy wages:*
> *Golden lads and girls all must,*
> *As chimney sweepers, come to dust.*

She didn't say it loudly, or declaim, just spoke gently, and it made the hairs on Ben's whole body stand up. He knew the verse: Althea had taught it to him and Cord, a little song to sing when they were afraid, having woken from a bad dream, or having to come back to a dark house before she'd had a chance to turn the lights on, when shadows moved and made them both jump. But, listening to it again, the verses scared him, rather than comforting him. We will all die, and come to dust. He bit his thumb, shaking away the bad memories again, helpless to stop them. It was like that, when they came: he'd be fine for days, weeks sometimes, and something would happen and he was strapped to the chair, watching it all unfold again. He balled his damaged left hand into the right one and swallowed, pushing down bile.

But then suddenly Cord, hidden in the shadows, started singing.

> *Fear no more the lightning flash*
> *Nor the all-dreaded thunder stone.*

She stopped, and cleared her throat just a little. Then she slid her hand into Ben's, squeezing them tight.

> *Fear not slander, censure rash;*
> *Thou hast finished joy and moan:*
> *All lovers young, all lovers must*
> *Consign to thee, and come to dust.*

She sang two more verses, hand still in his, her voice swelling as the final verse sounded loud, Belinda Beauchamp picking out a tiny harmony on the guitar, and when she finished there was silence. Ben squeezed her hand tighter still.

'I know you're afraid of things,' Cordy said to him, so quietly that even Mads, half asleep, wouldn't have heard. 'I wish you weren't, Ben. I'll always look after you. Promise. We're the Wildflowers.'

He said nothing; his throat was too tight. 'Did you hear me?' she said, still very quiet. 'I promise. I'll always look after you. We'll always be together.'

He nodded, still unable to speak, and squeezed her warm little hand again.

Belinda had put her guitar down. 'Cord,' she said, in a strange voice, 'who taught you that song?'

'Mumma,' said Cord, absently, still looking at her brother. 'She had to learn it at Central.'

'I mean—' Belinda blinked. She turned to Mumma, who was smiling at Cord. 'Has someone taught her to sing like that?'

Mumma was nonplussed. 'No. She's got a lovely voice, though, haven't you, Cord? Always has done.'

'Yes,' said Belinda Beauchamp quietly. 'Yes, she really has. I wonder . . .'

Olivia clapped gently. 'Hear, hear,' she said, and Guy joined in. 'Marvellous, Cordy, here, imaginary bouquets to you, prima donna.'

Ben knew Cord wouldn't like clapping, or flattery, she didn't do it to show off or get applause, she did it because singing was part of her. It always had been. His first memory of his little sister was of her in a cherry-red knitted cardigan with a rose on it, humming to herself as she lay back in her cot, waving her fat feet in the air. Belinda Beauchamp got up, stumbling a little on a loose floorboard. At the doorway she paused.

'You were born to sing,' she said. 'It's a gift, singing like that. You must use it.'

She went downstairs, and the others were left looking at each other. Cord said nothing, just stared at the French windows, where Belinda Beauchamp had been standing. Mads giggled.

'She's ever so dramatic.'

'Belinda? She's a funny girl, rather theatrical. But I'm fond of her,' said Mumma, sipping her drink. 'It was her great dream to sing professionally, you know. But she had a growth on her vocal cords. They took it out last year. She hasn't sung since.' Glancing at Cord, she said, 'It is a gift, darling, she's right.'

Ben said hotly, 'She's not a funny girl.'

He saw his mother turn to him, and felt himself blush, furiously.

'Sweetheart – I wasn't laughing at her.'

'She's not over-dramatic, she's just being honest, you wouldn't understand that . . .' He trailed off, his face hot, and there was silence. He couldn't say what he really wanted to. What he'd wanted to say to Mumma these last few years and never would. But this last week, meeting Belinda, had changed everything. Though there was seven years between them he was going to tell her soon that he loved her and the age gap wouldn't matter. Daddy was years older than Mumma, not that they were any example. Ben vowed he'd become rich somehow and she'd never have to worry about teaching again, and he'd find someone to mend her voice and he would look after her for everything else . . . Her gentle voice, her sweet nature, the way her breasts bounced against her top . . . She was natural and real. 'She's not a liar. Not like you.'

There was a thick, tricky silence. 'What do you mean?' his mother asked, eventually, and there was a dangerous note in her voice. He heard Guy mutter something to Olivia.

'You know what I mean, Mumma,' he said, his voice trembling.

They were on the brink, he knew, and he was about to step into the chasm—

But then he shook his head. 'It was all she wanted to do and it's been taken away from her. That's – that's all.' Ben shrugged, retreating from the edge of the abyss. But, *I know all about you and Daddy. I've known for three years now*, he thought, looking at her.

Guy muttered something about turning in and Olivia nodded assent. Ben saw her raise an amused eyebrow at Althea, who smiled. Rage coursed through him. They were all liars, all cheats.

Olivia stood up. 'Well done, Cordy,' she said, blowing Cord a kiss. 'That really was astonishingly beautiful. I'll be watching you at Covent Garden some day, I've a feeling in my bones.' She yawned. 'Gosh, I'm done in now.'

Mumma suddenly seemed to notice the time. 'Mads, you'd better sleep on the other sofa, since it's so late,' she said. 'Ben, go and fetch some spare sheets from our room.' She came over to them, looking down as she stumbled slightly. 'That floorboard is loose,' she said. 'We need to nail it up – why, Mads, you look done in, darling. Let me get you a glass of milk. Cord, go and help Ben fetch the bedding.' She touched Cord's chin. 'You made me very proud. Cordy? Are you listening? Go and help Ben.' She pressed her daughter's shoulder, lightly, and Cord shook herself.

'Yes, yes, of course,' she said. Afterwards, long after this, she would tell Ben what that moment was like, how everything was clear to her now, how she knew she had found the missing piece of the puzzle. She shook Ben's arm. 'Come on, let's go.'

She turned for the staircase and went downstairs, and Ben followed.

But Cord reached Mumma and Daddy's bedroom before him and put her hand on the door handle. Noiselessly she opened the door and was now standing still, staring into the room through a narrow crack in the doorway. The dim glow of the bedside lamp cast her into golden shadow. Her mouth fell open, into a small O. Slowly, she shook her head.

He moved towards her, afraid, and she tried to push him back but he stood behind her instead and stared over her shoulder. He screwed up his tired eyes, afraid now of what she could see.

Visible through the partly opened door was their father, pushing up against someone on the far wall. He was groaning, then he moved back and Ben saw it was Belinda he was pressing himself against. Daddy had his hands on her waist, her top was wide open, and he was kissing her, and her head was thrown back. He could see her small, even teeth. Her golden hair was all messy.

'No,' she was saying, wildly. 'Oh, Tony, I came down to tell you—'

'Shh, my darling, quietly,' Daddy said, kissing her neck, and he pulled down her gathered top, exposing her plump, beautiful breasts and with his big hands he held them, lifting them a little so that the soft white flesh spilled out on either side of his tanned fingers. He began kissing one breast then the other, Belinda sagging slightly, her eyes closed, and Ben thought he might be sick.

'All night, I've been waiting for this,' Daddy was saying. 'It's torture to watch you, do you realise . . .?'

Cord reached for Ben's hand, hanging beside her. He rested his chin on her shoulder. Her fingers tightened around his.

Daddy's hair was fluffed out at the back, and slightly greying. Ben had never noticed before. Mumma's nightie was on the bed, pink silk and oyster lace. She had a matching dressing gown. She'd bought it from Harrods with the first lot of the *Hartman Hall* money; Ben remembered the day she'd come back from shopping, swinging the bags as she got out of the cab . . . He looked at it, then back at them. Ben could see Belinda Beauchamp's nipples now, shell-pink and tight, the flush on her neck. He thought frantically that if he got an erection now, watching this, he would be the most disgusting person alive.

In the first few seconds it seemed unbelievable they hadn't been noticed. But the door was only open a foot or so and he found himself staring for a little longer, straining to hear their frantic whispers, the wild, hungry look on her face.

After another moment Cord backed out, quietly, not daring to shut the door again, and turned to him. Her heart-shaped face was white. Then she pursed her lips together, gave a small shrug: *What do we do?*

In answer Ben turned and went upstairs, and Cord followed him, slowly, silently.

'Did you know?' she whispered, at the top of the stairs.

Ben shrugged. 'Not really.' He ached to tell her what he had heard the night he'd run away. *They're both liars, as bad as each other.* Upstairs, he could hear Mads and Althea in the sun room, laughing at something.

Cord's eyes were huge. 'It's – it's awful. Daddy—' She rubbed her face. 'How could he?'

'That's what they do,' Ben said. He shrugged bleakly.

Her face was utterly white.

'Well, I won't be like that, like either of them,' she said. Ben smiled for the first time.

'How can you say that?'

'I can because I know.' She shook her head again. 'My throat hurts from whispering. What do we do about the sheets?' Her hands closed over his wrist; she stared up at him imploringly; she wanted him to make everything all right and he couldn't.

Ben went to the crowded dresser. He picked up an old stone paperweight, shaped like a bird, and held it in his hand. Cord stared at it.

'What are you doing?' she hissed.

Ben met her gaze. He stretched out his arm and dropped the bird over the bannisters that looked into the hall. It smashed on to the hall table, shattering the bowl that held the keys, shattering the ink-black silence of the floor below. Then, seconds later, he heard his father's voice.

'Jesus, what the hell was that?' Daddy appeared in the corridor, shutting the bedroom door behind him. Ben ran downstairs, glancing up at Cord.

'I knocked that bird over . . . it must have fallen off the dresser, and I kicked it through the bannisters.'

'That was Aunt Dinah's. Alulim. He's very old.' Daddy was crouched, sweeping up the bits. 'She dug him up. Jesus, Ben. Jesus Christ.'

'It was an accident, Daddy,' Cord called over the bannisters to him.

'I know it was an accident but please, be a bit more careful next time. Someone might have been hurt.'

'Yes, they might,' Ben said. His father stared at him.

'You could say sorry, darling.'

Ben said slowly, 'Sorry, Daddy.'

He made a vow never to call him *Daddy* again. Such a silly name for a person like him.

'I – I need to get some sheets from your room. For Mads.' Tony rubbed the top of his head; the hair fluffed up and he smoothed it over his balding spot. Ben remembered the times his father had scorned men like Uncle Bertie who combed hair over their pate.

'I'll get the sheets. You fetch the dustpan. There's broken bits everywhere but the bird's all right, thankfully. Good old Alulim.' He held it for a moment. 'King for twenty-eight thousand years, he was. She used to use him to weigh down the tablecloth when we ate outside, of all the prosaic endings.' Then he stared up at them, pinching the bridge of his nose. 'Don't come down. You might cut yourself.'

Ben nodded, miserably. 'Yes, sir.'

Cord moved towards the kitchen, and Tony's expression softened. 'It's all right. Fetch the dustpan, OK?'

In that one moment Ben suddenly felt somehow lighter, relieved of some burden. He could not love this man in the way he had, it just wasn't possible. He was able to shout at Ben about some old paperweight from some stupid old aunt when he'd just been doing *that* in the bedroom . . . Belinda's face, her flushed neck, her amber-gold hair tumbling around her as her fingers caught at him, pulling him closer . . .

Why's he like this?

Around the corner, Cord had begun singing to herself, her sweet voice low and sad.

'Fear no more the heat o' the sun—'

'Sorry,' Ben said to her, under his breath. 'I'm sorry, you shouldn't have seen any of that.' His father was crouched below him, picking up the broken shards of the plate, the paperweight still clenched in his hand. Cord carried on singing.

> *Golden girls and lads all must,*
> *As chimney sweepers, come to dust.*

Chapter Ten

Dorset, August 1940

Ant sat in the dark green Morris 8, looking for healing scabs, and when he found one on his shin, a fat, pinkish primrose, he picked at it with angry relish.

The car was wedged up beside a strange house. A voice came floating in through the open window, along with a faint smell of honeysuckle and briny seawater.

'Come on, old girl. Hhhup. *Hup!*'

Ant gritted his teeth, eyes narrowed with loathing, and pulled off the scab.

'Shut up,' he muttered, under his breath.

'That's my girl. *H-h-h-hup.* Oh dear. Oh dear, the planes – they're definitely getting closer, aren't they?'

Before his mother died Ant had thought he hated Hitler, and the anonymous men who shot down his father, and most of all he had hated night-time – the terrifying, enveloping cloak of dark that descended on London each evening with the blackout, when you couldn't see your hand in front of your face. But his hatred for this person who was now in charge of him was something else. *She can die for all I care*, he would mutter under his breath. *In fact, I wish she would die!*

Funny to think at first she'd seemed all right; he'd quite liked her in the hospital, with her tales about ancient tombs and living in tents. But he hated her now. He hated her height, her silly floppy straw hat, her ridiculous large feet which made her look like a clown, the shapeless brown-and-grey clothing she wore. She was like a man playing dress-up, unnatural, clumsy: she wasn't a mother, someone who made you cakes and listened to the radio with you and told you reassuring stories when you couldn't sleep. His mother had been only twenty-two when she'd had him, and had still seemed like a young lady when she died: delicate, dainty, immaculately dressed; her nails were perfect glossy teardrops, her shining hair always smooth. It was impossible to believe that this person was now effectively his only living family member, that she was related to his dapper, neat father.

Now that Ant was thinking more clearly and was more used to her he was able to put his great-aunt into context, not that there was much context. He'd heard of Dinah, throughout his childhood; Mummy rather disapproved of her. She'd stayed with them once, on her last trip back to London ten years ago. He didn't remember it, but apparently she had made a terrible mess and used to put her feet up on the arms of the sofa. Mummy had lost a silver cat charm in the chaos Dinah left; Mummy blamed her for this.

In the days before they travelled down to Dorset Dinah told Ant more about herself, some of which Ant remembered from her infrequent, extraordinary letters. He was used to people with interesting jobs – his father was an actor, after all, not a hugely successful one but still making a living from it (Captain Hook in rep being his greatest triumph to date). But his great-aunt's job was something else. She had lived for years in Damascus, then worked on the famous excavations of the ancient city of Ur with its horrifying death-pits and ziggurats, these massive structures the size of pyramids, the sort you saw in comic-book stories about great explorers. That was her.

Now she lived in Baghdad, where she worked for the British Museum, periodically travelling, before the outbreak of war, to help with the excavations of the magnificent archaeological sites of Nimrud and Nineveh, where the great Assyrian kings had built their palaces. In Baghdad she had a courtyard garden with blue tiles, and a date palm tree, and a telescope up on the roof through which she could see the Milky Way. She had a monkey who sat on her shoulder and ate pistachio nuts out of her hand. She had been to Egypt, had seen the Sphinx and the pyramids: she had actually *been inside* Tutankhamun's tomb. She had known Howard Carter, though not well.

Young Ant had no idea what pistachio nuts were, nor the Milky Way, but it was thrilling, all of it. Johnson had a piece of German shrapnel from where the house next door had been hit, and Rogers knew someone whose uncle was in the army and was going to kill Hitler with some poisoned tea, because apparently he liked tea. But he was the only boy at school who knew someone who'd been inside Tutankhamun's tomb. *Very, very hot*, Aunt Dinah had written.

> *And extremely small, every room. But you can feel it, feel the power of the place. My favourite site, however, is Nineveh, in a city called Mosul. Now it is all desert, but once the plains in Northern Iraq were rich and fertile. Lions roamed the land, attacking and killing people. An ancient king built his new palace there. He called it the Palace Without Rival, and ensured Nineveh became the most powerful and beautiful city <u>in the whole world</u>. There was a winged bull carved into the gates, to guard the city from attack. He is thrice the height of you and me combined. I helped dig him up.*

'When will Aunt Dinah come back? Will she bring me a present?' Ant used to ask his mother.

The last time he asked her she said, 'Darling, I shouldn't think she'll return to England while the war's on. But I'm sure she'll come back afterwards. For a visit, not to live. She doesn't like it here.'

'Why?'

He remembered that Mummy had smiled.

'The Wildes aren't great ones for putting down roots. Your father wanted us to travel the world, I wanted to live in London. I persuaded him I wasn't the type. But Dinah hates it here. Bad memories. Her family had lots of money once but it all vanished. Oh, now Daddy hates me talking about money, says it's vulgar. But there you are, it all went.'

'How?'

'Oh, darling. Her father, your great-grandfather, lost it all. We don't talk about it, I'm afraid.' Ant, not understanding, had nodded obediently. 'But Dinah has a flat in London, next to the Natural History Museum. And she has the Bosky, but it's all shut up now; I haven't been there since my honeymoon. It really is beautiful there, it's rather unfair she won't let anyone else in. Daddy says she's a terrible hoarder. When she stayed with us she took some doilies, I'm absolutely sure of it. And I still wonder about that silver cat charm, I really do.'

'I wish she'd come back.'

'I think she likes it out there. Goodness knows why. It's filthy, and she's all alone – so very eccentric. But apparently she always was like that. And,' his mother added, as though this were a minor consideration, 'the work she's done has been important. She found some room or other they'd all forgotten about, absolutely stuffed with old panels – darling, don't tell your father I said this, but he showed me the photographs and the pictures on the panels all look the same to me. Soldiers killing people. It always is. Still, she's very clever, I'm sure. I'm sure she's always saying she'll come for a visit. I'm sure she'll be back one day.'

In the end it took Mummy being killed to bring Aunt Dinah back from Baghdad.

Ant tried to ignore the sounds in the sky, the distant buzzing like swooping flies caught against a window. It was light, at the very least. Hours till blackout when he'd need to start worrying properly about what kind of blinds they had. He'd heard the countryside was even darker than town; Ant could barely imagine anything worse than the darkness in town. Very slightly, he began humming to block out the sound. Aunt Dinah was strong, but not strong enough to move a car by herself. As the Morris sat stubbornly in the yard-wide ditch, lopsided and looking rather drunken, through the open window Aunt Dinah's voice came in, louder now.

'Come on, old girl. You and me. H-h-h-h-hup, come on.'

Ant wound the window down a little further. He stuck his head out.

'Are you sure I can't help you, Aunt Dinah? I think we should be getting inside. The p-pl – the planes, they're quite near—'

His great-aunt peered around the side of the car, in alarm, head cocked. 'What's that? Help?' She tucked a clump of wayward hair behind her large ears. 'Goodness, no. You must stay *in* the car for your own safety. It's just that I can't open the blasted front door with the car wedged so close to it. Potholes, they're the very devil, aren't they? But no matter. We'll have you out in a jiffy.' Now she was muttering quietly to herself. 'I'll have to go and ask old Alastair. Damn it. I just hope he doesn't . . . Damn you, cracked earth of the southern coast! Oh, hell . . .'

When Anthony bent his knees as far as he could, the great browning scabs would crack and lift slightly, and one could see, in some seams, the skin peeling away, pinpricks of blood appearing. It was satisfying, to gently lift the edge up with one nail and to feel the rush of sharp pain. To feel anything.

The scabs on his legs were healing, though the wounds had been very deep, and he had had stitches on his left shin where the wall had fallen in on his leg. He and his mother had missed the air-raid warning – they'd been asleep – and so they'd run down to hide under the stairs. If they couldn't make the shelter they knew they'd be safe there. They'd hidden there enough times before. Mummy had even found a bottle of sticky, dusty blackberry wine Daddy had made from the blackberries on Hampstead Heath a couple of years ago which they'd never finished, it being too sickly sweet in those pre-war years, when sugar was something normal you simply had when you felt like it. On her birthday, only a week before she died, they'd made for the cupboard under the stairs when the siren sounded. She'd put little glasses in there too, and she'd let him have a tiny measure of the stuff, and they'd been almost jolly, as the terrifying, screaming sounds of destruction tore overhead, tore up the world outside. Bombs landing yards away, noise so loud at first you thought you'd never stand it, you'd go mad, you'd rather run out on to the street and die than stay here like a stuck pig, waiting for it . . . And the sound as it hit, the sound of homes and shops and schools being blown apart or flattened. Nothing could prepare you for the terror you felt, there in the dark, listening for the next one, trying to work out if this time it'd be you. And then feeling luckier because you were safe there, and you could giggle about blackberry wine and other things and that you might one day get used to this hell. Yes, they'd begun to believe they'd be safe there, under the stairs.

In hospital he'd sat pulling at the too-tight starched bed sheets, picking at the flecks of scab, taking them off one by one. 'Don't do that,' one of the nurses would say, slapping his hand away from the spots of pink, new skin. She was nice, blue eyes, plump lower lip. She had asked about Ant's dad, she knew he'd been in the RAF. She had a boyfriend who flew Halifaxes, and she used to sit on Ant's bed and talk to him about the pilots, how they were the bravest men, that they were winning the war for us, but she was vicious about the scabs. 'Stop picking at them! They'll never heal.'

Ant couldn't tell her the truth, which was that he didn't want them to heal. They were the link to the last night she was alive. If they healed, it'd be over and she'd be gone.

'Ant? Ant? Stay in the car, will you, dear boy? I'm going to find Alastair Fletcher. He lives just down the road and he'll be able to help us. Just one minute, dear Ant.'

Don't call me Ant. Anthony knew Aunt Dinah was wrong, that the Morris 8 was the last place one wanted to be. He was a Londoner. Get to a shelter. Get out of the car. Get into the cellar or under the stairs or the table. Perhaps Aunt Dinah was trying to be kind, but she was stupid. She didn't know *anything* . . . But he didn't care if he died or not so he curled up tighter, enjoying the pain, wishing he could stop shaking.

The hospital had wired her to come home – it had taken her a month, first the train to Basra, an actual cattle truck where she'd shared a carriage with four horses. It was agonisingly slow, and dangerous, then she'd had a wait of days at Basra while she tried to get a passage back to England. She'd come straight to the hospital and then collected a friend's car she'd arranged to borrow while he was away fighting. She hadn't even been to her flat in South Kensington. Her friend Daphne was looking after it; she was engaged with war work and keeping extraordinary hours and Dinah hadn't liked to turn up unannounced and take the sheets. So she'd been to Fortnum's and bought some supplies. Money didn't seem to be a factor with Aunt Dinah, not at first, not then. Later, she told him, later when things are more settled, we'll go to London, go to the Assyrian rooms at the British Museum, see the great treasures of kings, of Sennacherib and Ashurbanipal, some of these famous panels she'd helped excavate. We'll stay with Daphne. Yes, Daphne was ever so jolly, such fun. She'd be delighted to meet Ant. Dinah had spoken to her, she'd said so.

I don't want to meet bleeding Daphne, he wanted to scream. *I don't care about stones in museums, not now. I want everything to be normal again.* But Dinah didn't seem to be interested in things being normal. She didn't care that all his books were gone, and his toys, and the photos on the sideboard, and Daddy's cup for his local team's winning their local cricket championship, or that the pots and baskets Mummy hung out to try and prettify the little back garden were crushed, as though a monster had stepped on them.

She didn't seem to care, and she didn't ask him about them, or the things he couldn't stop picturing when he closed his eyes, when the dark clutched him tight and he was unable to make out his hands in front of his face, and she was all he could see.

Lying on the kitchen floor, thrown on to his back, legs in the air like an overturned tortoise, the night sky above him visible, and the walls smashed to pieces, he had looked over to the stairs and seen the cupboard door underneath them blown off, most of the stairs gone, and his mother against the back wall, facing him. One side of her was still a person, the other side of her blown right off, the brown Fair Isle knit frayed where she'd been torn in two, as though the monster had ripped a part of her away. The sinews on her neck, the splintered bone sticking out of her soft gold hair that curled around her head very white. The blue felt of her soft belt curling around and into the bloody, spongy mess of her missing stomach and sides, and as he watched, shock making him amazed at the force of transformation, he saw that dust, like grey-brown snow, was settling over the fresh red blood and clean white bone.

The scab lifted away at the edge, half an inch almost, revealing a plateau of slick red-raw skin underneath. All these things he'd seen and Aunt Dinah didn't ask him about them. No one did. And he desperately wanted to say them to someone. So that he wasn't alone, so that another person had heard about them. He told his mother everything, no matter how silly, and she listened, always knowing how to make it better – Anthony pulled viciously at the scab. It broke in two, one half gumming itself back into place on his knee, the other falling to the floor. Blood gushed up in the open wound and Ant hugged himself, angrily, as tears fell on to his knees, his hands.

Somehow, someone had found him his school uniform, which he hadn't been wearing when the bomb hit; he couldn't remember where his uniform had been or why it had suddenly reappeared by his bedside two days ago. Those were the only clothes he had now.

He'd never gone back to the house. They said there was no point. 'Nothing left of the place at all, dearie,' another nurse, not the nice one with the Halifax-flying sweetheart, had told him. She said it almost gleefully. He was supposed to be grateful Aunt Dinah had come to take him away. He'd been scheduled to go to the Boys' Home the following week if she hadn't turned up.

'I want to stay in London,' he'd told her when she'd returned to see him for the second time. 'I don't want to go to the seaside. I don't know anyone.' Besides, he had this idea that if he'd been hit once in London he couldn't get hit again. Anywhere else was dangerous. He knew the streets round Camden, and he knew the park and the canal and the swings that weren't ever bombed. He knew his way in the dark. The dark was the thing. He could cope with it, in London, where there were always sounds. 'Please, don't make me go there. I don't want to – to – l-l-leave.'

'Listen,' she'd said. 'We can't stay in London. Daphne needs the flat. We're going to the Bosky. My father built it. Your great-grandfather, Ant. It's my house, it'll be yours, it's our home now. It's what we both need. Fresh air, away from all the bad memories . . . by the sea. It'll be wonderful.' But she'd been chewing her nail as she said it, and he wasn't sure she believed it, either.

Now, waiting for Aunt Dinah and this mythical neighbour, all he could make out so far was a dirt track, and an expanse of choppy grey water, separated from him by rows of dingy beach huts, and on the shore a barbed wire fence, stretching along the bay as far as he could see. Overhead, in the distance, still miles away but nearer now were the German MEs and British Spitfires, coiled and unravelling, spinning crazily in the grey-blue sky, like moths after too much candlelight. He could hear the roaring phut-phut, next to the sound of birdsong coming from the woods behind. Ant rattled the door handle, trying to get out. He didn't care what Aunt Dinah said.

But as he opened the door the car began to move, violently, and he was shoved against the other window and fell, banging his head, and a small cloth package, dislodged from her bag, also flew out, hitting his ankle. 'Victory!' Dinah shouted, as the car moved forwards. 'Alastair, you're a marvel, a veritable marvel!'

'I wouldn't say that,' came a measured Scots voice. 'It's my pleasure, Dinah. I'm awfully glad to have you back again. I thought you'd never come back, not after—'

Dinah interrupted. 'Come out, Ant dear, come and say hello to Mr Fletcher. He's down the road at Beeches. You seem well, Alastair. We should give you a drink some time.'

'You should, though of what I've no idea,' said Alastair, nodding in welcome as Anthony climbed, shakily, out of the car, holding the package that had viciously hit his ankle. His arm was bleeding. Alastair Fletcher nodded, and his moustache wriggled on his lip, like a hairy caterpillar. 'Good to meet you, m'boy.' He turned to Dinah. 'Listen, get inside. There's another fight on, over there towards Bournemouth.' He nudged Ant, as though pointing out a great treat to him. 'I say, laddie, look at that. Damn Jerry's back for more again. I tell you, Dinah, it's been relentless, all summer. I don't know how much longer we can go on. Now, I'll be off to my shelter. Do you want to come with me?'

'No thank you, Alastair,' said Dinah heartily, showing no inclination to move. 'I'll get us inside, we'll be safe there.'

'Hm. Well, Anthony, I've a son and a daughter I think you'll get on with. Ian, he's two years older than you and Julia. They're back from school in a couple of days so I'll make sure they come over and say hello. You'd like that?'

Ant stared at him blankly, as the sound of the planes grew louder, buzzing in his ear. 'Yes.'

Alastair Fletcher leaned towards him. 'Did you hear me, boy?'

'Ian and Julia,' he said, and he actually thought he might be sick, the plane noise was so near now. 'Yes, sir. Sorry, sir. I – it's just I think we ought to get inside.'

The adults both glanced at his face. 'Absolutely,' said Alastair Fletcher. 'We ought. G'bye, Dinah. Good to have you here.'

'Righty-ho. Tinkety-tonk, old fruit,' called Aunt Dinah to his retreating back. 'And down with the Nazis!'

After he'd gone, Ant jerked his head back and looked again at the house. He pointed. 'There's no underground.' He knew he sounded rude but he couldn't help it. 'We can't be safe if there's no underground.'

'The living area is up on the top floor, looking out to sea. But the bedrooms are built into the sand dune, so we're sort of one floor down, here on the lane. We sleep down here, so there's no need to move when the siren goes off, you see,' said Dinah, blowing her hair out of her face with a puffing motion of the lips. 'Oh, look, they're moving off.'

And it was true that the planes were further along the beach now, heading towards Bournemouth. But Ant was not appeased.

'Is it v-very dark at night?'

Dinah nodded. 'But that's good. It means the Germans can't see as much. Promise. It really is safe as houses.'

Anthony kept staring at the sky. 'Houses aren't safe,' he said quietly.

Dinah put her arm around him. 'I know, dear boy,' she said, briskly, and her voice wavered. 'But this one is. I promise you. Let's go inside. I long for a cup of tea. While I was in Camden I swapped some sugar coupons for tea coupons with your nice neighbour Mrs Gallagher.'

'I hate tea,' Anthony said, churlishly. 'Mummy used to drink coffee.'

'Well, there's a war on, Ant dear—'

'Don't call me Ant.'

'Besides, there is no coffee.'

'Well, Mummy knew where to buy it, she—'

But Aunt Dinah interrupted him, smiling quickly, and he saw the flash of her white, even teeth in the late-afternoon sun. 'Listen, Anthony. We will get along more harmoniously if each of us *tries*. What do you say? If not, I'm afraid the situation will

141

rapidly become tiresome. We have both given up much to come here. *Try* to remember that, if you please.' He nodded, hanging his head, and she touched his chin with her finger, raising it up so their eyes met. 'All forgotten. Welcome to the Bosky.'

Dinah opened the door. Ant followed her. She lit a candle, and took him by the hand up the stairs. It was dark inside, warm and still, the musky feel of a place undisturbed for years. Dinah drew back the shutters at the top of the stairs and the sun slanted in through the windows, dazzling them both, and Ant looked around at the kitchen-cum-sitting room, blinking in the golden light. At first, he wasn't quite sure what he was seeing. Then he began to take in the rest of his surroundings, and gave a small gasp.

There was literally no room except where they stood, all the space taken up by . . . things. Beside them, stacked against a bare wall, were piles of teetering books, some of which had collapsed on to the floor, surrounded by their own confetti: creamy shreds of paper, scattered everywhere, which gave the room an almost festive air.

'Oh, gosh, the mice have been at my books,' said Dinah, shaking her head. 'I'd forgotten quite how much I left down here. Daphne wanted me to remove most of my possessions from the flat . . . Now, where are the miniature deer?'

Next to the books, a velvet dressmaker's dummy wearing a brocade dressing gown, both eaten to lacy patches by the moth, and by the French windows a stack of battered leather trunks and suitcases, covered all over in travel labels, against which leaned a whole host of wooden panels and framed pictures: some had fallen forwards, and he could see paintings and tapestry-work in frames, the latter also attacked by moths. A huge stone panel dominated the centre of the room, of men diving for fish. There was a stack of bronze bowls, a small stuffed monkey wearing a red coat and holding cymbals, a footstool with worn metal lion's feet, worn green with age, and a pair of birds of paradise in a glass case: blue, coral and pink, their tails as long as Ant's arm.

'Where did you . . . where's all this stuff *from*?' he said, eventually.

'Oh – here and there.' She waved her arms. 'Some of it I acquired on my travels. Some of it was my parents' from India; you know, my dear father was a colonel in the army. I grew up in the North-West Frontier before we – we had to come home.' Dinah stepped heavily over piles of folded damask in an acanthus pattern that faded from blue to yellow. 'Father had a little difficulty and we had to sell everything off but there was an awful lot that couldn't be disposed of at auction. Hey-ho, what finds!' Dinah picked up a smooth, polished stone, with wings and a beak carved into the side. 'The paperweight bird! Alulim, dear Alulim. Hello, old thing, and good afternoon.' She gave a small bow to the paperweight in her hand. 'I found him in Ur. Alulim was King for twenty-eight thousand years, did you know that?'

'Um – no,' said Ant. 'No, I didn't.'

Dinah took off the peacock kimono and slung it, like a cowboy arriving in a bar, across the back of a chair. She reached across and smiled at the monkey. 'Now. I call *him* Livingstone. How have *you* been, sir?' She saw Ant watching her and smiled that rather enchanting smile. 'Right, enough nonsense. Let's open the doors. Clear a path, Ant dear.'

'Yes, of course.' Copying her loping, pincer movement, Ant slotted one battered and bruised limb in between a box of records and a gramophone, landing on a marble tube which rolled, sending him flying. He caught hold of her arm, then bent and picked it up. 'What's this?'

'Oh, it's a marble cylinder. It was a means of signing your own name. You roll it on moist clay and it forms a pattern – look, can you see it? A man and a god, look at his wings.' Aunt Dinah lifted up a huge doll with a china face and unsettlingly soft, lifelike hair pinned in a bun. 'Hello, Eunice, regards to the family.' She put the unsmiling doll gingerly down on one side. 'Now look, there's the mah-jong set! I bought this in Mosul, you know, off a terrifying chap with only one eye. Wonderful. We'll need that when the bombing raids are on, I suspect.' Ant's stomach lurched, as she clutched a wooden box with a pattern in pearl to her bosom. 'Awfully good fun, mah-jong. Look, there's the teapot. Now, talking of cylinders, I spoke to Mr Gage in the village and he very kindly arranged for a gas cylinder to be delivered and fitted so we should be – yes, we have fire, oh, marvellous.' She emerged from the galley kitchen with the kettle on the gas ring, and picked up the doll again. 'It's yours. It was your father's. He used to play games with her when he was little. Acting out stories. Rather sweet.'

She thrust the doll at Ant, who recoiled. 'Oh.' He held Eunice's rigid body, feeling the stiff sharp horsehairs that protruded from her torso scratching his arms and stomach. His father had held her, had touched her cold white china face, had made up stories about her. He had been here. He knew it here. So did Mummy, less so but still, this was a place known to his parents. He patted Eunice's head.

Dinah pushed and heaved at the French windows and eventually shoved them open, almost launching herself outside in the process. 'Come on through. Come and see the sea.'

Following the glow of the evening sun, Ant limped slowly to the window. 'There,' she said, yanking him over the last part, a heap of gleaming brass pots and pans. They stood on the threshold, doors flung open. 'Look at that, they're still there.'

There was the sea, silver-turquoise in the afternoon sun, set in a curved, glinting bay, woods and greenery sliding away from them down to the water, a line of white cliffs and rocks off to the right. And off to the left, two planes danced about each other, small as buzzing flies.

Dinah moved out on to the porch; Ant grabbed her hand. 'Don't.'

'We're safe here, don't worry.'

'But they might—' He felt helpless, and he was so sick of it. The smells, sights of the new place swamped him. Its newness wasn't exciting now, it was overwhelming, and he put his hands to his face, terrified he'd cry in front of her. *I just want to go home*, he said to himself, but there was no home any more, of course.

She produced something from her pocket. It was the cloth parcel that had hit him earlier. He'd put it down on the table. She unwrapped it. 'Here. Pop this above the porch door, would you?'

He looked down: in his hands was the ancient angel gazing out impassively at him. He stared at her. Her calm, wide smile seemed to say, *I'm here. I'm here now.*

Anthony followed Dinah out on to the wooden decking and breathed in, a huge, deep, calming breath, and for the first time in his life smelled the scent of the rosemary that sprang from the sandy earth underneath mingling with the wild roses that frothed over the side of the house, and above it all the fresh salty sea air . . . He closed his eyes, holding the square stone slab in his hand.

'Now, open this,' she was saying, and she handed him the sack she had brought in with her from the car. 'There's not very much, but it's what I could retrieve.'

Ant peered inside. 'From where?'

'Your old house. I went back a couple of days ago. I rather thought I should have another look, see if there's anything I could salvage.'

'It was you who went back then. That's how you got my uniform.' She nodded, her eyes bright with tears, long pointed nose shining.

'Only clothes you had left, dearest one. The lady at number twenty-one had hung on to them. She'd been drying them on the line for your mother.'

'Mrs Ball, next to Mrs Gallagher. She got the sun in her garden . . .' Ant opened the bag, slowly. There, sitting on the top and wrapped in a piece of cloth, was a watch, a Christmas present from his parents. It had a navy leather strap, scratched, and there was a crack on the glass, but it was still working. He held it up to his ear, heard the faint, purring tick of the mechanism and then, for the first time in days, smiled at Aunt Dinah, his eyes shining. 'My watch,' he said. 'You found my watch.'

She nodded. With shaking fingers he drew out next a brass doorknob, the long screw slightly bent, a worn copy of *Peter Pan* covered in pencil scribbles and two buttons glued all over with paste diamonds; Mummy had had an assortment of buttons in her sewing box. After that, a black velvet evening bag shot through with gold thread, and a matching scarf folded inside. There were some Happy Families cards: Mr Thread the Tailor, Master Stain the Dyer's Son, Mrs Smut the Sweep's Wife. A silver fork, two tines hopelessly twisted and finally, and miraculously, a photograph of Ant and his mother in Brighton.

He stared at it, at her laughing face, her bright eyes, her hands squeezing his shoulders as they smiled at his father who was taking the photograph. She had touched this photo, used the fork, worn the scarf, played with the cards. It was all he had left of her, of both of them.

Ant said, as his trembling hands struggled to put on the watch, 'You got these from the house? How did you get in?' He and his friends were driven away by zealous ARP wardens and police every time they tried to go near a bombsite.

Aunt Dinah shrugged. 'I'm an archaeologist. I'm good at clambering over ruins and finding things. And I'm persuasive when I want to be. One should be prepared to be elastic with the truth, only if absolutely necessary.'

The watch was heavy on his wrist, after not wearing it for all those weeks. He stared at the photograph again, tears pricking his eyes.

'Do you know any Shakespeare?' Aunt Dinah said, after a short silence.

'Bits.'

She reached over the porch railings, pulling at a sprig of rosemary. '*There's rosemary, that's for remembrance. Pray you, love, remember.*' She rolled the needle-shaped leaves between her fingers and the smoky-sweet smell assailed his nostrils. 'Now, put that angel up in her place. She'll look after you, didn't I promise you she would?'

Ant reached up and rested her on the lintel above the door. 'All right?' he said.

'We'll put a hook up so we can hang her properly,' she said. 'Look how tall you are, you're so like your father and he loved it here, you know. I say, perhaps you could put on some plays here on the porch one evening like he used to.' She glanced up at the angel and gave a deep breath. Ant thought it sounded rather like a ragged sigh. 'Well, then, Ant dear. Here we are.'

Chapter Eleven

September 2014

When the doorbell rang early one Saturday morning in September, Cord almost ignored it. People you knew never rang the bell any more, just as people never called the landline unless they wanted money from you. She'd taken, lately, to shouting firmly down the telephone before replacing the handset, 'Aren't you ashamed of yourselves, trying to con someone out of their savings? Aren't you? I'm putting the phone down, now. Goodbye.'

The truth was that actually she'd rather welcome a phone call from an old friend, or someone she'd sung with years ago. 'How are you, Cordelia? I saw your number in my phone book and I thought I'd look you up.' But it never was anyone she knew. Never. Silly to think it would be, she'd tell herself sternly. This sternness, it made her feel old, like so many things these days. Snapchat, YOLO. The previous week she'd visited her favourite music shop in Kentish Town to search for some obscure Brahms lieder sheet music. With no luck — and besides, what was the point? Why bother to buy new music for her wrecked voice? As she closed the banging door gently behind her on the way out, a man idly flicking through his phone and leaning against a massive, stupidly gleaming black 4×4 Land Rover had called, 'That place is a rip-off.'

'Oh?' said Cord, astonished.

'Yeah.' He was chewing gum furiously and was bored, she realised. 'Got all my kid's piano music there before I remembered Amazon.'

'What a terrible, stupid attitude,' Cord had heard herself saying in that bellowing Stern Woman voice. He was probably only five years younger than her, but still. 'It may be cheaper, but what's the long-term price? Hm?'

The man had looked blank. 'There's no long-term price. Place like this'll shut in a few years.'

'And don't you *care*?' Cord had boomed at him.

He looked absolutely astonished. 'Course I don't care. Why should I?'

'Why?' *Why?* Cord was astonished at the rage that bubbled up within her. *Because it's everything that's wrong*, she felt like yelling at him. Small businesses going under because of big corporations, years of expertise lost – Lorelei who ran the shop knew exactly what double-bass string was needed or the best plectrum for your guitar, but no, no, expertise doesn't matter when the product is cheaper from Tesco or Amazon or wherever according to some idiot hedge-fund manager who drives a vast car that blocks narrow London streets and belches out vile diesel fumes that children inhale and . . .

Breathe, Cord.

She was able to smile at herself, most of the time, for the grumpy old lady she was turning into and the gay abandon with which she castigated those responsible. 'Here's a bag for your dog's shit,' she was used to saying, having run after surprised dog owners whose pets had fouled on her street. 'You must have forgotten one so I won't report you this time.' A wide, dazzling smile.

'Please don't shout at that waitress. It's not her fault there's no almond milk. Dairy intolerance has been promoted by an increasingly industrialised health-food industry. Unless you have a medically diagnosed allergy to it, cow's milk is good for you. Almond milk is irresponsibly resource-heavy to produce.'

'This scribble is a delightful addition to the railway bridge. I hope you don't mind me pointing out that you don't know the difference between "your" and "you are". I'm taking some photos – could you lift your headgear up just a little so I can see your face? No, I won't, thank you very much.'

And once, when a small, nondescript man in a blue bomber jacket and jeans rubbed himself against her on the bus, she had simply shoved him away, then grabbed his hand and, raising it high above her head, called loudly, 'Sex pervert on board! Go and do that at home against your door frame, you sad little man.'

There followed an excruciating twenty seconds when the man stood utterly still before jumping off at the next stop, turning to her and shouting, 'You pathetic fucking whore.'

'Yes!' Cord had yelled at him. 'Yes, I bloody am, and I don't care!'

('Sex pervert?' her friend Nalah had said in the ensuing awkward silence.)

She didn't care, it was the truth. Somewhere along the way she'd lost the embarrassment trigger. Life was harder with each passing year. Giving in to self-pity would drive you mad.

But this Saturday, the bell rang after she had ignored it and then, again, for so long and with so much determination that the rasping rattle of the metal sounded as though it might fray and come loose. Putting down her coffee with a sigh and stepping over piles of papers, Cord made her way gingerly to the hallway of her flat and pressed the intercom buzzer.

'Yes?'

'H-hello?' came a small voice.

'Who is this, please?' she said, flatly.

'Is that Cordelia Wilde?'

'Who is this?'

'Is that her?'

'Bloody hell!' Cord said, hackles already firmly risen. 'Tell me who you are and I'll tell you if Cordelia Wilde is here. I should warn you already that the answer's likely to be Probably Not.'

There was a pause, and the voice said, 'I'm her niece. Um – I'm Iris Wilde. She hasn't seen me for years. I'm Ben and—'

'Yes,' said Cord, leaning her head on the intercom, her throat closing up so suddenly that it hurt. She managed to say, 'I know who you are. What – what do you want?'

'Dad wanted me to come.' Her voice grew louder. 'He says you won't return his calls. He said I should try. I've got something to give you, something from Gramma.'

'Look. I—'

'Please, Aunt Cordy.'

Aunt Cordy. Over the years of silence and distance the name had stuck. Tears pricked at her eyes: she blinked them away, then drew her small frame up so she was standing straight. She pressed the buzzer. 'Come up. It's the third floor. Sorry about the mess.'

All Cord had ever wanted in the matter of her family was to be forgotten, so that what she knew, what she had seen, might not be known or even suspected by any of them. Waiting for the sound of steps on the stairs, she glanced frantically around her flat, seeing it through a stranger's eyes for the first time. Seeing not the cosy, sunny, elegant flat she had moved into all those years ago, with so many happy plans for the future. The papered walls were peeling, one pane of glass in the window was cracked, and every surface was crammed with junk: the organised detritus of a hoarder's sad little life, newspapers stacked high, the music in piles on every surface, music she would never sing. Wildly, she wondered if there was still time to hide. *I could just wait in the cupboard until she's gone.*

* * *

They were twins, Iris and Emily, both blonde, one with straight hair and an almost-heart-shaped mole on her cheek, the other with matted, soft curls. But that was twenty-one years ago, when they were eighteen months old, and though for a few years after their mother's death she had sent them birthday presents and Christmas cards promising vaguely to catch up and had in return had little pictures from them when they were old enough to draw which she had now stashed away in some cupboard or drawers, she hadn't actually seen them since that last, terrible weekend at the Bosky.

As her niece appeared, turning the final corner of the staircase, Cord stared at her. This was the one with the mole. Her hair was not blonde now, but jet black and bobbed, her eyes framed with black flicks of eyeliner, her shoes, jeans, layers of T-shirt, vest, jumper all in shades of black, white and grey, the only colour about her the coral-red matt lipstick. She was willowy and, in the direct, puckish way that she leaned forward to shake her aunt's hand, Cord realised she was exactly like her mother and began to see how hard this would be.

Five minutes ago I was drinking coffee looking at the travel pages, imagining the places I'll never go to, staring out of the window wondering if autumn is here yet. I was going to have a long bath and walk down West End Lane and buy steak as a treat. I was going to go to that concert of Hannele's in Highgate . . .

'Do you want some coffee?'

The girl nodded. 'Oh. Thank you.'

Cord sat down and gestured for her to sit too, sweeping some scores off a frayed old wicker chair. 'Milk?'

'Do you have almond milk?'

Cord raised her eyebrows. 'No, I don't. You know—' She bit her tongue, then looked at her niece, properly, and saw she was pale and the hand that touched her lips was shaking, and Cord forgot everything and impulsively touched her shoulder.

'Oh, Iris. It's lovely to see you. You're grown up. Of course you are . . . How's Emily?'

'She's fine. She's in LA, studying screenwriting. She wants to be – well, a screenwriter. Obvs.' She made an awkward, self-mocking grimace.

'Your dad's there now, isn't he?'

'He's just gone back to LA. Lauren's here. She's – working on something.' She said, 'Do you know Lauren? She's his wife.'

'I haven't met her, no.'

'She's really nice. She redecorated the house last year.' Iris cleared her throat. 'She wants to do the Bosky too. Gramma has said she can, before she . . . Gramma loves Lauren.'

These new family relationships, this extension to her old family. She vaguely remembered her mother as a granny: how surprisingly good she was, patient, fun, goofy. The lovely side of Mumma, her down-to-earth Scots-ness and lack of ego that was so at odds with her great beauty . . . Cord found she was clutching her stomach, the assault of memory actually painful. *Was she in much pain? That's good, that she likes Lauren. I hope Lauren makes Ben happy. All he wants is someone to love . . .*

Heartache, nausea, confusion overwhelmed her. 'Right.' Cord stood up. 'Do you live in the Primrose Hill house, then? With your dad?'

'Yes, I can't afford a place in London, and Dad wants me to get a job before he'll help me out. It's fine, I'm lucky. They're away loads.'

Cord remembered Ben's house in Primrose Hill – a vast, shabby Victorian terrace he'd bought after his first marriage, before Primrose Hill became a place for people who earned lots of money, not people who had interesting jobs. 'So you're on your own there.'

'Well, sort of. He sometimes has this friend of his living in the basement. Um, Hamish?' said Iris. She drank the rest of her coffee. 'He knows Dad's from – oh – oh, Aunt Cordy, the cup – you're dripping coffee everywhere.'

'Oh. How silly of me.' Cord brushed the liquid off her skirt and on to the mud-coloured carpet – when she moved in, twenty-five years ago, the carpet had been fitted by Harrods, no less, in the days when Harrods did useful things like fit carpets. She stared at it, properly, for the first time in years. *It's filthy*, she thought.

Iris said, curiously, 'Do you know Hamish?'

Cord nodded. 'I used to. Long ago.'

Iris didn't notice anything amiss. 'Emily and I like Hamish. He's just got divorced and he's a bit of a loser but he's nice. When he first moved in all he did was sit around in the basement playing loud French love songs—'

'Charles Trenet,' Cord said, very quietly.

'You do know him. I *thought* he said he knew you once. But Daddy was there and . . .'

'It was a long time ago. He's an actor. He knew my father.'

'Oh. I thought he was an accountant,' said Iris, puzzled.

'Hamish Lowther?'

'Oh, I dunno his surname,' said Iris with the vagueness of youth. 'He's an accountant, definitely actually, because he did Gramma's taxes for her last year and there was some bother about it. Are you all right?'

Cord put her hands behind her head, stretching herself. 'I'm fine. It can't be him, then.' She took a deep breath. A huge wave of relief that this accountant called Hamish wasn't another ghost from her past cropping up as well washed over her. 'Now, Iris darling. This is very nice, but you're not just here for a cup of coffee, I know that much. Why did you come?'

'Oh.' Iris's eyes widened, and she fumbled in the bag at her feet. 'Dad – Dad said this way was better than ringing because you wouldn't answer the phone. I've got something for you.' She stopped, hand halfway to the bag. 'But before that – Gramma's asking to see you. It's about the house. She wants to sign it over to you and—'

'I know, and I don't want it. I've told them.'

'Don't *want* it?' Iris looked astonished. 'How can you not want it? It's my favourite place in the world.'

My favourite place in the world. Cord tried to stay calm. 'I can't really explain. I have written to her, to tell her I don't want it.'

Iris shot her a look. 'Right. But she's dying. You . . . know that, don't you?'

'Yes, I – I know.' She thought of the last time she'd seen her mother, at River Walk, after Daddy died. Staring at herself in the hallway mirror, patting the skin under her chin when she thought no one was looking. Hollows under the eyes, skin porous and doughy, like bread starter left to pucker in sunshine. The downward turn of the curving mouth . . . Already, then, she was beginning a decline. To see her now – to sit across from her and lie about her years of silence . . .

Cord found she could hardly bear to think about Mumma. That was it, you see, opening it up just made more pain, more trouble. *Stick to what you've always told yourself. It's better she hates me. Better the blame is all on me.*

Iris's young, pale face was full of scorn. She pursed her bright lips together. 'How can you be like this when – when I know from what Daddy says that you all loved it down there? Daddy says you used to be the happiest little girl in the world.'

Cord stood up, and went over to the window. She looked through the grimy glass over the rooftops of West Hampstead, down towards the city.

'Iris,' she said. 'I can't really explain it all to you. But I don't want anything to do with the Bosky. Or the family. I'm so sorry.'

'But you sent us birthday presents.' Her niece's face was flushed under her fringe. 'Dad kept all the tags, and the cards. Why, if you didn't want anything to do with us?'

'I don't know. I wanted you to know I was still – still alive.' She knotted her fingers together. 'That if things had been different I'd have loved to have—'

'If things had been different you'd have wanted to be in our lives?' Iris gave a short laugh. 'But you won't say why, or any of it—'

'I can't.'

'Why can't you?' Iris demanded. 'I mean, is it that bad?'

Cord pressed a finger to the bridge of her nose. 'We grew up one way, believing they were gods, thinking we had this perfect life, and then he ruined it all. All. There, at the house. That's why I can't go back there.'

'But what did he do?' Iris dropped her voice. 'Oh God. Did he – was he – did he abuse you?'

'No!' said Cord. Then she stopped. 'In a way, yes. But not like that. Nothing like that.' She came towards Iris. 'My love, it's best – *honestly*, I promise you it's best – if we leave it. Please, let's not get caught up in it all because I'll have to ask you to go, and I don't want to.' Her tone was pleading. 'So – show me what you brought.'

Iris's face was even whiter than before. She drew her bag up on to her lap and took out a package, wrapped tightly in a huge swathe of cloth. 'Here. She wants you to have this. She gave it to Dad last week. They found it while they were valuing the house. Thought they'd better pass it on.'

Cord took it from her, and unwrapped the cloth, twisting the material around her hand like a shroud, reams of it falling away with a curiously loud thud on to the floor. She took out a small square of terracotta, and stared at the angel that had hung over the door for all those years, her wide staring eyes, the owls on either side of her, the huge feathered wings.

'Hello,' she said to it. A cold, creeping feeling stole through her. Some memory, trapped within, tapping furiously inside her head, trying to get out. 'Do you know what this means?' she asked, eventually. Iris shrugged. 'Of course you don't. But your mother knew. She understood.' Gently, she put the angel back on the table.

'Understood what?'

'That there's a curse. The angel was supposed to bring us all good luck and she didn't, she didn't keep us safe at all.'

'How do you know that?' Iris said. *She thinks I'm crazy*, Cord thought.

'I don't know. I can't remember.' She tapped her head with her fingers, lightly. 'Did I dream it? Did she – it didn't used to be there, that's the thing. It wasn't there when I was little, then it reappeared one day. It was Daddy's, you see. His great-aunt gave it to him.'

'I'm sorry,' said Iris politely. 'I don't really understand.'

'No, no,' muttered Cord. 'You wouldn't. But your mum knew. It's what killed her, I think.'

'My mother killed herself,' said Iris, her voice dull.

'I know,' said Cord, swallowing. 'I was there.' The angel's face, still half exposed, stared up at her. 'I loved her very much, you know,' she began, and then stopped.

Iris said quietly, 'Did you?'

Cord nodded, looking at the floor. 'You hear it all the time, but she really wasn't like anyone else. I used to think it was right she had twins, as though she had to have two girls to adequately reproduce all the complexities of her – her . . .' She trailed off. 'Sorry, I can't explain it properly.'

Iris's face wore a hungry expression. 'No, you are already. Explaining, I mean. No one talks about her.'

'Your dad—'

'Yes, but he's with Lauren and he's happy now. I don't know if my mum made him happy.' Iris pursed her lips. She looked suddenly very young. 'I just want someone to tell us more about her. Dad won't and Gramma doesn't really remember a lot of things now. You're our only other . . .' She trailed off, bowing her head.

'She did make your father happy, Iris. I know that.'

'Really?'

'Absolutely.' Pushing away her misgivings, Cord went on. 'What else? Well, I can tell you she liked Sting when he was in the Police, not afterwards when he got all serious. Bowie. And *Grease*. The film, not the country. We all loved it. Your dad had a leather jacket that made him look like Danny Zuko . . .' She was smiling. 'Most of all Kate Bush. She absolutely loved her. And marshmallows. She could eat a whole bag of them.' She smiled. 'She was smaller than me and Ben and her hair was like a cloak, it was so long and thick and it'd shimmer in the sun. So she was like a fairy, or a sprite, quick and magical. She could read a book faster than anyone I've ever known. She was very, very, very clever, did your dad tell you that? Are you both clever?'

Iris shrugged, her eyes cast down.

'She had a sad upbringing, and her father was awful to her, so she'd stay with us in the holidays instead. She was happy. I know she was, for that time . . .' Cord tasted bitter, acrid metal in her mouth. She swallowed. 'No, I can't. I'm so sorry, I can't say any more.'

Her niece's pale face hardened. 'I just want to know—'

Cord cut her off and swallowed again, wondering if she might be sick. 'I wish I could be what you want. But I can't.'

'How miserable it must be, being you,' Iris said, her voice

cracking. 'What a pathetic life, hardly seeing anyone, no career if what Dad says is right. You must be very selfish. Dad said you changed when you became a singer. He said you didn't used to be like that. Well, fine. Screw you.'

She actually held up a fist as though she would give Cord the finger, but she waved her arm half-heartedly, her small, pale face creased with sadness and then backed away, out of the room and through the door, slamming it behind her as she went.

Cord must have sat there in the old familiar spot in the corner for hours, not really doing anything, listening to the sounds of the city float in though the open window, roaring white noise. Just thinking. Then she stood up, turned on the lamp – it was late afternoon by now – and tripped over the reams of material in which the over-eager estate agents had wrapped the angel. There was something else there, in the cloth bundle. Cord lifted it up, letting it unravel, and a piece of cardboard fell out on to the ground, and with it a book. She picked it up.

The Children's Book of British Wild Flowers, it said. A children's book with a picture of some buttercups and ox-eye daisies in a clump on the front, a sort of folder attachment at the back, like it was a work-book, something Mumma would buy from Woolworths the day before they left for the Bosky as a holiday treat, an entertainment to keep the children occupied while it was raining outside . . . She stared at it.

Someone had added an *e* after Wild. Wild*e* Flowers. It was covered in cracked, drying tape.

Hands shaking, Cord pulled the tape off with ease, and opened the book.

The Children's Book of British Wilde Flowers

Madeleine Fletcher

It is a SECRET DIARY

Cord looked from the stone angel to the worn little book. 'Oh, you two,' she whispered. 'You two.'

She told herself she knew without opening one damp, thin page what the diary would say. Hadn't they been, until their divergence, so close for so many years that there was nothing she hadn't known about Mads? She didn't need to read it, to put herself through it. But the angel . . . what was it, this itchy, sandy taste in her mouth, this strange sensation of a memory, long buried, that fought its way clear? *You're the Wildflowers. Don't forget it.*

She stared at the book for so long her eyes became rough and dry with the sensation of not blinking. She picked it up, holding its fragile weight in one trembling hand.

Time to go back there, to walk knowingly into the pain and betrayal of Mads's sad, short life. Cord flicked through the pages, flinching at the sight of the small, difficult handwriting, spanning the years, childish even in adulthood. She blinked, trying to focus, and let the pages fall open where they might. *1981*. The handwriting said *1981*. The summer she had sent Mads away, the summer their adult lives began really, though Mads and Ben saw it long before she did.

Cord's heart hammered in her throat and she sank back down on to the sofa, hunching into the corner. There was nothing else now except the soft yellowing pages, and the spidery, silver pencil scrawl. Words, Mads's words written firmly and deliberately onto the paper for her to read after all these years.

Chapter Twelve

The Children's Book of British Wilde Flowers

1 August 1981

Hello, Book. Every year I think you won't be here and you are. And it's so strange when a whole year has almost gone by to simply pick up where I left off on the line below. 1980. I was preoccupied with my spots I see from reading above & with some nonsense at school but when I remember last year it's really the summer of Cord and me having identical cheesecloth shirts from Littlewoods and the hours spent on the steps of the beach hut here listening to the Radio 1 Roadshow & the day we got ALL of "Bits and Pieces" right. This year, I think from her letters and the phone call we had that it'll be the Police. She likes Stewart Copeland, I like Sting. Although I like Kate Bush better, but Cord doesn't really like Kate Bush. I've tried to get her to listen to her but she won't. I'm a bit bored of "Walking on the Moon" for the twentieth time, to be honest.

Ben likes Kate Bush. I heard him mention her once last year. I was fifteen, now I'm almost seventeen. More grown up.

When I can't sleep at school I think about you here underneath the house in your tin, wrapped up warm and safe. I like so much to think about you during the year, to know you're waiting for me, the only one I can tell it all to. The girls at school think I'm crazy. I'm not crazy.

I wish Aunt Julia was still here to ask these things.

I do miss her so much. I couldn't tell her quite how much because she'd have stayed & I know she wanted to go back to Australia. She's sick of this country. She hates Mrs Thatcher. She wants sunshine again. She only came back to look after me and I'm grown up. Well, almost. I do miss her &

They interrupted me! I was sitting on the porch writing away and they arrived! We had a good long chat & a walk along the beach. Cord still exclaims at every change. The Harrisons' beach-hut front door is red now, the sea grass has moved and spread over the dunes over there, there's a tree pitched and fallen into the water almost by Bill's Point. I went inside quickly with them, then came back to Beeches so they could unpack. I'm still always a bit terrified I'll be in the way and they won't love me any more or want me to come over.

Here's some things I noticed.

Althea's floaty floral skirt is from a shop in Beech Ham Place, I heard her say this. Her hair is goldier than before, it's definitely got dye in it.

Cord's pixie boots are from C&A and are very fashionable.

Ben is reading John Wyndham "Day of the Triffids" and I recommended it to him in a letter so that's wonderful

Tony is coming in two days after his play finishes. They told me his play is "The Seagull" which I suppose I must read even though it's by a Russian man & depressing. Still, I must and I will. Just in case, the old reasons, just in case.

Reminders:

Be relaxed with them and STOP being too keen. You are sixteen now & you are the cleverest in your class and probably the year.

Royal Wedding: I am not so keen on the Royal Family but everyone else is this summer, it's practically the law. I thought her dress was silly & it's jolly <u>strange</u> to have a train so long. Imagine if you had to run suddenly if there was a fire – what then? – but when I said that at Gwendolen's house the other girls were horrified. Gwendolen said I was unpatriotic. Which *made me want to snort with laughter. Gwendolen's mother has a picture of the Queen in the kitchen. Anyway, make sure to show them the Commemorative Silver Crown of the wedding given me by Daddy – so unlike him, but he was given it by someone at work to give to me. It is in its blue plastic casing (TSB not Midland, the Midlands one is black) and it is very large & thick, I want to spend it as it is 25p but everyone seems to think this is not the done thing. I tried to pay for an ice cream up at the shop yesterday and they said it wasn't nice to use that to pay for it. I couldn't tell them I'd come down here on my own & was staying in our house & that I didn't have any more money till the Wildflowers arrived. Cos I'd rather be in our house alone and a bit miserable waiting for them than at home with the ticking clocks, waiting for Daddy to come back from work, furious about something . . . I miss Aunt Jules. Don't be a sheep like everyone else when you grow up, she used to say. They're all sheep at the moment.*

2 August

<u>*Now They Are Here: More reminders.*</u>
  Ben may not want to kiss you again so try to work out if he does. Do you want to kiss him?
  (Yes.)
  Ben is different even after only one day of seeing them, I can tell.
  He hates Tony and I tried to talk to him about it yesterday. He says he's seen through him. I know Tony is weak, but that's partly why I like him so much. He makes you feel human. Cord is the same. They're sometimes rather selfish and like attention but what they really want is love and to be told they're doing the right thing. I can see it but Ben doesn't see it like that.
  Althea is different. Fame has finally changed her. She is a bit less fun, more thinking about herself & her appearance. She is on a diet all the time. She doesn't enjoy it as much as she used to I am sure. I cut out the

interview with her in "Good Housekeeping", it is at their London house by the river, there is a photo of her in the sitting room, she is wearing a silk shirt with a bow at the neck and silk trousers & she is spreading her arms wide. The room is beautiful, huge windows, photos of them all around, paintings on the walls, there are gold candlesticks and the wallpaper is of lots of flowers. It is like a more elegant version of the Bosky. I have only been to their London house once. I stared and stared at the photo trying to take it all in. She gets more glamorous as she gets older but less joy.

Finally Cord – I just smiled when I wrote that! My darling friend, it's so wonderful to see her again. She is the same & there is some reserve about her these days but she really does make it all worthwhile. I can live the rest of the year having had the sunshine of her company for a few weeks. In fact she asks me about me and wants to know all these things but I just want to hear her talk, or hear her sing . . . it's very funny as I often don't know what to say as I have no life beyond them really & working hard at school. Perhaps I should do more research into myself (only a part of a joke, perhaps I really should).

Bye, Book x x x

3 August

I love the Wildflowers a lot but I do forget I have to get used to them each year. I am a solitary little bean, that is what Aunt Jules once called me & it's true. I spend so long each year dreaming of them & then the reality is a bit overwhelming. Sometimes, they seem to be tearing themselves apart with these internal battles I don't really understand. Perhaps because I'm older I notice it more. Tony & Ben. Ben & Althea. Cord & Althea. Althea & Tony.

There's some row about when Cord goes to study singing, she wants to go early and they want her to sit A levels. There's some other business about Tony's friend Simon coming for lunch: Althea doesn't want him to come, and Cord says it's because she went out with him years ago. And Tony's still furious with Althea because of the business over the dress she wore for his investiture, & whether it was indecent or not. Some MP has even asked a question in the House of Commons about dress codes for ladies for official functions. WHAT A WASTE of people's time. It was a bit short, but who cares?

Tony says she was taking attention away from him on the day of his knighthood. It was 3 weeks ago & even I who think he can do no wrong think he's being a bit of a baby about it. Cord sides with him – of course. Ben is with Althea, although he also says she's no better than his father.

The girls at school are <u>desperate</u> to know what Althea's like as we all still watch "H Hall" every week even though it's gone downhill these days. I don't tell them anything about her & I like that. I like having secrets. I store up the summer memories to sift through them on my own when I need them. The place mats in the sideboard of old horse paintings. Cord's T-shirt, with a smiling sun on it. The faces of the kings and queens on the sticky old cards we play Racing Demon with when it's wet. The new mugs, from Habitat, brown and green, awfully chic. The taste of Benson & Hedges that Ben and I smoked. (We picked them because of Benson – Ben Son – because Ben kept laughing at it. I wish I wasn't his son, he kept saying.)

Like keeping a jar of sunlight for the winter, or like animals in hibernation until the sun comes. I think about all these things the rest of the year. Aunt Jules used to say everything can't always be magical all the time like Christmas every day but they are to me.

5 August

Ben, Cord & I went into Swanage today, on the bus. Ben went to the cinema to see "Clash of the Titans", all he does is watch films, talk about films! We went to Boots (the Chemist) and Cord bought a really disgusting lipstick called Sheer Pink Mink, she saw it in London and has saved up for it with birthday money and I couldn't say it's absolutely the wrong colour for you, she's so happy to have it. But it doesn't suit her at all and she just folds her lips in and runs it round them, no application in a mirror or anything, no practising. She's off the Police. Her music taste has got even worse in the last year. In fact it's abismell. She likes Shakin' Stevens, Olivia Newton-John, Elaine Paige! She owns the single of "Memory" & she's supposed to be musical. I keep trying to get her to listen to other people. We both still like ABBA and look at pictures of them though they are slowing down this year. We can sing "One of Us" together & do the harmonies, at least I sing the tune, she does the harmonies. She does have a lovely voice. It makes me want to cry when we sing it . . . it's beautiful, and being in love is awful, really.

(But "Memory" from "Cats" . . . no way. Still, for her I pretend to like it when we listen to it.)

She seems much younger than me, & doesn't talk about boys. I think of it like this that she keeps her heart locked away whereas I want to give mine to someone, I have all this love inside me that's never been spent, like money in a piggy bank. I like Baryshnikov. I have his picture up at school and she let me put it up above our bed too. He is gorgeous. I like Adam Ant too. ~~And I like~~

Her hair much better this year (plaits gone, hair longer & nicely wavy) and she is a little thinner & tanned. She was awfully tubby last year, puppy fat they all said but it seems to have come off a bit this year. Never would say any of this to Cordy who is beautiful anyway – her eyes, she has such beautiful eyes just like her father's, silver grey, utterly serious, thick black eyelashes / brows. Cord doesn't really care about how she looks, she likes lipstick & eyeshadow & pretty things but never spends hours in the bathroom. She is beautiful when she smiles and laughs which she does all the time but she's more interested in singing than shopping. She would practise all day if she could but she can't sing too much or her voice will be ruined.

Imagine being Cord and knowing what you want to do, having your life all mapped out already. I can see it – become a big star, be the best singer in the world, marry a handsome conductor, live in a huge mansion with loads of children & servants, sing at the next Royal Wedding when Prince Andrew gets married.

10 August

Althea & Tony had friends over for drinks, actors from some old play of Tony's who are staying in Studland, and their friend Simon & his wife & two old friends of Althea's, ex-models, they were sort of awful. A very late night. We mixed gimlets for them. Two women appeared at the bottom of the porch steps and asked for Althea's autograph! Althea signed it but Tony was Not Very Happy. He said they shouldn't have bothered them. Althea: They didn't want you, dearest, they wanted me. The others all laughed at that a lot.

*   More facts:*
*   Tony has a new shirt from Austin Reed. Very nice, two or three of them in fact, checks, greens and browns.*
*   New Panama hat he got from somewhere near the Ritz he told me. "I will take you to tea at the Ritz, you and Cord, when you're up in town some time Mads." He said that yesterday, I think he did it to annoy Althea, after the people who came for drinks. There was a big row after that I know.*
*   Althea has lovely headscarves she ties up just so, so only a peep of her shining gold-red hair shows.*
*   New garnet earrings from Tony for their wedding anniversary.*
*   She is reading "Princess Daisy". (NB. Read it too?)*
*   Mrs Gage is making coronation chicken sandwiches for us to take on a picnic tomorrow to Worbarrow Bay. I said to her, "You made corona-tion chicken sandwiches for our picnic there last year."*

"No, I didn't."

"Yes, you did."

"You don't know," she says, in quite a nasty way. "I didn't, that's all."

Oh, but I do. I wrote it down. I've got it all written down. I know about you too, Mrs Gage, that when you were little you had a lazy eye & you picked your nose. You were called Eliza Proudfoot and they wouldn't play with you, Tony & Aunt Jules & Daddy. Aunt Jules remembers it all, you see, and she tells me. She was in love with Gary Cooper, that's why Althea calls her Gary, do the other Wildflowers know that or even care? No, she's just always been Gary to them. There was a time Mrs Gage saw Aunt Jules crying under a hedgerow because of something terrible that had happened to her, and she spat at Aunt Jules, & she said she had it coming to her. Maybe I will never see her again.

13 August

I kissed Ben today. Properly, in a grown-up way.

Or rather I let him kiss me. Been meaning to for ages, to see what it was like. I let him touch my bra. We were at the beach hut & Cord didn't want to smoke because of her voice so she went back and we stayed out for a bit & I flirted with him, to see if he would flirt back. It's _very easy to do it with boys when you know how_. That is what I've learned this year!

So I leaned over and let my front brush against him, that's what it is. Also then stroked his arm & said thanks.

Ben gets erections all the time, he's such a boy still even with the I'm-so-grown-up wearing a leather jacket I got from some market in Camden. I can tell when he gets them — covers up with a cushion or something like a "Beezer" or a "Dandy" annual he always has nearby which is sweet because who reads those babyish comics any more.

We kissed for 10 mins? It was boring after a bit. He was nervous, shaking hands. Kept <u>licking</u> me & my face. He said he liked my eyeshadow. (The eyeliner.) He whispered 'Thank you' ½ way through. It made me sad. I don't know why.

I like him so much, and he's different now to me. He's grown up.

But weirdly while we were doing it I thought about Cord & how angry she'd be if she found us. Don't know why but I know she wouldn't like us kissing. Ben tried to push me back on the daybed in the beach hut and I pretended to be offended & said no. I would have let him do it to me only I don't want to lose my virginity to him like that. Although it might be a good way to get it over with. But I don't think I'd enjoy it just yet so I said no.

He is very sweet. He said I was the 1st girl he'd kissed. I said your first kiss? (He's my third, a boy at the Clifton College dance and someone at Bethan's party at Christmas.) He said something I didn't understand about other times & new starts. He doesn't make sense sometimes & he goes into his own world. He tried to take my hand on the way back, and I wouldn't, in case they saw us. But I said I'd meet him tomorrow.

18 August

Ben & I hold hands now when we walk to the beach, behind Cord so she can't see. Sometimes, when we are on the swing on the porch, we touch each other under the blanket if it's sure that no one else will see. I like it, and the secrecy of it, having our own secrets when it was always Cord before. Cord bosses me round more than ever, I wonder what she would think if she knew.

Today we walked as far along as the beach goes towards the chain ferry, for an hour or so, just talking about things. When we were sure no one could see we held hands. We sat on the beach & let the water go on our toes. Our shoes were next to each other, touching. Ben stroked my face and I held his hands and looked at his fingers, and the stump where he lost them. I kiss the hand & the stump, kiss it & hold it to my cheek. I can feel a pulse underneath, beating fast.

We both know we are having a holiday romance like the lady in Mrs Gage's advice column in "Woman's Own" who met a Spanish waiter that Cord likes to read aloud. We joke about it.

I would 'sleep with him' now if he asked me. I think about him more than any of them now. More than Tony for once & Tony was always the hero of my whole life. But really now I see he's an old man.

Ben has a glint in his eye when he smiles. He has big hands, and he's taller than I realised, when we lie on the couch in the beach hut his feet bang up against the wall. When he's above me his blonde hair flops in his face. His arms are tanned with little white spots on them. He has a line of blonde fuzzy hair leading down to his groin.

28 August

Writing this on the porch, & it may end suddenly because they find me. Everything is over & this might be the last time I write in you, Book.

I've made an M mark on my hand with a biro. I have drawn over it several times a day. It's bigger every day.

I hate myself, I hate myself.

M for Madeleine, moron, mistake, maybes.

When I get to school I can use the compass to scratch it in properly. So it's a scar I can look at every time & say, "That's for making such a mistake."

Everything is ruined.

Tony has gone mad, I think he has a disease of the brain. Ben was rude to him but Tony actually grabbed his arm and hit him & Ben is almost bigger than him now. (He has been lifting weights at school. Told me this the other evening at the beach hut. Said it was cos he has been pushed around in the past by bigger people & doesn't want to any more.)

Ben took some whisky. Whisky is disgusting, I have drunk it before, one of the girls at school smuggled some in a Body Shop bottle. Ben came up to the sitting room in the night while everyone was asleep & had a whole large tumbler size. He got really drunk and was sick on the porch. Tony heard some noise, came upstairs & found him. I think that Tony was horrible to him actually. He woke us all up by shouting at him. Said he was weak and a disgrace & had to learn to be a man not a boy. All that sort of rubbish T has never gone in for. Althea shouted at Tony, Tony yelled at her, he called her a horrible name. Cord yelled at them both, Ben just stood there arms folded, swaying, v. pale, looking miserable. Smelling of sick (unpleasant). But Tony really was furious with him. Face is very red these days. Eyes bloodshot. Vein ticks in his jaw. I'm really not in love with him now. Ben said he was just trying it out & wouldn't apologise. He said Tony had never asked him how he was after he ran away and didn't care about anyone else but himself.

Then he pointed at his dad & said, "I can't wait till I don't have to pretend any more."

Tony said, "What the hell do you mean?" & he screwed up his eyes.

Ben said, "You know what I mean, Tony."

Tony touched his face with one hand, like he was shielding his eyes from Ben.

Althea said, "Darling, stop it. Stop it," but I didn't know who she was talking to.

Tony started yelling, saying how he'd had enough of it all. That there weren't to be any more visitors this summer, no more people coming round, that it was his house, he couldn't stand the way she made a fool of him . . .

Cord, Ben and I cleared out early the next day, took a picnic up on the downs. Althea went up to London to audition for a play. That evening when the three of us were in the beach hut Ben said he couldn't sleep at night & that's why he went upstairs. He told me he hates sleeping alone & has nightmares, doesn't mind school for that reason alone, that he is sharing a room with 2 other chaps. (So I am the reason he has nightmares, because if I didn't stay with them perhaps he could be sharing with Cord. He was OK when she was around.)

The other reason I am leaving early and I am marking myself like this is to me much worse and it is that 2). Cord has found us out. She left me & Ben having our cigarettes in the beach hut (strangely there was no punishment for Ben as if Tony knows he went too far) & then must have waited behind because after a few minutes she burst in.

I was enjoying it this time as I do more and more and I think about him touching me and kissing me more and more and sometimes the days are v. long waiting for night-time here with him. That night changed everything about him. I saw him as a different person for the first time. Not the boy I used to play with. I wanted him to kiss me, we both did. I wanted to push against him and feel how close we could get, and to touch him and his skin.

He had his hand up my skirt, I let him put one finger inside me. (It was OK. I am keen on the kissing / holding, not so much into the finger bit.)

She didn't burst in actually that is too dramatic. She opened the door & we were ½ sitting / lying on the daybed. I saw her first. Over his shoulder. I saw her expression & I won't forget it for ages. Like she was confused. Like she couldn't work out what was going on. 2 little lines between her eyebrows. She said, "What are you two doing?"

I laughed. If I regret one thing for the rest of my life, it'll be laughing at her. But I was scared at her face and how she looked at me. I said, "It's nothing."

"Are you boyfriend and girlfriend?"

I said no, but Ben at the said time said YES, really loudly. (I feel we should have talked about that bit before.)

I said, "Cord, everything's still the same."

But she just said, "No, it's not. You've ruined it." & she turned round & left.

She has not spoken to me for 2 days. Pretends to be asleep when I go to bed. Ignores me when I ask her something at the breakfast table.

Pushes past me, jabs me with her elbow just as I pass her, so I bash against the corridor. No one has noticed, I wouldn't say anything, but I'm not one of them anyway, I have to remember that, for all their kindness to me over the years.

Anyway, I have gone home early. 2 nights ago I came to bed & she had left a note on the pillow: I am taping it in.

Dear Madeleine,

    I am writing this to ask you to leave Ben alone and leave the Bosky. I don't want to be friends with you any more. Daddy told me once that living next door to your father and your aunt Julia in the war was strange because they were so totally different from him and he couldn't really understand them and he tried but in the end it never worked. I thought it was good we were different, you and me, but now I see it is that you are so different it is bad.

    We used to be happy and now we're not and no one seems to realise it's you causing it all. I am sorry this happened.

    Cordelia Wilde

I lied to Althea and to Tony & said some science prize at school meant I needed to go back a week before term began. Tony wasn't particularly interested which was awful, but Althea believed me. She was even upset I was leaving. I'm still on the porch writing now, it's about to rain. The wicker is warm, sagging under my bottom, I can smell the flowers and the dry heat & the metallic feeling rain is on its way. The footstool that catches right where you want on one of the floorboards. The waves below. Crickets. The radio in the background. All dear sounds.

I need to put you away for the summer, Book. Althea is inside now getting ready to drive me to the station. She is a terrible driver. "We'll see you next August, darling, won't we? Don't line up anything else to do, we'll all miss you if you're not here."

That morning as I was in our bedroom looking under the bed Cord came in.

I said, "Here's this, I made you a present. I'm sorry." And I handed her a package which is so small.

She didn't even open it. She threw it on the bed and she said, "We don't want you here. So don't come back."

I think it's the worst thing anyone's said to me. Because I loved Cord more than any of them. When I was scared at night she used to get into bed with me and hug me and our toes would touch. She could brush my hair and not pull at the tangles. She knew when I was feeling sad about things, and she would find my hand & squeeze it. When she laughs, she throws her head back and her mouth wide open and she rubs her ribs. She is so definite about everything. I love them all but I truly loved her.

The thing is, I don't think what me and Ben were doing was wrong. Ben is sad, I have made him happy. Other way round too.

The M gets bigger and clearer with the biro ink going in & under the skin every time I scratch it a bit more.

I wonder if Cord has opened the necklace. I wonder if she will wear it. It is a shell, I found on the beach, and something has eaten a hole away in it and it looks like a heart. I put it on the chain from my necklace Aunt Jules gave me when I was ten. It is gold.

I don't know where I'll go. Will they let me back in at school a week before term begins? Think it'll have to be Dad's even though he's away in Sweden at some conference. I do not know where the key is. I will have to break into my own house. Which is sort of funny when you think about it.

She is coming. No more now. Thank you, Book.

xxxxxxx

Chapter Thirteen

August 1983

Althea knew Tony was cheating on her again when he invited her sister to stay with them for the summer. Other potential guests were thin on the ground these days: Guy and Olivia were in New York while Guy appeared in a cycle of the History Plays. Simon was definitely *persona non grata* and Bertie was unofficially banned from the Bosky; Tony wouldn't say why but a kindly fellow actress told Althea that Bertie had left Tony an empty bottle of champagne at the stage door as a belated birthday present with a cryptic note that said, *The fizz has rather gone, hasn't it?*

A lot of the others had drifted away; one didn't see people as regularly as one used to. So if he couldn't invite Bertie it would be Isla. Once, he had adored Isla, who in past school holidays when the children were young had been an infrequent but much-loved visitor to Twickenham and the Bosky. She was unimpressed by artistic folk, having grown up with her and Althea's father, an enormously charismatic but rather temperamental painter. She had a way of teasing Tony that he liked, and used to laugh at, once.

Once, long ago. When had that changed? He was less interested in charming Isla, or anyone, for that matter. There was someone new on the scene, not the actresses, not the little singing teacher – for the first time Althea didn't care who it was. It'd be someone young, pliant, adoring. Someone the opposite of her.

When Althea and Isla were children Isla had liked playing dolls and making houses out of anything she could find in their father's studio or in the tall, cluttered house. Her dolls lived an intensely rigid, boring existence to Althea, their bedtimes monitored, food dull and solid, constantly being washed with little squares cut from kitchen cloths. She'd never been interested in crabbing on the quayside with the other children, or playing hide-and-seek in the long thin garden that led down to the river, or making things up.

'Come and imagine there are sprites in the willow tree.'

'No. Flossie will be wanting her tea soon.'

She had grown into a good aunt, a warm, comforting person, shaped like a cottage loaf, with the same sparkling green eyes as her sister and a dry, sharp wit. She was headmistress of the local girls' school, lived alone, was utterly unflappable, and Althea found her company these days alternately comforting and discomfiting. Isla knew her little sister. She saw through her, with those beady eyes that took in everything. She rarely called her Dorothy (Althea's real name, discarded when she went to drama school) any more, except by accident but every time she said Althea, the latter always heard a little note of amusement in her voice. She rose early, when Tony got up late, she didn't like strong drink, and found theatre talk tedious. Her sister was, Althea knew, probably happiest in the kitchen helping Mrs Gage.

Tony was taking middle age badly. His behaviour had deteriorated. He was drinking more, was obviously bored by people and, most shockingly of all, she'd seen him freeze on stage, a few months ago. It was a worthy state-of-the-nation play on at the National about Thatcher and he'd hated it, but still: Tony *never* dried. He laughed at the dreaded stage fright that affected others. Always had. But lately he was different. *Guys and Dolls*, the National's most successful show to date, was on at the

Olivier Theatre next to his own; the roars and screams and whistling were audible in the interval of *Mother's Milk*. The stage-hands were caught going backstage to watch *Guys and Dolls*. As you filed through the concrete lobby out into the South Bank night it was easy to spot who'd been watching the glorious life-affirming musical that was the hottest ticket in town and who'd just left an angry, slow-moving play about a decaying mill town, an ageing couple and their two dysfunctional children.

What bothered Althea was that normally Tony wouldn't have cared. He'd have been glad for the cast of *Guys and Dolls*, or at least would have pretended to be. But not any more. He hated them, ground his teeth when talk turned to it, smiled thinly when friends asked them if they'd seen it, and once even left the room at a dinner for a retiring director when someone broke into a chorus of 'The Oldest Established'. 'Sorry, needed some air, and I do hear that song rather a lot,' he'd explained when he'd returned ten minutes later, smelling of cigarettes and whisky. 'I'm awfully sorry, Michael. Do forgive me.'

'Is Tony all right, darling?' people had started asking her. 'Seems rather under the weather lately.' As if he had a cold, a cold in the head.

And he had started going to the Bosky at weekends again. There were always affairs; she wasn't stupid enough to pretend there weren't. She'd come to expect it: a few weeks before the end of every run he'd stroll into the garden or the living room and say, casually, 'Any objection if I take off to the Bosky for a few days after the run's over, darling girl? Be good to clear my head.'

'Of course,' she'd say, not even raising her head from the magazine or the rose bush or whatever she was doing. 'Poor darling, you've been at it non-stop.' He never seemed to notice this turn of phrase but it made her feel better. *Is it that dark little thing playing Doll Tearsheet? Built like a boy, no hips, no tits, big eyes? Or the stagehand with the nose-ring and the floppy blonde mohican?*

He'd been there three times this year, and twice taken a little gaggle down – hangers-on from the productions, which he'd at least told her about. The other visits he had supposedly been alone, but that she didn't believe. She was forty-two and too old for him was what Althea also knew.

The first time he'd taken her to the Bosky, all those years ago, when he had sat her down on that bed and told her the truth about everything, she had given herself to him then, right there. That weekend they had made their vows, the ones that mattered, she always thought, not the ones they said at the registry office a few months later. She had told him, on that day, that she would never try to hold him too tight, that he must do what he wanted. And that the same went for her, too. That they would always come back together in the end. Hadn't they stuck to this agreement? Hadn't it worked?

A week after their arrival there was a dramatic storm in which lightning cracked across the night sky and fierce rods of rain lashed the old wooden building. The next morning, as puffed white clouds scudded across the bay driven by a sharp wind from the east, Althea looked up at her husband over breakfast, and saw him, staring at his own reflection in the glint of his knife, smacking gently at the tiny wattle of skin that was beginning to dangle from his neck. He turned his head right and left, unaware that he was being watched, no trace of humour on his expression, utterly and totally focused on himself. She saw him trace the eyebrow with one finger, flare his nostrils, make a tiny moue with his lips – it was almost funny.

Her sister was absorbed in the paper. Althea watched her husband, feeling a cold kind of horror slide over her. Where had he gone, the joyous, fascinating, hugely attractive whirlwind of a man who had overwhelmed her and made her love him? Did he see her? Did he see their children, one virtually estranged from them, the other interested only in her singing? And what about her? Did he wonder about *Hartman Hall*? About what her dreams were, her hopes for the future? He didn't seem to care and she thought constantly about him and what he needed. He was petty, too, wanting to be right all the time, and with very little to be right about . . . Other actors of his age and experience founded theatre companies, marched for peace, wrote lyrical letters of protest, attacked governments. Tony sat at breakfast and worried about his jawline.

A fresh breeze through the open window ruffled the hairs on her arms and Althea came to with a start, still watching her husband. She realised her head had been aching for a while.

'What's that you're reading, Althea?' Isla said, poking the playscript she had rolled in one hand. Althea looked up, trying not to seem irritated.

'Just a script. It arrived yesterday. It's for a new production. A reworking of . . . something.'

'For you, darling?' Tony said, looking up. 'A play?'

'TV, or a play. They're not sure . . .' She paused, about to speak, then shrugged.

'How exciting. Let me see.' He wedged a piece of toast into his mouth and, without asking, took the sheaf out of her hand.

'Here! Don't do that,' Althea said, grabbing it back. From downstairs, the sound of Cord doing her vocal exercises floated up to them, rising a tone at a time. 'I was reading it. Don't just snatch it from me.'

'Sorry, darling.' He raised his hands, as if guilty. 'Forgive me.'

'I didn't know you were thinking of the stage again, Althea,' said Isla, dolloping a plum-sized mound of marmalade on her toast and spreading it around with precision. 'That's a departure for you. You wouldn't leave *Hartman Hall*, would you?'

'Well,' Tony said. '*Hartman*'s been wonderful for Althea but it can't go on for ever, can it?'

Althea heard herself say, 'You'd like it if it did, wouldn't you? A slow slide into mediocrity, then totally forgotten? That'd suit you ever so well.' She stood up, ignoring Isla's prim pursing of her lips, and prised the script from his pinched fingers. 'I'm going to finish my coffee outside.'

Outside, with the sun still behind the house and the wind high, it was chilly. Althea pulled the rug over her knees, and sat for a while, staring out at the churning sea. She felt rather sick.

Last week, she'd been told she was to be killed off in *Hartman Hall*. No one else knew; it was to be kept a huge secret, a big shocker for the last episode of the series to send the ratings back up again for the subsequent, final series. Lady Isabella would be murdered by her brutish new American husband, under mysterious circumstances that would enable him to evade capture before being brought to London for a sensational trial.

'Wonderful to get out at the top, darling,' Tobias, her new agent, had told her. 'It's time for a change. It's terrific news, really. Leave on a high.'

But it didn't feel like terrific news. You didn't kill off your main character when everything was going well, did you? You killed off someone incidental and framed the main character for the murder. She knew why she was being bumped off.

They wanted someone younger. A new leading lady around whom they could frame a whole story to try and breathe life into the creaky old Sunday-night TV warhorse which had lost its way several years ago. Other, better costume dramas had imitated it since, and done it better: *Jane Eyre,* for example, with Tony as Mr Rochester – the irony wasn't lost on Althea there. To compete, *Hartman Hall* had started throwing any old plot at the wall to see if it'd stick and she wasn't sure when it had finally lost any credibility it might once have had: possibly when Lady Isabella had started seeing ghosts, or the ludicrous plotline in the fourth series when she'd become a smuggler.

She'd been 'resting' for so long before *Hartman Hall* that it wasn't like she had any other recent experience to fall back on. The programme had made her; without it she was nothing. She'd be starting again, at forty-two, and things had changed whilst she'd been off being a huge TV star. She'd been turned down for two parts in the last week, one the lead in a Granada drama for Sunday evenings, the other the wife in a new sitcom. The first one she'd not been that surprised by: Tobias had been frank with her. 'You're too old, Althea darling. They're looking for a fresh face. You know. Someone more . . . eighties.'

But the second had been a real blow. It was for a wife and mother of two teenage children living in a leafy London suburb who gets a job working again after fifteen years . . . in the same office as her solicitor husband. She *was* the mother of two teenage children. She lived in a leafy London suburb, albeit in an eighteenth-century town house by the river. And yet still they'd said she wasn't right for the part, and Tobias had as good as told her it was again because she was too old.

'I was actually pretty young when I had my children,' she'd

told him. 'Most mothers of teenage children are even older than me if you can imagine that, darling.'

But Tobias had merely given a nervous laugh. Oh, she missed Bertie, with his rude honesty and his lack of bullshit, and the way they spoke the same language, but she'd got rid of him to appease Tony. She was starting to despair of finding another part, wondering whether she'd simply slide back into obscurity, her only role that of Lady Wilde, opening fetes and simpering on Tony's arm, and the idea absolutely terrified her. Then the script for *On the Edge* had arrived.

She looked down at it now in her curled hand. It would cement her reputation or ruin her career; it was daring, in places highly suggestive, nothing like it had been shown on TV. She was Janey, a divorcee, considering taking a much younger man as a lover. It opened with her buying bras and featured a post-coital scene in bed. Real conversation, not nonsense like *Dynasty* where the men wore as much make-up as the women and the bed sheets were blue silk. It was hilarious, too, that was the thing she liked about it. Janey was a real woman; it was written by a woman. She could see every one of her friends enjoying it and in her limited experience that was a recipe for a hit. But oh, the risk . . .

It had been Simon's suggestion they send it to her – darling, naughty Simon, doing it to annoy Tony probably but . . . how clever he was . . . how dreadful if it failed . . . Althea felt slightly sick again, only this time with nerves. She had to decide whether to take it, one way or the other.

'*Ah, sorrow! Ah, sorrow!*'

Cord's voice, still faint, came through the open window; she was preparing an aria from *Dido and Aeneas* for her Royal Academy audition the following month. She practised for at least two hours a day, listening to tapes of celebrated recordings on the battered cassette player Uncle Bertie had given her all those years ago that she and Ben used to hunch over, listening to tapes.

Shaking her head – she couldn't think about Ben without beginning to cry – Althea pulled out the plastic hand mirror she kept in the little drawer of the porch side table and stared at herself, frankly. The pale milk skin, the blue veins, the lines that seemed hatched into her. The eyes, faintly disapproving of something. Had she always been this . . . this . . . *disappointed-looking*? *There was a time when men used to stop and stare at me when I walked by. And it's not as though I miss it*, she told herself moodily, raising her knees up under her chin and tugging the rug around her, shivering, suddenly. *I absolutely don't, of course not. It's pathetic, those women you see still chasing their youth. I had my time and it was wonderful, being that girl.*

She'd seen Ray Harrington, the Australian actor who'd played her husband and who'd been killed off at the end of the second series, for lunch. She'd never liked him – roaming hands, a nasty streak when drunk, and no subtlety as an actor: really, he'd only been hired because of his looks. Halfway through his salmon mousse he'd leaned forward, spittle flecking his chin, and said, in soft, venom-filled tones, 'You'll find it hard, getting old, harder than most. It'll be a real come-down for a goddess like you.'

He'd said it with such relish. She'd wanted to slap him right there in the middle of Langan's. He, with his paunchy stomach and his veiny nose, boasting about character roles he was being offered, stuff with meat, real substance, not like all those washed-up actresses who only had looks to trade on . . . Since that lunch, Althea had become more obsessed with that idea. The notion that scores of well-known actresses just disappeared, after a certain time, when they got to whatever cut-off point was allowable dependent on their fame. Men went on, men could be desirable onscreen till their sixties or even seventies . . . It wasn't fair, wasn't bloody fair . . . Althea jumped, as the French windows banged open and Tony appeared on the porch.

'Listen, darling, I'm sorry about being vile to you. I must have drunk a little too much last night. I'm feeling wretched this morning.' Tony dropped a kiss on her head. 'I'm an absolute pill. Don't let's fall out before breakfast is over.'

She carried on staring ahead, not ready to forgive him yet.

'What's the new script? Is it a play? Do you want me to read it?' He crouched down, and took one of her hands. 'Althea? What's up?'

She wished she could tell him. Wished they were a team the way Olivia and Guy were, how they each knew what was best for the other, wanted the other's success and happiness more than their own. Tears came into Althea's eyes.

'Are you feeling sad about Ben, my darling?'

'No,' she said, but it didn't sound convincing.

'He'll come back to us. I promise.'

'I . . .' Althea shook her head, and uncurled her fists.

Tony took her chin in his hand and turned her head very gently towards him. He was more tanned, his face had a healthier glow than of late and his eyes burned as they met hers. 'Althea,' he said quietly. 'Darling, you're as beautiful now as you were then. More, perhaps.'

She looked at him through narrowed eyes, breathing hard. 'Don't tell fibs, Tony.'

But he was staring at her with total sincerity. As though he could read her mind, knew what was in her heart. It was a trick he'd always had, damn him. 'It's true, darling. You have something you didn't then.'

'Crows' feet? Tony, it's not just – it's not just looks, for God's sake. I'm not some mannequin in a shop, I'm an actress, a bloody good actress, actually.'

He laughed and kissed her, moving his hand to the back of her neck.

'My beautiful girl, you're the best I know,' he said. 'I'm sorry you're upset. Is there anything I can do?'

Althea cleared her throat.

'It's *Hartman Hall*,' she said, frankly. 'I'm being canned.'

'Oh.' He nodded. He didn't offer fake sympathy but stood there thinking, eyes narrowed, for a minute. 'It's for the best. Yes, absolutely. We'll find you something else.' He looked down at her, reappraising everything. 'God, I'm sorry I've been such a heel lately, and you've been dealing with all of that.'

She shrugged, wearily.

'I used to care,' she said, bleakly. 'I used to tear myself to pieces, when we were first together. When I thought, oh, I can help him, after the promises we made each other . . .'

'Althea – darling. Don't say that.' He looked quite stricken. 'I'm sorry.'

She could hear Isla inside, clattering about with plates, hear the wash of the morning tide on the sand below. All normal sounds. She felt quite calm.

'It doesn't matter any more,' she said vaguely. She thought of *On the Edge*. He'd hate it. Tony stared at her, his hand closing around her wrist. 'I'm not sad,' she said. 'I'm not angry – it's fine.'

'Don't be sad about me. I love—' He cleared his throat. 'Dammit, Althea, I love you, you know I do, I always have.'

'Gosh, all this *Sturm und Drang* right after breakfast,' she said mildly, and he smiled.

'Don't be sad about *Hartman Hall* either. You're better than them.'

Althea looked up. She said, 'I'm not, actually. I'm going to do a sitcom, they've offered me the part. It's rather racy. It'll upset a lot of people, Tony—' She rooted around beside her. 'Here, let me give you the script—'

But as she turned to give it to him she saw he wasn't listening. He was staring out to sea, thinking hard about something. Then he pulled a large handkerchief from his pocket and rubbed his face with it, and she smelled the perfume first, then saw the lipstick on the pale blue fabric. Just a smear. She knew it could have been any number of things – jam, pen, his own stage make-up – but she knew it wasn't. It never was.

'Everything's a bit hard at the moment,' he said blankly. 'I'm sorry. Getting worse.'

Althea said slowly, 'How, darling?'

'The nightmares. I keep having them. Awfully tedious.'

'Does she come back?'

'Every time.'

Her heart swelled with sympathy for him, and yet – the chill came over her again. For the first time she could see a future without him, without the handkerchiefs or worse, the phone slammed down as she entered a room, the receipts for restaurants she'd never been to with him. Or the feeling, the indefinable but true conviction one had, that another woman had been in one's bedroom, had preened herself in the mirror one used, lain in the bed one slept in . . .

Althea lifted her head to him, and took his hand. She said softly, wearily, 'You are a great actor, the greatest of your day. You had a terrible time as a child. Unimaginable. It'll always be painful but remember, darling, it helped you become what you are.'

'Do you really think that?'

She nodded, wearily, forcing a kind smile. Tony kissed her forehead, excited as a boy that he had smoothed things over. 'I have to go to the station, to collect Hamish. I'll be back for lunch.'

'Who?'

'Hamish Lowther, precious. You remember. Prince Hal. I invited him to stay for the week. You were keen on the idea.' Tony's face assumed that slightly mulish expression that used to amuse her. 'You were the one who said we should ask him, I seem to recall.'

Now Althea sat up. 'I didn't think you'd invite him and then not tell me. What are we to do with him? A whole week? Oh, Tony, it's too bad. It really is.'

He got to his feet, impatient again. 'Darling, you're the one who draped yourself over him at Orso's and insisted he accept. I had to ask him. Anyway, he's just been ditched by his fiancée and he's terribly down in the dumps. Needs cheering up. He's a lovely boy, he can – Cord will like him, and there's . . .' Tony trailed off, the lack of Ben and Madeleine heavy in the air. 'He can go for walks with Cord.'

Suddenly Althea saw the funny side, that this handsome young man with whom she had, undoubtedly, flirted far too much on that night, partly because Tony was obviously screwing Hamish's girlfriend, a cool young blonde named Emma playing Catherine de Valois, and partly because – well, he was a beautiful young man. He was droll and unhurried, with wide grey eyes, light brown hair and a soft Borders accent that reminded her of home, of sweet gentle boys who wanted to kiss her when she was a girl, of warm nights and the smell of pine and the call of the fishermen unloading their catch on the banks of the Dee in the mornings. The breeze fluttered the closed script, her hair, kissing her fondly.

'Yes, he was rather lovely,' she said, smiling at her husband, frankly for once, acknowledging their imperfections. 'You're right. He can go for walks with Cord.'

Chapter Fourteen

Hamish was as handsome as she remembered, and as shy. In marked contrast to Tony, who carried something of the charisma he wore on stage off with him every night, Hamish could not have been less like an actor.

'In fact,' said Isla, gazing at him with approval and not a little admiration, two days into his stay, 'you'd never know he was there. He just seems to blend right in, doesn't he, the sweet wee lad.'

Althea couldn't help but notice the flush on his cheeks when he spoke to her, or the studied, calm way he handled things: his cutlery, a stuck door, a lost child who wandered past the house in tears. One evening they went to the pub and she watched in awe as he carried four drinks back to the table in the garden, two each in the palms of his huge hands. He was unfailingly gentle, reserved, kind; only sometimes, when she looked at him, and found he was watching her, did she feel herself begin to blush, too.

Of course, what no one had foreseen was that Cord would develop a painfully obvious crush on him: Cord who, at seventeen, had never really shown any interest in boys, beyond the usual lip service to John Travolta. But Hamish acted upon her like the proverbial thunderbolt, and much as Althea wished she could discuss this with her daughter, whose cheeks flared painfully red whenever she found herself in the same room as Hamish, she couldn't. She and Cord had never been the kind of mother and daughter to girlishly whisper confidences in each other's ears whilst shopping for make-up and it was too late to start now.

By contrast, Hamish seemed to be a wholly restful holiday companion; she thought he must be rather bemused by her own coolness towards him, but she knew she must back away from any further entanglements if she were to maintain the moral high ground with Tony. Hamish took a while to say things, and it wasn't until he'd been there a few days that Tony told her he'd had a stutter until he was a teenager, which acting had helped overcome. Now, he thought out everything he said, in contrast to the Wildes, like a murder of crows in a tree, chattering non-stop. It was only a couple of months after the loss of his fiancée – Emma had dumped him for her director whilst on a national tour of *The Norman Conquests* and Tony said he was still awfully cut up about it.

It would be good for Cord to get her first crush out of the way and do so on this sweet-natured, gentle man, someone who didn't yawn as Cord loudly, excitedly explained her thoughts on modern music and what singers she liked and why . . . It made Althea glaze over, but in this Hamish was a better actor than she was, and always listened attentively. Yes, she *was* glad Tony had asked him down.

Cord was waving a crisp in the air. 'Well, I think some modern music is wonderful but a lot of it just hurts my ears.'

'That's the point, I think,' Hamish said, smiling. 'To make as much noise as possible. That's why I like it. The chaos of sound.'

'Well, I don't. What about that ridiculous piece that's just turning three radios on and letting them play for five minutes. Or just sitting in silence for four and a half minutes. It's lazy! I like music to have a point. Er – to sound nice.'

Hamish just laughed. 'How bourgeois, Cord,' he said, smiling into her face. 'I expected more of you.'

Her father laughed. 'He's right. You have to have the new. People thought Mozart was horrifically garish once.'

'Well, but these days I just feel we need to preserve classical music,' said Cord, a little too loudly, red in the face. 'It's really important. There's too much on all this other music and I just think . . . I just think . . . anyway.' But, running out of steam, she stopped and stared at the ground, biting her lip in adolescent awkwardness. Althea's heart ached for her.

Hamish nodded, smiling at her. 'It's cool to be passionate about something. I like it. It means you're interested.'

'Thank you,' said Cord, formally, and she picked up the bowl on the table. 'Would you like some more peanuts and raisins, Hamish?'

'Yes, thank you, Cord.'

'Er, not . . . not at all.' A shy glance at him. 'Anyway, as I was saying about coloratura . . . It's very interesting because . . .' She trailed off. 'Oh. I've forgotten.'

'Another Martini, Hamish?'

'I'd love one, Tony, but I think not. You make them awfully strong, you know.'

'My dear boy – this is nothing. School measures.'

'Leave Hamish alone, Dad!' Cord, flushed, hit her father playfully on the arm. 'He doesn't want another drink.'

Hamish smiled slowly at Cord. His eye caught Althea's. 'I'll save myself for later, I think,' he said, slowly.

Althea felt the shock of attraction, of sexual certainty, pulse through her, as it hadn't for – oh, years, now. Was she imagining it? 'Good idea, Hamish,' she said, with a slow, cat-like grin, and he blushed, and his gaze returned to Cord once more.

Oh, God. To think someone young found her attractive again! She felt a pang for Cord, but only a pang – she'd already made up her mind not to do anything about it and it was good to see her daughter falling in love. She saw that Isla was looking at her and wished her sister didn't still, after all these years, know her so well.

'I'll check on the pie,' said Isla, standing up. 'I don't want to eat too late, what with my early start and all of that.'

'Oh, Auntie I,' said Cord. 'I wish you weren't going.'

'Well,' said Isla, disappearing into the kitchen. 'Yes.'

Althea, feeling guilty, got up and followed her. Mrs Gage had been quite specific about the pie, though her sight wasn't as good as it had been and sometimes she got the cooking times and quantities wrong, lacing their coronation chicken last week with so much curry powder it was actually inedible. She gathered up her skirts and peered into the oven.

'I can't tell, Isla, what do you think? Done or not?' She rubbed at the ancient, chipped, enamel-and-glass door.

'Oh, I'd say it's as ready as it'll ever be,' said Isla. She reached for the oven gloves. 'I'll take it out, shall I?'

'Thanks.' Althea took the ketchup from the cupboard. There was a short pause. She wished she could think of something to say to her sister, but time seemed only to deepen the furrows between them. 'So, you're off in the morning, are you? Sure you won't stay for lunch?'

'No.' Isla opened the oven door and a whoosh of hot air hit them. 'I'll be on my way after breakfast. I'll need a clear run to make it to Lancaster by teatime. I'll stop off with my sandwiches somewhere, have a nice picnic—' Althea's eyes glazed over, and she searched around for something else to do. 'Some lovely spots near the M5, there's a National Trust place I want to . . . Althea, is everything all right with Tony? I'm rather worried about him.'

Althea didn't hear her at first, and then she laughed. 'Tony? He's fine. Well, fine as he ever is. Why?'

'Nothing.' Her sister smiled at her, the old comforting smile, holding the pie in her hands. 'I worry about you, too. I'm your sister. And he seems different. There's something about him there wasn't before.'

Althea gave a short laugh. 'Really, Isla, it's a strange thing to ask.'

'Is it? Dotty, you know sometimes I think you live in a dream world. There's Cord, working so hard to get away from you both – she's almost a grown woman and you treat her like she's still Cordy who's eight and likes making lists. And there's Mads gone, as if she was never here—'

'That's her choice, she's working this summer,' Althea began. 'We didn't kick her out, Isla, she said she wanted to stay in Bristol this summer, and last summer—'

'That's as may be, but she needed you, and I think it's pretty disgraceful. And then there's Ben barely spoken of, as if he's dead, and here you are all day mooning around waiting to hear about some script.' She caught her sister's hand furiously; Althea pulled away.

'It's – I'll be fine.'

Isla said fiercely, 'Oh, I know, dear, *you've* always been fine. I don't worry about you. You're strong.'

'You make me sound like a brood mare.' Althea shook her head. 'Isla, don't. I'm Cord's mother, I know her best. And I miss Ben b-b-but he'll be back. And Mads – she wasn't ever ours, you know, we couldn't force her to come here . . . They're growing up, that's all.'

'I'll take this out now,' was all Isla said, and she turned around and left Althea alone in the kitchen.

As suspected, the pie was dry and mealy, tasting too gamey for chicken and under-seasoned, and Althea resolved to Have a Word with Mrs Gage about her cooking and things in general though she had no idea how she'd approach the subject. They sat in silence, all of them, and occasionally she'd steal a glance at Hamish, at the strong jaw working on the pie, at the huge gentle hands, the long eyelashes.

She wondered if it would be so very bad to kiss him. She wanted to, very much, though it disgusted her that she could betray herself in this way, and betray her own daughter.

Tony was talking to Hamish about a new production of *Othello* at the Old Vic in which Othello was white, and the rest of the cast black.

'I think it's very brave, but I'm not entirely sure it works. Besides—'

'I loved it,' said Hamish. 'I thought it was remarkable, not just the idea, but the rest of the cast besides Patrick. To see a range of black actors on stage, not just one or two token performers; I found it exhilarating. The reviewers did too, didn't they . . .?' He trailed off, as Tony muttered something disparaging and drained his glass. Hamish met Cord's adoring glance and returned her smile.

'Reviews!' Tony rolled his eyes. 'The longer I live, Hamish, love, the greater my conviction most reviews are no longer an exercise in critical thinking. They're for provincial idiots who haven't the first idea about culture or simpering spinsters who want someone to tell them what to think.'

'Don't be so pompous,' said Althea, pushing back her chair and lighting a cigarette.

Cord laughed, shaking her hair out of her face, her grey eyes sparkling. 'Yep. What a load of rubbish, Daddy. You don't say that when they're calling you the greatest actor of your train compartment, or whatever it is.'

Tony smiled at his daughter. 'You'll see what I mean one day, Cordy. You'll come to realise the review of one idiot journalist one night is worthless. Who cares, as long as you tried, as long as you worked as hard as you could at the role? Unless you *become* the role.'

'What do you mean?' said Hamish, quietly.

Tony leaned forward. 'You see, it's you escaping everything when you step on to that stage. On your own up there night after night, utterly believing what your character does, being them completely, on one level of consciousness.' He stared intently at Hamish, then Cord. 'It's you who controls them, who holds them in the palm of your hand. Macbeth's nothing more than a gangster thug, a low-life murderer. It's up to you to make them believe he's a poet, a tortured genius. If you can't keep their attention and respond to each audience in a different way each night you're no artist. And the only way is by utterly believing you're them.'

'You can't utterly believe it, Tony, surely not,' said Althea, pushing her glass towards him for a refill, avoiding Isla's watchful gaze from the other end of the table. 'You'd drive yourself mad if you thought you were actually Macbeth every night.'

'On one level, isn't that what I said?' He poured more wine into her glass, then his. 'Not the whole. There are layers, you see? But yes, on one level one has to become him.' He looked up at her, and his expression was terrifying, his once-handsome face purple-black in the dark, moonlight throwing it into ghoulish shadow, like a cheap, Grand Guignol monster. 'Then one has to learn to preserve the rest of one's soul if one's to stand a chance of remaining sane.' He gave a short laugh. 'Perhaps that's pompous too. But it happens to be true.'

Isla did the washing-up and then retired promptly that night. Cord, with whom she was sharing a room, disappeared with her to help her pack and take her largest bag to the car, chattering fondly to her aunt as they went down the stairs. Tony went to bed early, saying he was tired, almost cheerfully admitting he'd drunk too much, so Althea put the dishes away alone. She could see Hamish hanging about, smoking on the porch and looking out at the full moon. He had offered to help but she'd refused and yet he stayed nearby, his long, lean body illuminated by moonlight that seemed to cover the whole bay with a phosphorescent silver.

Althea sang gently as she padded around the kitchen, killing time before making her next move. Suddenly she felt calmer.

Five or ten minutes after everything had sounded quiet downstairs she turned off the lights in the kitchen and, moving towards the French doors, paused to look at him again, in the darkness. The promise of youth. The promise of abandonment, of being wicked and feeling something again, after all these years. Was it so bad, to want these things? Lips parted, pulse beating at the base of her throat, Althea opened the door, silently.

He had vanished.

She froze, then saw a movement, and realised he'd gone through the wild flowers and was padding down the dark sandy path towards the beach huts, into the silver, glittering night.

Althea followed him. A few steps along, she trod on a partially broken pine cone, and the jagged edges tore into the thin skin on the arch of her foot, which was unbelievably painful. She had to pause for a moment or two, biting down on her hand, leaning against the beach hut two along from theirs. She almost called out to him then, but still – something stopped her – what if someone was watching?

So she began walking the final ten yards, or rather limping, trying not to smile now, because it was ridiculous, and wonderful too. Once or twice she thought he seemed aware of her behind him, and when he got to their beach hut, he stopped, so she stopped too.

'Hello?' she heard him call, a laughing mischief in his voice. 'Is that you?'

Heart in her mouth, Althea whispered softly, 'Yes—'

But he didn't hear her, and walked up the steps.

'I'm here,' he said. 'Did you wait long?'

Althea was about to answer, and she might have utterly made a fool of herself had not Isla's words suddenly come back to her.

You live in a dream world.

She stopped, behind the hut next to theirs, peering around the edge to watch him ascend the steps. There, waiting at the top for him, was a figure, silhouetted in black, moonlight shining on one side of her face.

'I've been here for ages,' said the figure, with a small, soft laugh.

No. Althea clutched the side of the beach hut, utterly still: as though an arctic blast had turned her into ice. Her eyes stung; her bowels lurched.

'I was waiting for your ma to leave. She took ages. Oh, Cordelia—' The steps creaked; Hamish's low voice was urgent. 'I wanted you all night.'

'Me too, and you shouldn't have been touching me like that at supper. I'm sure Mumma suspected something.'

'She didn't. I'm starting to wonder if she thinks I fancy her.'

'Oh, no!' A gurgle of mirth. 'Poor Mumma. Though to be fair to her, people used to.' Cord's outline swung towards Hamish, who caught her and slung his arms around her waist, kissing her hair, her neck, her hands, and Althea shrank back as far as she could.

'I don't want to talk about your mother.'

'Don't lie! I'm sure you do too. They're both actors, remember, I know what you're all like.'

'Look at her? When you're here? No, my beautiful prim angel, I don't. I don't. I don't fancy you, either.'

Althea could hear the catch in her daughter's voice – it was still, there was nothing else. 'Oh, dear.'

'I don't, because it's for people playing games. I love you. I'm in love with you. You know I am.'

'Darling Hamish—' She heard the door creak open. 'Don't talk nonsense. Let's go inside. It's cold out here.'

'I can't stand the daytime. It's d-d-driving me completely mad. Waiting to be with you . . .'

His voice was thick, his stutter trying to assert itself. *He really does love her*, Althea thought, absolutely astonished. She stared at the silhouette of her slim, happy daughter, relaxed and grown up. *I don't know her at all.*

'I thought they'd never go, and when Isla said I should take her bag out and get to the beach hut from the front—'

'She's b-been a brick. She really has. I'll write and thank her. When it's all out in the open. When can we tell your parents?'

'Never.'

'Don't joke, Cordelia—'

Her tone was light. 'Hamish, I told you from the start of this. You can trot out all those lines about loving me but really it's – it's not that simple, is it?'

'I don't know how you can talk like that.'

'You know how. You're twenty-five, Hamish, I'm seventeen.' Cord's clear voice carried on the night air. 'I'm starting at the Academy in September, and that has to be everything . . .'

Hamish was asking her something, his gentle voice determined.

'But oh, Hamish, you really don't understand. Mumma and Daddy! They're wonderful but they're not good at . . . parent-y things. Trust me. Dad will take it as some assault on his masculine good looks and age and have a crisis and order you out of the house, and Mumma will sabotage it somehow. They're both children, that's the trouble, they behave like children. Ben worked it out ages ago, it took me longer.' She sounded so matter-of-fact. 'And we're adults now, that's the thing. I'm an adult and

I've got into the best place in the world for singing and all I want to do is sing. I'm absolutely not doing what Daddy and Mumma did, mixing everything up, so you're not sure when you're on stage and what's real.'

I should go, Althea told herself. *Now, before I hear more . . .* Shame burned her cheeks; still she could not move.

'C-c-come on, Cord, dammit. Can't I see you in London?'

Say yes, you idiotic girl, Althea wanted to scream.

She couldn't hear what Cord said, and then there was silence, and then he said, 'Don't you want to?'

'I want to be with you.'

'That's not what I meant.'

'Don't,' she said, and there was more low mumbling, and laughter. 'I – Oh, Hamish, I don't believe it, I can't believe it's real, here, you and me . . .'

Her voice faded away. After a moment's stillness Althea made a vow. That she would never, ever betray that she had heard any of this. She would from this moment pretend everything was as normal. She would take the role in *On the Edge*, even if it terrified her to be playing a desperate ageing actress who stood in front of the mirror in her underwear, who got drunk, who kissed a younger man, who got turned down for parts all the time. They must see she could laugh at herself. She must play the role of glamorous, fun-loving, game-for-a-laugh, former dolly bird down on her luck . . . she must wring the last drop out of it no matter what it cost her. And she would give it everything. Tony was wrong, you didn't become the part, you disappeared into it for a couple of hours so you weren't yourself for a little while. She would disappear into the part of Janey, and she would forget this evening entirely.

Her foot throbbed now, pain flooding her senses. Althea wrapped her arms around her shivering body. She must never tell anyone what a fool she might have made of herself, how much this hurt, worse almost than anything.

Althea walked away from them down the bay until the beach met the lapping sea, and she was sick then, heaving the dry chicken and wine in a molten mess on to the sand, and she stayed there, bent over, saliva hanging from her mouth in drooling lengths like a dog, for the longest time. Eventually she turned back to the house, where all was still in darkness. She stubbed her toe on the door frame and cursed quietly, then more loudly. It didn't matter who heard her now, did it?

At the top of the stairs she flicked on the light switch and stared at her face again in the mirror, for what seemed like an age. She could see the curve of her brows, the apples of her cheeks, the deep, disconcerting green eyes. All these small factors that made up her beauty. Every day, hour, second, ageing, changing, so that she was decaying in front of her very eyes . . . She could smell the stale vomit on her breath. Staring at herself, Althea slowly dragged her one sharp nail down her cheek, drawing blood and leaving a fine red stripe, almost exactly straight, on her white skin.

The house was perfectly still. There was a line of gold light under the door of her and Tony's bedroom. She told herself it would soon be over, summer was coming to an end. And she was glad. Something had shifted; she couldn't see what it was.

Chapter Fifteen

Eight months later
Spring 1984

Most days, Ben would stave off loneliness by walking around Bristol. He had grown tall like his mother and, though he was an affable young man, ready to make new friends, he didn't care for team sports. The other chaps in his halls of residence reminded him of his dreaded ex-schoolmates: competing over the amount of beer drunk at rugger matches or arguing about Gower or Gooch. They were mostly Oxbridge rejects, pretending the faux-Gothic Victorian hall of residence was an Oxford college, organising balls and black-tie dinners where blonde girls wore puffball-shaped brightly coloured taffeta dresses and the boys similarly coloured bow ties to mark themselves out as fun, crazy, up for it. Ben noted it – he noticed everything – but from the sidelines. It wasn't his scene.

He'd wake early, missing home, yearning for the old house by the Thames, and the sound of Cord singing as she got ready for school, or the smell of rush matting rugs and Mumma's scent. His heart would ache a little in his tiny, dark, stone room and he'd realise he had to get up, walk it off.

So at first light he would set out across the downs, noticing with some embarrassment the mud caked to his trousers – somehow the washing never got done when you had to do it yourself. Up on the wide-open space at the top of the city he'd walk until he reached the spiralling descent that took him through

Clifton, past the Avon Gorge, an apocalyptic chasm so at odds with the demure cream and sugar-pink Georgian terraces clinging to the sides of the rock. Ben liked the drama of Bristol, the contrasts within the city that were alive there today. He'd wander and walk, waiting for the builders' café that served a full English from six every morning to open so he could settle in with his notebook and a mug of sweet tea and start to write. Only he never did.

One part of the Drama and Film Studies course was to finish a screenplay in the first year. Ben had the idea of writing about a boy who runs away and is locked in a barn for three days whilst his family grows ever more frantic, intercutting between the isolation of the barn and the panic of the family home. It was a neat idea, he knew, but he couldn't seem to write it – his own experience would get in the way, and the scenes he wrote never seemed urgent, terrifying. In his lectures he was regularly told of the importance of placing one's characters in peril – but the running-away bit wasn't perilous, it was the family the boy came from which seemed the more dangerous, and the characters wouldn't behave the way he wanted them to, either. They kept saying things in his father's voice, or that of Mads or Mrs Gage.

Away from River Walk and the Bosky, freed from the shackles of school, he had hoped he'd have a fresh start, become his own person, not so much in the shadow of his famous parents and boisterous younger sister. But all he could think about was them, all of them, and how he wasn't really a part of it all, never had been, never would be.

He had wanted to love Bristol, to embrace the experience fully. But lately he was afraid he was starting to hate it.

But then came a miracle.

* * *

One particularly unproductive morning at the café, Ben looked up as a sharp wind knocked a hanging basket against the glass. He saw a caped figure rush by, red shoes on her feet, hair like spun toffee sugar blowing out behind her.

If he hadn't looked up then would he have seen her again? Would they have bumped into each other? Fate would say yes; Ben, however, was never sure. When he was older he would try to write about it, write about her, and he could never quite capture her. She was always, to him, just out of reach, and it always for ever afterwards seemed a miracle to him that he saw her that day.

'Mads!' He pushed aside the table, knocking over his white china cup and saucer and dashing for the door. '*Mads! Hey!*'

Down a vertiginous lane that wound through the heart of Clifton he followed her, past secret driveways and high-up white stucco terraces edged with black railings. She kept disappearing, the navy cape or cloak she was wearing swinging like a bell around her, her shoes flashing jewel red under trees far down the lane. He called and called to her but she never turned around; she obviously didn't want to see him any more. He had even begun to plan out what he'd say to Cord in the letter he'd write her.

Damn you, Cordy. Mads wouldn't even say hello to me. Who are you to play God like that? Why do you care if we kissed a few times? We weren't doing anything wrong but you made her go away as if she was a criminal. She wouldn't hurt a fly.

'*Mads!*' he bellowed, one last time.

And then it happened. She stopped at the edge of the road and took a pair of headphones off, carefully wound the wire around a Sony Walkman – red like her shoes – turned and looked up at him, perched on the pavement. That silvery hair he'd dreamed of flew about her small, frowning face and then, eyes searching for what she had heard, her gaze settled on him.

'Oh!' she cried, the cape rippling around her as she lifted both arms up, hands frantically waving now. 'Ben? Oh, my goodness, it's really you. Ben!'

Her blue-grey eyes, molten silver like the sea in the bay after a storm, her flushed cheeks, normally so pale, her thin small hands with bitten nails and tiny deft fingers that could lift a beetle carefully by one leg or pluck an eyelash from a cheek – Ben stared at her helplessly, as she came into focus, running up the steep hill. He didn't know what to say. All he was aware of was a thrumming ache in the stump on his hand and a rushing feeling that rooted him to the spot.

Life so far had taught Ben to be pragmatic but he had thought of Mads all the time since their last meeting a year and a half ago. And now as she was almost in front of him he couldn't think of a single thing to say.

'What were you listening to, Maddy?' he asked as she reached his side. He nodded at the red Walkman.

'Kate Bush,' she said, panting.

'*Never for Ever*?' he said.

'*The Kick Inside*. I finally got it on tape for my birthday. I'd forgotten how amazing it is. "The Man with the Child in His Eyes".'

'I don't listen to her any more. I miss her.'

'Oh, Ben, do you? Do you really? I am absolutely obsessed with her at the moment. I think she's a proper genius.'

He nodded. 'So do I. But *Never for Ever*'s better than *The Kick Inside*.'

'No, no way,' she said, but she was grinning and he grinned back at her and there they both were, as though no time had gone by but they were adults now. 'Ben, did you know, she's working on a new album? They had it on the radio last week, and—' She stopped, putting her hands on the railing next to them, and looked up at him. 'Forget all that. Why are you in Bristol? You don't live here, do you?'

'I'm at university. I'm doing Drama and Film Studies.'

'No, really? So am I. I'm doing Engineering Design.'

'But you're from Bristol!'

'What can I say,' she said, shrugging. 'I'm a home bird. Bit too scared to go anywhere else and I can live in Aunt Jules's old flat.'

'What about your dad?'

She shook her head. 'He died – didn't you know, Ben?'

'Oh. No, I didn't. My – my condolences.' *My condolences?* He blinked, wishing he was mature, a man of the world who could negotiate complex situations like this, and rubbed at the stump of his fingers. 'Um – I'm really sorry. What happened?'

'He had a heart attack,' Mads said, shaking her head. 'He was driving back from Filton, and he pulled into a siding, and they found him dead there, two days later. I had to go and identify him. Had to organise everything and – well, we weren't close, you know—' She shook her head and looked up at him with a small smile. 'He wasn't very nice. You know that. That was what someone said to me at the funeral. An old colleague. Aunt Jules didn't even come back for it. There were only seven of us there in the end. Me, the vicar, two colleagues of his from the factory in Filton, a cousin from Dundee, an old man whose name I didn't get and a lady who lived on our street.' She bowed her head. 'He wasn't very nice, but it was a pathetic gathering. Aunt Jules always said it wasn't his fault entirely, that it was their dad who messed them up, you know, that he sort of fell apart after their mum died. But I still – I can't forgive him.'

She coughed, and pushed her canvas rucksack, covered with chemical symbols and peace signs, back over her shoulder. Ben found himself taking her hand.

'I'm sorry. I know it was bad, but I don't think Cord and I ever really understood – we were too sheltered from it all.'

'You shouldn't have known, no one should. Your parents tried, I loved them for it.' She nodded seriously. 'But even they didn't really understand how bad it was. You know, he wouldn't give me water once – he locked me in my room on the hottest day of the year because I'd interrupted him while he was working—' She smiled at Ben's expression. 'Yes, he did. I asked him to fetch a cup of water for me and he wouldn't. I was five, Ben. I was in there for a day, I didn't go to school, didn't eat, I peed on the carpet because I was so desperate for the loo and my throat – it was like sandpaper. All I could think of was water. I sort of passed out eventually.'

'Mads . . .' Ben shook his head, pain compacting in his chest. He squeezed her fingers. 'Didn't anyone say anything? Didn't the school ask where you were?'

'That's what I don't understand. They used to just ignore it, if I wasn't in for a day here or there or I had a black eye because he'd hit me or thrown me down the stairs.' She was speaking rapidly now. 'He did that once and my hair was so tangled it got caught in the newel post at the bottom of the bannisters and it broke my fall but half of it was pulled out, this side. And I never knew what a newel post is before then. They told me at the hospital. But they sent me home to him again. You know—' She rubbed her eyes, tiredly. 'He didn't calculate it. He wasn't a sadist. He just had no emotional fallback, no way of calming himself down. If something annoyed him he'd just lose it. I reminded him it was my birthday once and he hit me. He said I was bad and that's why we didn't do anything for my birthday.

He punched me, Ben, in the face – I was seven years old and he knocked a tooth out.' She pulled aside her mouth, and he could see one empty black square in the row of teeth. 'It was a new tooth too, I was so proud of it. But then I came downstairs later and he was crying. Sobbing and sobbing, very quietly, this hissing sound, and his hands were in front of his eyes. He was such an unhappy man. I think that's when Aunt Jules came into the picture. I think he must have called her in then. They had a ten-year deal. She came back from Oz to look after me and I went to boarding school, too. I think he knew he'd kill me or do something stupid. And—' She clutched his hands. Her little face was white. 'I can't believe I'm saying all this to you after all these years. I want to stop but I can't. I haven't really said it. Ever. How are you? How's everyone? Tell me – how's—'

He interrupted her. 'It's OK,' Ben heard himself saying. 'Forget them for a minute. Forget them, Mads.' He curled his stump into her palm and linked the forefinger and thumb around her thumb, and led her up a steep, curling path where he'd wandered a few days previously on one of his peregrinations. His heart was thumping: anger, sadness, sheer joy at seeing her again, all these things. He felt lightheaded, but also very calm.

There was a tiny pub, perched on the edge of a dilapidated crescent that sold cider in half-pint glasses because it was so strong. At this time of day it was still shuttered up, the empty ashtrays turned over. They sat down on the bench outside on the cobbles, staring out over Brandon Hill, down towards the docks.

They were silent for a long time – a minute or so. Eventually Ben said again, 'It's awful. I'm so sorry.'

She shook her head. 'It's awful not to be sad that your dad's died. But I wouldn't have met all of you if he hadn't been so horrible. And now I'm free of it.' A watery, pale sun flickered over the city below. She turned to Ben.

'You know, my friend Johnny said something to me, in the pub the night after the funeral. Johnny's really wise. He said, "From everything you've said about your dad he was stopping you living properly. He was stopping you from falling in love, or dreaming about the future, having a career, or children, or any of those things . . . He was like a stop on your heart." And he said, "Well, now he's gone and you can start to live." And I – you see, it's exactly like that. He was born that way. Born sad and mean, and just not very nice.'

'You know, I'm not sure if it helps but my dad used to say something similar about him too,' said Ben, biting his lip with the effort of not asking who Johnny was.

'Darling Tony.' She clasped her hands together and smiled at Ben and his heart sang. 'He was right, as always. Daddy hated him, and it always seemed so petty. He caused so much trouble with Tony and Aunt Jules in the war. She never forgave him.'

'What did he do?'

'I think it's more what they did, if you know what I mean,' said Mads, and she looked up at him again, and raised her eyebrows, and he laughed.

'That makes sense, where my father's concerned,' he said.

'Well, she always was a free spirit, Aunt Jules, you know. You'd love her.' Her smile faltered. 'Tell me, how's your mum?'

'Very well, thank you. This new sitcom she's made, it's quite something.'

'I read an interview with her last week in *The Times*,' she said. 'They were extremely disapproving.'

'It's never been done before. An older woman talking into a mirror and going out on dates and drinking a bit too much, imagine!' Ben smiled. 'I went to a taping. She's in her bra for a brief shot. That's what's got them all in a tizzy. If it was a skimpy bikini it'd be no problem. Talk about double standards.'

'Is it good?' said Mads, seriously.

'Yes. It's fantastic. Really different and new but of course it's her and she's something of a national treasure, I suppose, so it scares the horses that she's being so daring. She totally carries the show.'

'Your dad—'

'Oh, yes, well he's delighted for her,' said Ben, a little too quickly. 'Says he told her all along she should take the part.'

Mads nodded. 'And – how – how's Cord?'

'She's OK, I think.' He tipped his head from side to side, a movement of uncertainty. 'I don't know. I haven't seen her since Christmas. I go and stay with them back in London but . . . I don't see much of any of them.' He looked out over the rooftops. 'She started at the Royal Academy in September. She's pretty busy.'

'Oh, that's wonderful.' Mads nodded emphatically. 'I didn't know – she wouldn't answer my letters . . . I just want to know if she's OK.' She cleared her throat, recovering herself.

'She's absolutely fine.' He reached out, wanting to touch her arm. 'I keep asking her if it's like *Fame* and she has to wear a yellow leotard and leg-warmers with people warbling in the corridors and dance routines up and down the front steps. It makes her furious. She's taking it *very* seriously.'

Mads gave a gurgle of laughter.

Ben paused. Then: 'Um. You know, I told her she'd been an absolute idiot about all that business and I think she agreed.'

'About what?'

'You – and me—' He could feel himself blushing, the memory of those ecstatic fumblings with Mads at the beach hut, the thrill of lifting that heavy sheet of silken hair away from her neck, peeling back her T-shirt, of their bruised, throbbing lips,

her skin, soft and cool, of the rapturous innocence of it all . . .
'It was none of her business. She used to act as though she owned you. That you were *her* friend. I told her it was rubbish. That you were a member of the family.'

'Family members don't do what we were doing, Ben,' she said drily, her eyes glinting with mirth, and he shifted around on his seat, embarrassed, smiling.

'Humph. Anyway, she's mellowed a bit, that's all. She's got a boyfriend.'

'Oh, really? Who is he?'

'He's an actor friend of Dad's. Few years older than her, he's twenty-five. He's completely mad about her, it's so strange,' said Ben, big-brother callous. 'My father was in *Henry V* with him and he'd just been dumped, so he took pity on him and asked him down to the Bosky last summer and that was it, apparently.'

'This is the most exciting news I've had all term.' Mads wriggled on the seat, shaking out her hair. He'd forgotten how little she liked talking about herself, how much happier she was in their lives, not her own. 'Is he nice? What's his name? What are they like together? Oh, my goodness.'

'Hamish. He's a nice chap. Got that sort of quizzical expression like he's amused most of the time. He thinks she's hilarious. He's kind. And he adores her.'

'Lucky Cord, how wonderful!'

Ben hesitated. 'It's weird . . . oh, Mads, I don't think she's as keen on him. Had a letter from her a couple of weeks ago. He tries to hold her hand when they walk down the street.'

'Dear me, that's not Cord.'

'No. She says she wants to devote herself to her art and she can't fall in love, it's the enemy of woman's ambition. She's got this professor, Italian bloke who's very short and yells at her and rings up Mumma and Daddy to yell at them if she doesn't take care of her voice. Thinks she shouldn't live by the river, it's too damp for the vocal cords. According to him she ought to focus on singing and there's no room for anything else in her life.'

'Imagine that,' she said, shaking her head.

The front door of the house next to the pub opened. Its owner emerged, looking suspiciously at both of them. She double-locked the door and hurried past them down the hill. The air was suddenly a little chilly.

Ben found himself saying, 'You don't have to go anywhere, do you? Will you have breakfast with me?'

'I have a lecture in five minutes,' she said. 'I'm late.'

'Oh, a lecture,' he said dismissively. 'You can miss that.'

'We scientists actually have to go to lectures most days, not like you arts people who just sit in cafés looking out of the window.' She bit her lip, trying not to laugh. 'But – oh, Ben.'

She understood everything, everything. She always had. 'If I hadn't been looking out of the window I wouldn't have seen you, and that would have been terrible,' he said, and squeezed her hand. She was shaking very slightly, he realised. 'Later, then? I'll make you dinner, if you like,' he said. 'I'll come to your flat. If – if you'd like.'

'Dear Ben,' she said, eyes bright, her head on one side, looking at him. 'There you are. Right there, in front of me. We were just playing before, weren't we? All those years there and now it's different.'

'What do you mean?' he asked, his heart in his throat.

But she just shook her head. She scribbled her address and phone number down on a piece of paper. 'I must go.' She thrust it into his hand. 'Come tonight. Come before that, come as soon as you can.' She ran down the street, her bright feet pattering on the cobbles. He looked down at the address, her scrawling writing, his heart leaping for joy.

'I'll come straight after I've been shopping. I'll bring some food.' He hesitated and said again, 'W-W-would you like that?'

'Yes, I'd like all of that,' she was calling, as she ran out of sight. 'Yes, yes, please.'

Chapter Sixteen

June 1941

When it was going to be a nice day you knew because there was one tiny chink in the stick-on gauze that got through the blackout blinds and if the sun was out it shone a direct beam, like a laser from one of Dan Dare's baddies' guns, on to the bedroom floor. 21 June 1941, Midsummer's Day, was a day such as this. It was also Anthony's thirteenth birthday and he was woken very early by the sound of someone outside his bedroom window, scuffling about on the ground.

He lay there for a while, wondering what Dinah was up to, and whether he should investigate or try and sleep again. It was too dark to see his watch but he was glad. It was almost a year since his mother's death and thankfully the crack on the watch face had not grown; it kept time remarkably well. Though he had worn the watch every day since he'd come here, Ant had already planned that today he would simply leave it on the dressing table. It had been a present from his parents, for his twelfth birthday. If he could have gone back a year and told his newly twelve-year-old self where he'd be in a year's time, he'd – well, he knew what he'd do. He would have made sure he'd died beside her, that night. In his lighter moments he could at least smile at the idea that Aunt Dinah had taken him away from London to the safety of Dorset. There were more air-raid alerts here than any he'd known back in Camden, the sirens from Swanage ringing out most nights.

The noises from outside grew louder.

'*She was despised! Despised and rejected! Rejected of men!* This rope is not thick enough, Dinah. Oh, it doesn't matter, who'll steal the thing? He'll be up in a couple of hours.' A pause. 'But you don't know who comes by here, perhaps a dishonest sort who might take a fancy and swipe it . . . Oh, dear, the sooner we give it to him and it's inside the better. *A woman of sorrows . . . and acquainted with greeeeeeeeeef.* Oh, *what* a glorious day it is.'

Ant bit the tip of his finger, blinking. He got up, patting the velvet dressmaker's dummy which stood sentinel by his bed every night, and peered out of the window, squinting through the chink in the gauze. There she was, scratching on the dirt in the lane outside, skirts gathered in one arm, those huge feet in their big flat shoes planted firmly in the dust at right angles like a clown, rear end pointing up in the air. Little daisies and late violets bedded in the cracks at the edge of the house bobbed about in the fresh summer breeze.

Anthony shook his head. If he went outside and remonstrated with her (mildly, of course; they were always polite to each other) for making this racket this early in the morning she'd have some answer. She always did; he'd never known anyone so certain about everything they were doing and it was comforting, even if sometimes he wondered whether she was telling the truth all the time. The fact was, since the previous August, he did feel more warmly towards her. Perhaps he – he even liked her, a bit.

There had been dark days, moments when he'd thought he wouldn't be able to survive, here or anywhere. The winter had been worst: the house was so cold and windy they both had chilblains, and the ache of missing his mother and father seemed to have settled in his heart; it was like a shard of ice, it hurt when he breathed. The Bosky was still crammed full of bric-a-brac and though Dinah sighed about it she made no effort to clear it. For one who was constantly busy she could also be curiously ineffective.

That first summer they had taken walks on the sand but during the autumn and winter the beach became inaccessible: littered with mines, covered in barbed wire, the land rising away from the shore up to the house lined with dragon's teeth – pointed blocks of concrete in sturdy lines, designed to slow down the enemy. An invasion was expected that day, that week, that month and the word was if the Germans came they'd land at Worth Bay. And though Ant told himself he didn't care about dying it was hard not to be scared all the time. Everyone was: they pretended not to be, of course. There were dogfights in the sky, night after night; German planes had been shot down at Harman's Cross and right there in Worth Bay and the pilot of the latter had never been found: alone each night in the awful, thick, silken darkness, shivering with cold and yet still clammy with sweat, Ant would wonder: what if the pilot *hadn't* drowned in the bay, what if he was still out there, waiting to come and kill them in their beds at night?

Then spring came, and somehow his suffering was eased in a tiny way by the lighter evenings, as well as the sweetness of the warmer air, the lambs out in the fields, the villagers who knew him now and were kind to him because they liked Dinah and were glad the Wildes had come back. Some of them even remembered his dad when he was young. Philip Wilde had put on plays and charged people to come and watch them and Tony loved hearing these stories, just as he loved hearing about Dinah's father, Colonel Wilde, who liked firing shots off the porch on to the beach at sunset.

'Oh, we wasn't scared, we thought it was just Colonel Wilde having his fun, poor fella,' Mrs Proudfoot told Ant once. She liked Ant and would give him twists of precious boiled sugar wrapped in waxed paper when he called to sweep her drive. Dinah, when Ant asked, was silent about her father, but that was no surprise. Another neighbour called Mr Hill let Ant choose a kitten of his own when his cat had a litter; Ant loved it and called it Sweep and it did a marvellous job of driving out the mice and rats that had taken up residence in the Bosky, chewing books, living amongst the junk of Dinah's family and her former lives.

But mainly it was Dinah herself who made things better, by virtue of being gloriously certain about everything. Though the truth was that he didn't understand her any more now than a year ago: she ate with her fingers; talked in strange languages when she washed the dishes; she knew nothing about film stars or radio programmes but knew hundreds of songs, some of them utterly filthy, that she'd picked up on digs. She liked cheese and attempted to make it with the curds gifted to her from the farm. She disastrously kept bees (the swarm flew away) and hens (rats ate the eggs; foxes ate the hens). She grew vegetables that either never came up or instantly bolted: she would lean on her spade in the tiny garden to the side of the house, strong slim hand on her forehead, loose tendrils of hair around her face, frowning at the tilled earth. She had tried to join the Home Guard and was disgusted when they laughed her away.

He was never sure what she understood about him. But she had somehow come to see his fear of the darkness, so had taught him to play mah-jong in his bedroom (in later years Tony realised the version he knew so well bore no relation to actual mah-jong, that she'd bent the rules so it worked for two people, made it up to suit them, like so many things). They'd stay up late into the night trading beautiful mahogany tiles inlaid with mother-of-pearl patterns, until he was drooping with sleepiness and the wick on the oil lamp had burned almost to nothing and Dinah could creep out and leave him, fast asleep. She taught him the rudiments of astronomy, with the ancient telescope the mysterious Daphne had grudgingly sent down from the flat in South Kensington and such books on the subject as were available at Swanage library. Her facility for acquiring knowledge astonished him – yet simple things, like clearing a space to walk from the sitting room out on to the porch, or remembering to shut up the hens, or keeping the milk in the larder, were utterly beyond her. And so every time he believed he understood her views or her approach she'd wrong-foot him. At first, she told lies – he wished she wouldn't – just small ones, about where she'd been: 'I was up at Bill's Point,' when he'd seen her in the village because he'd been there himself. Or about where food came from, or sometimes her stories of life in Baghdad that didn't quite make sense. But Ant had been at school with a boy, Peters, who'd lied only when he was flustered or nervous. If you questioned him about it he lied even more. It was like that with Dinah. As life at the Bosky settled into something resembling a routine, she made things up less. And Ant didn't see what harm it did, really. It was a diversion, after all. Life with her was curious, funny, frustrating, exhilarating – but never dull.

As Ant climbed back into bed, kicking the mah-jong set under the bed, the shuffling and the low singing faded away. He stared at the photograph of him and his mother on Brighton Pier, which sat beside his bed at all times. With a feeling of gloom he wondered with horror how his great-aunt celebrated birthdays, and Midsummer's Day. She was a great one for marking occasions, big or small.

Though she rarely attended church herself she made Ant come with her on high days and holidays like Christmas and Ascension Day, when she would embarrass him terribly. Her knees knocked against the narrow pews when she sat down and her powerful voice boomed around the ancient stained glass; she had a beautiful voice, low and pure, but she sang far too loudly, enunciating every word. ('*When I survey the wuuuhndruss cross . . .*' '*Christian! Dosst thou see them? On the holee grrrround?*')

The vicar, the Reverend Ambrose Goudge, was a kindly man with expressive eyebrows. Transplanted by the war from his High Church parish in Pimlico to a sleepy English village which now nightly feared either obliteration by a ferocious assault from the air or a German land invasion, he gave himself the not inconsiderable challenge of taking the residents' minds off the war in whatever way he could. He had formed a local drama society which had already staged a sold-out production of *Mother Goose* and was full of ideas for what to do next.

The vicar adored Dinah and took to coming round for tea. Most men liked Dinah, Ant saw that early on, but in a strange way, different from the way they liked his mother. They treated her as an equal, not someone whose hand ought to be delicately kissed like Mummy's. Mummy would laugh gently at their jokes, and then ask them whether they thought it would turn to rain later, or whether they might be awfully kind and fetch more milk – Aunt Dinah wasn't like that at all. She told Mr Hill, the local solicitor and noted local historian, that she believed in fairies, and that as a child she'd seen a witch land on the roof of this very house, a witch who'd carried away sprigs of rosemary for her potions. Mr Hill had nodded and asked for proof, folding his arms and listening carefully as Dinah told him about sightings of white witches in Dorset. She asked the vicar for evidence of transubstantiation, only the vicar just laughed, and said if she wanted evidence she'd missed the whole point.

That Easter there was a tiny piece of chicken each for lunch, courtesy of Alastair Fletcher from Beeches. His garden was large and he not only grew vegetables but kept chickens too. Ant was scared of Alastair, who could be kind but who he'd discovered could also be extremely stern. He could do things like fix kites and, directly after Ant and Dinah arrived, he had offered to help him with his bowling in the sandy lane, though he had a tendency to grip Ant's too-thin arm tightly and tell him he needed to build up his muscles, or that his spin was pathetic. It wasn't much fun and, after a while, Ant rather avoided him.

Like the Reverend Goudge, Alastair had been too old to be called up, and was an enthusiastic member of the LDV instead. And also like Reverend Goudge he would sit on the porch in the light summer nights before blackout looking out over Worth Bay, laughing at Dinah's droll stories. Alastair had studied Greats at Oxford, which meant Latin and Greek, Ant discovered, and could talk for hours of places with exotic, magical names: the Mausoleum at Halicarnassus, the ancient minaret of the Umayyad Mosque in Aleppo, the Temple of Baal. He was at his happiest then; he was a serious man, serious in his interests. Dinah, who'd known the Fletcher family for years, said he hadn't been like that always. His wife had died of influenza several years ago and her death, their children, and their care, seemed to lie heavy on him; he was extremely strict with Julia, who was treated like a Victorian debutante to be chaperoned everywhere even though she was only twelve, and perplexed by his withdrawn son, Ian.

Ant didn't really like either of them. Julia was annoying, she talked too much and recited poems in an awful 'knowing' way, and Ian was strange. He had toothbrush hair, spoke in grunts if he spoke at all, and stared at Ant in almost open loathing. 'No one likes poor Ian,' Dinah said once. 'The boy must have some redeeming features but it's hard to know what they are.'

So the first couple of summers, Alastair was a reasonable neighbour. And it cheered him, Dinah believed, to sit on the porch and talk of inconsequential things unrelated to war and children. The dear, jolly vicar enjoyed both village gossip and discussions of ancient tombs and clay fragments, and he was the only person Ant knew who could tolerate Aunt Dinah's dreadful elderflower wine. Ant would hear the three of them, as he lay in bed at the bottom of the house, and it made his fear of the dark seem more manageable, knowing that if he woke up the sounds of conversation would often still be floating down into his room.

These days even without mah-jong he regularly fell asleep straight away, for he'd be tired after another day of schooling. Lessons with Aunt Dinah were not remotely like the ones at his old school. English was Shakespeare, nothing else. Geography was crawling across the downs, looking for butterflies and their pupae, examining the plants and the rocks. History was the best: full of Sultans being murdered by their sons, or mad inbred kings with tongues the size of snakes, or Marie Antoinette's clothes in prison: no Corn Laws or tedious naval battles. Nothing about living with Dinah was tedious.

Ant stared at the watch next to him. Suddenly, grief at his mother not being there to wish him a happy birthday settled on his chest so heavily he could not move. He decided he must get up. He would fetch a slice of bread from the pantry, go and find Sweep, who often slept in the kitchen at night, and take him back to bed with him, the bread, and his book. He was reading *The Hobbit* again; he'd read it twice now.

Silently, and not without a struggle, he put on his dressing gown – it was too small and smelled of oil from when he and Dinah had tried to mend the car and used the dressing gown as a rag. She had rinsed it in the sink afterwards but not successfully: he'd never admit it, but he liked not minding so much about pressed clothes and everything being just so all the time.

Creeping up the stairs, which were apt to creak, he came out into the sitting room and, pushing aside the blinds, gazed out at the view of the rising sun. Pearlescent ropes of cloud hung across the raspberry-red-and-turquoise sky and he smiled at the sight, pulling the dressing gown more tightly around him.

'*One-two two-two three-two hup! Up and down and up and down and . . .*'

Ant turned to see his great-aunt lying on the floor, eyes fixed on the ceiling and apparently oblivious to his presence, alternating sit-ups with strange cranking arm movements in which she swung her arms behind her. She lifted herself off the floor with one hand.

'*Up and down and three and four! Come on old girl do some more!*'

Anthony said, 'Morning, Aunt Dinah.' Dinah jumped, and her arm gave way. She collapsed on to the ground in surprise.

'Oh, dear me, you gave me a shock.'

'You gave *me* a shock.' Ant felt this was unfair. 'I thought you were outside.'

'I was outside. Silly me!' She shook her head and leaped to her feet, catlike. 'Happy, happy birthday, old fruit.' She gripped his shoulders, and kissed him firmly on the forehead. 'Dear boy.'

'Thanks,' he mumbled.

But she stepped back, releasing him, and her eyes were shining. 'What a glorious day to have a birthday. Your darling mother was clever, having you on Midsummer's Day. Well, we've a host of activities planned. I have a picnic all ready for us. Ham, Ant dearest. I've got us some ham. Don't ask me where.' Her eyes twinkled. 'And tomatoes from the garden.'

'No,' he said, curiously. 'Real actual tomatoes? Not from our garden?'

'It must be some kind of miracle, for my reply is yes. Our garden. I've picked four. And there's a cake with real eggs.'

He stared at her in disbelief. 'Where from?'

'Mrs Proudfoot brought it over last night. It's her present to you.' She clapped her hands. 'But the cake's for later. The vicar and Mrs Goudge and various others are all coming for tea this evening. Alastair's coming too. His children are back early, their school's been evacuated.' Ant scowled. 'Dear, but I thought you'd be pleased. Some children to play with.'

'They're not my sort of people. Ian gives me the willies. She's cracked, too.'

'You can't celebrate reaching your teenage years solely with me. You have lessons with me and you live with me!'

Without really thinking he answered, 'But I don't mind all that. I like being with you.'

Dinah's face flushed ridiculously and she raised her hands to her cheeks. 'Dear Ant. Now, don't you want to know where we're going for our picnic?'

'There?' Embarrassed, Ant pointed to the sandy patch of half-dune before the dragon's teeth and wire on the beach, one hundred yards hence, trying not to smile: where else could it be? Petrol was so dear these days the car had been up on bricks for months now, to protect the tyres, and as for buses, they were rarer than hen's teeth.

She shook her head. 'Aha! No! I have you, you see. I thought we'd go to St Aldhelm's.'

This was an ancient chapel perched on top of cliffs the other side of Swanage. The views were magnificent, stretching for miles in every direction, and the walking particularly fine, but – Anthony hesitated. He didn't care about views much and he remembered the time Dinah had made him walk to the Square and Compass Inn, in Worth Matravers, not far from St Aldhelm's, on a broiling hot day the previous September. The heat didn't bother her; years of living in Iraq had made her resistant to most privations: lack of electricity, of hot water, of cool weather. Ant's feet had bled and still she'd kept on walking, hat jammed on head, waving her arms, pointing out interesting barrows and rock strata, cooing in great excitement as the vista of the Purbeck Hills opened up before them. Eventually he had collapsed in tears against a milestone, refusing to go any further, almost hysterical with exhaustion and anger at her. She had had to flag down a car to drive them back. Once they got home, he was violently sick and had to spend the next day in bed.

'How will we get there? Because, Aunt Dinah, I don't want to sound wet, but it's rather a hike and on one's birthday one maybe doesn't want to . . .' He trailed off. She was watching him with a strange smile on her face.

'Ah, I see. Well, why don't you come with me,' she said, leading him gently by the arm. They went outside on to the lane.

A bicycle, its frame dark blue, its handlebars polished dull silver, sat outside, propped against the house. She had tied a silk scarf around it in a bow. On the dirty sand around it she had drawn, with a stick or some such, the legend:

HAPPY B DAY DEAR ANT XXX

There were swooping curlicues framing the wonky writing. For the rest of Tony's life, no matter how long afterwards, whenever he looked outside into the lane by the Bosky he would see that patch of the road, could see the letters forming again in the dirty ochre-coloured sand, hear the sound of her scratching them out, on that fine midsummer morning.

Anthony looked up at her. 'It's really mine?'

'It's really yours,' she said, smiling at him, and he thought again how lovely her long, eager face was when she smiled.

'Oh, Aunt Dinah.' He rang the bell, trying it for sound, fingers gripping the handlebars. 'Thank you. It's terrific, it's whizzo. But how—'

'Some things are worth outlaying a little cash on,' was all she'd ever say on the matter.

The bike was second-hand but in good condition – the daughter of the ironmonger in Wareham had joined the Women's Land Army and had left it behind with instructions for it to be sold, and it was virtually new. For the rest of his time in the Bosky during the war, and to Sweep's disgust, it was Anthony's most trusted companion.

Aunt Dinah had done him proud on the picnic. Cold ham, mustard, bread and home-grown tomatoes are all one needs for a really good feast and she'd managed to make some strange drink with mint from the garden boiled up with the tiniest amount of sugar. It was delicious, even though they were picking pieces of soggy mint leaves out of their teeth for the rest of the afternoon. The tomatoes were entirely edible, if still a little green around the edges, and adding to her horticultural triumph there were also five or so tiny strawberries, and – the great surprise – wrapped in her large men's silk handkerchief were two gobstoppers and a square of chocolate for each of them. Sweets were very dear and used up many sugar coupons; Anthony was touched.

As they lay on their backs on the sheep-nibbled turf watching the gulls soar over the edge of the clifftops and the roaring, crashing turquoise waves hundreds of feet below them, Anthony felt totally at peace. He could feel the warmth of the sun beating through the wind, feel it working its way through his shirt and tank top, feel it on his bare knees and forehead, looking up to the sun. He knew that across the Channel lay war and dreadful conflict but perhaps it was not to be worried about on a day like this, and the cramping coiled creature of fear which lay curled up inside him, jabbing him painfully and making him feel sick, was quiet today.

The sky was endless, a clear blue. Ant wondered about Mummy and Dad. Whether they could see from where they were, whether they were watching him. He hated the thought that they might be in heaven and worrying about him, as he would worry were he to have died instead that day, leaving Mummy alone. He wanted to stand up and shout out to the sea and the sky, *I'm all right. I'm safe, I'm all right.* He stared up into the blue. *I miss you both. I do wish you were here.*

And he felt something, a breeze ruffling his hair, a touch of something on his forehead: sea spray, he would tell himself later, but at the time it felt as though he were being kissed by something invisible. He touched his head gently. Next to him, Aunt Dinah sighed in contentment.

'I like it here,' he said, turning towards her.

'It's a glorious spot, isn't it?' she said, misunderstanding him.

Harebells nodded in the breeze; brilliant blue butterflies fluttered nearby. He smiled. He wanted to say, *Thank you for looking after me.* But he didn't. After a minute or two, he rolled on to his front. 'Aunt Dinah, can I ask you something?'

'Of course.'

'Do you love Alastair Fletcher?'

'Alastair?' She laughed, and rolled over too, so she was looking at him, tendrils of her soft brown hair around her face and her eyes shining. 'Goodness, no. What made you think of that?'

He scratched at the back of his head. 'Don't know. He's always offering to help. Mummy used to say beware of men offering to help.'

Her expression grew sober. 'Lavinia was right, as ever.'

'But he's always coming round, lately. And you two laugh together.'

'Well, he makes me laugh.' She sat up. She never got cross, there was nothing you couldn't talk to her about. 'He's so sensible and serious but he's such a funny chap too. I wish he—'

'What?'

'I was going to say I wish he wasn't quite so lonely, but of course he has the children and I imagine one is never lonely when one has children, even if they're away at school.'

'Do you think that?'

'I don't know. I always believe it to be true.'

'Were you lonely in Baghdad?'

'Not really. One's never lonely when one can escape into another world. I'm myself there, you see. Here I'm an eccentric old lady and the daughter of a gambler who's no use for anything.'

His throat tightened. He said, 'Will you go back there, then?'

'Yes, darling. I've always said I will, haven't I? But that's years off.'

'But it's in ruins, they said. When we retook the city. There was that photograph in Reverend Goudge's *Times,* you remember? I don't think you should go back. You probably don't have a home any more.'

But Dinah looked out, over the cliffs to the sea where two vast ships in the distance broke the still calm of the horizon. 'Have I told you yet the story of Gilgamesh?' He shook his head. 'It's the greatest story of Nineveh. I'll take you there, one day. The palaces are rubble now, or they're hidden under modern cities, but what you can see . . . it's miraculous. Gates, higher than three men. Stone lions they had guarding them, with vast wings, absolutely terrifying. And the kings, the tablets they produced, the stories of their deeds . . . Miraculous. Gilgamesh was a ruler of a city like that. He was proud, and fierce to his people, and they suffered under him, though he was a strong king. But he had a friend.' She paused. 'A friend called Enkidu, a wise, kind man. And he was *created by the gods* to show Gilgamesh how to behave. He was better than most men. And Gilgamesh came to love him, and they were great friends. Enkidu made him a good man. Do you understand?'

Ant stared down at the tough, cropped grass. 'Um . . . maybe. His friend made him better.' He wanted to ask if this applied to her but somehow knew he shouldn't.

'That's it. You must hope for that, one day. A person who makes you better in all things. Who helps you to become a better man.'

'A wife?'

'Yes, or a friend. Or a child, like you. I've never – there's never been – What am I trying to say? You've made me into a better person, of that I'm jolly sure.'

'Oh.' Ant felt uncomfortable – there was no emotion with him and Aunt Dinah, just practical conversations about food and ancient Egyptian tombs and the like. She never got into a bate about things. He never saw her upset. Since he'd known her she had been constant, always cheerful. For the first time he wondered if she, too, liked their life together and the companionship it provided.

'Were you very good at finding things in the desert, Aunt Dinah?' he asked, as they cleared up the picnic.

'I was,' she answered. 'It was what I was good at. I wasn't

any good at school, hopeless with maths or the meaning behind some poem. But I can remember things, and I've got a sixth sense, I suppose it is, for where things might be hidden.' Her eyes shone under her floppy straw hat. 'The moment when your hands clutch hold of something. Something that's been buried for thousands of years, that might have been in the Bible. The temple's survived under the sand for centuries, it'll still be there in centuries. I like that. Everything else in one's life is rather unpredictable.'

'I understand,' said Ant, gravely.

'I'm sure you do,' she said, smiling at him, and they cleared up, wrapping everything carefully in the tea towels and putting it into Aunt Dinah's wicker basket at the front of her bike. She caught his hand. 'Happy birthday, dear Ant. What a lovely day this is.'

Ant scratched at his knee and nodded, unable to look at her.

On the way home they sang 'It's a Long Way to Tipperary' on a loop, sticking their legs out and freewheeling down the narrow, verdant lanes, and even though the wind on Anthony's cheeks was cold, he felt warm, and quite full, inside.

Dinah had gathered wild flowers up on the downs and in the hedgerows on the way there and back, and she tied them now to her handlebars and the rear seat of the old bike, and as she cycled leaves and petals and buds flew off, creating a gentle floral whirlwind behind her, like the last leaves leaving a tree in autumn.

He never compared her to his mother, but in later life he came to see how particular Mummy had always been, crying when a linen tablecloth was torn, furious at a slight mark on the dresser, how she was always wanting him nearby, making a pet of him, and how he had begun to chafe against it. With Dinah he was allowed to grow how he wanted to, to choose his own path. In later life when he thought of her, it was in this moment on his thirteenth birthday, bedecked with dog roses and daisies and lavender, the peacock kimono flying behind her like a cloak, legs thrust out, mouth pulled wide in a beatific grin.

He watched her approach him and had a moment of clarity, a definite sense then of how everything was familiar, safe, once again. He knew this lane, these wild flowers, the corner of the Bosky jutting out to his right, the sound of wood pigeons in the trees. He felt safe.

You can be free here, Aunt D, he thought to himself as she grew closer. *You don't need to leave. Here's free, here's fine. We're fine. You mustn't leave me.*

Chapter Seventeen

That evening, Ant sat on the edge of his bed and slowly slid the drawer of his bedside table out. He took the watch his parents had given him from its black box, and fastened the strap. He wound it up and set the correct time, then covered his wrist with his other hand, remembering the day they gave it to him, feeling the soft ticking through his fingers, up his arm, seconds of time passing that took him further away from them and his old life.

Upstairs, the large radio rumbled with news. The Home Service had a report of bombers attacking southern coastal towns. They didn't say where; they never did. But he and Dinah had both heard the planes as she was preparing tea.

He could hear Dinah welcoming a guest; he thought it might be the vicar. Ant's arms were warm and crisp with summer sun and he was tired from the long cycle ride and wished he could stay downstairs. But he climbed the steps anyway, touching the walls, for he loved the warmth of the wooden panels after the sun had been on them all day.

Suddenly he heard scattered noises like gunshots and he froze, heart thudding painfully before he realised the sound was clapping, not gunfire. He went out on to the porch and there was the tailor's dummy, dragged up from his room and dressed with a paper hat, Alulim the ancient stone bird paper-weight balanced on a side table, and Livingstone the stuffed monkey, Eunice the doll, the birds of paradise in their case.

'They're all out here too. They wanted to wish you a happy birthday,' said Dinah, pushing her hair out of her eyes, and smiling at him. Ant stared at her, bewildered, then saw a knot of people beyond them too.

There was Reverend and Mrs Goudge, and Mrs Proudfoot holding a cake, and her daughter Eliza with the squint and her young man Joe Gage, and Alastair Fletcher and his children, Julia swinging from the porch balustrade, waving at the setting sun, and Ian, hands in pockets. And Phoebe and Roy, two other children from the village of his age with whom he used to hang around and the curate Bob and – oh, he couldn't see who else was there. They all clapped as he appeared and he felt his cheeks smarting with embarrassment as though he'd been slapped, and then Mrs Proudfoot handed the cake to Dinah, who held it up, with the thirteen candles ablaze, and led them all in 'For He's a Jolly Good Fellow'.

There were crystallised rose petals, yellow and pink, to decorate the thin buttercream layer on top of the cake. They spelled out 'A'. The cake rested on the old willow-pattern cake stand that had belonged to his grandmother, Dinah's sister Rosemary.

Julia Fletcher sang louder than everyone else, adding annoying trills and low rumbling harmonies to the song. Ant ignored her.

When they'd stopped singing and Ant had blown out the candles Dinah said, breathlessly, 'Everyone chipped in. Jane made the beautiful sugar petals,' she gestured at the vicar's wife. 'The eggs are from Mrs Proudfoot, and Joe and Alastair shared their sugar ration, and I got the cream and butter from old Roger Hardy's farm up past the village. His son, Derek, brought it over.' She smiled at a thin, sour-faced boy who sat, arms crossed, on the edge of the porch as though he wished he were anywhere but here. 'Everyone chipped in, like I say, Ant. It's all for you. Happy birthday.' Her eyes shone and her beads clinked as she hugged him. 'Happy, happy birthday, dear boy.'

'Oh, yes, Ant, happiest of lovely delicious birthdays,' said Julia, flinging her arms around him.

Ian muttered, 'Shut up and stop being so jolly embarrassing, Jules.'

He pulled her away and she fell back, with a giggle.

Ant ignored her. She *was* annoying. But she couldn't spoil this lovely afternoon.

There had never been such a cake and he could remember the taste of the fresh eggs, the cream and butter, for as long as he lived, years after eating such things became an unremarkable event. And there were sandwiches, on thin Victory loaf bread, with either local crab Julia had caught at Chapman's Pool – which was decent of her – or tiny scrapings of meat paste and dripping provided by the vicar, and there were strawberries, and an extremely undercooked vegetable pie that Alastair had made and handed round, and was chaffed about and took in relatively good humour. The atmosphere was genial, magical even – there was something about that evening, when the light refused to fade and they might suddenly all have been bombed or gunned down, something glorious about it. Some of the guests dragged the old wicker chairs down the porch steps and on to the sand, others remaining on the porch or on the stairs. Derek, the farmer's son, excused himself, Ian hung around looking miserable, and Julia chatted to Dinah about their shared belief in fairies.

When sunset came they set the candles and the paraffin lamps along the porch balustrade and they all 'did' a bit. Mrs Proudfoot sang, 'When Father Painted the Parlour' with great gusto which earned her an enthusiastic round of applause. Alastair recited, very seriously, '*There's a one-eyed yellow idol to the north of Khatmandu*', to awed silence. Julia, rather shyly, sang a short verse of 'O for the Wings of a Dove' in a low, surprisingly sweet voice.

'That was good,' Ant told her as she hopped off the porch.

'Oh, darling boy, you're too kind,' she told him, flinging her arms round him and he recoiled, regretting that he'd found her momentarily not annoying.

Then, at much urging, the birthday boy himself was pushed up on to the stage, made to do a speech. Though he was learning more Shakespeare every day with Dinah, the only piece he was confident he knew by heart was Prospero's speech from *The Tempest* which his father had always done at auditions.

> *Our revels now are ended. These our actors,*
> *As I foretold you, were all spirits and*
> *Are melted into air, into thin air.*
> *And, like the baseless fabric of this vision,*
> *The cloud-capp'd towers, the gorgeous palaces,*
> *The solemn temples, the great globe itself,*
> *Yea, all which it inherit, shall dissolve*
> *And, like this insubstantial pageant faded,*
> *Leave not a rack behind.*

He was nervous, and unused to it, though he used to love acting at school, before Daddy died. He had to clear his throat twice to be able to get through the bit about '*the great globe itself / Yea, all which it inherit, shall dissolve*', for Daddy had always done a little action with his hands, miming the disintegration of everything, but then he forced himself to stop thinking about that, just pretend he was Prospero, standing on the steps of his own magical mysterious cabin looking out to sea, looking out at the horizon, and with his strange, otherworldly subjects about him, half real, half imaginary. And suddenly it was true. He was not a newly teenage boy standing knock-kneed on a porch on a summer's evening. He was a sorcerer, an exiled duke, a master of magic, able to control tides, conjure up storms. In the distance, Venus shone steadily in the violet-peach sky. He fixed his gaze on her, and when he finished, there was respectful applause, but Dinah was staring at him, with a curious expression on her face.

'You're very good,' Jane Goudge said, kissing his cheek as he came down the steps and stood amongst them rather awkwardly. The others stood up, murmuring. Dinah handed round more elderflower wine.

'Thank you,' said Ant. 'It's just remembering words, really—'

'It's a bit more than that, dear boy,' said Mrs Goudge, hugging a cushion to herself and looking at him appraisingly. 'He's got a lovely speaking voice, hasn't he, Ambrose?'

'I should say so,' said the vicar.

'Yes, old bean, you really have,' came a voice from the shadows of the setting sun.

Ant jumped. A woman was standing to the side of the Bosky, a little pigskin case in her hand.

'Good – evening,' he said, and the vicar and his wife stared at her. 'How – may I help you?'

'I should say so. I'm looking for Dinah Wilde, is she about?'

The Goudges went into the kitchen together to fetch her, leaving Anthony alone with the strange woman, who stepped forward, raising her face to him, and Ant had to stop himself from giving a low cry.

She had an elegant, swirling crop of blonde hair, which curled at her neck. Her eyes were blue, her white skin stretched over slanting cheekbones which might have given her the air of an ice princess or a sprite, Ariel come to life, but the hard squareness of her jaw offset it. There was something mannish about her, something ugly, though the eyes were almost turquoise and glittered. In the fading light he could only see she was dressed all in grey.

But none of that was what shocked him. There was a scar, running down her right cheek, a fine line like a seam, but for the end by the mouth where the red stitching was obvious. He blinked heavily, the excitement and emotion of the day catching up with him, and nodded at her.

'You must be the famous Anthony,' she said, in a strangely rich, clipped voice. 'Well, this is awfully nice. Party, is it? I'm Daphne. Daphne Hamilton,' she said, and she held out a slim white hand, each digit dotted with dark red nail polish. 'I'm a very old friend of your aunt's. You *are* Anthony, aren't you?'

Alastair Fletcher was staring at Daphne, trying to size her up. He said tersely, 'He's Anthony, all right.'

'Yes,' Ant said, slowly, but it sounded unconvincing, as though he were lying. She held out a hand, and he took it and shook it. It was cool, soft, heavy and almost limp in his, as though she could barely be bothered to expend the effort on him.

'I've heard a lot about you, Anthony. I say, where *is* she? Don't tell me she's done a runner again.'

At that moment, Dinah appeared on the porch, smiling in mid-conversation at something someone had said, half turning back to the house, and then she saw Daphne and stopped short, two crystal glasses in her hand, green stems glinting in the lamplight.

'What are you doing here?' she said. Ant looked at her, surprised; he'd never heard that tone in her voice before.

'Evening, darling!' Daphne called, gaily. 'Gosh, well, I've come to see the great treasure-hunter in semi-retirement, if that's all right.' She held up a half-empty bottle of gin. 'Bought some

Booth's Dry with me. Thought it'd be jolly to catch up. It's awfully boring in town at the moment. Everyone's either orf fighting, or evacuated, or run away like cowards, or they're bloody dead.' Her languid gaze took in the burning oil lamps, the cake stand empty but for crumbs, the glasses knocked over to the side. 'I obviously made the right decision, coming here, even though the trains were terrible, darling, I had to take four of them and it took all day, that's why I'm so late. You've grown your hair. I liked it short, I must say.' She looked around and laughed. 'I say. I *can* stay, can't I?'

'Oh.' Dinah put down the glasses. 'Well – of course you can, Daphne dear. It's not awfully convenient but—'

'I had to beg a lift off an extremely suspicious chap at the station,' said Daphne as though Dinah hadn't spoken. 'Looked at me as though I was a Hun.' She glanced around the porch, bird-like eyes taking everything in. 'Anyway, darling, I wanted to talk to you about Ishtar.'

'Ishtar?' Dinah said, frowning.

'Do listen, Dinah. You understand what I mean.'

'Yes,' said Dinah, nodding furiously. 'Absolutely I do. But come inside, dear, I'll show you your room . . .'

Conversation between the other guests had melted away and there was silence. Daphne looked around – she was always in control, he was to realise that later. 'Hello.' She raised a hand to the assembled group. 'I like your brooch,' she said to Mrs Goudge, who'd reappeared from inside.

'This is my dear friend, Daphne Hamilton, assistant curator of Assyrian antiquities at the British Museum,' said Dinah, needlessly loudly. 'Daphne, do come in, darling.'

They walked inside, the stranger's hand on the small of Dinah's back, guiding her across the threshold of her own house, leaving Anthony alone on the porch.

'Who is that, pray tell?' came a voice at his elbow and he looked around to see Julia Fletcher doing balletic arm movements next to him.

'She's my aunt's friend,' he said. 'From London.'

He leaned over and stared round past the house down to the lane, looking at the scuffed lettering of Dinah's birthday message in the sandy dirt by the dusk light. It was almost all gone. From inside the house he heard lowered voices, and then a soft laugh. He hesitated, not sure why he did so, and then followed them inside.

Chapter Eighteen

London, 2014

One week after her niece's reappearance Cord went back to the Royal Academy of Music, for the first time in years. Her old singing teacher, Professor Mazzi, who'd stuck by her and was one of the few who believed her voice might one day return, had invited her to take part in a panel discussion on singing careers post degree. Cord would have done anything to get out of it.

The old broken-backed book held her captive. Autumn was in the air and every evening, despite herself, she would carefully open a page at random, and start reading Mads's difficult, tight handwriting for the second, fourth, eighth time. She was only vaguely ever at peace when she was reading it, yet she dreaded opening the pages each time, fearing the pain it would cause to read it all again, and from the point of view of one she had loved, and hurt, so very much.

She could not undo what had happened and she could not tell anyone what she knew. That autumn she began to dream again, to wonder, to see patterns emerging down the years, and it was terrifying, opening it all up again, because for so long she'd survived simply by closing her mind to the whole business of her parents, Ben, Mads, Hamish, her voice, the Bosky, the person she had once been. She was intelligent enough to have not repressed it utterly, but she had cut most of her past life – the part that makes us who we are – out of her present life for years. Now she could not seem to stop the two mixing together.

The dreams were strange, sometimes horrific, dreams where she was back there again, where she saw the old witch on the beach who looked like Daddy's aunt, where wild flowers grew up around the house and smothered it, where she conjured up ghoulish sights: her brother and her mother kissing, a shelf of water engulfing the house and the wild flowers and the beach huts, washing it all away . . . Night after night she came home and reread Mads's words, read again the diaries of a terrified little girl and the warmth she had found with Cord's family. And Cord began to understand. But she couldn't go back in time and change what had happened.

The news was all about the appearance of a terrifying group called Isis, taking over vast swathes of Syria and Northern Iraq seemingly with no opposition. There were pictures on TV bulletins of men driving into Mosul, hacking at the stones of ancient Assyrian cities nearby like Nimrud and Nineveh, winged lions they said were idolatrous, statues of kings who had lived thousands of years before Mohammed whom they said were infidels. Cord felt protective over her little angel, who she liked to imagine had been rescued from just such an Assyrian city, and had cleared a space for her on the cluttered mantelpiece. Now the angel stared down at Cord as she ate breakfast or shuffled ineffectively through papers looking for music or articles she had lain aside, or lay on the old sofa rereading the diaries late into the night. She liked the owl's baleful stare which reminded her of Professor Mazzi, in fact. Most of all she liked the way the small square sat neatly amongst her rubbish, as though it belonged there. Just sometimes Cord found herself wondering if the angel was actually watching her, waiting for Cord to do something, trying to tell her something. And then she'd tell herself she really was going mad. *I'm not going to see Mumma. I'm not going back there. Nothing's changed*, she'd tell herself, but for the first time this withdrawal and isolation felt not like a necessary position she'd had to take to save herself, save them all, but like an excuse.

The other two members of the panel were a mousy shy young counter-tenor and a baritone who – with tours, albums, appearances on chat shows – had done very well for himself though, Cord privately thought, more with bombast than with actual talent.

The questions ranged from the technical – how to warm up the voice when singing chamber music in a large venue – to the optimistic – when should I get a manager? – and she was pleased to be asked as many questions as the baritone, whose slightly bumptious, self-referential manner and commercial success had not particularly endeared him to the audience of serious young students arrayed in front of them. She loved their confidence. They knew they were good, the best – they wouldn't have got to the Royal Academy of Music if they weren't. Cord regretted many things but didn't actually mind growing old, having grey hairs, twinges in her knee, or a lack of knowledge about pop culture because she had always been old before her time in any case. But here, in the warm wooden hall surrounded by portraits of former principals and successful old students, she felt a sudden primal, blazing envy for these young people and their unsullied careers, what was there for the taking if they so chose. What she wouldn't give, not for their unlined skin but for the chance to go back and do it again. To choose differently . . . to still have her voice. To open her mouth and to have back the glorious, peerless sound that once came out . . . The afternoon sun shone in shafts through the tall windows like searchlights, and she blinked, suddenly overwhelmed.

My darling friend it's so wonderful to see her again . . . I can live the rest of the year having had the sunshine of her company for a few weeks. In fact she asks me about me and wants to know all these things but I just want to hear her talk, or hear her sing . . .

'Time for one more question,' said Professor Mazzi, who was chairing the event. He pushed his glasses up his nose irritably. 'Yes—' He pointed to an eager girl with enormous round wire glasses and a large forehead, in the second row. 'You. Oh.' His voice changed, took on a tone of resignation. 'Soo-Jin. What question do you have for the panel?'

'My question is for Miss Wilde,' said Soo-Jin, leaning forward. 'Thank you very much for coming today, Miss Wilde.'

She paused, and Cord, thinking that was the question, laughed awkwardly.

'Well, it's my pleasure, although I'm not sure that's actually a—'

Soo-Jin interrupted her. With devastating clarity she said, 'I wanted to ask you what happened when you ruined your voice?'

There was a quick in-draw of breath from someone and then a heavy silence.

'Sorry, could you be more specific?' said Cord, softly. She could feel the counter-tenor next to her stiffening and even the baritone stopped checking his phone and looked up. Professor Mazzi looked more owl-like than ever, but said nothing.

'Your voice used to be perfect. We had an English Song class last month and they showed us a clip of you singing Dido when you were twenty-two and it was very inspirational.'

Imagine being Cord and knowing what you want to do, having your life all mapped out already.

Soo-Jin was still talking. Cord blinked again, trying to recall herself to the present.

'But I heard you at a performance of the *St Matthew Passion* in June. Your voice doesn't sound like that any more. It was very bad, really. You cracked on the high note and you couldn't make the end of the run and—'

'Soo-Jin, that's enough.' Professor Mazzi was glaring at Soo-Jin who sat, calm and mildly curious, her arms folded. 'I do apologise. Cordelia, you don't have to answer the question.'

There was an awkward silence. The roar of traffic outside seemed to grow louder, like a swarm of approaching bees, and Cord wanted to press her hands to her ears. Not this, not this now, not as well as everything else. She kept nodding, idiotically, trying to buy time . . .

'Anyone else want to ask something instead?' said the baritone suddenly, for which Cord was grateful.

But, before she could stop herself, she'd raised her hand, and greatly to her own surprise heard herself say, 'It's fine. Really. Listen, Soo-Jin. Do you know what the epithelium is?' Soo-Jin shook her head. 'No? Well, you should learn it. It's the membrane that covers the vocal cords. I had a lesion on it, eight years ago. I had it removed and during the operation the epithelium was torn. It can happen, it's a very delicate procedure. Now if I was a teacher, or an accountant, or anyone with a normal job it wouldn't have mattered. My speaking voice would have sounded the same. But it tore and afterwards I discovered—' She couldn't finish the sentence and so she swallowed. 'It had badly damaged my singing voice. That's what happened.'

There was a silence, broken only by the shuffling of feet on the varnished wooden floor. People looked down, not meeting her eye. As though she were polluted, contaminated.

Soo-Jin, however, nodded. 'OK. Thanks.' She added, 'That really sucks, I'm sorry.'

'Thank you.'

'Do you know what caused the lesion in the first place?'

Cord swallowed again. 'I – I noticed it one day.'

'How come?'

I loved Cord more than any of them. When I was scared at night she used to get into bed with me and hug me and our toes would touch.

She looked down at her wet palms, smearing the wooden table, her shaking hands, and folded them in her lap. 'I shouted at someone. It was a bad day.' She looked up but they stared blankly back at her, embarrassed. 'I had the nodes on the cords already but they weren't that big. Nevertheless, I'd seen a specialist, and I was considering the operation. They weren't sure I needed it, that the risk was too great. But I was very upset and I—' She broke off, unable to go on.

'So you're saying we mustn't shout at people, that's correct?'

Someone gave a nervous titter. Cord hunched her shoulders almost up to her ears.

'I had a row with my dad.' She felt her throat swell, and tears came to her eyes. 'I found out something and I was devastated and I lost control. Anyway, the reason doesn't matter – to you. But that's what happened.'

She felt lighter, suddenly. She had said all this out loud.

'What bad luck,' the baritone said quietly in her ear and he patted her arm. 'You poor sod.'

Bad luck. She had never been able to see it other than as utterly bound up in her own fortunes, some retribution, some part of the myth of her family. But what if it wasn't? What if it was just that: bad luck? She had damaged her voice, she had had an operation, the operation hadn't worked, and it was bad luck. Nothing more.

She smiled at Soo-Jin, who was writing furiously in a note-book, and let her shoulders drop. *How strange*, she found herself thinking. *They asked me and I told them the truth. And it's OK.*

Cord's always been so full of purpose. I find that very comforting, someone who always knows what to do. She always has.

She didn't want to get on the tube: it was a beautiful day. Cord lingered in the hall after the panel was over, not wanting to get caught up with the dispersing students. Eventually she was just leaving, the heavy door she remembered so well swinging hard behind her, when she heard a voice calling her. She kept her head down and carried on walking up to York Gate and into the park, over the bridge underneath which the sludgy green water mooched lazily along and the trees were still, the sky a piercing autumnal blue.

Suddenly a moped screeched to a halt just in front of her and Professor Mazzi, removing his helmet, said crossly, 'I nearly got killed crossing the road. What a way to die. Cordelia, don't you listen? I was calling your name. So many times.'

'I thought you were a student wanting to ask difficult questions.' Cord took his helmet, smiling. 'I'm so sorry, Professor. How can I help you?'

'By listening, as before, as I used to beg you to, when you were a young girl and so sure of yourself that you never listened, even then, always with your opinions,' said Professor Mazzi. '"Here, and there, I sing like this, I walk like this."' He shook his head, frowning. 'Maybe we sit down here, if you have a minute?' He gestured to a bench past the bridge and flicked out the moped's kickstand.

'Oh – OK.' Cord looked at her watch.

'What?' said Professor Mazzi. 'You are busy? You have somewhere to go, a new concert, an interview? No. You are going home to wallow in the mire as the poem says.'

'I'm teaching a class later,' Cord lied.

'Don't tell untruths to me. Now, listen, please. I am a patron of Goldsmith's Choral Union. They have commissioned a new work for next summer from Alfred Gatek; you know him? He is a brilliant young composer.' Cord nodded. 'They are performing it at the Royal Festival Hall. It will be a grand event. The piece is called *Nineveh*.'

'*Nineveh*?'

'Yes, you have heard about it?'

'No . . .' Cord shook her head. 'My great-great-aunt – oh, it doesn't matter.'

'I have suggested you as the mezzo. I said I would ask you about it.'

'Me? No,' said Cord. She put her hand on the professor's arm. 'Professor Mazzi, you're very kind, but my voice—' She gave a bittersweet smile. 'That girl in the class, she was right. My voice is ruined.'

'This is it, you see, you are wrong. You recovered badly from the operation.'

'No—' Cord shook her head. 'It was torn, Professor Mazzi, they couldn't fix it. Don't you remember?'

'Yes, I remember, of course I remember, I remember that one of my best – no, my best student – I remember that her voice was ruined,' said Professor Mazzi, furiously. '*Stupido. È molto incredible – Chiedere questa domanda. Allora, una donna che . . . Incredible . . .? Certo, certo . . . Bah.*'

He thumped the bench angrily. 'All right then,' said Cord, mildly. She just wanted to get away, really, to be back at home, reading the diary again.

'You don't have any interest in this, what I say? You don't care! You are single-minded. You make up your decision and – *è finito*.' He sliced both hands through the air. 'Like that poor boy you broke your heart over.'

'I didn't break my heart over him, Professor Mazzi,' she said, smiling gently. 'We split up. He went abroad . . . It was for the best.'

'No, no, *cara mia*.' The professor stared at her. 'I remember it differently, then.'

She closed her eyes briefly, turned away. But he went on.

'I always took such an interest in you. From the moment I see you and I see – aha, this girl is Sir Anthony Wilde's daughter. So she is born with this gift of her father, perhaps. I saw him in *Macbeth* when I come to live in Londra, in nineteen seventy-seven, and such art. Such mastery of art. And then I meet you and it is the same. The dedication, the control of the voice, it was perfection.'

Cord waggled her jaw from side to side.

'You don't want to hear this, you pretend to not listen. But I remember. There was the concert at the end of the year and Sir Bryan Linton, he pick you for the solo recital. And as we are waiting backstage, you remember what you said to me?'

Cord shook her head.

'You said, "Should I be nervous? Because I am not. I want to sing to them." Do you understand? It was the most important performance, everyone out there who could shape your career and you knew . . .' He pointed his finger at her. '*You knew how good you were, carissima*.'

Cord nodded, trying to block out what he was saying, but

she found she couldn't. All she could hear were the words of the diary in Mads's quietly intense, heart-piercing little voice.

Just for one day, one day, I would like to know a feeling where you are totally, utterly happy with nothing else but happiness in your heart, no worries about anything else. Just once, just one day.

She squeezed her aching eyes shut, and then forced herself to listen. 'It is this that I can't believe, Cordelia. That you haven't looked into this and thought about it, when it could help you so much.'

'Thought about what?'

'Agh. You don't even listen to me. Thought about having the operation again. The success rate is optimal. Yes, even for you.'

'What operation?'

'My dear,' said Professor Mazzi. 'You are a severe trial to me. The operation on your vocal cords.'

'Oh, that.' She shook her head. 'You are kind. There's no point, though, is there?'

'I have gone so far as to make the telephone call, and to speak to that man Khan, at Imperial College Trust. He assures me it would be worth your coming to see him.'

'What? No – oh.' Cord pressed her hands to her now-burning cheeks. 'Dear Professor Mazzi, I wish you hadn't. It's very sweet of you but—'

'Dr Khan remembers you and he has looked into the operation. He says it would be easy to correct. He thinks you would suffer a slight adjustment to the range – you would be a mezzo, not a soprano – but I have always longed to see you as Cherubino, *cara mia*. Anyway, I say to you that Dr Khan is hopeful.'

'Mr Khan,' said Cord, after a few moments. 'He's a surgeon. It's Mr Khan.'

Professor Mazzi raised his eyes to heaven, pointing a finger upwards. 'I do not know why I try to help you, Cordelia. You are a bull-china young woman.'

She leaned over and kissed him on the cheek. 'Young woman indeed. Thank you, Professor.'

He reached along the bench, took her hand. 'Do you understand me? He thinks he can help you get your voice back again. If you want it, that is.' His grasp tightened gently; his own voice softened. 'That is the question, isn't it, Cordelia? Do you want it back? Do you actually *want* to sing again?'

Cord walked home through Regent's Park. It was gloriously hot, more like late summer than autumn. She turned into the rose garden. Funny, talking about Hamish again; this was where she and Hamish often used to have lunch when he came to see her in a break from his rehearsals. Oh, it looked fine on a day like this, with the last roses still blowsy and full, the scent of fallen petals on the ground, the trees still rustling and heavy with leaves. Hamish would pick roses for her. The open ones, lemon-yellow at the centre, blushing pink at the petal's edges. 'We're helping them flower,' he'd say. 'We have to pick them so they flower again.'

The vast cream houses lining the inner circle glowed in the afternoon sun. She remembered that one of Daddy's friends, an ancient old actor whom they'd been to visit once for tea, had lived in one – which one exactly she couldn't be sure. She supposed it showed her age if nothing else for it would have been in the days when actual Londoners still lived in Regent's Park, not absent billionaires or sheikhs or both. What was his name? He'd adored Daddy, who had played his son, Hamlet, and he Claudius and the Ghost. Every night he'd walk across the battlements humming very softly the theme to 'Hitler Has

Only Got One Ball' – Daddy had loved this story, bringing his knees up and guffawing with laughter when he told it. His laughter was childish, infectious; it was at the centre of her earliest memories, the sound of Daddy laughing.

'I would give you some violets, but they wither'd all when my father died. They say he made a good end.'

Inside the park she peered past the ticket office of the Open Air Theatre. It had been one of her and Ben's first theatre trips as children, when they'd seen Olivia as Titania, and Daddy as Bottom. She'd had to hold Ben's hand all the way through – he got so scared of things. And the memory of Daddy, at the curtain call, pulling Olivia and Guy forwards with him as the cast held hands, peering into the audience, spotting the children at the back of the stalls waving furiously at him, throwing his arms wide and calling out, 'Hello, darlings! Did you like it?' in front of the whole theatre, and Cord pulling Ben to his feet with her, the pair of them clapping even louder, Ben so happy now, hands cupped around his mouth as they both called back to him.

'Yes! Yes, Daddy!' The other theatregoers, turning to stare at them, smiling as they all shuffled out: 'His children. Isn't that lovely? Weren't they well-behaved? What a lucky man.'

In the broad sunlight Cord blinked back tears, yet still the light feeling continued. She had not thought of her father with affection for so many years now, this man for whom she had formerly felt only pure and total adoration and more than that, understanding. *Simpatico*, Professor Mazzi used to call it. She walked through the rest of the park, past the children playing football, past the croaks and roars from the zoo. He'd taken them there too, on Ben's birthdays, when Mumma was away, and he'd impersonated all the animals. Even the stick insects . . .

'There's rosemary, that's for remembrance. Pray you love, remember.'

Do you actually want *to sing again?*

Suddenly, Cord crossed the road and, instead of turning off for home, walked up Primrose Hill. She sat right at the top of the park and looked out over the city, her arms resting on her knees. She was shaking. Without asking herself why, she turned out of the park and began to make for Ben's house. *I might as well do it now*, she said. *While I think I can. After all, someone asked me about my voice today and I told them the truth, I didn't run away.*

Ben's road had been bohemian and even rather down-at-heel when he'd bought it after their move to London: book publishers, actors, academics who had lived there for years. Now it was grand, box hedges everywhere, gleaming black Jeeps in each driveway, and very still. No children playing in the street, curtains drawn: no signs of any inhabitants at all.

Cord knocked on her brother's bright red front door. Her hands were shaking. *Please be in. Please* don't *be in.*

'Hello,' she said, when Iris answered.

Iris held on to the door with long slim fingers, her pale face flushed in the afternoon sun. She stared at her aunt. 'What are you doing here?'

'I had a thing near you so I thought I'd pop by.' Cord shook her head. *Pop by*, as if she were one of their multimillionaire neighbours wanting a teabag.

'So you've changed your mind,' said Iris, her tone neutral.

'I don't know,' said Cord, simply. 'Look, can I come in?'

Iris turned around without speaking and walked down the corridor. Cord followed her inside.

She wouldn't have recognised the place. It was extremely grand – of course, it should be, she had to keep reminding herself of this. Ben was a big shot, married to a – was she a set designer, his wife? He certainly wouldn't have kept the eighties album posters, the frameless frames stuffed with photographs of days gone by, the sixties art nouveau posters of concerts and albums of which Mads had been so fond. Now it was all tasteful muted colours, expensive prints on the wall. Cord remembered that Lauren was a set dresser. The house looked like a set.

Cord plunged her hands into her pockets, wondering if it was a mistake to have come. She paused at a flight of small steps.

'Let's go into the kitchen,' said Iris, gesturing. 'Oh, look, there's Emily.'

Her sister had appeared at the bottom of the stairs. She stared at Cord. 'Hello?' she said.

'This,' said Iris, 'this is Auntie Cord.'

'Oh, my God.' Emily, who was all pre-Raphaelite curls in contrast with Iris's geometric black-and-white-ness, was still for a moment. 'Sorry. Hello.' She turned to her sister and stuck out her jaw, an infinitesimally small gesture of anger, but Cord saw it, and that made up her mind.

'Maybe I should go,' she said. 'I only came by to see – to see . . .' She trailed off. 'I'll fix up a time again—'

'You were right, Iris,' said Emily, and she turned back to Cord. 'So you're off because now you're here you can't quite hack it? Wow.' She pushed her curtain of golden-red hair over her shoulder; hair so like Althea's Cord wanted to smile.

'I only mean it was a mistake to turn up like this, I should have rung . . .' Cord shook her head, cornered, overwhelmed.

'Emily, be quiet,' said Iris, and she put out a slim hand. 'Please stay, just for a quick cuppa. It's great that you've come, Auntie Cord.'

Could she just say it now?

You don't understand. I'm not your aunt.

Cord rubbed her forehead. 'OK.'

The twins looked at each other; she saw how alike they were, despite their differences. *I'm the only one alive who knows the truth,* she thought. *I have to do this for them.*

She followed them into the kitchen where Emily sat down at the breakfast bar, hands cupped under her chin while Iris put on the kettle and fussed in the fridge, taking out food and offering it to Cord, who shook her head every time.

'Just a cup of tea, please.' She sat down on a bar stool next to Emily. 'So. What do you want to know, in particular? How can I help you? If that doesn't sound too formal . . .' She trailed off. 'Oh, I don't know what's for the best. Tell me what you want to know.'

They looked at each other and she saw how young they still were in the darting, awkward glances they exchanged. After a moment Iris, obviously the one who spoke for them both, said, 'Can we start with how our mum died, please.'

Her voice had the tiniest crack in it. Cord's stomach lurched. It was too warm in the perfect glass box of a kitchen. Could she tell them that they'd inadvertently given her their mother's diary and that had the truth in it? No. Never.

'There's a reason you haven't seen much of me, you see—' she began, and stopped, her throat so dry something seemed to be scraping at the back of it. She swallowed and started again, her voice low, eyes cast down on to the table. 'I killed her. You can't prove it, but I'm pretty sure I did.'

I killed her – it sounded so melodramatic, there in the pristine interior of the sunny room. But Emily shivered, and looked at her sister, biting her lip. Her eyes filled with tears.

'What do you mean?' Iris demanded. 'What did you do?'

'I told her the truth,' said Cord. 'What I thought was the truth.'

'But wh-what is the truth?' Emily leaned forwards.

'I'm not even sure, any more,' said Cord. She swallowed and looked at them both, both so young, so like their mother, whom she had loved more than anyone else for so much of her life.

Oh, Mads. Why did you go and do what you did? Why did you break us all apart?

Her heart swelled with love for them, for these beings in front of her who were her flesh and blood, no matter what happened, and somehow, it was done, it was over, the isolation. She could no more walk away from them now than she could forget the diary. But she could still ruin their lives, if she accidentally let slip the truth.

Cord put her hands out towards them.

'Look, I'll tell you what I know about your mum and dad. I always wanted to push people who loved me away, I've never learned how to let them in. I don't know why. My dad, probably. But, girls, I promise you something, you have to understand this most of all: they were mad about each other. They were so happy, before it all fell apart. They really were.'

Chapter Nineteen

1986

Cord had booked the tiny Italian restaurant on a narrow lane off Brewer Street: it was a recommendation of Professor Mazzi's. After the arthritic waiter had cleared the coffee cups – all four of them self-consciously drinking espresso and saying how much they liked it – he brought four thimble-sized glasses filled with a cloudy yellow liquid to the table. Only Hamish knew what it was.

'It's *limoncello*,' he said, giving a thumbs-up to the restaurant owner, who stood behind the swing doors in the kitchen, watching for their reaction with almost comic anxiety. 'Thank you! Oh, it's delicious.' He smiled at Cord; they had a joke that he liked old-lady drinks: sherry, crème de menthe. 'I first had this in Naples when I was filming a swords-and-sandals epic. I had one line, *Sire, the phalanx won't hold*. I got the giggles each time I had to say it and eventually the line got cut. I was devastated. But there was a lovely restaurant in a tiny piazza near our hotel and the owner's wife was Scottish. Cheers.' He raised his glass, as the others laughed.

'Stop!' Cord put her hand to his mouth. 'Don't drink. We should make a toast. Happy birthday, Mads.'

Mads shrank back into her chair, as the others pushed their glasses together. 'Oh, no,' she said, tipping her head forward so her hair covered her face. 'I hate birthdays.'

But Ben tucked her hair behind her ear and kissed the ear,

gently. 'Come out of there, Mads.' He put his arm round her. 'We should make a toast—'

'Yes,' said Cord. She reached over and took her friend's hand. 'Happy birthday, darling Mads.'

As they clinked their glasses together, the operatic aria playing in the background swelled to a climax, and they all smiled at each other, and drank. *It's so easy, the four of us together*, Cord found herself thinking, and the back of her neck prickled, and her head ached.

'Is that you, Cord?' said Ben, gesturing towards the record player. 'She sounds pretty upset about something.'

'She's about to throw herself off a building,' said Cord. 'Her lover's been shot.'

'Fuss fuss fuss,' said Hamish. 'She shouldn't have got together with an artist. They're the worst kind of boyfriend.'

'Actors are better, then. OK.'

'Oh, yes. Very reliable. Steady income. Normal-sized ego. My advice to anyone seeking a life partner is – go with an actor.'

Cord laughed, squeezed his thigh. He took her hand, held it tightly in his.

'The three of you, and Tony and Althea, with your strange occupations,' said Mads. 'I'd like to point out I'm the only one who has an actual job.'

'You got a job?' said Cord. 'Where? That's wonderful.'

'Yes!' Mads grinned. 'At Rolls-Royce. I start next month after we're back from Australia.'

'You're going to Australia?' Cord said, not sure if she'd misheard.

'Yep. We're going to visit Aunt Jules. She wants to meet Ben.' Ben nodded, Mads nodded in sync and Cord thought how alike they seemed these days. Their blonde hair the same colour, their eyes – his blue, hers a deep dark grey – with similar expression, the jawlines both set, determined, the mouth quick to smile. 'Going to Melbourne, Sydney, the Gold Coast and then home. Four weeks. I can't wait.'

'Me neither,' said Ben.

'Are you going to stay in Bristol?' Hamish asked.

She nodded. 'Ben wanted to move to London, but I said not yet. He's got these two productions lined up in Bristol and a film job, haven't you?'

'Where?' demanded Cord. 'That's wonderful.'

Ben said, 'It's just doing a bit of second AD work. It's a comedy, they're filming at Pinewood. Friend of Simon's. You know, Cord, Simon Chalmers, Mumma and Daddy's old mucker.' He hesitated, about to say something. 'Who knows. But it should be good experience. And it pays, which is something.'

'Simon Chalmers is a terrific director,' said Hamish. 'I saw his production of that Shaffer play last year. Great stuff. You are funny, you Wildflowers, you know everyone.'

There was a slight pause, and then Cord said, 'Shall we get the bill?'

'We could go for a drink somewhere, have a look round Soho,' said Ben, hopefully. 'We're staying at Mumma and Daddy's tonight – the later we get back the better.'

'Don't say that,' said Mads, as Hamish asked curiously, 'What do you mean?'

'Oh, there's always some drama on with them, you know,' said Ben, casually. 'Daddy'll have been drinking, Mumma won't like the new script they've sent over for *On the Edge*, they'll pretend everything's fine in front of us . . .' He trailed off and looked across the gingham tablecloth at his sister, who smiled.

'Where were you thinking of going?' she said.

'I don't know. What about that pub Daddy took us to before

the matinee of *Cinderella*? We walked past it on the way here. It looked pretty much the same, funnily enough.'

Cord nodded. 'Great idea. Although this time, please don't be sick with nerves in the loo.'

Ben laughed. 'I won't. Actually—' He looked at Mads, who nodded. 'Can we just say something, before we go? We really do want to toast something, toast it properly. We wanted to tell the two of you before we tell the parents.' He moved closer to Mads.

'We're engaged,' she said, and leaned back, as if dodging a blow.

Hamish stood up, hands clapped to his face. 'Madeleine! Benedict! This is wonderful news.' He stepped around the tiny table, knocking against another diner. 'Sorry. Apologies.' He put his hand on the shoulder of the lady he'd hit; she smiled up at him, her eyelashes actually fluttering. 'Give me a hug. I'm delighted.' He embraced Ben, enfolding Mads in with him. 'Wonderful!'

Cord sat still, watching him, keeping a smile on her face. Ben disentangled himself from Hamish's embrace, patting him on the back. He stood on the other side of the table from his sister.

'Are you pleased, Cordy?' he said. Mads, still in Hamish's arms, looked back at her, her eyes darting from brother to sister.

Cord blinked. 'Of course,' she said. She stood up, stumbling slightly. 'Of course I bloody am.'

She came around to their side of the table and hugged Mads, feeling her thin frame, the silky sheet of hair on her own cheek, the smell of her, almonds.

Ben turned round to accept the congratulations of another diner behind him. Cord leaned as close as she could to Mads and whispered, 'I love you, as if you were my own sister, you know that.' She touched her forehead to Mads's, and wanted to cry, though she didn't know quite why exactly.

Then she hugged her brother. 'Oh, Ben. Lovely brother.'

'We thought you might be a bit funny about it,' he explained.

'Course not,' said Cord, wiping one eye. 'I'm not a jealous teenager any more. I'm—' She looked at her watch. 'You know what, I actually can't go for a drink,' she said, and pushed her hair out of her eyes. 'Dammit.'

The other three stared at her. 'Really?' said Hamish, first.

'I have an audition in the morning,' she explained. 'First thing.'

'You never said.'

'It's – it's top secret.'

Mads nodded, politely. 'How exciting. You can't tell us anything about it?'

Cord hesitated. 'No, I can't.'

'That's convenient,' said Hamish, quietly.

She turned to him. 'What does that mean?'

'Nothing.' Their eyes locked. 'I'm sorry.'

'I don't lie,' Cord said, quietly. 'It's true.'

'She doesn't, she's right,' said Ben. 'Never has done.'

Hamish put his scarf around his neck. 'I want to celebrate with you guys. Shall we go and find that pub? Cord, can you come for one drink?'

'I—' Cord was torn. 'I'm sorry. I did promise them. I really did. I'll walk with you towards Charing Cross Road. I can get the bus from there.'

They walked down Berwick Street, busy on a Friday in late July. Tired, tawdry young women stood in doorways. Brackish liquid pooled on the pavements. Down the road towards Piccadilly, the lights from the Windmill and the Raymond Revuebar glittered.

'It's not very nice round here, is it?' said Mads, looking round with interest. 'Where are we?'

'Soho,' said Hamish. 'It used to be nice. It's a bit crummy these days. Still, all of human life is here. Where's your dad's pub?'

'On Wardour Street. The Moon Under Water,' said Cord, and the four of them walked, in silence, Mads and Ben in front.

The atmosphere was different. *It's all my fault*, Cord thought. *I can't tell them about the audition, can I? They'd go mad if I did . . . it'll come to nothing, I'm sure . . . But just in case . . .* She squeezed Hamish's arm, as if trying to let him know, via ESP, that she was sorry for behaving badly. He squeezed it back, his warm fingers on her skin, and began humming 'La Mer'. He was always humming, usually songs by French singers, or trying to sing them in execrable French. His fingers tightened around hers. *I could just lean in to you, and never stop leaning,* she thought and again the prickling feeling started.

'Well, it's a great night,' Hamish said, in his soft voice. 'I'm glad we could all celebrate your news.'

Cord wished he wouldn't say things like that. Childishly she broke her arm free of his grasp. 'The pub's just here.'

'Oh,' said Ben. 'Oh, it's not the one I'm thinking of then.'

'It's busy,' said Mads, doubtfully.

Cord suddenly felt responsible for the evening. 'Look, I'll come in for a blackcurrant and soda. Let me just see if there's any room—'

She left them and went across the road, standing on tiptoe to peer into the window of the pub. She was still, pressing her nose against the dirty glass, breathing fast, and then came back across. A motorbike dodged past her, and hooted.

'There's no room,' she said. 'Let's – let's go somewhere different.'

But there wasn't anywhere else – it was almost eleven, and other than brothels and private drinking clubs, there was nowhere open. 'Are you sure?' Ben asked. 'Not just a tiny table we could all—' He stepped off the kerb.

'No!' Cord called, angrily. 'God, why don't you believe me? Don't, just don't.'

'I only wanted to—'

She nodded. 'I'm sorry. Anyway, you know, you'd better go if you're catching the last train to Richmond. Otherwise you'll be stuck on the night bus.' She caught her brother's hand, pulling him away from the kerb so that his back was to the pub. 'Look. What about if you come back to my halls? I've got a bottle of whisky from Aunt Isla. I have to sleep but you guys could—'

'Stand in the street drinking?' said Hamish, wryly.

'Oh—' said Mads. 'That'd be so lovely, but you're right, it's getting late—'

'I'm not sure where the night bus goes from—' Ben began. 'Perhaps we had better get the tube. It's just—'

Cord breathed a sigh of relief. 'I'll show you how to get to Embankment tube. You'll remember, won't you, Ben?'

Ben said, 'I don't know.' He looked deflated. Hamish was staring at Cord, disappointment on his face.

'We'll celebrate properly soon!' Cord said. 'After you've told Mumma and Daddy. How about that?'

'Yes,' said Ben. 'Our last night down here's tomorrow. How about you plan to come over then, both of you?'

Cord laughed. 'I can't. It sounds like I'm avoiding you, but I really can't.'

'What is this thing tomorrow?' Mads said, curiously. 'You really are being so mysterious. Are you going to the moon? Are you singing for the Queen?'

But Cord just shook her head.

They walked down Charing Cross Road, past the theatres, thronged with crowds, lights blinking. Cord saw them off towards the District line of the tube, and then she and Hamish turned around, towards Covent Garden and the deserted streets around Seven Dials.

'Do you want to come to mine?' Hamish said. 'We should have got on the tube with them, I suppose.'

'No, I'd better get back.'

'Can you tell *me* what it's about? Just me?'

She said, 'No, Hamish.'

'Are you seeing someone else?' He was half joking, but there was a strained tone to his voice. His jaw was tight. 'Just tell me if you are, Cord.'

'I'm not. Don't be silly.'

They were on a quiet street, lined with Georgian houses, down a tiny cul-de-sac. She looked around her, confused; she'd never been this way before.

'It's not silly. You won't fix dates. You won't return my calls. You tell me you love me. You want me. I know you do, you can't make up the way we are together.' His hands were clenched. 'I know your family – I know it's hard sometimes. I know you think I'm too old for you.' She was shaking her head. 'But . . . You break up a nice evening like this, you want everything on your own terms and it's not always like that, Cord. Grow up. This is real life.'

She swallowed, her hand on her throat. 'I am grown up.'

'You're twenty. You're a baby.'

'Why are you with me then? Why do you say you love me if you think I'm a baby?'

'Because you're behaving like one now! Refusing to go into the pub. Acting so weird with them about their engagement. Making up some excuse about needing to go home.'

'I didn't want to go in there. And I need an early night.'

Hamish said gently, 'I know why you didn't, because of the

smoke, because of your voice. Well, that's fine, but you can't let it stop you doing—'

She laughed. 'I can't? Don't tell me what I can and can't do, Hamish.' He tried to reply and she held up her hand. 'Don't ever tell me that. Ever. It's my life, singing, I've told you that before. It always comes first. It *always* does.' She felt as though the dam had burst, that she was free to say what she wanted. 'It's my life, and you're always trying to get me to do what you want, what you think we should do, what you think is best for me. I have to do this tomorrow, OK? You'll know, you'll know soon enough. And as for the pub, I don't ever want to go in there, and it's none of your business.'

She was shaking; he came towards her, his eyes dark. 'I want what's best for you because I thought we loved each other. I want to look after you, and vice versa. And you do, you are the kindest person I know. You need someone who watches out for you, who you can lean on, Cordy! I want you to be happy. You need someone to—'

Cord stepped back. 'That's it, though, that's the thing. I don't need someone. In fact, I – I really don't.' She stared up at him, tears running down her cheeks. 'I don't want to be with you any more. I want to be on my own. I have to – I have to be able to do what I need to do. I'm sorry, Hamish. The voice—'

'The voice isn't everything. It's not a person. It doesn't love you.'

'God, what a cliché. You don't understand, darling, darling Hamish—' His dear angular kind face, the thick sandy hair with the tuft that stood up the wrong way . . . She wiped her nose on the back of her sleeve, looked down, cleared her aching throat. 'Professor Mazzi says for the rest of your singing career you have to lay an extra place at the table for your voice. And I will. It's everything, to me.'

'Everything?' His voice was hollow.

'Everything.'

He put out one hand towards her, then let it drop, and they stared at each other, in the moonlit silver-and-dark street.

The next morning, at eight o'clock, Cord walked up the wide steps below the Albert Hall, looking for Door 11. It was a warm morning, but she had a scarf tied round her neck. There, waiting for her, were Professor Mazzi and Sir Bryan Linton, the director of the Proms, and as they saw her, they started, and moved towards her, eagerly.

Sir Bryan clasped her hands. 'My dear Cordelia,' he said. 'I trust you got some sleep.'

Cord smiled. 'Not much. I'm afraid I – I couldn't.'

'It doesn't matter. You'd be unusual if you did. Now, come with us, my dear. The orchestra is waiting.' They were walking along the curved corridors of the vast circular building, picking up pace. 'Not all of them could make it at this hour, and we don't have much time, as they need to start packing up the previous night and unloading for tonight. Here we are.' He opened a pair of doors and they walked down, through the rows and rows of red velvet seats, through the open Prommers area, and Cord stared up at the huge mushroom acoustic diffusers hanging from the vast ceiling, like flying saucers.

'Have you heard from Isotta Cianfanelli?' she said.

Sir Bryan shook his head. 'Not a damn word. My dear, I fully expect she'll come to her senses and go on tonight, but we can't assume that, not when no one's heard a peep from her since she arrived and that was two days ago. I'm afraid she's very angry with us.'

Professor Mazzi spoke for the first time. 'She is an artist. This is how they will behave.' He held out his hand to Cord, and she realised they had reached the edge of the stage, where steps had been pushed into place for her. She went up, followed by the two men, and the orchestra started clapping, or banging their bows on the music stands, until Sir Bryan called for quiet.

'We do not know whether Miss Cianfanelli is able to sing tonight,' he said. 'And her understudy is, as you may or may not know, at home with a broken ankle. The Proms has a fine tradition of debuting new artists. We have asked Miss Wilde to step in and sing the part of the Countess in *The Marriage of Figaro*. She has just left the Royal Academy of Music, and has performed the role several times there, but we must crave your indulgence, and thank you for supporting her.'

There was another smattering of applause. The orchestra members gazed at her, some shyly, some openly curious.

The conductor, Pierre Besson, nodded at her.

'My dear, it is a great honour to conduct your Proms debut.' He turned back to the orchestra. 'I have heard this girl sing the Countess before, at the Academy, and she will be one of the great singers of her age. If she goes on . . .' There was a murmur of amusement. 'An impossible situation but we will carry on. Thank you for coming this early, to run through the work with her.' He tapped his baton, and Professor Mazzi squeezed her arm, and he and Sir Bryan melted away. 'Now, this is a concert performance, so there are no stage directions, but clarinets, if you could gesture Miss Wilde as she walks on as we agreed I would be very grateful. And at the end of *"Sull'Aria"* remember we are still *allegretto*, no *rallantando* as Miss Wilde will not slow down . . . do you usually slow down at the end here before we lead back into the recitative, Miss Wilde? Miss Wilde?'

But Cord was staring around the vast Victorian hall, imagining it filled with people, seeing their faces, waiting for her to open her mouth and sing. The prickling feeling, the sweaty, tight panic she got lately, every time Hamish mentioned meeting his parents, or visiting hers, or talked about a weekend away with Ben and Mads, or even moving in together – all of it had gone. It had gone, truth be told, the moment she'd peered over the window frame the previous night and seen her father, holed up in a corner of the Moon Under Water, kissing some girl. Cord knew who she was – she'd met her in fact – she was a young actress, daughter of an old friend of Daddy's, and she'd got a part in *Richard III*, playing his wife, Lady Anne. She was, however, twenty-five years younger than Daddy. Of course she was . . .

It was how little he seemed to care, there in that smoky, dingy pub, there amongst the pissed office girls with their white shirts and red lipstick, and the yuppie boys in their wide suits. As she'd stared at him, his hands moving over Georgina's body, slipping under her clothes, then moving back, holding her face as he passionately kissed her, and she him, Cord had seen a man nudging his mate, over by the pool table, both of them smiling at him. She knew they didn't recognise him. She knew they were smiling at this drunk, dishevelled man, fondling a young woman in public.

These images – Mads's sweet smile, her brother's gentle pride, their father . . . the long, long walk across the floor of the Albert Hall to this stage, in the early morning chill . . . She closed her eyes, as Hamish's kind, bewildered face appeared before her. *You need someone who watches out for you, who you can lean on.*

She struggled to blink back the tears, gritting her teeth, and she gently cleared her throat. *It's better on my own.*

'Yes, Sir Bryan. I'm so sorry. I'm ready now,' she said, and the conductor nodded at her, and raised his baton, and the orchestra began to play.

Chapter Twenty

1941

The third Christmas of the war was difficult for Ant. London seemed a distant dream to him; he could recall his life there still, but bits of it were becoming blotted over, like rain dropping on to a chalk painting. It bothered him and he took to testing his memory at night, trying to see exactly what he still knew about Kelly Street, the time before his father's death, his mother's death. He couldn't remember the privy at the back of their house, for example, or the colour of the eyes of the sweetshop owner's granddaughter, who had thick brown plaits and liked sherbets. He remembered the smell of coal in the air, and the burned-caramel scent of the roasted nuts in stiff paper cones sold by the man next to Mornington Crescent tube station. And the scratchy blue seats at the opulent Bedford cinema when he could escape his mother (who didn't like him going, she said he'd catch fleas), and the particular fug of Turkish cigarettes, and the skinny old usherette who clipped your ticket. But he couldn't remember the outside of the Bedford or where on the high street in Camden it was. He couldn't remember whether his father had had a moustache the last time he came home on leave or not and this especially bothered him. They'd argued about Ant going to boarding school – his father was adamant it was best for him, that he couldn't stay at home with his mother all the time. Ant had shouted at him, and refused to say goodbye. He remembered that.

He missed London but the truth was that he was at home

here now. He loved the sea, and the sand, and the lanes where you could cycle everywhere, and Playland in Swanage where you could go on rides and play on the slot machines with your gaggle of friends, boys and girls you picked up en route into town, many of whom were staying in Swanage as their whole school had been evacuated. People were still dying every day and the planes buzzed overhead constantly but you got used to it. Ant could recall beginning to feel guilty about this but you had to. You squared your shoulders and carried on. That was all you could do. He had Aunt Dinah, after all, and she had always known how to make things better. He'd believed that, after a while.

Although, sometimes still . . . take Daphne, for example. Aunt Dinah said Daphne was an old friend she didn't see much, and Daphne had stayed that first weekend of his birthday and had been quite jolly, helping make beef hash fritters and charming Mrs Proudfoot in the village into giving them a cup of sugar which she had heated up on the gas ring and somehow made long strands like filaments which she twisted into toffee-coloured bundles. She had a sweet tooth, and Ant noticed she ate most of the sugary hair herself.

Then Daphne said she wanted peace and quiet and to do some sailing, so she came back in a few weeks, then again and again. Ant didn't understand why when it was anything but peaceful here and there was nowhere to sail, not with the beach and sea bristling with troops and fortifications. But still she kept coming down. She'd bring her ration book with her but it wasn't worth much as she'd always used up most of her coupons. She was lazy, she lied, and, over time, Ant grew to dislike her. And he wouldn't ever have admitted it to himself but he was disappointed that Dinah was in awe not just of her intelligence but also her superior social status – it was rumoured that Daphne was the daughter of an earl, that she had eloped with an Italian count to Monte Carlo when she was eighteen and had been excommunicated by her family as a result. 'She used to be fabulously wealthy, before they cut her off without a penny. She moved in the best circles, Ant dear,' Dinah told him once. 'We were in Venice before the war for a conference on Sumeria and Daphne was staying in a palazzo on the Grand Canal. Guest of a duke there. Mallowan and Desmond and I were in a terrible *pensione* on the Lido and we all got bed bugs. She misses being rich, one has to feel for her. And the people she knew. I mean, she knows everyone. I saw her kiss Oswald Mosley at a party once.'

'He's not exactly the best people, Aunt Dinah.'

'Oh, dash it, Ant, you know what I mean,' Dinah had said crossly. 'My point is she moves in the finest circles. I know she can be a little selfish, but it's only what she's used to. And I owe her.' Her face fell, and her eyes were solemn. 'I owe her a great deal. I can't repay her.'

Ant didn't believe this. He thought Daphne came because she wanted something and Dinah wouldn't give it to her.

Christmas Eve was a bitter cold day and frost glittered on the sand. Dinah and Ant cut holly from the lane by the church together and were twining it in and out of the piles of boxes still stacked high in the sitting room at the Bosky in harmonious silence as darkness fell. There came a ferocious knocking at the door.

'Mary and Joseph?' said Dinah curiously, going downstairs. 'Oh!' he heard her say, as she opened the door. 'Daphne! How – how wonderful.' Tony's heart sank, but he rearranged his face into a polite expression of surprise. Daphne came upstairs into the living room, wrapped in a large fur coat, the usual air of insouciance and prurient curiosity. She flopped on to the sofa, as she stretched out her arms.

'What are you doing here, dearest?' Dinah said behind her, scurrying to relieve her of her possessions. 'I thought – the advice was not to travel by train this Christmas unless urgent.'

Daphne pulled her gloves off, one by one. 'Well, dear, the museum's been hit. Absolute carnage.' She said this almost with relish.

'Oh my dear. Oh no.' Dinah turned pale. 'But the marbles, and the panels, the statues – where – where was everything?'

Daphne looked around, lowered her voice. 'It's just us, isn't it, darling? And him?' She jerked her head at Ant. 'Aldwych tube station.'

'No, darling. Really?'

'Absolutely, yes. Isn't it a scream? The most priceless treasures in the British Museum, the Elgin marbles, most of the Assyrian reliefs, all stacked nicely away in the old tunnels from the line that goes up to the BM. Some of the other stuff's gone out west, we're not allowed to know where.'

Dinah rubbed her hands together, and exhaled. 'How marvellous, how clever they are. That's one in the eye for them. They'll never find them, not even if we lose. Can you imagine if they got hold of the Elgin marbles.'

'Oh, they'd slap them all over one of Speer's ghastly Führer schlosses.' She shrugged off her mink coat and said, 'Too ghastly. The old place took quite a hit, I'm afraid. *Everything's* ghastly, isn't it?'

'Mr Churchill's in Washington,' said Dinah, who had a huge, almost religious-like faith in the Prime Minister. 'We must hope that his meetings with Mr Roosevelt will produce some new direction of hope for our two peoples.'

'What rot. We're all scuppered, Dinah. London's a smouldering mess, virtually nothing left. It's over – all we should do is drink and be merry for tomorrow we all die.' She yawned, heavily, the scar on her cheek puckering as her muscles pulled downwards. 'What's for supper? I'm famished. Ant dear, is there any gin?'

Ant looked at her coldly. 'No gin, sorry. You don't seem that upset about the museum, Daphne.'

'Ant!' Dinah said, furiously. 'Don't be rude.'

But Daphne appeared not to have heard him. She sank down on to the sofa and looked up at Dinah with her big, clear blue eyes, rubbing her hands gently together in a curious motion, like a satisfied spiv.

'Listen, old bean. That's not why I came, I'm afraid. Dinah, poppet. I'm awfully sorry to bring bad news. The flat's been hit.'

'What flat?'

'Your flat, darling.'

Dinah paused in the act of stuffing some holly into the handle above the window seat. She turned round, her mouth a large oval O. 'Oh – oh, dear. Is it gone?'

'Whole building now a pile of rubble. Everyone in it at the time killed. Absolutely rotten show, D, I'm so sorry.'

She had stopped rubbing her hands together and Ant saw the palms, as she flexed her fingers. They were flecked with black and grey, bumpy, as though she had taken in the gravel and rubble herself.

'The barrage balloon, though . . .' Dinah's expression was bewildered.

'Oh, darling. As though that'd make a difference. Haven't you been listening to the news? Don't you know how bad it's been? Elizabeth Senior was killed two weeks ago, did you hear? Direct hit on her flat, her sister was in the other room, escaped without a scratch.'

Dinah put her fingers to her mouth. 'Oh, dear Elizabeth – oh, no.'

Daphne pressed her palms down on her lap, and said, 'What they'll do now with the Prints and Drawings department I've no idea. There's that awful Stanley Robinson gone off to fight and old Gadd isn't up to the job – it'll come down to me now, I know—' She saw Dinah's expression and said quickly, 'I am sorry, D.'

Dinah was still. 'Everything, really everything has gone?'

'Darling, it was an incendiary bomb. Normally they can put them out in time but not this one – burned the place to the ground.'

Dinah slumped down into the window seat, staring at nothing, and after a moment she said, 'I'm selfish for being so upset when there's others who have absolutely nothing. Just rather a blow. Some dear memories in the place and – and money, you know . . . were you all right, dear Daphne?'

'I was out. Dancing at the Café Royal – thank God. Boyo was with me, he was an awful brick, helped me clamber over the rubble to have a look and see if anything was salvageable . . .' Daphne gave a small smile. 'Listen, I told the ARP I'd tell you. You'll have to go up to town to see what's saved . . . not much, I think.' She was watching Dinah carefully. 'I think most of your papers, all the research on Nineveh – it'll all have gone.'

Dinah slapped a box under her feet. 'No, some of it's here. It's the personal things. Some of them were awfully . . . special.'

She turned to Ant. As though covertly checking to see if he was listening. Then she got up and went into the sitting room, holly in hand. In a minute or two Ant could hear her, singing, louder than he'd ever heard her before.

'*The holly and the ivy! When they are both full grown!*'

'This is awful.' Ant didn't understand why Daphne wasn't being nicer to his aunt. 'It's her flat. It's her home and now all of it's . . .' He trailed off.

Daphne said quietly, 'Your aunt isn't like you, sad because you've lost your home, Ant. She has homes all over the world. She takes things and leaves things everywhere. Don't worry about her too much.'

'But she's lost almost everything.'

'I'd hardly say that.' Daphne waved an arm around the cluttered sitting room, then stood up. 'War is misery.' She came over to Ant, took his chin in her cold, firm hand. 'Do you like it, living with Dinah?' she said.

'Yes,' said Ant.

Daphne put her head on one side, looking at him with her curious, sparkling eyes. 'Why?'

'Because she's my family. And she loves me. And I love her.'

'Sweet.' She made a small moue with her mouth.

'I don't have a family. She's the only bit of it I've got. She doesn't have any family either. It's her, and me, us together, you see.'

'Yes. You know, Ant, your aunt –' Daphne screwed up her eyes as though she were about to say something difficult, but then she opened her mouth so it made a small O and then stopped.

'What?'

'This rather changes things for her, losing the flat. Fewer options. She doesn't like being pinned down. Trapped.'

'I'm not trapping her,' said Ant, hotly. 'We just – we jolly well rub along together, that's all.'

'No, no, no, of course you're not! I understand that. But I'll be living here now too, you see. Hope that's all right. We'll have to be friends, you and me, Ant,' she said.

'Only Dinah calls me Ant now,' he said. 'It's Tony, actually.' He stared into her cornflower-blue eyes, and she slapped his cheek, gently.

'Run and find me a drink, will you, *Tony* darling? Doesn't

matter about the gin. Just anything you've got.' He could smell her scent now, that peculiar musky mix of floral scent and something else. Years afterwards he realised it was caraway seeds, and cigarettes, though why the former he had no idea, but then he had no idea about Daphne, who she was, where she came from, why she did what she eventually did.

'How do you know Daphne?' he found himself asking Dinah, one afternoon several months later. It was March, a beautiful spring day, and Dinah and Ant were outside, gently detangling the old dead branches of creepers, roses, tendrils of bindweed and honeysuckle that enmeshed themselves up the side of the house and along the porch and needed a firm prune every year.

Dinah paused in the act of pulling a skeletal set of long twigs, like Struwwelpeter's fingernails, from the wild rose that climbed up the side of the Bosky and flowered a beautiful sunny yellow every May. She waved the branch at him.

'I met her at the British Museum. I was back here for a time after the season at Ur, before I went to Baghdad. She was helping to catalogue the Assyrian seals. She'd just come down from Somerville with a First in Ancient History, and she'd got rid of the terrible Italian count by then, you know.' Ant didn't know. 'These were only two other girls in the whole place. They'd had two women before but both of them had been made to leave when they got married.' She shook her head. 'All those brains, that ability, what they could have offered the museum . . . gone. Anyway, I knew no one in London and a lovely woman, dear Elizabeth who died last Christmas, she worked in the Prints and Sketches department. Well, she took us both under her wing. Daphne was very different from me – aristocratic, glamorous, ran with a fast set – but we rather palled up. It was thrilling to have a chum.'

'You didn't know anyone else in London?'

'No, not a soul. I grew up in India. Father was a colonel in the army. Waziristan, then Kashmir, then we lived in Damascus.'

Ant said, 'With your sister. My grandmother.'

'But I didn't really know Rosemary that well, she was eleven years older than me. She went back to England when I was five. I grew up practically as an only child, Ant. I was a mistake, you see.'

'What do you mean?'

She laughed. 'You'll find out. Or I should say, hopefully you won't. I didn't come to England until I was eighteen. I grew up dreaming about it. And when I got here it was so green, like the ancient plains of Assyria used to be, when the lions and hoopoes were plentiful, before they all died out last century – such a tragedy, when you look at Ashurbanipal hunting all those noble lions and the trees around and the grasses, and now it's all desert . . .' She chewed a nail, and Ant waited patiently. 'Anyway, England appeared to be like paradise, when I first came here. Regent's Park – it seemed like the Hanging Gardens of Babylon.'

'I've never thought of it quite like that,' Ant said.

'Well. No pomegranate trees or waterfalls, or any of that, but the lushness – I thought we'd be so happy here, at first. I really thought things would be different.' She stopped. 'My father brought us down here, to the Bosky, the first summer we came back in 1908. He'd had it built for Mother as a surprise.'

Ant was pulling at a firmly attached rose creeper entwined around the porch overhang. 'A whole house? That *is* a nice surprise.'

'Daddy was rich then. He'd had a run of luck. Somewhere. Biarritz, I think. Not really sure.' Aunt Dinah turned away and started hacking at the ground. 'We moved so often. He'd get asked to leave his regiment, gambling debts and all that, but he was so charming they'd often find him a new job somewhere else.'

'Did he have many debts?'

She nodded, cleared her throat, tucked a loose tendril of hair behind her ear. 'Oh, yes, and a debt of honour is the most serious of all. We'd have to leave quite suddenly, sometimes.' She smiled, but it didn't reach her green eyes. 'But when his luck was in . . .' Dinah smiled. 'We lived high on the hog, not that there's much hog in Syria or India. He was the most generous man. That's the thing, you see, about gamblers – often they do it to make people love them, make them happy. Poor Daddy. Even after he died, I felt desperate for him.'

'How did he die?'

She shook her head. 'Oh, Ant. You never knew? He shot himself.'

'No.' Ant was horrified.

'I'm afraid so.' She swallowed, closed her eyes. 'He spent a month down here, kitting it all out, he ordered everything himself. Daddy! He always was wonderful with homes, knew how to make them cosy and beautiful, Mummy just wasn't interested in that sort of thing, she'd rather have been outside with the horses. Daddy found the man to build the house, someone who'd built villas in Simla, up in the mountains in India. He chose all the furniture, he went to the Army and Navy and even picked out the dinner service and the cutlery. All by himself. It was his grand project. Then we all went down there for the summer. I hadn't seen dear Rosemary for years and years. That's the first time I met your dear father, he was just a baby then, such a cherub. Oh, we all had a wonderful time. It was – yes, it was the happiest I think I'd ever seen my father. It was the happiest I've ever been – but it was all a lie, you see.' Her eyes were fixed on a point in the distance, out to sea.

'We caught crabs. We played endless mah-jong, the proper rules for four.'

'What do you mean, the proper rules?'

'Never mind. Well, and we sailed, at Brownsea. He was a wonderful sailor . . . He'd got a new commission with a regiment in Yorkshire. I think Mummy thought the worst was over.' She cleared her throat and looked around, back in reality. 'Then he disappeared one morning. Gone off to the Riviera. Gambled the rest away and was so in hock they arrested him. Had him brought back to England and then it all came out, the house, everything in it, all paid for with money he didn't have, money he owed . . . They as good as gave him the gun. We were here . . . having a picnic on the beach . . . We heard the shot and we ran back up to the house . . . Mummy found him on the porch . . . One does feel rather angry that he did it there. Silly, really.' She let her hands fall to her side. He watched her as she turned and looked at the house, as if seeing it again for the first time in ages.

'I'm so sorry, Aunt D. I never knew. Daddy never said—'

'Well, we just didn't discuss it – one didn't, you know.' Aunt Dinah smiled sadly. 'But that first summer . . . Gosh, yes, then it all changed. He died, and Rosemary moved up to Northamptonshire and Mummy went with her, and I was in London studying at Bedford College – I didn't see them for years and years . . .' She trailed off. 'It really was the end of our family.'

There was a silence. 'Poor us,' she said, after a short pause. 'Don't gamble, Ant, not even once. It gets into the blood. It's bad for you. Let's change the subject, shall we?'

'How did you become an archaeologist?'

'A good question. Oh, by bothering people. I went to stay with an old family friend in Damascus after I'd taken my degree and then the Great War broke out and I was rather stuck there. So I palled up with a nice chap who was studying the columns of the temple at Baal, and then I travelled along the Silk Route to Babylon, and then on to Ur. By camel, Ant dear, it was marvellous. The Gate of Ishtar, Nebuchadnezzar's palaces and treasures – he besieged Jerusalem, you know. The start of history, and it was all there, just under the ground, more and more appearing every day. I stayed to help and I went to Ur for a season too and I became rather a talisman – one had a run of luck with finding a few things and so one was rather more welcome after that.' She shrugged, as though a lone female travelling by camel from Syria to excavate ancient Babylonian sites was utterly normal. 'So when I came back to London to help catalogue it all they gave me a job at the BM and that's when I met Daphne. She lived in a terrible serviced flat in Kensington, costing an arm and a leg, and the porter used to try and put his hand up your skirt. Honestly, Ant. In the lift. Don't do that to girls when you're grown up, will you? Don't ever do that.'

'I won't,' he said, fervently.

Dinah handed him the branch. 'On the pile with the wood that can be dried out, not the wet leaves that can be mulch, please. Where was I? Yes. She was running with rather a fast crowd, not terribly nice, to be honest. She's rather easily led . . . I – anyway. I asked her to move in with me. And we lived together for two years before—' She broke off. 'Forget-me-nots. Lovely. Look, they're out.'

'Before what?'

'I dropped a stone tablet on to a little table by the sofa. She was having a nap. Table had a glass top.'

Ant shook his head, not understanding.

'I remember seeing the cheek open up, the line awfully clean, that's the thing about glass. I gave her the scar.' Ant dropped the branch he was holding. 'Very bad business. Had to have it stitched back up and they did a wonderful job. Still, she caught an infection, was ill for ages.'

'No – goodness. How did it happen?'

Dinah said firmly, 'I was tight. My fault entirely. We had had a row about something – the tablet I was holding, I think. I couldn't regret it more. A silly row.' Her eyes swam with tears. 'I can't remember what and I wish I could. Poor Daphne.'

'I rowed with Papa the last time I saw him,' Ant told her, to make her feel better. 'About boarding school. He wanted me to go, and I didn't. I was horrible to him, and then he left, and he died two weeks later. I wish – if I could just change how we left it. One silly thing.'

'You can't though, can you?' She put her head on one side, looking thoughtful, and hitched her fringed silk shawl around her shoulders. 'Your father was rather keen on you attending his school, wasn't he? He wrote to me about it, when the war broke out, since I was your guardian. Hadn't heard from him for years. I think he wanted to make sure you had the best . . .' Ant's jaw clenched shut, and Dinah pushed a lock of hair out of her eyes. 'Listen, we all make mistakes. I went to Baghdad to escape mine. They'd got a place for me on a dig at the start of a new season and I've always loved Sennacherib, you know, he moved the capital to Nineveh, he built the palaces, the magical gardens . . . that's where I found the angel, you know.' She glanced up at her, above the door. 'Where was I? Yes, so I let Daphne stay in the flat, seemed only right considering it all. And she – she and I—' She stopped. 'I keep having to remind myself it's all gone. I'm free, really.' She smiled, slowly.

'Free?'

'Free of certain obligations. I'd got myself in something of a mess, and now it's all fine.' She cleared her throat. 'So, Ant, will you come back with me, back to Baghdad?'

He thought she'd gone mad. 'Me? Baghdad? How, Aunt D?'

'Not now! When this cruel war is over.' She was rubbing her hands in the cold spring air. 'Baghdad is wonderful. Peaches you pluck off the trees, and bridges made of boats, and minarets shaped like unicorn horns with curling staircases around the outside. You can buy anything in the great bazaar, things you didn't even know you needed, things on the very edge of history – a carpet woven in Isfahan for a queen, or a glazed tile used to decorate a harem in Babylon, or a lovely hoopoe in a cage, I had one for ages. Zoltan used to keep interesting things for me, such a lovely man, he was a Magyar, you know, descended from Attila the Hun. And the food – fresh watermelons, and dates, and meat cooked so it melts in your mouth.' Ant's own mouth watered, the constant hunger, the dream of delicious food. Normally, they tried not to talk about foods they missed. 'Chickens grilled on spits, and lamb, falling to bits off the bone . . . You can buy gold, and frankincense, and myrrh, Ant, we'll live like ancient kings. You'll love it, yes, yes, you will. I'll buy you a camel if you want.' She was smiling. 'Honestly. There's a Bedouin chap near the edge of Damascus who sells camels. And silver teapots.'

'Aren't they awfully uncomfortable?'

'Teapots? Oh, camels. No, perfect shape. I could sit on them for hours.'

'I never know if you're telling the truth or not,' he said, daringly, because she was relaxed and they were telling each other things.

She gave a small, rather sad smile. 'Do believe me, darling. Will you think about it?'

'I will – I—' He was flustered, but he knew it was a lie, that they would never go together to Baghdad. 'Look, I say. Daphne hasn't got anything on you, has she?'

'Oh . . . she wants something but she's not going to get it.' She hesitated, then said with bravado, 'Nothing for you to worry about, dear boy. Promise.'

He didn't believe her, but he slipped his hand inside hers anyway.

Chapter Twenty-One

In 1942 after Daphne moved in for good, Dinah became obsessed with her nephew's schooling. Ant's father had gone to a well-known boys' school in Sussex; there was a full boarding place available the following September. The school was good, it had not yet had to be evacuated, and the number of teachers currently fighting in the war was relatively low, meaning the disruption to lessons was minimal.

'I can't go on teaching you for ever, you know,' she'd said to him at Easter, when this idea had first been mooted.

'Yes, you can,' said Anthony, horrified. 'I don't want to go to school, I don't want to go away.'

'It's what your father wanted. You said so yourself.'

From the moment Ant had let slip about the final time he'd seen his father, he'd regretted it. He ground his teeth from side to side, anxiety pricking him. 'I'm not likely to learn the ways of the world cooped up in a school with several hundred other boys. You're always saying that. You said public schools were a stain on the British psyche.'

'I did, didn't I?' she'd said.

'Do you *want* to send me away?' He glanced from her to Daphne, who had her head in a book, a cigarette in one drooping hand but who he knew, from a certain kind of tension in her still frame, was listening.

Dinah's eyes widened. 'No, no, Ant, dear. I don't want to

send you away, but I think you ought to go. Downham Hall is awfully good, and it's what your father wanted for you, you know that. And I have the money—'

'How? How have you the money all of a sudden?'

'Don't worry about that.'

He said quietly, 'Please don't make me.'

'Oh, Ant, dear. You can't stay here for ever,' she said, gently.

'I know that. But I wouldn't feel right, leaving you alone, in wartime.'

She'd had her back to him, rearranging the mats on the dresser. 'I've got Daphne.'

'I don't think Daphne'll be much help if the Germans attack.'

Daphne looked up from *Gone with the Wind*, which she had borrowed off the vicar's wife. 'Dinah only wants what's best for you, Ant—'

'It's Tony. Honestly, Dinah—' But his great-aunt had turned away from him, and was humming. Almost as if he weren't there.

Yet there was good news, too. With the arrival of summer, gradually Ant became aware for the first time of the sense that the country was fighting back, that they might be up to conquering the enemy. Years later, he would try to explain it to his children, this idea that the outcome of the war was so very perilous for months, even years of his life, and that they all expected at any moment for the Battle of Britain to be lost, or the bombing to inflict enough damage for the country to be unable to defend itself. They never believed him. 'Don't be silly, Daddy, the Battle of Britain was a glorious victory,' Ben informed him once in a solemn voice.

'Yes, but only because we very nearly didn't win,' Tony had told him.

'That's very unpatriotic. Miss Beale says it was being patriotic that helped us all fight Hitler and win the war.'

Tony couldn't explain to a nine-year-old the terror of hearing the planes go over, wondering if this time would be it. The dreariness of dreaming of food, of constant hunger. The cold – it was always cold. The nightmares of his parents dying . . . How at one point he'd remembered saying to Dinah, 'We will win, won't we?' and she replying, 'I don't know, Ant dear. I'm afraid it might all be over for us.'

But the nightly bombing raids had slowed – just a little. Some evacuees had gone back to London that summer. The Germans were losing in Russia – word was they couldn't take Stalingrad. The army was already exhausted, and that was before the Russian winter set in. The Americans were in the fight now, fresh and unbattered. Something, steadily, was changing. With the arrival of summer and the introduction of Double Summer Time, to give people even more time to do things in the evenings, there was a feeling of hope around, you could smell it, taste it, for the first time in years and years.

The big event of the summer was that Reverend Goudge had taken it upon himself to put on a play. The village drama society had suffered from the onset of war and almost folded. The previous year the village hall had been strafed by guns from a low-flying Messerschmitt and caught fire, burning down to nothing. The hall was where wakes, wedding parties, choir rehearsals, Girl Guides and drama society productions had once taken place and now Reverend Goudge, with his usual enthusiasm, had decided that, for the good of the village, the drama society should be resurrected. He would direct a production of *A Midsummer Night's Dream*.

A stage had been made using driftwood from the beach and wooden beer crates donated by the village pub. It was July, unnaturally hot even for the time of year, still and humid. The group was of all ages, a ragtag mixture of evacuees and those locals either not fighting or not old enough to work, yet even so Ant was flattered – and very surprised – to be given the part of Bottom.

'But I'm only fourteen,' he protested.

'Well, we're short of men, dear,' the vicar had said briskly. 'You're fourteen but you look twenty these days and the voice is wonderful. Bottom's the key to the whole thing. You'll be marvellous. Just pretend you're doing one of your plays out on the porch.'

He would play Bottom again, and Lysander, and Oberon, to great applause, and he would direct the play too, but it was this production that he always remembered, when details of others had long been forgotten. The donkey's head, made out of an old brown cushion of indeterminate hide, the smell of grease-paint and damp and sweat, the thrill of transforming, of becoming this utterly different being, a dolt, a lascivious fool, sloughing off the sadness and confusion of things. It was addictive, this sensation, with only one drawback: for the entire length of the run – three nights – he'd have to pretend to be in love with Julia Fletcher, who was playing Titania.

This summer Julia seemed even more grown up, wearing voluminous see-through clothing in layers and walking out early on the hills, declaiming poetry and the like. She picked flowers, and called them by their names, making up rhymes about them. She was always saying hello and trying to get him to come over to their house for tea, or to go on bike rides. Ant was shy. She was annoying, even if she did have a nice actual, real laugh and always shared her sandwiches. Dinah said it was difficult, living with Alastair Fletcher.

'She's a young girl. Everyone tries on different clothes for size before they decide who they're going to be. Who cares if she wants to wear long dresses and waft around pretending she's the Constant Nymph? She'll grow out of it. There's no harm in her. I think she's a sweet girl.'

Even worse than Julia was Ian, her brother, who still popped up at odd moments around corners and seemed to be watching you all the time through his hooded, slitted eyes and who said things like, 'Is your aunt happy now her friend's here, her friend Daphne? Hm? Did you hear me, Wilde?'

After most rehearsals Ant would leave as swiftly as possible to avoid walking home with them: it was a great fiction still maintained between Alastair Fletcher and Aunt Dinah that their charges got on well. If he couldn't get away quickly enough, he'd hang around until they'd gone, and talk to the ladies assisting with the production, or the vicar, then help to put the sets and props away. He liked old ladies. He liked vicars. He liked the gentle reassurance of village life, the humming sense of making do and community that bound them all together in those difficult days, and he'd rather spend his time with them; sometimes one of them might slip him a piece of cake, give him a warm kiss or share some story about his father when he was little.

One night, however, as he was walking home in the evening dusk after a nice chat with some of the ladies who were making his costumes, his luck ran out. He was waylaid by Julia Fletcher, who dragged him off the road into a lay-by. She'd obviously been lying in wait for him, half an hour or more.

As Anthony rebounded against the springy turf-and-ivy of the built-up hedgerow she gripped his upper arm.

'Here, let go,' he said, recovering from the shock of being abducted like this, and by a girl. And he couldn't say what he wanted to, which was, *It'll be dark soon. We have to get back before it's dark.*

But she said nothing, only smoothed her wild hair back with her nail-bitten hands.

'Look here – are you all right?' Anthony had asked, rather alarmed at her strange expression and silence.

'I say, are those pink forget-me-nots?' she said, waving a small flower yanked from the hedgerow at him. '*Hope's gentle gem, the sweet forget-me-not.* Beautiful, aren't they? Aren't they? Don't you think? I *love* flowers.'

'Oh. Don't know. Don't really mind them.'

'Mind them! Ha!' She gave a too-loud, world-weary laugh. 'Such a boy!'

'My aunt likes them. She uses them. Camomile in tea, and that sort of thing.' Ant peered at the flower she was waving at him. 'That's not a forget-me-not, anyway. That's deadly night-shade.' He removed it gently from her hand. 'You really should learn what's what. It's fearfully poisonous, Julia, I wouldn't – oh!'

For she had pushed him against the hedge and kissed him, messily, frantically. Anthony was taken wholly by surprise, and stood rigidly waiting for her to finish, and when she broke away, she laughed and said, 'Oh, goodness. I got you all wrong.'

'What do you mean?' he said, stung.

'Well, I wanted to have a passionate interlude, and I thought you'd be ideal. But you've never kissed anyone before, have you?'

Surprise made Ant honest. He shook his head. 'Course I haven't. Who is there to kiss around here?'

Julia laughed again, theatrically, and kissed him again, and Anthony found, this time, that the position of her body against his was different and he liked it. He found he liked too her soft but firm tongue in his mouth, and he moved his head a little so they were actually kissing, and then put his arms around her, and felt her move against him, and that was even better. She tasted of something bitter and stale but her mouth and lips were wet and full, and as she sucked at him he found himself kissing her back, sliding his tongue into her mouth: he didn't have time to think about it, because that was obviously what you did.

After an awfully long time – his erection was cramped in his slightly too-tight shorts, and starting to hurt, and he was worried that he might embarrass himself over her if she didn't stop – he pulled away from her, and she fell back, pushing her hair out of her eyes again in a dramatic fashion. 'There, damn you,' she said, self-satisfied. 'There you go, isn't that what you wanted?'

'No,' said Anthony, truthfully. 'Not at all. But I liked it when I got used to it.'

Julia looked a little disconcerted, and annoyed; this kind of talk was obviously not in the dramatic scene she had written in her head. 'That's all you're going to say to me?'

'Oh, well,' said Anthony. 'I say, in that case, thanks.' He glanced at the violet-and-blue sky. 'We should get back—'

'Are you afraid of the dark?'

'Course not,' he said quickly. 'Don't be silly.'

'Oh. 'Cause if you are I collect glow-worms. I keep them in a jar. You can have some if you want.'

'What for?'

'Well, they glow, don't they? I keep them outside the front door for when I'm coming back from walking in the lanes at night. Or in my room. They just . . . glow.'

He couldn't help it; he laughed, and she smiled back at him.

'Glow-worms glow,' he said. 'I'll remember that.'

'They're lovely. Makes a bit of light. Not enough to break the blackout,' she added hastily and she gave him a smile, a natural smile this time, and her face shone. 'But enough. I'll find you some. You'll see.'

He shrugged. 'Fine. All right, then. But look up deadly night-shade in the library, or ask for a book on flowers for your birthday, or something like that. Honestly, you'd die if you ate those berries.'

'Oh, you bloody little fool,' said Julia, spirits undampened by this admonition, and she walked on a little way ahead of him. Ant wondered where she got her conversation from – she talked like someone who'd copied phrases into a book to be reused. But he followed her back home again, down the verdant lane, heavy with the scent of late-summer honeysuckle. He was rather surprised but not displeased with the turn the evening had taken and absent-mindedly nudged his crotch with his knuckles, wondering if the events of the last hour would ever happen again. His lips tingled. When she turned off towards her house with a cheery wave of her hand he waved back, and turned to watch her go in, her halo of hair bouncing between her slim shoulder blades. Gosh, he thought. I wasn't expecting that.

He walked down the path, hearing the sound of the sea sloshing in the bay below, the constant pull and pluck of the tide. He was thinking about Julia's lips on his, the feeling of her body against him, wondering why she was *like* that – when he heard voices.

'I'm sure – dear Daphne – I don't. I can't.'

'You can, Dinah. Just one more. Come on, dearest.'

'I've said before, you know I have! Let's not talk about it any longer. I don't want us to fall out . . .'

The waves and the wind were too loud, and he came closer to the house, and the sandy crunch of his feet on the path seemed unbearably loud.

'. . . have to do it once more. I'm sorry but you do. For him.'

'Yes.' There was a long pause. 'For him. You will – you will be extremely discreet, won't you?'

'Oh, yes. They don't suspect a thing. A nice English girl like me.'

They must have moved about for he couldn't hear the next few exchanges. But as he crept to the balustrade of the porch, straining to hear, Dinah said, 'I suppose in wartime everyone does what they must.'

'Tell yourself that, darling.' Daphne gave a low, amused laugh, which chilled Ant to the very bone. 'Go on, do.'

The French window opened, and he shrank behind the house, out of sight, and saw something being thrown out into the shivering mass of wild flowers and nettles by the house. It shook, rattled in the wind.

Hair. Human hair.

Ant began whistling loudly, then climbed the steps of the porch. He swung into the sitting room, banging the door casually loudly. Daphne looked up at him, in annoyance, alarm.

'You're back early.'

'Well—' he began, and then saw his aunt. All her hair had gone, cut into an uneven bob. Ribbons of grey and brown lay on the parquet floor. Dinah patted her neck.

'It feels very odd. But it was Daphne's idea.' She turned towards him, and she seemed intensely vulnerable, her eyes huge, cheekbones jutting out. The hair around her skull was greyer, the muscles at the back of her neck fine, and fluted. 'I used to have it like this, it's rather nice to go back to it . . . It's all right, isn't it, Ant? Not too dramatic?'

He felt very angry. She looked totally different. 'It's lovely, Aunt D. Very dashing.' He turned to Daphne. 'Why?'

Daphne shrugged. 'I was bored.' She gave a small smile. Ant realised then that he hated her.

Chapter Twenty-Two

It was Reverend Goudge who had first pointed it out to him, the final night of *A Midsummer Night's Dream*, leaning against the wall, eating a greengage, plump face shining in the sweaty close heat of canvas. 'You should think about acting, Anthony dear.'

He hadn't understood. In fact, as he struggled out of his thick theatrical tights which Mrs Goudge had proudly unearthed at a jumble sale, Ant thought he was castigating him for something. 'I – yes, sir. I did *try* to.'

He tugged at the gusset as the Reverend Goudge made a choking sound. Swallowing the final piece of his greengage, he said, 'I meant as a career, dear. You are very good, in fact: you make Bottom interesting. The man's an idiot and I don't know what you did but it was something to make me care about him.'

Ant paused and then shook his head, smiling the disarmingly charming grin which Daphne had once told him he possessed and advised him to use whenever necessary. As often with Daphne's advice, it was useful, even though it made him feel as though he were acting offstage, too, something he didn't ever want to do. 'Oh, well, thank you. Thank you very much, sir.'

'It's true.' The vicar stared at him appraisingly. 'It's the same with the little plays you used to do on the porch. Always the same. Doesn't matter whether you're playing a young village maiden or a hunchback or a fat old vicar like me, you always make them seem real, Ant dear.'

Around him, in the makeshift tent erected in the vicarage gardens, which acted as 'backstage', rather in the manner of a Restoration troupe of strolling players, bohemian chaos reigned. It was the last night of the run (of three, but they considered themselves professionals now) and a heady atmosphere prevailed: Jane Goudge had produced some elderberry wine, and Ant had been allowed a glass of his own. Helena and Demetrius, respectively the village schoolmistress and Jim the postmaster from Swanage, who had only one leg, were dancing slowly together next to two candlesticks, which sputtered in the gloom. Joe Gage had remembered all his lines, and in fact had unintentionally brought the house down on successive evenings. It was still not yet dark.

Ant felt exhilarated, joyful at the applause and the attention. Despite the fact that he didn't at all care for his character either, he loved the play. He knew all the lines. He loved being backstage and watching the girls transform themselves, the excited chatter, the glimpse of the audience filing into their seats. Only once had a siren disrupted proceedings, halfway through the second night, and he had led the cast offstage and to safety in the cellar of the vicarage, then come back to direct the audience to safety.

'What a nice young man,' someone had told Dinah and Daphne as they made their way out of the front row.

'He's my great-nephew,' he'd heard Dinah say. 'A most *satisfactory* one, too.'

This, the broken voice, and the regular kissing sessions with Julia Fletcher which were now an accepted fact of walking home after rehearsals, all made him feel unexpectedly potent for the first time, the ruler of his own domain. 'The cock of the walk,'

Daphne had called him at breakfast a couple of weeks ago, and Dinah had laughed.

'What does that mean?' he'd said, unsettled by their chuckles.

'Oh, my dear Ant,' Dinah had said, 'she's only teasing. You're suddenly rather grown up this summer, that's all.'

He didn't like it when they talked in riddles, or laughed together at him: the summer had gone on, hot and curiously calm. Somehow, and he wasn't sure when, Dinah had won the battle over schools and he was off to Downham Hall in September, much against his will. He didn't remember agreeing to this: Dinah knew how to avoid unpleasant topics, he didn't know how, but she just did. Those who underestimated her, who saw her just as a silly eccentric in long baggy clothes who talked too much, were fools. For starters, she wasn't old. She was still quite young, compared to the vicar or Alastair, and her face, now it wasn't hidden by all that hair, was quite young and pretty. She wasn't silly, either. She knew and understood far more than Bob Dolney, the rather pompous young curate who had flat feet and was a Communist and spent a lot of time talking about Stalin. Or Mr Hill, the local solicitor who professed to know everything about ancient history and whom she'd listen to politely even when he was telling her about things she herself had probably dug up . . . And she knew other things, too, like how to barter with the man at the garage who looked after their car, and even though she was hopeless around the house, Ant wondered if sometimes, just sometimes, she cultivated this air of eccentricity. Just a little.

Walking back this time in the purple haze of night, listening to the crickets in the hedgerows and the faint, very faint sound of merriment from the vicarage fading into the distance as they approached the barbed-wire beach, Tony was silent, thinking about the glorious days of the play now behind him and about what Reverend Goudge had said, *You should think about acting*.

Beside him walked Julia and Ian. He could tell Julia was desperate to get rid of her younger brother; she kept sighing dramatically and making crude attempts to shake him off. 'Oh, Ian, I've forgotten my bag, could you be a *darling brother* and run back to the tent?' Ian, apparently oblivious, was clinging to them like a limpet. Tony himself was deep in thought, only half listening to Julia's story about a poem she was writing about a symbolic poppy in an English hedgerow – she kept flinging a scarf around her neck, red and trailing, which didn't go at all with her rather pretty cotton dress – and Ian's strange, stilted replies.

It had never occurred to Ant before then that he could be an actor, like his father – Philip Wilde had been away so often Ant had no clear memory of his father, nor what exactly he did: he really had been a self-absorbed little boy, he thought, treated like a prince by his mother when he was actually very ordinary. He could remember his father's one big part, as Captain Hook in *Peter Pan* in the West End, decked out in the obligatory wig and cutlass. He used to practise his fencing steps in the kitchen. Ant had found this thrilling; he'd read *Peter Pan* and this was something about his father's strange job he could understand; but he couldn't remember anything else about it.

Besides, who knew when the war would end and if it ever did would there be theatres, and would they want actors, or would they want dancing girls and films instead, not old-fashioned plays? He couldn't really remember life without it; only last week Dinah and Daphne had both laughed, and Dinah had hugged him impetuously when he'd said, 'But what will happen to newspapers after the war? They should carry on printing them.' He had thought newspapers had been invented to report on the war: he couldn't recall a time when there was different news. And the other children couldn't, either. Julia had told him she'd asked Alastair at Christmas if Hitler had always been leader of Germany and was surprised when her normally unbending father had hugged her, tears in his eyes. No, he'd said. No, and he won't be for much longer, I promise you.

The grimness of starting school, of breaking the spell of life with Dinah, hung over him like a cloud; he couldn't shake off the feeling of dread he had about it and, now the play was over, leaving the Bosky was edging towards him around the corner. It would be dark and cold, and he wouldn't know anyone. He couldn't go back to being Wilde who mucked around with other stupid boys and listened to their stupid stories. He didn't like boys, he didn't like the atmosphere of boys together. He liked women, and being with them. And he liked living with Aunt Dinah.

'Got cramp,' he called to Julia and Ian, sitting suddenly down in the road and untying his laces. 'It's these boots. Go on without me.'

'Oh,' said Julia, stopping in surprise. She put her jar of glow-worms down on the ground. 'Do you need help?'

'Damn it. I'm off,' said Ian, striding grumpily ahead, and Tony could hear him swearing under his breath.

'Oh, well,' said Julia, shaking her hair out, and smiling down at him.

That night even Tony was surprised at the sudden ease with which they were alone and he proceeded to go as far as he had yet done with Julia. This time was slightly different: this time it was both of them shuffling into the shelter of the siding off the lane, pressing one another frantically against the gate, and for once it was he who fumbled with her clothes and told her what to do and she, at first rather unsure – she was keen on being the director in everything – who acquiesced, gratifyingly quickly. The floral dress was unbuttoned within minutes, and she insinuated his hand into her cotton briefs, and let him waggle his finger around. It was wet and thrilling and she brought him to a climax with her clumsy hands – his penis jutting out of his shorts – all too quickly.

'You ought to do it back to me,' she said, after he'd recovered, head sagging on his chest, breathing heavily.

'Do what?' He reached for her; he wondered if they could do it again, and could kiss in the meantime.

'Make me feel the same way. You should do it to me. We do it to each other at school.'

Tony obviously looked confused. 'Do what?'

'Stop saying Do What! That!' Julia pointed down at his limp penis, at her dress, covered with his fluid. 'You can make girls feel like that. And you should, if you rub it harder, if you try a bit harder.'

'I didn't know.' He felt as though he'd made a major social faux pas; obviously this was something one did, obviously he'd got it wrong. 'I'm sorry. Show me then.' He reached for her brassiere, but she began buttoning herself up again.

'No, not tonight. I'd better go back. Ian will tell Dad if I'm not back soon. He'd love to catch us out one day, you know.'

'Your father? He likes me,' said Tony, confidently.

'He might like you because you're Dinah's nephew but if he thought you were fiddling with me in a hedgerow he'd probably strangle you. He's one of those Victorian types who thinks the piano legs should be covered up. Sees sex absolutely everywhere, poor ducks, probably because it's been so long since he's known the ways of woman.'

'Julia, don't,' he said. 'That's your father, after all.'

'Gosh, you sound like him when you get that stern look on

your face. It's all just bodies, isn't it?' She smiled at him; he thought how nice she was especially now she wasn't trying to be dramatic. Her teeth were even and white, and her freckled cheeks were flushed. Suddenly, he felt a rush of foolish affection for her, and wished she wouldn't go.

'What'll we do now the play's over?' he said, half to himself, a dreadful flatness seeming to fall on him, from somewhere high above. He felt awful.

'How about a bike ride tomorrow?' said Julia. 'We could sail over to Brownsea. I was going to go anyway; they've an old fort there I want to sketch for my art teacher. She told us to draw monuments in case they're bombed and lost to the nation. We could take a picnic and swim off the side. I say, would you like to?'

It was said with such artless enthusiasm he grinned at her. 'I'd love to. Thank you.'

'We'll leave Ian out of it, shall we? He's packing for school anyway.'

'Don't mention school,' said Tony, the old sick feeling returning to his stomach again. 'I don't want to go.'

'Fine, we won't talk about it at all, we'll just have a jolly day. Bring some bread if you can, I've some fish paste and heaps of strawberries and greengages. Bye then,' she said, almost cheerily, as though they'd been out picking wild flowers or something, and then she ran off into the night.

Ant followed her down the lane, face raised to the sky, feeling the breeze on his cooling skin. The night was dark with no moon and he negotiated the path and side steps up to the front of the house; he was used to walking in the dark now, where formerly it had terrified him. Entering the Bosky from the entrance on the lane, he ascended the stairs to find his great-aunt standing looking out of the still-open door on to the porch.

Her arms were planted on her hips; she was bent slightly at the waist, as if wanting to bend forwards, but unable to.

'Hello, Aunt Dinah?'

She hadn't heard him come in and she turned slowly towards him; he couldn't see her face. 'Ant dear . . . yes, of course. How was it?'

'It was terrific. Reverend Goudge, he said I should think about – I say, are you all right, Aunt Dinah?'

Looking at her, he understood for the first time the cliché 'white as a sheet'. Her skin was a ghastly colour, chalky and deathly pale, as though she had aged many years in one night. *I wouldn't recognise her if I walked past her in the lane*, he found himself thinking.

'I'm sorry we didn't come, Ant dear. We were home – yes, I should have come.'

'What's happened?' He looked around, his euphoric glow draining slowly away, and then he noticed for the first time the disorder of the sitting room. Two glasses knocked over and smashed upon the floor, Aunt Dinah's spectacles twisted and broken, lying atop a novel, which had been damaged, as though stepped on. The cushions of the sofa were disordered. The great wooden wireless had fallen backwards, and sputtered intermittently into the silence, and all the boxes, the ones still to be sorted through, were opened, contents spilling out on to the floor.

Dinah said nothing. Ant bent forwards, picked up her spectacles. 'Aunt Dinah,' he said, handing them to her, and as he did he saw the droplets of blood on the old and worn sofa cushions.

'What's that?' he said. 'Are you hurt?' It was her stillness, the frozen quality of the scene, that scared him the most. 'What happened? What did you do?'

At last she said, 'She tricked me. She tried to make me – but I wouldn't.' She looked down at him, her large face haggard with misery. 'We had a row.'

'What about?'

'Telling the truth. I'm not good at it. You must forgive me, Ant. I've lied to you. And I lied—' Like a child, she wiped her nose with the arm of her sleeve. 'I lied about that, too!'

'There's nothing to forgive, Aunt D—' He came around, and sat next to her, and put his arm around her thin shoulder. Her shapeless khaki blouse was stiff with grime. She'd always been relaxed about washing clothes, and personal hygiene; lately, though, even he, a teenage boy, had begun to find the smell of her a bit much.

'I say, where's Daphne?' he asked, wrinkling his nose. 'Why don't we have a celebratory—'

'She's gone back to London. She – she was angry with me. I wouldn't do as she asked.' Her thin shoulders shook. 'She said it was the last time, and then she asked again, and again . . .'

'What do you mean?' Ant bit one finger, and stared at her; it was awful, seeing her this upset.

'I – I made a mistake. Gambled at long odds. Please, Ant, dear—' She broke away, pressing her shaking hand to her mouth, suppressing a sob. 'No more, not now.'

She pushed him aside, and thudded downstairs, her tread on the stairs shaking the whole house. The door to the porch slammed shut, in a sudden breeze, leaving him alone in the unrelenting darkness.

Chapter Twenty-Three

1987

On the day of his wedding, Ben woke up at 5 a.m. wide awake and knew he wouldn't be able to get back to sleep. He lay in his childhood bedroom, wallpapered in pastel zigzags, the tattered posters of Bowie and Roger Moore in *Live and Let Die* opposite him. He could hear the wood pigeons cooing out in Marble Hill Park, smell the distant and distinct scent of autumnal damp from the river. He stood up, foggily, and looked out of the little window. He'd stayed away so long. It was on autumn mornings like this that the river was perhaps loveliest of all.

For a while he lay there, thinking about all that had to be done that day. He knew, as did his parents, that Mads was apt to worry and become close to hysterical if overwhelmed. She found large gatherings terrifying – he hadn't really realised this until they'd started going out in Bristol, having previously only really seen her at Worth Bay where everyday life was fairly relaxed: his parents, he saw now, had this wonderful ability of making everyone believe everything was running smoothly, that life was grand, whether it was the truth or not; it was immensely comforting. He'd had to reject them and move away to discover how hard a trick that was to pull off.

In crowded student pubs or gigs Mads was pale and silent, trying to pretend all was well. 'I love it!' she'd say, bouncing up and down with enforced enthusiasm at a group of shaggy-haired, leather-clad, guitar-wielding youths and turning that huge smile on him. 'Don't you? Isn't it great, Ben?' He'd take her hand and find it was icy cold and clammy. Gradually he came to realise she was doing it for him, because she wanted him to enjoy himself. So much of what she did was to make him happy. Ben, full of young-man swagger, found this alarming, and then immensely touching. He thought of it as a privilege to be loved by her. Knowing what he knew now about her grim childhood it seemed to him to be a miracle that she could trust anyone. He and Cord had been too young to fully understand the truth about the strange clothes she wore, how hungry and thin she was, how dirty.

Mads told him and Cord one summer that she ran away from her father, when Ian Fletcher had left the kitchen window open. It wasn't until after their engagement when they went back to Beeches before it was sold that he went inside the drab, miserable house and saw the window in question – the size of an A4 sheet of paper, high off the ground. 'I stood on some old books to climb out of it,' she told him as they stood in the dank kitchen. 'I think that's why he hit me when I came back, because he didn't like his books being disturbed.'

'Where did you run to?'

'Oh, well, that's the thing, I didn't know you all yet, so I couldn't run to you. I ran up and down the beach for ages and then I was so tired, I fell asleep on the sand, and in the morning, I woke up, and there were all these families arriving on the beach, to play and have fun, and they all stared at me like I was . . .' She had shaken her head, hair flying around her. 'Rubbish. Scum. This mum, she had a lovely flowery pinafore on, and she was giving the children a pear each. It looked lovely. And she looked really nice. So I smiled at her. I was all covered in sand and she pulled the children close towards her as though I'd give them a disease.' He had pulled her close to him, then, his heart lurching. 'So I went back. I didn't know what else to do. Who'd believe me? Where would I go?'

'Oh, sweetheart. How old were you?'

'Seven. Maybe six.' She had considered the question seriously, staring up at the kitchen window. 'It was her face. I realised no one would help me. Then I found you lot . . . I found you . . . And Aunt Jules came back.' He had held her tight, but she pulled away from him. 'I've been very lucky, really.' That was always what she'd say. 'I'm so lucky.' And he didn't believe her, not for a minute.

Ben's first job, working as a lowly second assistant director on a British comedy, which Simon had got for him, had gone well and he'd stayed in touch with the director. He was writing scripts in his spare time, and going in for meetings with whoever would have him for, even though he was young, he knew he wanted to direct. Big, splashy *Jaws*-style films, small, intense art-house films – anything and everything. Always had done. Through the director of the comedy film Ben was recommended for a gig as assistant director on a very successful soap made by BBC Wales. Everyone said this would be the best kind of experience, but it meant he had to relocate to Cardiff for three months; they pushed the wedding back a year. He found being able to concentrate on his job and on the screenplay he was writing an enormous relief, and Mads, who had just started working as a design engineer at the Rolls-Royce factory in Filton, confessed on one of his weekends back home in Bristol that she did, too. 'I wish it was over already,' she'd said, clutching his hand as they sat on the pavement of a crowded Clifton pub drinking strong cider, the very pub outside which they'd had their first conversation after all those years. 'Already married, snug as bugs in our little flat, nothing else to worry about other than being together.'

Despite that she had wanted a large wedding, a party. That was what you did, of course, these days, though Althea kept pointing out that in her day weddings weren't the five-ringed circuses they'd become today. 'I was married in a dove-grey bouclé suit at Chelsea registry office with no bridesmaids. I wore the suit for years after and there were fifteen guests and we had lunch afterwards at the Arts Club and then we all went home,' she was fond of saying to absolutely anyone who'd listen whenever the subject of the wedding came up. And to Ben, she'd add: 'Mads wants a huge wedding because she thinks it's what you ought to do, not because that's what she wants.'

Ben agreed, but he thought it was more than that. Mads wanted what Cord had called a 'Look, I'm Officially Part of This Family Now' party and though his sister had said it in a rather cutting way, there was truth to what she said. So the bridesmaids were four old friends of Mads's from school whom he'd never met and Mads scarcely saw, who were to be decked out in huge coral taffeta affairs with crowns of baby's-breath; the church was vast, enough to hold Mumma and Daddy's theatre friends, and just right for Cord's voice for while she had point-blank refused to be a bridesmaid, she'd reluctantly agreed to sing.

'I don't want people looking at me, when it's your day,' she'd said.

'I do,' said Mads. 'The more people looking at you the less they're looking at me, and you don't mind it, and I absolutely hate it.'

The reception was at Marble Hill House, a few hundred metres from River Walk, and they would come back to his parents' house afterwards for more drinks and music, and a lunch for family and close friends the next day – Ben made a note to check that the chaps from Oddbins had put the champagne in the vault, where it would remain cool.

That set him to wondering whether, if they hadn't, there would be enough time to chill it later, and eventually the director in him realised it might be best if he got up and did it himself. He knew he wouldn't sleep any longer. Ben pulled on his Levi's and a T-shirt and padded silently downstairs, past the cavernous drawing room, scene of so many Wilde parties but now still, grey-yellow in the morning light. In the hall he put on his old wellington boots, gazing up the stairs at the huge window that ran up the back of the house. The first time Madeleine had come back to River Walk, only a few months ago because they really weren't in London that often, she'd been rather over-whelmed.

'I stayed here once, the night before I went off on a French exchange. I remembered you lived in a massive house,' she said, squeezing his arm as he guided her over the porch and into the kitchen. 'But, God, it's actually rather terrifying, isn't it?'

To Ben it was just home, where he'd spent most of his life. He neither loathed it the way he loathed walking through the gates of his school, where the legend *Huc Venite Pueri Ut Viri Sitis* (they come here as boys, but leave as men) in huge letters greeted every boy as he arrived; nor did he adore it and dream of it the way he did with the Bosky, the way they all did, wishing away the dull and grey months of winter, praying for summer to come so they might be there once again . . . River Walk was where his Lego was stored and his school books stacked neatly into the bookcase in his room; it was where he had slept the most nights in his life, but after he'd left home and gone to Bristol University he'd barely thought of the place, much less come back. It was just easier to stay away.

The champagne was perfectly safe in the chilly, damp vault under the garden at the rear of the house.

Not quite sure what to do with himself now he was up, Ben walked through the long, dew-sprinkled garden and let himself on to the lane which led down to the river. It was very quiet and, when he reached the Thames, utterly still. It seemed as though the weeping willow at the bank was being sucked into the water, inky black and hardly moving. Across the river, the side of Ham House glowed a fierce flaming red in the rising sun's glare. A moorhen moved silently through the water. He could hear a dog barking, far away. Ben sank his hands into the pockets of his jacket and gave a deep sigh, which juddered as he exhaled.

He was twenty-three, and he would be married today, and after that everything would be different. To many of his friends it was a ridiculous age to be settling down. Several of them were still studying. A couple of them had never been to a wedding at all and were incredulous.

'Why do you need to get *married*?' his old school friend – his one friend from school in fact – Bingham, had asked him, only the night before. They'd gone for a drink at the White Swan on the banks of the river. Bingham was heavily into metal, he'd even been to Berlin to watch Motörhead and had a tattoo of the Ace of Spades of which he was inordinately proud. By day George Bingham was a trainee solicitor. He had a girlfriend called Louise, also a Home Counties girl, who was now a punk, with an actual safety pin through her ear – Ben had met her, and she'd taken it out for him, described in minute detail the process of piercing her own ear. She was training to be a nurse, so she'd known what she was doing, she explained. It seemed so normal to them, to be living that life, where you worked and then you played in the evenings and didn't care much about other stuff.

'Why?' Ben had answered. 'Because – I love her, and she loves me, and we want to start our lives together. You know, when you can see the horizon—'

This was how Mads had explained it to him.

'You're the horizon. There's a big empty space in the sky and you're what I've been walking towards my whole life,' she'd told him one freezing winter's night in her little bedroom in Bristol, not long after they'd got together.

Most of Ben's friends who'd studied Drama and Film with him lived in squats off the Gloucester Road and went on marches and had Nelson Mandela posters up on their walls, and watched *Spitting Image* whilst recovering from hangovers on Sunday evenings: it was just what you did. But Mads had a huge South African flag draped out of the window in her tiny flat that she shared with another Engineering student, and a calendar marking the days Mr Mandela had been imprisoned. She wrote letters to the South African embassy every month and to the Chinese about political prisoners, and to the Turks about the Kurds – she wrote a lot of letters. She felt things deeply, he'd always known that about her. Since she was a child.

Ben sat on the curving branch of the willow, shivering in the chill, and watching the light change on the river.

He felt strange, not quite right. He wished he could talk properly to Cord. But she was never there. Since her triumph in *The Marriage of Figaro* she had worked non-stop. When Ben looked back on it, it made complete sense: Cord was born to be a star, a diva on her own terms.

And she used her fame, and her busyness, as a shield to keep them all away. She was quieter, the jaw less firmly set, and her dimmed blue-grey eyes had a weary tinge; her lovely, curving mouth drooped now.

He and Hamish had gone together to the Albert Hall, after she'd telephoned him that day to explain about the previous night.

'I'm so sorry. I couldn't say a thing. Not in that restaurant either – I was sure there was a critic behind us. But I'm going on, Ben, I'm going on. Isotta wouldn't leave her hotel room. Said it was too cold in London and they hadn't provided a driver for her and she couldn't risk getting a black cab.'

Mads was too nervous on Cord's behalf to go, and Mumma and Daddy wouldn't Prom, and couldn't get hold of a ticket, so contented themselves with organising a party-cum-reception back at River Walk. So Ben and Hamish had stood with the other Prommers jammed in towards the back of the oval arena. Ben was glad he was with Hamish. He liked him.

The Countess doesn't appear in the first act. She opens the second with one of the most beloved and difficult arias in opera, 'Porgi, amor'. Ben and Hamish, pushing their way towards the front as the music began again, to the utter disapproval of their fellow concertgoers, had stopped as Cord began to sing, standing stock-still.

There she was, in a long, bullet-grey dress of raw silk, her dark black-brown hair swept in waves away from her heart-shaped face, her serious eyes so grave the blue in them was almost gone. When she sang it was extraordinary: everything seemed to be right with the world, and yet the sound was so sad.

'Restore to me my loved one – or in mercy let me die.'

The surtitles that appeared above the stage as she sang pierced his heart, the slight catch in her voice, the bowed head, the clasped hands . . . she was Cord, yet something else, and her voice was pure, old, everything beautiful.

In that moment Ben loved her completely, but knew that she

had left him, that she was different now. He could never explain it out loud – a higher plane seemed so pretentious. But she was special, to be set apart, because of the gift of her voice, and he understood that. He, Ben, was nothing special, a clever chap, with ideas and drive, he knew that. But he was Mads's and she was his, first and foremost.

What it also gave him, starting that triumphant yet melancholy night, was an understanding of his father, too. He saw, in a way his sister could not yet, that Tony was touched by some genius that he, Ben, didn't have, that Althea, talented as she was, also didn't have. That it tortured him, defined him in some way. And from then on he tried to forgive him for things, to love him. He tried.

The following day the *Evening Standard* alone had had three separate mentions of Cordelia Wilde, daughter of Sir Anthony Wilde, and the ravishing performance she gave having stepped into the shoes of the now miraculously recovered Isotta Cianfanelli. They said she was the next Kiri Te Kanawa. The *Times* critic said she was the most richly enchanting and heart-breaking Contessa he could remember, the perfect blend of acting and singing combined.

> I have no idea how she is able to reach out and so profoundly clutch at my heart when I am seated more than thirty yards away and in the deadening goldfish-bowl acoustics of the Albert Hall. But she does, and it is wholly moving, and electrifying. Yes, I do not know how she does it.

But Ben, hardly breathing, squashed in on either side there in the audience next to a totally still Hamish, had known the answer. He understood then that it was her, that it was simply

Cord being herself up there, singing for the love she desperately wanted but was unable, for whatever reason, to take.

He and Hamish had walked together to the tube station, in silence, and at the entrance Hamish had shaken his hand.

'I've an audition tomorrow so I'm not coming back to your parents'. I've phoned them,' he said. He clapped Ben on the shoulder; he was tall and strong, and it made Ben wince. 'Goodbye, Ben. Give her my love.'

'Give it to her yourself,' said Ben, trying to sound light.

'No, no,' said Hamish. His jaw was set. 'It's not our time. That's it, really.' He took out his wallet, fiddling with something in it, not meeting Ben's eye. 'I've told myself she might have loved me, in another life, if she hadn't had her singing. And I wouldn't want her to be without it, would you?'

Ben shook his head, not sure if he agreed or not.

'Oh, Ben. Good luck to you, laddie, and your lovely Madeleine. I hope you'll be happy. Look after her.'

And he'd walked away, past the V&A, his tall frame setting him apart from the other pedestrians crowding the streets. Some of them gave him admiring looks, and he was oblivious; it was one of his nicest qualities, that he was so unaware of his own presence.

That audition was for *Afternoon of the Raj*, the TV series that would, when it was released the following year, make his name. It took him away from England to India for seven months' filming and was where he met his wife, Sunita, whom he married a year later in Bombay. Ben had heard from him, a battered postcard sent a couple of weeks ago wishing him luck for his own wedding and telling him of the marriage, of their impending parenthood. No mention of Cord. It was as though he had put as much distance between them all as possible. As though he'd known he had to get away from them while he could . . .

Ben shook himself. No point thinking about that on a day like today. He stood up, swinging his arms around him, smiling at the thought of Mads, still sleeping soundly, with any luck. He hoped she wouldn't have lain awake, worrying about things. Biting those thin, furious fingers, those fingers that never ceased activity, whether pulling at hair, touching anything that caught her eye, making him groan in ecstasy. He had seen her in the lab at Bristol once, utterly still, like a dancer, lowering a filament of metal into a test tube, other hand steadily holding the tube. The rest of the time, she was intense, impatient, nervous, and when she did sleep, it was like a child, curled up, feet tangled in her nightdress, hair wrapped around her, face utterly peaceful for once. She was his future. Him and her.

'Ben?' A voice behind him, far enough away that at first he thought he was hearing things, and then again, 'Ben, darling boy, that's you, isn't it?'

Ben jumped, guiltily, as though he'd been caught misbehaving. 'Dad?'

Through the dripping fronds of the willow he could see his father, standing at the end of the lane by the towpath, peering at him. He was in his old gumboots, as he always called them, and the faded blue smock he wore around the house, covered up with an ancient mac that hung by the back door. 'What on earth are you doing up at this hour?'

Ben stood up. 'Oh, I couldn't sleep.'

'Fair enough.' His father took a cigarette from the smock. 'Want one of these?'

'No, thanks.'

'Swig of this?' Tony waved a hipflask, produced from the other pocket of his smock. An old bloke bicycled past them, staring at Tony; Ben flushed. His father did look rather eccentric.

'It's six in the morning.'

'Is that a yes or a no?'

'No, thanks, Dad.'

'Oh. Mind if I do?'

Ben shrugged, in a neutral fashion. By mutual unspoken assent they began to walk south, the rising sun covering them with golden light.

'How are you feeling?'

'Nervous. Bit nauseous, actually.'

'Yes, I remember it well.'

'Do you?'

'Absolutely. Your mother had an ear infection on the day itself. I took her to the doctor. And I was glad, really, though I felt sorry for her of course. But I'd been sitting there in my tiny bedsit feeling sicker and sicker and when she telephoned to say I had to take her to the surgery in Hammersmith it's no exaggeration that I was halfway to running away.'

'No.' Ben looked at his father. 'You didn't mind that it might be bad luck?'

'How so?'

'To see her on the wedding day.'

'Oh, that. Well, we're so superstitious already, we actors. I think that one sort of passed us both by.'

'I never knew that,' said Ben, wondering. 'About the trip to the doctor's.'

'Didn't you?'

'No.' *I know nothing about either of you really, Dad*, he wanted to say. 'Didn't she have family, someone else who could take her?'

'Listen, weddings weren't the productions they are now, cohorts of bridesmaids, cakes with twenty tiers, eight-piece bands and the like. It was small. We wanted it that way, both of us.

Nice lunch afterwards, at the Chelsea Arts Club. Bertie made a speech . . . Her family retired at about five. We pootled off in the car to the Bosky that evening.' Tony's head sank on to his chest, his lips pursed, and he looked upwards. 'I do remember it. So well. Wonder if she does.'

Ben said, suddenly, 'What about your family?'

'What about them?'

'I mean, who was there from your family?'

'Oh, Simon, and of course Bertie, Guy and Olivia, and dear old Kenneth –'

'But your *family*. Didn't you have anyone there of your own?'

There was a short pause. 'Nope. My parents were dead. And Aunt Dinah – well, she wasn't there.'

'Was she dead too?'

His father gave a small smile. 'Do you know, I didn't used to know. But I do now. No, she was alive. But she didn't come. It was a long time ago.' He looked up. 'Well, it's your wedding day. She's not too sad there's no family coming from her side, is she? Old Ian, dead, not a great loss, alas, but she'll miss her aunt, won't she?'

'Aunt Julia? Yes, she's been wonderful to her.'

'She was a good old girl.' He sighed. 'I screwed her, you know. She was an absolute firecracker.'

Ben could feel a flush breaking over him, prickling uncomfortably on his skin. 'Oh. God, Dad.'

'Yes, she made me – well, she knew what she wanted, I can tell you. What a summer we had of it! Dear Jules.' He chuckled, and took another swig, and Ben could feel the old, familiar anger again.

'It's my wedding day, Dad,' he said shortly. 'Cool it on the fruity memories, will you?'

'Sorry. Ben, I do apologise.' His father was silent, and then he laughed bleakly before saying, 'Nothing was fun, then. Nothing. We were afraid, all the time. I used to laugh, when the Cold War was at its height, and young people would say how scared they were. Nothing like it. This was real, gut-squeezing fear, not knowing if we were about to be overrun, conquered, killed in our beds. We knew it was right, too . . .' He trailed off. 'Ben, you know how my mother died, don't you?'

'No, Dad. Of course not. You never talk about her.'

'Well, I survived and she didn't. A bomb. We lived in Camden,' he added, inconsequentially. 'When she came out she had – she had no—' He broke off.

'No what?'

'I was twelve. It's a long time ago. But I still see it, you see. She had no face, on one side, Ben, her face was gone, and no arm or shoulder . . . I could see her bone, her – her bones, splintered, sort of – ah. Very white. Sharp. Sticking out through the cloth, her – her cloth dress. Filthy. *Isn't that stupid*, that's what I kept thinking. She hated mess and it was all so filthy.' He looked down. 'They dug her out and I watched them and then they told me I was *lucky*.' He smiled at his son. 'Lucky, do you hear? My father had been shot out of the sky a few months back and my mother was there on the ground, two yards away, and the only way to identify her was her engagement ring, but they said I was lucky. I couldn't even remember if he had a moustache that last time or not, you see. Couldn't remember.'

He lit another cigarette, with a choking cough. Ben took his hand.

'I'm sorry, Dad.'

'Well, you see. That's where the Bosky came in. I was sent off to live with Dinah and oh, she was wonderful. For a few years it was wonderful, I adored her . . . and then she was gone.'

'What happened to her?'

'I honestly don't know.' His father pushed himself away from the wall. 'Let's not talk about it, not today. Do you have a speech prepared?'

'Well, it's fairly rudimentary.' Ben hesitated, rubbing his arms, for it was cold in the early autumn chill of the day. 'I want to show it to Cord – I meant to ask you about her, Dad,' he said impetuously. 'Doesn't she seem sort of . . . quiet, these days? Have you noticed?'

'How so?'

'Oh, she's so distant. And thin and tragic-looking.'

'She's lost her puppy fat, that's a good thing. She's beautiful.'

'She is – but she seems so sad. Don't you think?'

His father shook his head. 'Nope.'

'Really? You don't think she misses Hamish?'

'She's not you and Mads, Ben darling. She doesn't want to be in love. I should think she enjoys leaving it all behind.' Tony threw a stone into the river. They both watched the ripples spreading outwards till they were lost in the silvery water. 'That idea of dressing up and escaping who you are. This heightened reality where you are only truly present onstage, a controlled dream, and you utterly believe it—' He halted. 'Never mind.'

'No,' said Ben. 'Dad, don't stop. Go on. A controlled dream, you mean like you are only yourself when you're onstage?'

'I suppose so. I imagine it's the same for her.'

'But she doesn't seem very happy.'

'Yes, yes.' His father seemed to accept this as fact without any regret. 'I'm afraid that's the way it is, though.'

'We're so different,' Ben said. 'I never realised it, but we are.'

His father looked at him. 'Yes, darling. You are. In more ways than you think.'

Ben's heart thumped in his chest.

'I know,' he said.

Tony's gaze raked over Ben. 'Ah. You do, do you?' he said, almost to himself. The silence between them was suddenly electric.

Ben cleared his throat. Nerves, adrenaline flooded his body.

'I do,' he said, and he put his hand on Tony's arm. 'I do, Dad. I've known for years.'

'How long?'

'Years, Dad.' *The night I ran away. Why do you think I ran away? Why didn't you ever ask me?* Ben rubbed the stump of his missing fingers, the worn, safe patch. He thought of when Cord had first seen him, in the hospital, and she'd taken his hand, with the black stitches sewing up the torn skin, and she'd kissed his palm. 'I'm so glad you're not dead,' she'd said, three times in a row, her soft cheek rubbing his fingers, the huge grey eyes fixed on him, trembling with tears. 'I'm so glad, Benny. I ate all your pear drops, by the way, I didn't want to but I was worried they'd go sticky and if you were dead you wouldn't want them.'

'How did you find out?'

'It doesn't matter, Dad. It's a long time ago.'

'Don't you want to know—'

'No,' said Ben. 'Like you just said. Let's not talk about it, not today.'

Tony said, 'Ben, darling, look . . .' He looked out over the river, glinting in the morning sun. 'I know I screwed it all up. I wanted the best for you and I kept thinking I knew how to do it and by the time I realised . . .'

Ben kept stroking his finger stump, and he swallowed, and then he put his other hand, his 'good' hand, on Tony's knee. 'Dad. Don't. I mean it. I know you didn't mean to hurt me.'

'I have no control, that's the trouble.'

'I know.' Ben felt the faint stirrings of irritation. 'We all know.

314

But –' He stared at Tony, and felt something shift, the balance of power, something fundamental – 'it's really important you understand I don't want it to change anything. I spent years trying to forget all about it. Not today, all right?'

Tony gave a quick smile. 'Of course, darling. You don't want to ask your mother about it?'

'Absolutely not.' Ben shook his head vigorously.

'What about Mads?'

'I haven't told her . . . not yet.' Ben shifted on his feet. 'I need to, I think.'

Tony nodded, suddenly practical. 'Yes. You should. Does Cord know?'

'I don't think so. But I haven't talked to her properly, not for ages. It's strange,' he said, taking up the thread of Cord again. 'She's a different person now. Her voice – it makes her special. Like you need to look after her, protect it. I wonder where it came from. Mumma says she gets it from her side of the family.'

Tony roared with laughter, hugging his knees. 'My darling, I love your mother very much but the first time I heard her sing I nearly called the wedding off.' He wrinkled his nose, pleased with himself. 'Sounded like cat's guts haling souls out of bodies. What's the line? *Much Ado*. Something like that.'

'Sheep's guts.'

'What? What?'

Ben said with certainty, '*Is it not strange that sheep's guts should hale souls out of men's bodies*. He means lute strings, you know. Not that some woman sounds like a gutted cat.'

'You sure?'

Ben laughed shortly. 'Absolutely. I directed a production of it last year.'

'Really?'

'Yes, Dad. At a pub theatre by the docks in Bristol. It went down rather well.'

'You did?' His father sounded amazed.

'Yes – I—' *I told you, I sent you the poster*, he wanted to say, but it'd be pointless. All his rage towards Tony, built up and calcified over the years, had gone, as though it were a carapace covering them both that had suddenly shattered.

Ben glanced at him as they turned into River Walk, narrowly avoiding another morning cyclist. The profile, so like Cord's, that perfect straight nose, the strong jaw, the lines around the eyes, the grizzled hair . . . But he was an old man now. Tony turned, and caught his hand.

'I'm proud of you, Ben love,' he said. 'You're a good boy. My boy.'

His hands were calloused, and cold, but strong – Ben flinched at the force of their grip. 'Thanks,' he said, and would have said more but Cord appeared at the back door, pulling the sash of her dressing gown around her waist as Ben kicked off his boots. 'Hello, darlings. Have you been for a father-and-son prenuptial walk?'

'Cordy.' Their father kissed her on the cheek. 'Something like that. How are you today, my darling?'

'Wonderful,' said Cord, brightly, twisting a lock of wild dark hair around one finger. 'Looks like a beautiful day for a wedding, Ben. Come in, let's have some breakfast. Mumma's up already.'

The two men came into the kitchen, glad of the warmth after the sharp cold of the autumn morning. Althea was sitting at the kitchen table, pulling flakes of croissant away and popping each delicately into her mouth, as she flicked through the paper.

'Hello, you two,' she said. 'I was extravagant and bought us all croissants from Harrods yesterday. I thought we'd need a special breakfast. And Mrs Berry says she's coming in specially today to make you bacon and eggs, Ben. She wants to give you a kiss and wish you luck. You always were her favourite boy.'

Ben shrugged, rather embarrassed. He hugged his mother, and sat down.

'Feels strange, doesn't it,' Althea said, smiling at him and pouring him some coffee. Cord leaned against the dresser, arms folded, watching them.

'What?' Ben said.

'Knowing you're getting married and everything feeling normal. Like Christmas Day when you're a child, you keep thinking there should be angels. Or birthdays.'

'Or going to the Bosky, because you've looked for it for so long and when you're there it's mundane, cleaning your teeth and eating breakfast,' said Cord, with a trace of her old self. She stopped. 'Something like that, I imagine.'

'That's exactly it,' Ben said, smiling at her. 'That's exactly how it feels.'

'We're all together,' said Althea, patting the seat next to her. 'Cord, come and sit down, darling. Let's have breakfast.'

'Not for me,' said Cord. 'Just coffee, thanks.' She cupped her chin in her hands. Despite what his father had told him Ben still thought his sister was too thin, her eyes huge, with dark puddly circles under them, the hollows under her cheeks too pronounced. 'When was the last time we were together, just the four of us, I mean?'

'I can't remember,' said Althea. Tony looked up.

'No idea, darling.'

Ben shrugged too. It had been long, too long, and he had been the one who'd left, not run away like the first time, more distanced himself from them, left behind the grandeur of River Walk and the suffocating feeling of his family to try and be his own person and here, back again on his wedding day, it was

OK. Because he loved them all, and none of them was perfect, but they were all here and that was what mattered, and later, he and Mads would be married.

What Ben didn't know, couldn't ever have guessed, is that they would never, all four of them, be together again.

Chapter Twenty-Four

15 October 1987

Hello, Book of Wildflowers! Dear old thing.

I should have thought I'd have long stopped writing in you by now. There's ten or so pages left . . . It scares me, the idea of finishing this exercise book. As if something permanent will come to an end. The question is, will I buy a new book after that? Will I still be writing in you in twenty years' time, creeping down to sit out on the steps and scribble away undisturbed by the rest of them? Will we still come here? Will we play Flowers and Stones and will the rules still be hung up in the beach hut or will there be other games? What will we look like, as a family, Book? I wish you could tell me. I've given you so many secrets over the years I think it's about time you gave me some back.

I married him. I can call myself Madeleine Wilde now & I think I will. I married him, he was there, he smiled at me the whole way through and I still can't quite believe this happiness is mine. Someone or something will take it away, I feel sure. I married him in the chilly Victorian church by the park in Twickenham – I'd never been there six months ago, I knew virtually no one in the congregation, I had nothing to do with planning it all. But I didn't care. I married him, and right behind him as I said my vows were Tony & Cord, smiling at me, the whole way through. Cord sang for us. Althea wore a hat the size of a table dressed for a tea party, flowers and boxes and all sorts spilling over the brim and down the side; of course there was a photo of her in <u>The Times</u> the next day. The headline was "A Rather Wilde Family Wedding" and they had a picture of her and Cord, and another one of me linking arms with Tony and Ben, only my head is turned away, back to Annie to give her my bouquet & because of the veil you can't see my face. That's the photo they wanted to use because I'm not the big draw, the rest of them are, and I couldn't be happier – having my photograph in the paper terrifies me and yet they couldn't care less. Oh, the Wildes.

We are the Wildflowers.

There it is.

We are.

I write this three days later at the Bosky. It is clear the summer is over, but down here the warmth lingers, and we have walked on the beach most nights. It's strange, being here alone with Ben, the place to ourselves. It's strange dashing to the hut so I can scribble all this down, Book. It's strange, being a bride. I didn't like it much. I kept catching sight of myself in mirrors. I don't know the Wildes' London house well enough to know yet how to avoid them. Ben doesn't know I often can't look in mirrors, that I can't bear to see myself or what might stare back at me.

He knows he's rescued me but I'm sure he doesn't know quite how much is wrong with me.

Yesterday I reminded Ben I want children right away. I want them while I'm young. It's the one thing we always talked about, the moment we met again in Bristol. He came over to my flat that first day, and we kissed and had sex that first night, and we knew, and if I write more about it then it takes the magic away from our secret special world, and I can't seem to put it down on paper. But he knew then and I wasn't afraid to tell him, because it's Ben.

He said, 'But I thought you were going to design spaceships and aeroplanes.'

'Build them, not design them,' I said. 'Yes, but I want children as soon as possible and then I'll go back to it. And I want them to have a dog and a big garden and to have holidays like we did. And I want them to have a mummy who does something she loves and a daddy who does too, so they understand that's important. And I want to read to them every night, stories about nice things, so they're never scared of the dark, so they fall asleep and don't have nightmares.'

'Sounds like you've thought it all out,' he said, and I could only think then of Aunt Jules, who used to hold me when I woke up screaming, because the girls at school wouldn't and I got moved to a room by myself eventually, which was better for them but only made me more scared. Daddy would shout at me to shut up if I did at Beeches, but I couldn't stop. The only place I slept well was at the Bosky.

Aunt Jules sent a telegram for the wedding – they read it out at the reception. Funny because no one else knew who she was, they were all Tony and Althea's friends. So people talked over it and that was the only bit of the wedding that mattered to me. I am pasting it in here my book.

```
To my darling niece on her special day. This
is the happiness you deserve and I prayed for.
I wish I could be with you and Ben to celebrate
but illness keeps me in Australia. I send you
all my love, balloons of happiness that float
up into the air - Never forget you are golden
and the Wildes are lucky to have you. Your
loving aunt who adores you and misses you,
Julia Fletcher
```

She always was a bit overdramatic, she loved writing poetry, I thought that balloons part was a bit much.

And Tony read it out which was nice but he read it in a soft sad voice and the room was loud and the guests, these strangers, talked over him, which is so odd for Tony, the last person in the world you'd expect to be talked over.

So I felt, with Ben, that we both wanted to make our own family, that we had the right beginnings. I knew he wanted to be a father. To create a new generation. So we're not the runaways, the disappointments, the mistakes, the oddities. So we're the caring ones, who devote ourselves to their happiness, who make sure they have everything, absolutely everything they need.

* * * *

February 1989

Well, Book, it's funny reading that, written eighteen months ago. One year married. (Paper. Time for a new book for when this runs out? Or will I never write in any book but you?) We did nothing but have sex on that honeymoon. Well, we went for strolls, drank at the Calke Arms, we hiked up to Bill's Point – we ate like lions. Every morning I'd get dressed and stare out of the window at the back of our room on to the dirt road up to where Beeches is. It's an old people's home now. They've rechristened it "Driftwood". You can see them, shuffling about sometimes on the lawn. I fear it is still a depressing place.

Oh, everything changes . . . It's Valentine's Day today and our first day in our new house in Primrose Hill. It was five old bedsits & is a strange warren of locked doors. Ben likes the road. He likes the area. I don't know it at all so I hope it will be an adventure.

I look back on the honeymoon all the time. We were happy. And I found myself wondering for the first time if it's the pull of the place, whether there's something about it, some dark magic that made us want it all the time, both of us. On the porch where we'd sit until the stars were out. In the sitting room – where the ghosts of other summers seemed to drift into and out of view as we twined around each other on the tiny yellow silk couch where we'd lounged in our childhoods, scabbed legs & sunburned arms, watching the Ashes and old Westerns, where we were now husband and wife trying to make our own family and sometimes I would find myself out of my own body, watching us and wondering if he found it as strange as I did. The only other sounds the waves and the wind & the wood pigeons calling out to each other.

We were making a fresh start, we told ourselves this, as the honeymoon went on. I was in no doubt that we'd pack up the house & return to Bristol with our child inside me. And we'd always know they were made here, my Book. Where we first met. Where I found my family. Where you saved me, Book, and they did too . . .

But it's eighteen months later now. And no children have come.

* * * *

15 August 1990

I always start by saying it's been a long time since I wrote in you. Well, I'm running out of space, Book. And when I look all the way back in this book, back to the start of it all, oh, it breaks my heart. You are like my child, Book, I wrap you up safe every time to keep you away from harm. My only child.

The lab called today.

They gave me the test results. Annie said not to tell anyone – she could be sacked for testing a friend. I said, well, they can't do that, we're not friends. I tried to joke about it. It's hard to have conversations at the Bosky, there in the hallway where anyone could be listening. I don't think Tony would care, but Althea moves silently & Ben must know something's up, mustn't he?

Book: will I tell Ben? I wish you'd decide for me. I think I know him so well but this – this waiting and not understanding, it's very hard. For both of us, for I am used to science being able to explain what I can't understand & he is used to action, to directing what happens next. Neither of us can make sense of it. In fact, Ben is more convinced than ever that it's going to happen. It's since these new pills we're taking, some rubbish the actress on his new film got him into. You go to a Chinese herbalist in Willesden Green – she sends you away with a huge bag of strange-smelling herbs. All these women, alone, in the waiting room. Just there for hope. Because this might be the answer – who knows? I'll look at the women and they'll avoid my gaze, as though no one wants to admit why you're there – you're not working properly because you can't make a baby.

You pay £50 a time for this bag of herbs. You boil them up into a huge soup and drink it and it makes a baby come – whoomp. Ben's convinced of it. Oh, Ben. ~~Sometimes I wish you~~ I'm doing it for him, I don't believe in it. I should be glad he's not shagging around like Tony, but a tiny part of me has begun to wish he'd do that instead of making me drink this vile stuff every morning.

Sometimes when he touches me I want to scream. And when he strokes my stomach, and whispers in my ear that one day we'll have a baby in there . . . I feel sick now about it, not excited. He's the one who won't have IVF, or consider sperm donors, he wants it this way, but he won't even talk about what might be wrong. Or consider it might be him – that's funny, isn't it? He won't talk about it but he wants me to do all the work on it. Just wants it to be sorted out, like a box that's ticked. Oh Ben, I thought you were perfect, of course you're not, are you?

That's why I've gone behind his back. Because I have to know. I can't stand this much longer.

It's not too much to ask, is it, Book? To sit here on the porch with my children. To feed them proper food, macaroni cheese, soup, to sew name tags into their clothes, to read them stories. I'd do it well. I'd do it better than Althea, who spent their childhood drinking cocktails and flirting with Simon and Bertie. That's awful, that's not kind. Sorry, Book. Sorry sorry sorry.

But it's not fair.

<u>I have to make that family. I can't keep living like this.</u>

Every month, thinking my breasts hurt more than usual and finding it's just PMT. Every month, taking my temperature like the women's magazines say and judging when it's just the right moment to do it with him. Which isn't sexy, let me tell you. Every month swearing off drink for two weeks so that people raise their eyebrows and say, casually, "No wine, Madeleine? OK then."

I wish there was someone I could talk to. Apart from you, Book. I hate living in London.

We're in Primrose Hill, because that's where Ben wanted to live. We've been there two years & I don't think I know a single person on our street. Ben is always away, first shooting the Irish film and now in LA doing that idiotic-sounding robot film. So I'm alone a lot. I'm used to it but I miss Bristol. In Bristol, we had his actor and director friends and my lab friends and I knew the city from school. I had the memory of Aunt Jules, too. I wish I could talk to her more. I don't call her enough.

Work is dull. I don't want to work for Glaxo, I don't like driving to Brentford every day and wandering round an industrial park for my *lunchtime. I want to solve things, crack mysteries, understand diseases. Not make more money for rich men.*

How did it become like this? That's what's funny. All the dreams I had on the morning of our wedding are still true but becoming thin, sad, I hate it.

So yes, I wish I could talk to someone. & we're here, and it's gorgeous to be here again but I can't seem to relax. & you're supposed to relax – it helps, along with the vile tea and the lying with your legs in the air and taking vitamins. (Again from some doctor in LA that Ben has been put on to by this time the screenwriter of his new stupid film. I hate LA people. I knew I would and I do.) Relaxed people make babies. That's what they say. So be calm. Serene. Don't do aerobics, don't have hot baths, don't eat this, don't drink that – and above all, relax. I want to scream. SCREAM AT THEM, <u>I have never been a relaxed person in my life!!</u> I have been too busy looking out, watching, seeing what comes next and what I need to do to protect myself before the world caves in.

I was six when I first saw Cordelia & Benedick playing on the beach the morning after I ran away. I never told them this. I sat on the steps of someone's beach hut and watched them for what seemed like hours. They were playing Waves – we played it lots over the years. (You have to dodge the waves. That's it.) I practised when they weren't there. Just in case they saw me and wanted me to play with them. Just so I'd be prepared, be ready. I have always been ready. I am now. And nothing happens.

I feel totally on my own again, isn't it strange. Ben is so busy annotating his script and keeps having to go downstairs to fax his producer in LA. The machine whirrs and spits, slowly, beeping and threatening. Cord is supposed to be arriving tomorrow—

Perhaps I could talk to her about all of it. I should try. If I don't, I'll go mad, or explode, all these things I want to say inside me, it's worse than ever, Book. But I still have my old habit of trying to learn everything about all of them, especially her, & she finds it irritating, I know she does, when I ask her about playing Dido again or some more technical question about the score or singing with Thomas Allen or meeting the Queen. I don't know any of these things. I've looked them up and saved them to roll out later as always, like a squirrel hoarding nuts for winter.

"Don't crawl, Mads," she said to me once. "You're family now, you don't need to sneak around." It hurt me so much, her talking like that. But I can't help but ask. I want to know. I used to think she didn't know how much it hurt me, when she was brusque and cutting with me. But the last couple of years I think she does. I also think she, of all of them, understands the most that I'm damaged beyond repair. Shoddy goods like the way the mum looked at me that day on the beach.

That sounds mad!

I can't discuss it with Althea. I adore her, but she's like a beautiful picture on the wall, delicious to look at, lovely, rather wonderful, but increasingly not an actual person you can talk to. She's bonkers, really, staring for hours at the mirror and lying on the porch swing practising her accent – she is in _The Glass Menagerie_ this autumn & rehearses most of the day with Tony. Tony is scared, I know, because she's good. He is playing Hamlet again, doing his first great role. At his age. I can't help thinking it's a strange thing to do but . . . He's directing it too.

What about talking to Tony? Oh, I love him but I can't exactly confide in him about my problem. "Hello, Tony darling. Me? Oh, fine, thank you. I spoke to my friend Annie at Imperial College today. She's confirmed the lining of my cervix is thin and that's part of what's wrong but not all. The actual problem is Ben's sperm. (Collected in a condom, when he wanted sex and I told him I was worried I had thrush – you see, I am as cunning as ever when I want to be and Cord is right about me.) They are abnormally low, according to Annie, & the motility and morphology are also poor. In the meantime, in short, there's no chance we'd conceive naturally. So that's that then . . . How are rehearsals going?"

Still, Cord arrives tomorrow. Then we'll all be together again. Three weeks. I must convince myself of what I know, deep down: it'll be like the old days again. She needs rest, I know she does. Althea and Tony need to learn their lines; here's the perfect place to do it. And Ben and I could still yet make that baby. I've seen the pathology & I know it doesn't look great, but a will to win can move mountains. We can still have a baby, it'll just be harder. But it has to happen. I will make it happen.

17 August 1990

There has been some terrible news from the other side of the world, Book. Darling Aunt Jules is dead.

She's dead.

Dead, dead. She fell in her garden, they said, and hit her head.

A rhyme.

She felt fine and then died suddenly the following day, in an ambulance.

It was fast, they said. There are worse ways to go. But she was only sixty. I always thought she'd come back one day. And I'd be her family. I'd look after her. She'd help me look after my children, the way she did with me. We talked about it. It would have been nice to look after her and to have my own bit of family again. And it's strange to think I won't ever see her. The funeral was over there – they said the church was full and that her dog Schmitty went, wearing a black bow. He howled during the hymns – she'd taught him to sing, she'd play the piano when we spoke and he'd howl away. Oh, Aunt Jules. She was not like others, bit of a free spirit, you might say. She didn't care what other people thought. Truly—

She had curly hair and a gap in her teeth and pink cheeks. She was slim, and always on the go, typing furious letters, striding out of the house, plucking weeds.

She loved Australia, and hated England. She read _Oz_ and _Private Eye_ and didn't trust governments. She wrote poetry & had a beautiful garden. I've a photo of her in her garden – she's in pink and turquoise and so are the flowers.

I should have gone to see her. Shouldn't be mouldering here worrying about every month going by, every new chance to make a baby. I should have seen her again.

20 August 1990

There's one extraordinary thing in Aunt Jules's will. I'm the sole beneficiary, not that I care about that.

"To my dear niece Madeleine Fletcher I leave my estate. With the sole instruction that she should try less hard, care a little less, eat a little more."

I'll write the rest out:

"I direct that after my death my ashes should be scattered on the beach at Worth Bay in the Isle of Purbeck, in Dorset, by Sir Anthony Wilde (if he is willing to perform the task), in sweet memory of our summers together. Will he, please, recite that verse from The Tempest he performed so long ago one of the first nights we met. Our revels now are ended. They were revels, weren't they? Please inform him of my wishes and excuse him should he decline to carry out the task."

Aunt Jules & Tony? Apparently so. I remember after our wedding, Ben said his father had hinted as much to him, but I never really paid it much attention, head full of wedding nonsense. Dear Tony. Dear Jules. I wonder what happened. I really can see them together, even though they're so different. They have a zest for life. They had, I should say. Darling Aunt Jules, oh, how I miss you. Something dies with you. Something that can't be brought back.

Well, I'll ask Tony today – & today's the day, time to get Ben to do his duty.

Chapter Twenty-Five

Dorset, July 1943

Down the dusty lane he dragged his trunk, through the beautiful, familiar little meadow of nodding wild flowers, the cheery yellow ragwort, orange and red poppies, and baby-blue scabious – Dinah called them pincushions, Ant didn't know their name. He had been travelling for twenty-four hours to get home and had wondered whether he'd ever make it, but now he was here, after the months and months of longing for the place. The sky was a soaring pale periwinkle blue; swallows looped above him. From here you could not see the dragon's teeth concrete defences that led down to the shore, only the sound of the sea below him, the wind in the grasses.

Instead of coming in from the lane Ant hastily hauled his trunk up the porch steps, hoping to surprise her and – there she was, standing over something in the kitchen! He raised his hand to knock on the French windows, but then suddenly paused and looked back. Something wasn't right.

He saw now the porch was filthy, covered in bird droppings – rat droppings too, if he wasn't mistaken – and littered with books, books splayed out obscenely on the wood, spines cracked. One even had pages torn out, and these had been blown into the four corners of the wooden railings.

The yellow rose that smothered the side of the Bosky, that was gone too, cut off entirely so that all that remained was a brown fork at the base of the house. It made the place seem bare, open to the world.

Dinah was singing, snatches of something, and she moved furtively, in odd, fast little movements, so unlike her usual expansiveness. She took a cylindrical-shaped piece of marble out of a wooden box and, crooning gently, wrapping it in muslin, put it into another box on the floor, and whispered something, smiling to herself. He peered intently at her, suddenly and unaccountably unable to alert her to his presence . . . Then she looked up and her expression changed, and Ant was terrified, and he didn't know why.

'No one's been here for ages – I've become rather lazy,' Dinah said, by way of explanation, as though that accounted for the dirty plates, the stale air, the shrivelled dead flowers in the glass vase on the dresser. 'I've lost track of time, Ant dear – I should have prepared the fatted calf and there's no tea.' She laughed in a jittery way. 'Rations are awfully slim at the moment. I did try keeping chickens again but they only lasted a few days, the foxes got 'em. I hope it was foxes, anyway.' She looked up and around, slightly blankly, then wrapped the worn peacock kimono around herself. Moths had devoured it; huge bare patches bloomed across the pattern. 'I'll just put this in your room.' She picked up the handle of his own trunk and pulled it along the parquet floor, carving a large scratch into the wood.

'Aunt Dinah—! Careful,' he said, impulsively.

'What?'

'The floor.'

And she called back to him, a little sharply, 'Don't be a maiden aunt, dear. That's my job. Gently she goes, into her cloth, hey ho.'

Ant was very tired. He'd come from London where he'd gone with two schoolmates to see *Blithe Spirit*, a birthday treat for one of them, Campbell. In a little over twenty-four hours he'd taken six different trains with a wait of around an hour between most. On the last train they'd been held at a signal for over half an hour near Southampton. Ant had stood sandwiched between a group of raucous Land Girls, who'd tried to flirt with him in a way that made him uncomfortable as he didn't understand many of their jokes, and a slightly sinister-looking husband and wife, who were identical and who kept asking him where he was going and whether he'd be all right. He wasn't confident enough yet to deal with either of them, and he was exhausted with the effort of assessing the behaviour of other humans.

The show had been wonderful; Margaret Rutherford was awfully funny. But going back to London – seeing it in ruins, the false gaiety everywhere, the eerie calm now the bombing had stopped for the most part – had been more than strange; it had disturbed him deeply. For it was clear just how much time had passed, how everything was different. His schoolmates, Campbell who was half decent, and an idiot called Bailey, had both gone into a chemist's and bought French letters – he had gone along with them, and bought one himself, because they'd teased him so much about not buying one, dead-arming him, laughing and ruffling his hair. This was what he hated about school – the crudeness, the cruelty. He'd never have told any of them about Julia, and he suspected from guarded, half-questioning boasts they made that not one boy in his class had any experience of girls, bar Elwood and he lived in a castle and had once forced a maid to kiss him, and that hardly counted.

He hadn't gone back to Camden – how would he explain it to his schoolmates? And besides, what was there but ghosts, and a neat gap in the terraced row of houses, like a tooth missing from a child's mouth?

'I might just get some water,' he called, awkwardly, moving towards the kitchen. A fly buzzed unhappily amongst the listless curtains that hung over the window seat.

'Sorry,' Dinah said, reappearing. 'I've been rather preoccupied. I wanted to make it all fine for you when you got here, dear Ant. And it's not.'

'It is,' he said, weakly, staring round at the dingy kitchen where the thin curtains were still drawn and the mess of several days' plates and meals adorned every surface of the kitchen. 'Are you – is everything all right?'

'Absolutely! I'm putting my house in order. A saying, and an actuality . . .' She gazed at him, almost hungrily. 'Gosh, I have missed you. You're so grown up, dear. I'd hardly know you.'

The school had been evacuated in the New Year to the Lake District and he hadn't been able to come home. It was a day's travelling from London to Dorset, but even longer from Dorset to Windermere.

You sent me away, he wanted to say, but didn't. *Of course I've changed.* He felt a vibrating soft mass against his leg and looked down. 'Sweep!' He scooped the fluffy, gangly bundle up, and Sweep purred even more furiously, urgently pressing her face against his hands. 'Sweep.' He nuzzled the soft spot between her ragged ears. 'Ah, you're older.'

'She keeps me company. She's no trouble. She sleeps in that enormous wardrobe in your room.'

Ant set the cat down on the floor again, and she immediately jumped into a box of old books and sat looking at him with unblinking glass-green eyes. 'How's Daphne?' he said, without really thinking.

'How should I know? Ant dear, I haven't seen her for an age, not since she abandoned us last year.'

'I just thought you might have heard from her.'

She looked up, her thin shoulders hunched. The hair that Daphne had cut so short the previous summer was now past her shoulders, greyer and wilder than ever, and she didn't put it up as she formerly had done, so it hung in lank streaks around her face.

But her green eyes flashed suddenly as she said, 'I don't need to hear from her. I can tell you what she's up to, Ant dear. She's having fun. Dancing. Seeing who'll buy her dinner. You know dear Daphne. She wouldn't cross the road for a good cause but she'd jolly well cross the country for a good party. Oh, yes. Now, I absolutely must feed you.' She went over to the kitchen counter and began slicing clumsy hunks of crumbling National Loaf. 'We'll have dripping and toast for tea, and I've some actual tea leaves from the Rev.'

'Good old Rev,' said Ant.

'Oh, he's a darling man, a good friend. And what luck, Ant, we've a few plums he brought round this morning from their orchard. We'll have a real feast. And afterwards – ah-ha!' She slapped her hands together. 'What do you say to a game of mah-jong?'

He nodded happily and their eyes locked. 'Sounds marvellous.' Her eyes shone and she was Dinah again, caught up in the joyous enthusiasm of the moment. Ant honestly believed then that everything might still be all right.

They sat in the kitchen with the remains of tea and a soporific warmth stealing over both of them as the afternoon sun gave a golden glow to the wooden room. A vase of dying dahlias, velvet red and hot pink, bent under their own weight, scattering pollen on the slightly sticky table. He found he could ignore the mess. He smiled, gazing out of the window at the bay and the sky, and when he looked at his great-aunt she was smiling at him. She wiped her eyes with the sleeve of her kimono.

'I want to talk to you about something, Ant dear.' She got up, and opened the French windows. 'That's better. Some fresh air.'

'What is it, Aunt D? Want me to find another game I can beat you at, is that it? Happy Families is over there—'

She laughed, then hesitated for a moment, looking out at the sea and back at him. 'Ho – no, thank you, dear. Listen, Ant. I'm afraid it's rather serious.' And Dinah cleared her throat. 'I told you about my daddy, didn't I? Your great-grandfather? He built the Bosky for my mother, as a surprise.'

'Yes, I know.'

'He was a gambler, Ant, did I ever tell you that?'

'Yes, you did.'

'Good. Well, don't forget it, dear boy.' She gripped his hands, suddenly. 'Oh, Ant. He gambled, he won, and he built this house, and then he gambled again and lost. Lost everything. And it killed him. Well, I took a sacred oath in the Temple of Ishtar. I stood there, I held up my hand, it was all terribly dramatic. "I won't be like him."'

She got up, and said bleakly, 'Well. I failed. I'm his daughter after all, you see. I've gambled, Ant. And I've lost everything.'

Ant didn't understand. 'You've lost the – the house?'

'Not the house. Not yet. That's what I want to talk to you about.' She stood up, moving towards the sideboard slowly, as though she were lame, or in pain. She took out some papers. 'Ant dear, I wonder if you would sign these. I had them drawn up by Mr Hill. I'd always have given the place to you anyway, but if you sign them then all will be fine.' Something more was muttered under the breath. 'It will all be fine.'

Ant moved towards her, took the papers from her and set them on the kitchen counter. He glanced at them briefly. '"Title Deeds". "Transfer of Assets". I don't understand—'

'I'm giving you the Bosky,' she said, jutting out her chin. There was a martial light in her eye. 'Then they can't take it away from me.'

'Who's "they"?' he asked, with a creeping, nauseous feeling of unease.

'Oh – people who want to destroy me. She came back for it,' she

335

said, slowly. 'Couldn't find it. Even thought it was right under her nose, hanging there, all the time. Above her nose, I should say . . .'

'Aunt Dinah . . .'

She put out one shaking hand. 'It's yours. Then you'll always have something. No matter what happens. No matter what they try to do.'

And she pushed the sheaf of thick papers towards him.

'Oh,' Ant said, shrugging, and feeling rather sick at the sight of the official words, the huge seal at the bottom of the letter. 'Aunt D, let's not worry about this right now. You boil the kettle. I'll go and put my old pair of flannels on. Why don't we go for a walk? We can plot the summer—'

Dinah slapped the folded papers down in front of him. 'No. Please, dear. Here,' she said, opening one page and then flattening it down with her outstretched palm. 'Sign here, and then it's done, and it can't be changed.'

'But it's your house, not mine.'

'Please,' she said, urgently. 'Dear Ant, for me. Do it for me . . .' She watched as he scratched his name in his looping hand by the black-inked 'X' and then gave a great sigh. 'Wonderful,' she said, and she smiled at him, raising her shoulders and letting them drop, as though releasing herself of a great weight. 'That's that!'

Ant handed the fountain pen back, looking at her. 'I wish I hadn't.'

'Nothing will change,' she said, and she stood up and put the sheaf of papers on the sideboard. 'Nothing at all, dear. It'll still be my house to all intents and purposes, but if they come for me, or try to take it away—'

'Who'd try to take it away from you?'

She gave a thin smile, and scratched her nose. 'No one! It's just silly talk, a precaution. But what if I have to travel and you need to stay on here? Well, then – it's yours. It's always yours and everything in it. We'll just carry on as normal, yes? You understand?'

He didn't, and he wouldn't, not for a while, but he nodded, and just then a face loomed through the French window, and he started.

'Ah,' said Dinah, with satisfaction. 'She said she'd call round. Come in, dear! He's here!'

There, knocking happily at the window, smiling broadly, was Julia. At the sight of her Ant blushed, the impure thoughts he'd had about her all year since the previous summer rushing back. She rattled at the metal door frame, trying to open it, her curls bouncing around her head, and when nothing happened Ant stood up to help her. He pulled at the heavy cold handle and eventually the door gave way, and she stumbled into the sitting room, almost landing on the floor but for Ant's arm.

'Oh, I say – thanks.' She leaned heavily against him, and smiled up at him, her eyes gleaming with delight.

He smiled back at her. She was tanned, and the halter-neck strap of her swimming costume was slightly too small, cutting into her plump, golden flesh. He tried not to stare at her breasts. She had grown since last year, was taller than ever and her breasts were larger too. Her slim, strong fingers gripped his arm; there was a smattering of freckles across her nose, on her cheeks.

'Hello, Julia,' he said, and she squeezed a little harder on his arm, moving against him.

'Well,' she said, in that low, clear voice of hers, full of laughter, 'hello, old bean.'

'Julia's been here most days, asking when you were arriving – haven't you?' said Dinah, and Julia nodded, unabashed at this display of enthusiasm – indeed, it was one of the things he'd always liked so much about her, that she never tried to be aloof.

'We broke up ten days ago and came straight down and Ian's already driven Father almost to distraction. I've been so utterly bored, waiting for you, Ant,' she said, and he could smell the salt on her skin and the faint sweetness of her. 'We missed all the action

– did you hear about the Mustangs crashing over at Smedmore in May?' She turned to Dinah. 'Did you see them, Miss Wilde?'

'Yes,' said Dinah vaguely. 'Terrible.' But she had picked up an old, gold-tooled book and was flicking purposefully through it; Ant glanced down, and could only see pictures of burial chambers and rows of skeletons, golden headdresses, the shine on the photographic paper that gleamed in the darkened room.

'You had your hair cut,' Ant told Julia, touching the bouncing bob of curly hair. 'It suits you.'

'Run along, why don't you, and go for a walk by the dragon's teeth,' Dinah said, glancing up. 'You must be dying for some fresh air, Ant, cooped up on trains all that time. Watch out for the barbed wire – they've repositioned some of it, and it's a nasty shock if you're not careful. And I know it doesn't need saying, but *don't* go on the beach. They've evacuated everyone down at Shell Bay, did you know? Joe saw them moving the concrete in the other day. Big army nobs down here all lined up inspecting the bay. Something's happening there. I'm sure of it.'

She tapped her nose and Ant nodded, but he wasn't sure if she was telling the truth or not.

'Maybe they'll come for us next,' she said. 'Tell us to move on.'

'Oh, Miss Wilde, I'm sure they won't,' said Julia. She glanced over at Ant. 'Well? Shall we go?'

He didn't want to leave Dinah alone, but Ant realised he couldn't bear the stuffy, dirty, too-hot house that was now his, not for a moment longer. He nodded. 'I'll see you later, Aunt D,' he said to his aunt, picking up his blazer. 'Won't be long.'

'Take your time, all fine,' she said, in a sing-song voice, and she stood up, and began peering into the boxes again, lifting things out, putting other things in. 'Never fear, Ant dear, never fear.'

Chapter Twenty-Six

He didn't lose his virginity to Julia that evening, or the next, but a few days later, in the sand dunes, as evening came. He had been back at Worth Bay for five days by then, trying to settle back into life with Aunt Dinah. The weather was still, clear, hot, the nights thick with stars, the Milky Way visible over the Channel towards France, brighter than ever on those blackout nights. In later years Tony would stand on the porch and try to see that pale swirl of countless stars, as on those cloudless warm nights, but he never could.

It was on a night like that, amongst the dragon's teeth high up towards Bill's Point along the coastline, that they did it. Julia had already prised from him the existence of the French letter, and he was desperate for her, wild almost, and both of them thought it made sense. It seemed like a natural thing to do, in this world where concrete pillars and bollards lined the bay, where planes strafed the sands, and where danger was still everywhere.

They didn't think it was wrong, or that they were too young, or that they were deceiving anyone. It was as natural to them both as kissing had been. Afterwards, as he lay still inside her, panting and worried he might pass out, she began to giggle and then, moving her head back so that the curls mingled with the sand, properly laugh, her small white teeth shining in the gathering gloom.

'Well, what's so funny?' he said, grinning at her.

'Oh, I don't know. That I've done it with you. You're just divine, Ant, and you seem to have no idea. I can't believe it.'

'Can't believe what?'

She slid her body up so she was free of him, pulled on her knickers, then nestled back against him. He stroked her freckled forearms. 'If there was more choice, you wouldn't choose me,' she said into his chest, quietly. 'But I'd always choose you.'

He could feel the tips of her nipples, hard again, and her thudding heart, and he held her to him more tightly. 'That's rubbish, Julia – don't say things like that. Anyway, I thought we were in it together, both of us.'

'Oh, yes, of course,' she said, and then she closed her eyes, slowly. 'Us against everything. Especially the Nazis. And Pa.'

'And school.'

'And school. And being selfish and petty. The greater good.' Julia sat up and he could see she was about to start on again about equality – she was jolly obsessed with it, this idea that women were given a raw deal. 'We should all be fighting together. Miss Bright has a friend working in a munitions factory, in Liverpool, putting the sulphur into the shells. It's turned her face and hands bright yellow – they call her Canary – but she loves working, she was at home doing nothing before except cleaning and cooking for her husband who didn't even work. And the minute the war's over she'll lose her job. The men'll want it back. Men want everything for themselves, the power, the money, and they keep women down in a position of servitude. When you get married, you resign from your job. Can you imagine that, Ant?' She actually shook a fist at him. 'These awful magazines like *Woman* telling girls they need to wear stockings and wave their hair and silly things men don't have to do. Women are the objects . . .' Ant nodded, and she trailed off, looking up at him through her lashes. 'Talking of objects. Honestly, Ant, I don't want to hark on about it but you really are awfully handsome now.'

'Now!'

'You know what I mean. You were a boy when we met. Now, you're not. You're a heartbreaker. A matinee idol. How's the acting, by the way?'

'I was a servant in *Antony and Cleopatra* last term.'

He hadn't told anyone at school that he liked acting. He'd been picked to be a soldier in the end-of-year production of *Antony and Cleopatra* because he was tall. 'You and the other poofs, eh, Wilde?' Johnson had said, when he'd seen him in his Roman soldier costume, queuing to go into the ballroom, which was now their hall, of the old country house on the shores of Lake Windermere to which they'd been evacuated. 'Ha! Look at Wilde, chaps! He's got make-up on! Dressed up like your mother, Wilde. She'd be over the moon to see you using her eye pencil.'

How dreary, how pathetic to be this Johnson, with his small, small tales of life in a large house in Surrey and the father who taught him to shoot and the big brother who was out in Cairo 'doing his bit'. The tennis court 'rolled every week in summer by our gardener, Philpott', holidays in the south of France before the war, the tedious Christmas family traditions he insisted on telling one about. He would grow up pink, baby-faced, querulous, snide, small-minded, mean, idiotic. Ant knew this. He found lately that he knew more than his contemporaries, as though tragedy had widened his world view, made him see and understand more. Ant had promised himself right then, shivering in his costume in the cool of a Cumbrian July, that he would never ever be a Johnson. He would be wild and curious and open to everything.

'I'm certain you were wonderful.'

'Not really, Jules. I stood at the back with a spear.'

'I'll bet you held the spear jolly well.' She slipped her plump breasts into her brassiere, fiddling with the hooks. 'No, no, don't worry. You'd better dispose of that,' she said briskly, pointing to the condom, elongated and ridiculous-looking. 'Wrap it in your handkerchief, chuck it away later.'

'Have you done this before?' he said, smiling up at her with his hands behind his head, and she hit him.

'No! Of course not. You're the first, and if Pa or Ian knew we'd be for it, absolutely. He didn't even want me to go to school but Mummy's aunt paid so he had to accept. He really can't stand the fact that I'm brighter than Ian. I am. I'll go to Girton if they'll have me. He'll never let me, of course.'

'Really?' Tony was surprised. 'Even your father? But he's all for education and everything—'

Julia gathered her cotton floral frock and pink cardigan together. 'Since we've been back, I've noticed, he's become much worse. A Land Girl fixed his car in the ATP the other day, on the way back from the station. I thought he'd die of anger, he was so ashamed.'

'But he loves Aunt Dinah. And she's – well, she's like a man, in lots of ways. Does exactly what she wants.' He was proud of her for it.

'He's a hypocrite. I think he doesn't understand it, this new world, and the war, and it makes him furious. That's what Miss Bright at school says, anyway. She says men hate us having the freedoms they've got, and that's how we know it's worth fighting for. Miss Bright was in prison for Votes for Women, you know. I'd go to prison for it.' She leaned over him, and the smell of her, salty, sweaty, sweet like roses, the feel of her firm, soft skin almost undid him. She kissed him. 'We must be careful, but gosh, there's a war on, and life is short.' Her face shone in the light from the setting sun, rippling on the sea. 'Wasn't this nice, anyway? I thought it was awfully nice.'

'I should say.' He sat up, grinning shyly, and fumbled in his blazer pocket. 'Here. Would you like a cigarette?'

'No, thanks,' said Julia, pulling her dress back over her head, her springy hair emerging first with a bounce. She scrambled into her sandals, and it struck him then how funny the business of it was, the taking off of clothes and artifice, and how natural it was to be naked as they had been five minutes ago, to put himself in her as she had spread herself for him, brushing her hair out of her eyes, moving down to meet him as he pushed inside her, and both of them at the same time saying to the other, 'It's lovely.'

It wasn't at all how he had imagined, it was kind, and sweet, and moving . . . Julia was, for all her am-dram quality, entirely natural.

'Don't go. Stay a while. Please,' he said.

Her fingers deftly fastened the straps on her sandals. 'Be awfully sophisticated to sit here watching the last of the sunset with you, but I promised Daddy I'd boil up the bones from the duck carcass. Duck soup. Don't know if that's bathos or pathos or something like it – we learned it in school last term.' She pulled her cloche straw hat on and looked down at him, blinking heavily. 'I liked it awfully today. Tomorrow?'

Anthony put his fingers around her smooth ankle and nodded. 'Tomorrow.'

'Marvellous,' said Julia, and her smile was brilliant. 'What a summer it'll be.'

Chapter Twenty-Seven

London, August 1990

Oh, the lovely newness of the carpet! And the curtains: a peacock-feather pattern in gorgeous purple, turquoise and pale green, in a heavy printed silk bought from Liberty in a rash splashing of cash she'd received for an album, and so expensive but there they were, in the wide bay windows of her beautiful new flat, and they looked gorgeous. 'Last you a lifetime, those will,' the curtain fitter had observed as he packed away his things. 'I guarantee you'll still be drawing these when you're seventy.'

Cord was amused that he thought she'd still be drawing the same curtains in the same flat in forty-five years' time. Yet, as she looked around the place on the night before she left for the Bosky, she had to admit she rather liked the idea. She was in love with her home of six months and now, when she was away, she longed to be back there playing house: being a grown-up and listening to the (new glossy black stereo) radio in her (brand new blue velvet) dressing gown, smelling the fresh air through the open French windows mingling with the faintly delicious smell of paint. The place had been thoroughly redecorated before she took up residence, having previously been the home for many years of a housebound old lady who had eventually died there. Cord had kept the Arts and Crafts touches – the leaded windows with curlicue latches, the curving door handles, the fireplace with its sunflower tiles – but had rid herself of everything else and any associations with the previous owner. She had the whole

344

place painted in light colours, creams, fawns, blues and yellows. She wanted it to be sunny, and warm, and safe, like the Bosky had been when she was little, only this was her place, earned with her money. When her friend Amanda, a fellow singer, had seen it she'd said, 'Cord, you could have a new career doing up flats.'

'Oh, I absolutely loved it.' Cord had rubbed her hands and smiled. 'If the singing lark fails, maybe I should.'

'Ha ha,' Amanda, fresh from another failed audition, had said drily. 'Cordelia Wilde, fallen on hard times, becomes an interior decorator. Highly likely.'

It was a fresh slate, empty and waiting for her to make it into a home. She would have musical evenings. Crowd the walls with photos, fill the shelves with books. She would invite her family round: Mumma would come now the sitcom had ended, they'd go to galleries together and come back here for tea. Mads and Ben's children, if they ever materialised, should know the place as well as their own home. There was a dear cupboard in the hall with a heart cut out of it, where she'd keep her new little suitcase, ready to be picked up or dumped when she got back from trips abroad. There were heart-shaped hooks on the door for coats, and a turn-of-the-century hall table for her new telephone and a beautiful art nouveau mirror above it, which she'd found at an estate sale in Glasgow before a recital – it had been in a Charles Rennie Mackintosh house. There was a fridge in which she always kept a spare bottle of champagne, and tins of pâté and biscuits in the little cupboard above. On the newly painted mantelpiece only one housewarming card had been allowed to remain, from Ben. A picture of Agnetha in silk knickerbockers, cut out from a newspaper or a book, glued on to card.

Dearest Cordy, you Super Trouper, Ben had written inside in his difficult hand. *Wishing you many happy years in your beautiful new flat. With all our love B&M*. The postmark was Los Angeles.

The little suitcase stood by the door now, all packed, but this time she was going away to the Bosky, early the following morning. Cord couldn't wait. Summer in the city, even in her quiet, leafy part of West Hampstead, was still torture, every year, for a girl who had grown up spending July and August in jelly shoes, running in and out of the sea. Lately, for the first time she could remember, she had been feeling tired after performances, her throat hurting. She was twenty-six; she had been performing non-stop for six years. Her diary was booked up as far ahead as 1993, with engagements at concert halls and opera houses around the world. The previous week, she had sung the role of Countess Almaviva for the fortieth time – she kept a record of every performance in a black leather notebook, true to the Cordy of old who loved lists and order. She wasn't bored – never that, she could never be bored of singing. But lately, she was bored of herself. Of talking about herself all the time, of thinking about her own voice. Being the star gave you an inflated view of your own importance. She told herself it'd be good to get to the Bosky, be one of a crowd again. See Mads, have a proper chat with her, find out how she was – the last time she'd seen her, too long ago now, Cord had known things weren't quite right.

She was heading for the kitchen to treat herself to a single glass of wine when the phone rang and she answered, wondering who it could be – it was nine-thirty, a little late for a call.

'Hello?'

'Ben?' came the voice. 'Hello, is that Mads?'

The response was instant: Cord felt her body tense, stiffen.

'Who is this?' she said, sliding one finger into the phone cord, staring at herself in the new mirror. She wasn't used to it and saw herself then as a stranger: free for once of stage make-up; her flushed high cheekbones, mouth partly open in surprise, the hair, wild, thick, dark, down her shoulders, her back. *I am slim*, she found herself thinking. *I am not a stocky ten-year-old. I am that willowy girl in the mirror.* 'I think you've got the wrong Wilde. This isn't Ben's—'

There was a pause.

'Oh, God. Cord. I'm so sorry. Of course, I know you're not your brother. I looked his number up in the phone book – I must have dialled you by mistake.'

She said, 'It's fine.'

'You know it's me?'

'Yes, Hamish,' she said, trying to sound chirpy. 'Of course I knew it was you.'

'This is wonderful.' His voice was warm, soft, liquid. She pressed the phone closer to her ear. 'How are you, Cordy?'

The front door buzzer sounded – she pressed it, swiftly. 'Absolutely fine. Great,' she amended. 'I've just moved. Enjoying summer. Trying to avoid catching a cold, oh, and mad cow disease of course . . . Got some new flip-flops. Um—' She flushed.

'Still singing?' There was a silence. 'Jesus, what a stupid question. I'm sorry. I'm flustered. You've made me flustered, Cordelia, but you know, you always did.'

She laughed – she couldn't help it.

Was he still as blonde as ever? With the smattering of freckles, and the pale grey eyes? And the dimple in his chin, and the smile, that smile . . . Footsteps thundered up the stairs towards her, and Cord cleared her throat. 'Oh, you flirt.' But that wasn't fair – he wasn't, hadn't ever been; he wasn't a player, hadn't ever been. 'How are you? How's – is it Sunita?'

'Yes, that's it. She's fine, thank you. We're back in the UK now. Our daughter is almost one, Cordy, one year old.'

'Ah,' she said. 'Lovely. What her name?'

'Amabel,' he said.

'Annabel?'

'A*mah*. Amabel.'

'I heard you. Annabel. How lovely.'

'No. Ah-*muh* for mother. Amabel. Amabel Hester Chaudri-Lowther.'

Cord found she was almost glad to feel that this was ridiculous. She wanted to snigger, to say, *What kind of a name is Amabel?* She wanted to find him silly, stupid, not her kind of person. Before, he'd been her kind of person, the one who was entirely good. 'Um – lovely,' she said dumbly again, and she turned away from the mirror.

'Her – Sunita chose Amabel. She wanted something Scottish.'

'Amabel is a beautiful name.'

'Yes. Cordy . . .' He trailed off. 'Why are we saying Amabel over and over? I've now lost all meaning of it. You've made me lose all sense of my own daughter's name. Good grief.'

'Honey?' came a loud, deep voice behind her. 'I got fish and chips. Is that right? I went to a place near Marylebone. This guy, the guy in the shop put vinegar on it, I told him I wasn't sure. But he did and—'

Jay, beautiful, barely out of breath after four flights of steps, standing in front of her, holding aloft a white plastic bag taut with takeaway food. He grimaced when he saw her on the phone and whispered.

'I'll wait in there.' He pointed.

'Thanks,' Cord mouthed.

'Sure,' he said, and as she turned back to the phone he came up behind her, wrapping his arms around her, kissing her neck, his skin against hers. She saw the two of them in the reflection, his dark skin pressed against her pale body. 'Sure thing.'

'I ought to go,' said Cord, into the phone, as Jay applied himself to kissing her neck.

'Yes, you've someone round. He's rather hungry by the sounds of it,' said Hamish and Cord smiled, and her heart ached, and she shifted her weight from one foot to another, pushing Jay away.

'Did you want me to give Ben a message? I'm seeing him tomorrow.'

'It's only about the script. I wanted to talk to him – tell him I'm not sure how I'll climb that scaffolding in heels.' There was a pause. 'I'm joking. It was a joke.'

'Oh – I – sorry,' Cord apologised. 'I—'

'I'm nervous,' he said. 'So stupid.'

They were both silent, neither sure what to say next. In the kitchen, Jay whistled as he took the food out of the bag. She watched his coffee-coloured arms lift, move, his muscles work as he opened cupboards, removed plates. Later, she would have Jay on the new bed with the new blue-and-yellow patterned duvet, peeling his clothes off slowly, revelling in his body, his hands, his difference to her. She would leave him behind in bed tomorrow morning as she left for the Bosky, and she wouldn't know when she'd see him next. That was how it worked.

'I have to go,' she said quietly. 'Hamish – it was lovely to talk to you again.'

She could hear, at his end, a little voice, chirping in the background, something about a puppy. She strained to hear more, but he simply said, 'I'm sorry to have bothered you again. Take care, sweet girl. Take care of yourself.'

And the line went dead.

'Hey. Come and eat,' Jay called. Cord said nothing, and he repeated himself, his voice louder, till she shook herself, smiling up at him.

'Sorry.'

They'd been on and off for over two years now. She had met him in Chicago when they appeared opposite each other in *La Traviata*. Professor Mazzi, always pessimistic, had warned her against

349

him. 'Jay Washington. No! He will steal the show from you.' But her agent and the Chicago opera were both incredibly keen and they had been right, Professor Mazzi wrong, and she was glad to ignore him, glad to be able to say, *I know what I'm doing, just butt out for once.* He always knew best, and it annoyed her, sometimes.

The chemistry between her and Jay was electric, the revival of an old, old touring production acclaimed to the rafters. Jay was from Detroit, and the combination of the local boy and the English star had been potent. They queued round the block for returns.

And he was like her – he didn't want anything more than sex, which he took immensely seriously, and the added benefit of companionship. When he was in Europe, he'd come over, or she'd fly out to see him, if she felt like it, and wasn't sick of flying, of never being home. That was before the new flat. Now, she could no more see Jay on the sofa next to her in ten years' time than she could her and the Prince of Wales. The two of them, watching TV, pushing a trolley around Waitrose – no.

She watched him humming something lightly to himself – he was always singing, like she was. He'd never met her family. She knew he had a sister in Oakland and a mother still in Detroit. He sent her money every month and Jay claimed she'd promised him she'd up and die if he ever brought a white girl home. She knew he'd lost his dad in an accident when he was five. That he liked steak dinners, and English football, and walking in city parks – he loved open spaces. Wherever they were he'd make her go with him to the local park, and they'd walk through the Borghese Gardens together in autumn, or Hyde Park in Sydney when they were together in *Tosca*, and most of all he loved Regent's Park.

'It's so English.' 'It's hilarious, it's so British.' 'It's like Mary Poppins.'

He said something like this every time and every time it annoyed Cord, and he'd laugh at her.

Now, Jay looked up as she watched him, watched the new curtains stir faintly in the breeze. 'Everything OK?'

'Yes. Sorry. That was . . .' She trailed off.

'Old boyfriend, right?'

'Actually, yes, it was.' She came in and put the plates down on the table.

'Hah!' Jay clapped his hands. 'I knew it. So he's been down to your place by the seaside, I bet. I bet you took him to meet your parents. I bet you let him screw you down there.'

She shook her head, smiling. 'He knew my father. I met him down there. And yes, I let him screw me down there.'

'Oh.' Jay was fascinated by her family, the fact that her father was Anthony Wilde, that he was a sir. He opened the fish from its paper bag. 'Oh, OK.'

'Daddy invited him down. They were into that, picking people up, bringing them into the circle. Hamish's fiancée ran off with someone. Daddy felt sorry for him.'

Jay shrugged. 'The guy kinda sounds like a sap.'

'He's not.' She smiled. 'He's nice. The nicest man I ever knew.'

'That's so fucking rude when I'm right here,' said Jay, unperturbed, and she grinned at him. He piled chips into his mouth. 'You guys. Your French fries are gross, but they're incredible at the same time. You British are so weird with your food, you make something called pease pudding that looks like yellow diarrhoea and yet you also make this. This – it's amazing. So, what went wrong then? You and Sap Guy, I mean.'

'He wanted to make me happy,' Cord said, almost to herself. 'That's what went wrong. He wanted to look after me and I was too young, and he was older, and it wasn't right.' She sat down at the little dinner table, and poured them both some wine. Jay shook his head, and pushed his glass away, but she drank from hers, feeling the ache in her voice numb a little as the alcohol slid down her throat.

'That's a cop-out, honey,' said Jay, wolfing down more fish. 'He just wasn't right for you, that's all.'

Cord stared out of the window. 'No. I wasn't right for him.'

Chapter Twenty-Eight

'Ha, ha! Are you honest?'

'My lord?'

'Are you fair?'

'What means your lordship?'

'That if you be honest and fair, your honesty should admit no discourse to your beauty.'

'Could beauty, my lord, have better commerce than with honesty?'

'Ay, truly— Hm, Althea.'

'Yes, darling?' Althea's tone was slightly acid. Tony put his hand on her arm.

'Wonderful, it's really wonderful.'

'But . . .?'

'A little more coquettish. She's hard, Ophelia.'

'She's being driven mad by Hamlet, Tony. She's not hard.'

Tony was nodding seriously, not listening. 'Yes, yes. If you could just try it my way—'

Althea gave a small, pointed sigh. 'I'll add more, if you really feel – But Delia should do it herself, in rehearsal.'

Tony nodded absently and bent over to write a note. Althea left the sentence unfinished, and let the paperback of the play drop on to the swinging chair. She ran a hand along the back of her neck, up and over the orange-and-black scarf tied around her shining hair. Tony glanced up then at his wife, and Cord saw with a start how his eyes rested on her with something like annoyance – perhaps even indifference. She might have been a stranger, invited in to read the part with him.

It's all fake, all of this. The black-and-white photographs lining the walls of the Bosky seemed to have multiplied in size the last few times she'd been down. A tapestry showing how wonderful it had once been: a young Mumma and Daddy hand in hand on the beach, the children on the steps of the hut, Olivia and Guy and Bertie sitting on the porch with Martinis, Mads and Ben on their wedding day – all so relaxed, so casual, you had to look ever so closely to see the careful way they'd been staged, how Tony and Althea were always perfectly groomed, looking gorgeous. There weren't any photographs up there of Althea late at night with smudged eyeliner, or Tony kissing the hired singing teacher, or Ben's left hand with the missing fingers . . . It was rather wretched sitting here pretending everything was all right. Ben's face was blank and tired and Mads was stranger than ever, wired tight and impossible to talk sensibly to.

She had arrived after lunch. Madeleine had gone into Swanage in the morning and bought crabs. They'd eaten them that evening with mayonnaise she'd made herself. 'So in case you were wondering, no, I'm not,' she'd said with her strained, sad smile. Cord hadn't understood.

'What did she mean about "No, I'm not?"' she asked her mother as they washed up later, when Mads and her father were outside on the porch making desultory conversation, and Ben had gone off to bed for an early night.

'Oh—' Althea looked over towards the open door. 'You're not supposed to eat mayo these days. Or crabs. Bad for the –' she whispered it – '*baby.*'

'But there is no baby,' Cord said, stupidly.

Althea looked at her sadly. 'No, darling.'

354

Cord hugged herself. 'Poor Mads. Have you asked them about it?'

'A little. If you ask me, I think she's rather too obsessed with it though. Can't see the wood for the trees.'

'What do you mean?'

'She's got Ben and he's doing so well – he's just signed on to direct the robot thingy sequel . . . She doesn't need that job she hates in London any more . . . you know, that girl really has come so far when you think about her childhood. I don't think we know how bad it really was for her, poor darling – she never talks about it—'

Cord remembered waking up and seeing Mads's rigid little body, quivering with fear, stiff as a broom in the bed next to Cord those long-ago summers. Her small mouth chewing on great clumps of her moon-coloured hair. 'I'm just lying in bed thinking about things, it helps me go to sleep,' she'd told Cord, as Cord lay back down with her, stroked her trembling shoulders, singing softly. 'Just going to sleep, honest. I sleep really well here.'

'Poor Mads,' said Cord, sadly. 'She wants to make a new family, a sort of separate one from the one she came from. One day,' she said, vaguely.

Her mother wasn't really listening. 'Oh, darling, don't be down in the dumps about it. You'll find someone.'

Cord shook her head and smiled to herself. She thought of Jay and tried to imagine him here, amongst the old willow-pattern dishes and the worn chintz sofa, restlessly rocking backwards on the cane chairs that looked out to sea. He would love Althea, and Ben would love him – he'd be fine here, fit right in.

What's wrong with me? she'd started to wonder, in the last couple of days, away from the flat and able to see the emptiness of the rest of her life. *Why don't I want to be with anyone? There must be something wrong with me.*

She leaned on the tea towel, looking down at the worn printed image of Corfe Castle, wondering how many dishes after family lunches this towel had dried. All these things in the house that they forgot about when they went away, then reclaimed again the following year. The board games, the old Georgette Heyers and green Penguins on the bookcase, the salad bowl in the shape of a lettuce leaf, the chopping block where once Mrs Gage had sliced off a little of her finger . . . dear Mrs Gage, dead for three years now and Cord had missed her funeral because she was in Leipzig, performing at the Bach Festival.

Like the black-and-white photographs, the house seemed to her now part of the past. And as she looked at her mother's carefully made-up face, the heavy eyeliner that ringed her once-sparkling eyes, the restless hands that tapped on the counter, Cord thought then rather sadly that her mother had completed a transformational stage, like the life cycle of a butterfly. She had become the person she most feared, and Cord was afraid the same was happening to her, too.

The following day, she got up early and walked along the beach, a scarf wrapped tightly around her neck, then they all had a late breakfast, and Tony and Althea rehearsed again, even though Althea wasn't in Tony's directorial debut, a daring new production of *Hamlet*. She was about to go into rehearsals for *The Glass Menagerie* instead, and clearly thought Tony's production ideas were terrible. Mads wrote in her notebook-cum-diary that she kept with her all the time – what, Cord wasn't certain – and Ben shut himself away again, talking to important people on the phone. Then it was lunch, and afterwards everyone dozed, and then in the early evening Mads and Tony went out to scatter Aunt Julia's ashes. They were gone a while.

'We walked up to Bill's Point, chucked most of them off and a funny little cupping wind carried them up and over into the sea – it was the strangest thing,' said Mads happily. 'And there were peregrine falcons nesting there. She'd have loved that.'

'She loved it up there,' said Daddy, and he glanced around at them all. Cord thought it was as though he wasn't sure where he was. 'Who's here?' he said. 'Right, let's drink.'

He opened a bottle of champagne he'd put in an ice cooler beforehand and poured out five glasses, holding the bottle with one hand at the base in that way he always did that the children had found so impressive. They all toasted. 'Julia.' He and Mads clinked glasses first, smiling at each other. Then they all clinked, and Althea rolled her eyes, but said nothing.

'She'd have liked it all, Tony,' said Mads, and she kissed his cheek, and then Ben's. 'She'd be very happy if she could see us now.'

But Cord's father was staring out to sea and didn't seem to have heard her.

Dinner was fish pie, and more wine. Althea drank and didn't say much, and Tony was virtually silent, frequently refilling his own glass, the actions of the afternoon sitting heavily on him. Mads was sad and subdued. It was Cord and Ben who kept things going, Ben telling them about the famous people he'd seen in Hollywood, the action-hero actor he'd had a drink with who had worn a wig throughout which had slipped to one side about which no one had commented. Ben hugged himself when he laughed, sometimes rubbing his face in the sweet way he always had. He made Cord laugh too, and she told them in exchange stories of her travels, not that they were as good, but Ben wanted to know, even if Mumma started looking bored early on. *We're OK, Mumma*, she wanted to say. *Look at your children, we're doing well. Really well.*

Later that night she lay on her side in bed, very still, listening to the rasp of her eyelashes against the pillow when she blinked, and the beating of her heart pounding against the mattress. She wondered what Jay would say if he could see them all. If someone, an outsider, could assess it, for she found she couldn't any more. In the silence of her thinking she realised she could hear Mads and Ben in the next room, as she had done the night before, the rhythmic shunting and creaking of the bed, the groan of release from her brother, Mads's urgent murmuring afterwards. Then silence.

She tried to sleep, but couldn't, not for a long time.

By the third night she was feeling slightly mad. Her mother was still patiently rehearsing *Hamlet* with her father but Tony didn't seem to want to remember that Althea wasn't in the play with him. When she said, as she did often, 'You'll have to get Delia to do that in rehearsal,' he'd ignore her, and simply say, 'Can we try that scene again?' And Cord saw for the first time that she'd given up trying. That she was just going along with him for an easy life.

'Well, that's it for today, I think, my Prince,' Althea said as teatime came, and she stared into the little mirror hanging on one of the wooden slats. There were, Cord had noticed, mirrors everywhere in the house now. 'I've been Ophelia and Gertrude today and that's enough for any woman. Let's get a drink.'

'I really must go for a walk while it's still light,' her father said, putting down his copy of the play and rubbing the back of his head. He had had his hair cut quite recently, she saw; it stuck out at the back where he rubbed it, almost comical, like a grey and brown duck's tail.

'Darling, it'll be dark any moment. And Ben and Mads will be back from their walk soon – we can eat when they're here,' said Althea. Cord knew what she meant was that she could drink freely then. 'Don't go now.'

'Oh, for God's sake, Althea!' her father said, flaring up. 'I know! I was out there yesterday with Julia, it was fine. Please. Leave me alone. If you want a drink have a bloody drink. I must walk for a while, clear my head a bit.' His voice softened. 'Sorry, old girl. Have a drink if you want. See you – soon.'

He strode into the gathering gloom down the path towards the sea, and Cord saw Althea sigh and glance into the mirror. Cord watched him go, her heart aching. How she would love to run after him as she would have done once. To catch up with him. 'Daddy, can I walk with you?'

And his face would have lit up, because she was his world. 'Cordy, of course.'

'It's the anniversary,' her mother said quietly behind her. 'It's always bad, today. But he might, just this once – oh, damn him.'

Cord turned to her. 'What anniversary?'

'The day his aunt went off. August the seventeenth.'

'Aunt Dinah?'

'He told me once he almost died the night his mother was killed but Dinah brought him back to life, and then she left and part of him died for ever . . .'

Cord frowned. 'But, Mumma, what happened?'

'She went away.' Her mother shrugged, as if this was a frivolous detail. 'Oh, it's old news now. Years ago when I started coming here with him, someone in the village told me she brought it on herself. But Daddy simply wouldn't talk about her.'

'Did he never see her again?'

'I don't know. Sometimes I wonder if he did or not.'

Cord scratched her cheek. A muscle under her eye was ticking. 'She just disappeared into thin air? Never contacted him again? Didn't she . . . I mean, didn't she *love* him?'

'Oh, she was an absolute disaster, darling. Shouldn't ever have been in charge of a child if you ask me. Sounds very charming but she was hopeless. Mess everywhere, odd people turning up, very shady past . . . She bunged him in a school and took off, best thing she could have done. But he was very fond of her. Always been a hard day for him.'

'I never knew she did a runner.'

The idea of Daddy now walking alone on the beach like that, no way of telling anyone how he felt, locked in this prison of his own making, moved Cord's soft heart. She stood up, slipped on her flip-flops. 'I'll catch up and walk with him for a bit.'

'Oh, what a nice idea. I say, get him to come back quickly, will you? I'll lay the table.' Her mother began humming.

Cord tripped down the steps and through the first row of beach huts. She could see a solitary figure down on the beach, walking south-west towards Bill's Point, towards the sunset. She felt as though she were chasing the past, running to catch hold of the person he had been.

She walked for several minutes, following the lone figure, squinting to see if it was him or someone else altogether – it was too far away to be certain. As she walked she hugged herself, thinking over the last few days, the strangeness of being here again. And with every passing minute dusk seemed to enshroud her.

Did he feel like this every year, or was it with him all the time? What had happened to his great-aunt? Cord screwed up her eyes, trying to remember what it was about mysterious Aunt Dinah that tasted so funny in her mouth, like Proust's madeleines; madeleines of Worth Bay. What did she know, what had she forgotten?

Then she realised she'd lost sight of the figure; it had vanished in the gathering gloom and the shadow of the bay. She stopped, unsure whether to follow him or not. She was quite far now from the house, so she turned back and retraced her steps. The sun was about to slip behind Bill's Point, the horizon amber gold and gunmetal grey. When eventually she reached the beach hut Cord looked up, more out of habit than anything else. Flowers and Stones, she thought. I'll go in there, get the old rules down. We can have a game tomorrow. It'll be fun. Silly . . . something old . . .

But the light was on and the door ajar, which was odd. Cord walked up the steps, before she'd thought about whether she should or not. Her mind was full of stories: her father as a child, Aunt Dinah, the haunting familiarity of her, the cold feeling in the pit of Cord's stomach that assailed her when Mumma had described her. She walked towards the lit interior of the hut, not really wanting to go back to the house. Perhaps her brother—

There was someone inside. As she opened her mouth to speak she heard noises, and she gripped the door handle. It had already pushed open a little – the old, swinging door that moved freely – and so she saw it before she could stop herself.

At first what she saw through the two-inch-wide crack made sense, though she recoiled at the sight. *Oh*, she thought, stepping back as she saw the figures on the daybed, her sister-in-law's shoes on the scuffed wooden floor. *Ben and Mads are here.* It was where they'd first kissed, where they'd come all those illicit evenings without her. For a brief, surging second or two she was overwhelmed with memories, sensation of those summers past. She could hear them, and this time Mads's voice rose above his. She was talking, talking urgently.

Then Cord looked inside again and saw the back of his head,

and the hair. Short hair, grey and brown. Sticking out like a duck's tail.

'More like that . . . like that . . .' Mads's voice was low, urgent, frantic. 'Don't stop . . . More . . . more like that . . .'

Cord frowned, not understanding. She was stupid. She saw them move on the daybed, and then she understood.

It wasn't Ben.

It wasn't Ben.

Her father was there with Madeleine, her father's head, seen from the back, like those other times, a kaleidoscope of images jumbling in her mind . . . his shoulders curving over Madeleine underneath him, her own silvery hair spilling over the worn old cushions on the daybed, thin knees drawn up, clutching him between her legs and that was all she could see in the crack through the door. She heard her father mutter something, groan, a desperate exhalation. This all happened in a few split seconds and Cord felt a force in her chest that made her stagger slightly backwards. She steadied her hand on the railing, then ran down the steps again on to the sand. Their sounds rose a little, carried out to her on the still evening air.

'Oh, Tony . . .'

She saw it was night-time now, the stars pricking the pure, periwinkle sky. Cord tried to run, but the sand held her back.

Cord would relive this moment in a dream every other week or so for the rest of her life. Their rising, peaking sounds of sex, hoarse and furtive. The sight of her bare feet, blue-grey in the light of the moon. Trying to run away, but stuck, trapped in the heavy, sinking sand.

She left the next day: an urgent rehearsal had come up, she said, and she had to leave. She went after breakfast, waved off only by her brother. Mumma and Daddy were continuing to eat muesli in mutinous silence. Mads was, Ben said, still asleep.

'So sorry you have to go,' he said, but there was a hardness in his eyes and a tone to his soft voice she hadn't heard before. 'We've hardly seen you.'

'Sorry, Ben,' she'd said, climbing into her battered old Golf. 'I – I have to go.'

'You're always leaving, Cordy. Forget the rehearsal for once. I've given up stuff to be here. I should be at a script conference in LA, but I'm not, because I wanted to come. For us all to be together.'

She'd pulled the car door shut and wound down the window, stared at him, unblinking. Her big brother, who was the one she had to love and protect, whose hand she had held when he was scared.

She just said, 'I'm sorry, Ben. I'm so sorry. For all of it.'

The car lurched up the bumpy track, clouds of dust rising behind her so that they obscured the view of her brother in the rear window. When they cleared, as she reached the main road, she saw he had gone.

Cord drove almost to London without a break. But, going through Richmond Park where the grasses were bleached almost yellow-white in the late-summer sun, with screaming, delighted children randomly popping up between rolling swathes of bracken, she suddenly pulled the car over in an open lay-by and was sick once again, her stomach reflexively heaving for a long time afterwards until it was entirely empty. The heavy scent of straw, bracken and petrol hung in the dusty air. She would think she was finished, and then would start to gag and be sick again, only there was nothing left. Fluorescent-yellow acid burned her throat; it was sore for days. The following evening, at the Wigmore Hall for a concert of Handel arias, it hurt to sing and she received the only bad reviews she'd had to date.

Though she told herself she wasn't to blame, a part of her knew that wasn't true. And she kept thinking of the postcard in the lavatory at the Bosky, of the cartoon of the old man visiting a dying friend, obviously a fellow actor. She'd never understood it as a child, then barely noticed it for all the years afterwards, until that night when, returning from the beach hut, vomiting silently into the toilet bowl, her throat burning, she had raised her spinning head and seen it once more, for the first time in years, and now she understood it.

For on that night she'd gazed at the black-and-white, roughly sketched men, one sitting by the other's bed. 'It's jolly hard, dying, old chap,' the ill man was saying, gazing up at his Garrick Club-tie-wearing pal. 'But it's not as hard as farce.'

Chapter Twenty-Nine

April 1991

It was a glorious spring that year. She would sit for hours on the porch in the daytime in her ancient fleecy blue sweater whose cuffs were chewed and loose, wrapped in a blanket like a whale beached on the shore, her long thick hair covering her: yet another layer. She'd eat endless toasted cheese-and-tuna sandwiches Ben made her and read murder mysteries, while Ben worked on his script. The spring wild flowers at the Bosky were totally different, the house was totally different from the dry heat of summer. Buttery primroses and glossy celandines around the house and on the sloping grassy verges before the grass gave way to sand, the lanes edged with bobbing, pretty, baby-blue forget-me-nots and hot-pink campions. Blackbirds sang in the hedgerows beyond the house; she could hear them in the morning and at night, when she lay shivering and uncomfortable in bed.

The old wooden house was no good at retaining heat and Mads suffered. For it was still bitterly cold come evening, the stars glittering and hard over the bay. A waxing moon rose early over the sea towards the end of their stay and hung, shining ice-white light, towards the Bosky in a jagged path across the waves. By day it was peaceful but when she got up in the night as she did frequently she could always hear up above her the strong spring tides lashing the beach with violent force. They could not go on the sand except at low tide. It was for the best:

the two babies inside her might come at any time, they said. They could not accurately measure them and so weren't sure when they were due. In any case, she should not be scrambling over the dunes. And so she stayed in the house, waiting for the building work in London to finish, waiting for these children, so looked-for, to come.

'Isn't it strange, how different it is here in spring. Like another house,' she said to Ben on their last night there as they sat inside in the cosy, timber-lined kitchen-diner, looking out over the bay at the rising moon. She shifted in her chair, trying to make room for more pasta, unable to get comfortable as one persistent foot repeatedly jabbed under her ribcage, as if it were trying to escape.

'Yes,' said Ben. 'We came here once for Easter when I was little. It *was* strange. I've never forgotten it. The grass all fresh and green, and the flowers and everything else.'

'When was that? I didn't know you'd been here at Easter.'

He eyed her with a twinkling smile. 'Didn't you keep a detailed record of our visit in your diary?'

Mads kicked out her foot and he laughed but she said, passionately, 'Oh, don't tease me about it. I liked things being orderly. It wasn't like that.'

Ben took her hand, still smiling, and stroked it. 'It was, Maddy, and that's why I love you so much.'

He kissed the hand, then shifted his chair over, and put both his own hands on her huge bump.

'One's kicking. There's a foot right up there.'

'Hey,' he said, talking to her stomach. 'It's Daddy here. Stop kicking your mother. I can teach you karate when you're out. We'll watch *Karate Kid*. Just chill, for the moment. Be calm. Not like Mummy.' He looked up at her mischievously.

Ben's hands were still on her. She pressed them against her mound even more firmly. 'Ben . . . I'm scared.'

'I know,' he said, looking down at the bump. 'I know you are. It's huge. It's twins.' He rubbed his face; he looked very like Althea, horror mixed with wry amusement. 'But we've got money now. We're not penniless students eating our baked beans out of tins any more. We can have help. A nanny. Nannies, plural—'

'No,' she said, shaking her hair; like a creature in a fairy tale, it seemed to grow thicker, more lustrous with each day of her interminable pregnancy. 'I said this before. I don't want nannies. I want to look after them myself. And I'm not stupid, I know it'll be hard. But I – I didn't know my mum. I was two. I know she was called Suzanne and she was from Worthing and she was married to my father for six years before she died having the other baby—' Her lip quivered; lately, she couldn't stop thinking about her mother. She remembered nothing of her apart from the suggestion of a tiny figure with long hair and firm thin fingers, a smell of lilacs, and she knew nothing apart from a few bland little letters she'd written to Aunt Julia that Mads had inherited (*Dear Julia. Thank you for your letter. I am glad to hear all is well in Sydney. All is well here. Ian is well. Your niece is called Madeleine Ann. She is very good. I enclose a photograph. We will be pleased to see you in the summer. Love, Suzanne*), a quaint sixties photograph of her parents' wedding day, her mother decorous and shy in a lace wedding dress, her father impassive behind horn-rimmed spectacles as her mother smiled timidly at the camera. 'They're having a mum and a dad who are there, who love them, not people who've been paid to love them.'

'I understand. You know I do.' Ben nodded. She could hear the nervousness in his voice as he added, 'I'll be away, though, you know, this Irish priest thing I'm doing and it's at Pinewood but it'll still be—'

'Of course, we agreed, I know that. I'll do it myself. And

you'll have breaks between films and you'll see them. But they'll be mine and I want them to myself and I want them to be looked after by me.' She heaved herself up. 'I'm their mummy.'

'I know. But—' Ben took her plate of pasta and started shovelling it into his mouth and she watched him in distaste. 'Don't be a control freak, darling. I know you like to understand everything, to know everything and have a list and everything all ready but – God, you know, when I visited Hamish and Sunita they spent thirty minutes getting the baby ready to go out to the park for a walk and then she did this poo that sort of went everywhere, all over her clothes and the pram, and they had to start all over again and that's all they were doing for the two hours I was there, changing her, feeding her and then cleaning all this shit up off surfaces. I thought Hamish was going to fall over at one point, he was so knackered. And that was two of them. And only one baby.' He looked pale. 'It was – it was really intense.'

Mads stared down at him. She was very tired. Ben finished the pasta.

'Say something,' he said.

'You've got ragu on your mouth,' she said eventually and, collecting the plates, she went slowly to the kitchen counter. 'I might go to bed.'

'Are you feeling OK?'

'Actually, I feel a bit sick.'

'Oh. How long for?'

'Just now.' She leaned against the counter. 'Just now.'

He came over, and she rested her head on his chest. 'I can't hug you,' he said, kissing her hair. 'But I can hold you like this.' He wrapped his arms around her shoulders.

'I – I don't know if we've done the right thing,' she said, in a very quiet voice.

'That's normal.'

Her blood felt like ice, as so often these days. *Normal.* He was running his hands through her hair, the way he had when they were children, the way he had the first time they met again, and she felt better immediately, the soft, sensual tickling sensation calming her. *Normal.* She blinked away the memories that flashed in front of her now with increasing regularity and potency . . . the sight of him, that night, the way he knelt down and wept silently, pressing his palms into his eyes like a child.

'Julia,' she had heard him say, softly, brokenly. The catch in his voice as she helped him to his feet again and held him, and kissed his cheek and sort of missed so half kissed his lips, for a moment too long, so that they broke apart and stared at each other, in recognition of something they had never before understood . . .

The moment of pause, inside the beach hut, as the sea washed the shore outside and he put his hands on her hips and pushed her gently against the wall . . . those old veined hands of his, that she suddenly realised she didn't know at all, on her breasts where she was used to Ben's missing fingers . . . the glazed, terrified look on his face as he plunged into her . . .

And then it was too late and she was enjoying it, and that was the worst part of all. It wasn't a mistake – it was what she had always wanted, since she was aware of studying her own feelings carefully, tacking it against information about female desire gleaned from seamy library books, Victoria Holts and Shirley Conrans. She liked information, and she knew that she desired Tony, that she wanted this, that he was barely himself, a shell of what he had been. That this might help him. She knew that she wanted him, in a way that was unlike her need for Ben, her love for her husband. That was the greatest shame of all.

A fortnight later, her scientific knowledge gave out on her

and instinct kicked in. After they had returned to London, and she had gone out jogging in Regent's Park, and had had to sit down on a bench very suddenly, she understood instantly then that she was pregnant. She was never alone with Tony after that, never spoke to him about it, but she knew he knew too. It was obvious, wasn't it? Wasn't it obvious to Ben, to Althea?

Apparently not. They were deliriously happy and happiness, as Mads already knew, obscured many truths. But it had happened, and she had got what she wanted. This is what she told herself, every day, every hour.

Now she pulled herself gently away from her husband. 'I'll get ready for bed. Can you pack up the kitchen? I think we should leave in lots of time tomorrow. I'll need to stop and pee every hour at this rate.'

'Of course, and then we'll get back home and the house will be finished and ready for us and all you have to do now is enjoy it. Have some people over. Do a bit of shopping. Relax.'

'People?'

'Well. Friends. Family.'

'My family's all dead. I don't have any friends in London, I'm hopeless at shopping and I bloody hate being told to relax,' she said, ticking them off her fingers. He closed his eyes penitently.

'I know. I'm sorry.'

'No, I'm sorry.' She bit her lip. 'Darling Ben, you're trying to be kind. I love you—' She put her hands to her burning cheeks. 'Sometimes – oh, sometimes I wish with all my heart it was just you and me in our little bedsit in Clifton again, all snug and cosy and no money except for my job and your lovely sofa you filched from home. Don't you?' She gazed at him.

Ben said slowly, 'Look. Perhaps I could get Mumma and Daddy to come over and pay you a visit once a week? They're not busy since Daddy's disaster with *Hamlet*. In fact, they're twiddling their thumbs slightly till Mummy goes off to America to reprise *Glass Menagerie*.'

'No,' said Mads. 'Not your parents. Not at the moment.'

He put his head on one side. 'Maddy – I'm leaving you for two weeks. I hate the idea you're on your own . . .'

'Cord?'

He rolled his lips towards his teeth in a grimace. 'Haven't heard back from her. I've tried. It's like she's vanished.'

Mads arranged things on the counter. 'Me too. Do you think . . .' A thought, unbidden, pushed its way into her mind and she pushed it away, with vigour – she was having to become increasingly good at this, the forcible ejection of thoughts that threatened to overwhelm her, these days. 'She can't mind. I don't know . . . I don't understand it,' she finished, her tone high so as to eliminate the catch in her throat.

Laughter, that's what she missed most about Cord, and the Bosky holidays. They'd laugh and laugh, Cord with a proper gurgling giggle that entirely overtook her. About the funny faces Althea made to herself in the mirror when she thought no one was looking, or the way Tony tried to charm Mrs Gage to her total indifference, or the small boy on the beach peeing unseen into a bucket of seawater that his oblivious brother later threw over their parents. Or Cord's ABBA routines, her poems she'd make up about communism, or the time she got a rash from spraying on too much Charlie Girl perfume . . .

She felt very tired. *I miss her. Oh, what a bloody mess it all is.*

'I should call your parents. I just want to be alone, that's all. They've been so kind, I owe them so much, but sometimes . . . sometimes they . . .' Tears filled her eyes at the idea of distance from them, this family she'd loved so much. *I've fucked it up. Properly, truly. Every one of them, I loved them so much and I have absolutely ruined everything.* 'I don't know what I'm trying to say.'

'You do really love us all, don't you?' he said, staring at her. 'The only one who does. No, I won't tell you. It doesn't matter, in the end.'

'Tell me what?'

Ben stood under the light; it gave him a golden halo around his head. 'The reason I ran away. The reason I lost the fingers.' He held up his hand: light from the bulb above shone on it dramatically. 'I've never really told you why.'

She swallowed. 'Tell me. Tell me why?'

He was silent. Then he reached over and pulled the curtains across the window, and the view of the bay vanished. 'No, I won't tell you. It doesn't matter in the end.'

'Ben—'

'I can't see how it makes a difference.' He kissed her again. 'And I wish I didn't know, and he doesn't know, and so perhaps it's best to let sleeping dogs lie. He . . .' He coughed, clearing his throat. 'He's my father, after all.'

Mads pressed down on the kicking foot that jabbed up into her once again. 'Yes,' she said, as images danced through her aching, throbbing head. 'Yes, he is, isn't he.'

Birth Notices

To Benedick and Madeleine Wilde at UCH on 15 April 1991, twin girls, 4lbs 7oz and 5lbs, EMILY SUZANNE and IRIS JULIA. Granddaughters to Sir and Lady Anthony Wilde, nieces to Miss Cordelia Wilde.

Christening to take place on 29 May 1991 at St Paul's Church, Covent Garden, WC2.

Chapter Thirty

29 July 1992

It happened today.

Iris walked for the first time – three steps. (That's not what happened.) Very unstable, like she's drunk. Emily watches her from the corner of the kitchen, bemused. Tony and Althea were here, doting grandparents that they are. Althea clapped, she took pictures. She loves the girls, it's strange quite how much. Tony stared at Emily, watching her sister walking across the lino, and I knew he'd seen it. <u>Seen what I can see</u>. Iris's legs are crooked. The doctor says, with a note of irritation in his voice he doesn't try to hide any more, that it's simply the way babies walk but I wonder if there's something wrong with her – with both of them . . . More worries. I have these worries, Book. Emily watches her, & doesn't move – the doctor says that is normal too – and Althea scoops her up & covers her with kisses, cooing at her and whispering secrets in her ear. Emily has curls around her head, fine and damp after she's woken up. Her cheeks are like cool, plump, soft pillows. Two more weeks till Ben's shoot is over. I had three hours' sleep last night. And that was a good night. Do you know what lack of sleep is like, Book? Let me try & write it down. For weeks you just feel terrible, and then the mind games start, because you're still as tired as ever but your body is used to it. So you feel human some days & then you will start shouting at one of them when they cry, shouting in their faces so they stare at you in surprise, or you suddenly stab the table with the kitchen scissors when you can't open the damn milk. Or when the van driver almost knocks you over as you're waving your in-laws off, then yes, you will press yourself against the windscreen hammering with your fists & you will scream at him, scream till he drives off, you swearing at him in the road. The neighbours think I'm crazy. <u>It's true, I am</u>. They had such high hopes for us at the start: Tony Wilde's son & daughter-in-law & their delightful twin daughters. Instead they've got me. I look like a drug addict or a homeless person, in baggy worn jog bottoms with holes in them, and my hair has tangles in it I can't begin to brush out so I don't bother any more. I have bruises under my eyes: I can see them, but I can't stop pressing my fingers into my eye sockets, when I start to see things I don't want to, again. Like Tony's face. Like Iris, walking. Like Ben, as he said bye. Like Emily's sweet head nestling into my chest. I've got eight pages left. Book, my Book, what will I do with you when I've finished writing in you? I'll do something. My father always used to tell me I looked like a scarecrow. 'My little scarecrow'. He hit me once bc he said I was so dirty. I had been playing Flowers & Stones with Ben and Cord most of the day, in and out of the flowers by the house, then Dizzyman by the shore as the tide came in and went out. I fell in a couple of times. We were almost sick with laughter (Ben actually was sick, back at the house after lunch) and we were soaking and covered in sand, and then we'd gone to look at the rabbits in the field where the grey mare lived behind the lane. I can't remember her name, Book, & I'd been crouching on the sandy, dirty field trying to coax one towards me but they're very shy, rabbits. They really won't come near you not even if you have chocolate, which we thought they'd like (Cord said they did). When I got home, I was filthy, smelling of seaweed and rabbit poo & probably sick but I was happy, really, really happy for once, tired in the way you only can be if you've been laughing all day. Crying has the same effect. My father liked everything just so. Always has. He was drunk when I came in. And he hit me. He said I was a little slag for hanging around with them all day, that Ben Wilde

374

would try and do to me what his father had done to Aunt Jules and that's why she'd had to leave school early and never got her school cert. He wouldn't stop talking. He said that's why she'd moved to Oz for all those years & was now fat and bitter & sad and never came to the Bosky any more. He hit me so hard I fell against the corner of the table and he said I wasn't his problem. He was sick of having to worry about me. The next day he was sorry. He actually gave me a kiss on the head at breakfast. "That's a bit of a lump. Listen, I am sorry I walloped you, but it's for your own good I hope. I just want to warn you. You really must understand what they're like, that lot." Oh, Daddy, what would you have done if you'd seen me, all those years later, doing the same as Aunt Jules did with Tony Wilde, then? That's what she did, wasn't it? Making the same mistakes she did, only that's the thing, it wasn't a mistake, it can't have been because look at what I have now. It is the culmination of everything. It has to be. Perhaps they're not his. Perhaps they're Ben's. I never asked Tony about it. I know Tony, I know he wouldn't have treated someone badly. That's the thing about him, that years later even when I was in the middle of it with him, when he was on top of me, putting it in me, staring at me helplessly and rather sweaty – 'Are you sure, darling?' he said, the faintest stirrings of doubt blooming in his eyes & I nodded and gave him a little sigh to let him know how much I liked it. Because I did like it, even though he was slower, and rather older and purpler than in my life-long fantasy, I still believed he wasn't doing it to play a trick, to tick me off a list. But because he needed it. I don't know if he knew it was me, and not Aunt Jules. Poor Tony. I think he is trapped somewhere in time as a 14 yr old.

I can't remember how it happened, except that I love Tony, I always have and he was so desperately sad, and I wanted him then. I have started to wonder if the reason Ben couldn't get me pregnant was because I didn't want his baby. Because my body somehow wouldn't seek out the right sperm to make his baby & it's my fault. Because I am <u>BAD</u>, & sent to tear them *apart, to take revenge on them for what happened to Jules years ago – is that it? Giving me twins, laughing at our joint fecundity . . . Men take their pleasure, & the consequence is mild guilt. Women take pleasure, and they are punished for the rest of their lives. I took Ben's name when we married, and I wish more than anything I had not. So those doctors, with medical statistics and helpful leaflets, they were all wrong. I needed one night, the right time of the month, one roll of the dice: and well, didn't it work? I didn't get my baby, I got two, 2 2 2! I have a family, my two girls, my babies, and they're mine – and his. I'm sure they're his. Sometimes I look at my little plump Emily, with her thick curling hair and her nose like a button and her funny dark eyes that flash and sparkle, & a small Tony Wilde stares back, and I wonder why no one else has noticed it. Why Althea or Ben or Cord don't say anything. She is so like Tony it's funny really, mercurial, charming, somewhere not quite with you all the time. Iris looks like me. I look at her sharp, watchful face and her darting little eyes and her solemn expression and how she won't impress anyone just for the sake of it by cooing or gurgling and I could shout for joy. She picks things up precisely between one white slim finger & one white slim thumb. She is like him too, determined and quixotic & charming, both of them are charming of course, I understood them both perfectly the moment I saw them – also I knew the moment I saw them that what I'd done to get them here was wholly wrong & awful. A sin – I don't believe in God, or anything like that, but I believe in sin. I have sinned. Tony did too but oh, I'm the one who made it happen, & I am living with it now. I've never given Tony or Ben reason to suspect, we have never repeated what happened that night. But I saw how he looked at Emily. He saw it. I've got them. I've got what I wanted. <u>Now I simply have to live with what I've done, for the rest of my life.</u> Try to forget all the broken pieces of things I stepped over on the way to get here. I have to simply get on with living, and the truth.*

The truth for once? I'm not sure if I can.

5 August

*Ben is back, we go to the Bosky tomorrow. He says he has been
"thinking". He says things have to change. He is insisting on a nanny.
He won't listen to me. I am much better now than the last few weeks.
But he says I'm not coping. I thought this would be a relief but it's not.
It's not because it means it's real & I am doing it as badly as I
thought. Iris was in bed with me when he came back, fast asleep under
the duvet – she had wriggled down there in the night, Book, she
wouldn't sleep in her cot so I took her in with me. He shouted at me.
He said she could have suffocated. I don't know. I don't know if he's
right. He brought the girls back huge dolls in frilly dresses that the
studio gave him. One's all in pink lace and called Pretty Lil Flirt with
a pink hairband and the other one's in a green-and-brown smock and
she's called Lynda and she has a trowel and watering can. I don't know
why but this makes me laugh and laugh and laugh, Ben stares at me, I
can see him looking at me. He doesn't think it's funny. When they're
grown up, I wonder if they'll look at the dolls & ask themselves why
we gave them each the one we did.*

7 Aug

*When I write, the biro presses through the last three pages on to the back
cover of my book. When I turn to the front and read the opening pages
I see that 18 yrs ago I said I'd write down things I noticed about the
Wildflowers & Book is nearly finished.*

17 Aug

*Something strange is happening to me and it doesn't work to write it
down any more which is good – the book is nearly finished. We got here
3 days ago. Ben is still bossing me about. He has forced Cord to come
down too, the first time we've seen her for months. He says she must*

help with the babies too. Cord did help. She can do it, she just knows how to and I don't. She knows how to hold them, how to stop Iris wriggling and, when no one is around, she sings to them, as she's putting their night things on. "Stay Awake", from _Mary Poppins_. "Little Jesus Sweetly Sleep". Everything goes on as normal and yet it's not. I'm leaving this book under the floorboards of the porch. With the strange birdman doll that is buried there. He has a bird face and wings & is very old. Book will be under the porch. It's where Cord and I spent hours & hours on the steps predicting the waves, making up stories about the clouds, painting our toenails ridiculous colours, doing "Bits & Pieces" from the _Radio 1 Roadshow_.

You see, she almost as good as told me I had to end it all myself and I am grateful she has done it that way, it makes it all easier. I saw her – at the beach hut, last night, when I was sitting there trying to work out what to do. Feeling guilty because I had left the babies with Ben and Althea. She knows – I didn't realise she knows about Tony and me, and the girls. She said such horrible things to me. She said I was a slag – a slag. It's such a nasty word & it's what Daddy used to call me for hanging round with them all those years ago. She said I was a twisted, evil person, that I had wormed my way into the family and was eating us away from the inside. That I was the reason everything had gone wrong. She blames me for everything. Book, oh Book, oh Book.

She said she looked at the girls in the bath that evening and couldn't stand it any more. She said it's because they're so beautiful and pure. That they are marked with a stain, & the stain is all my fault and it will ruin their lives if I'm still around, that I am what will tear them down eventually. She said she kept away because she didn't ever want to hurt Ben but now he'd practically dragged her down there she couldn't stay silent, not to me.

Everything you touch turns rotten," she said. "I thought you were a good person. But you weren't. You lied to us and you crept around hoping to be our friend. You lied to Ben and pretended to be all doe-eyed and passive to kiss him when we were young. You made my mother wish she had a

*daughter like you, all long hair and simpering, instead of the daughter she
had. You couldn't get Ben to give you a baby. I think you must have driven
my father mad, mad over the years. I'm not surprised he went along with
you." I SAID to her, Cord, none of that's true, but the noises hammering
in my head, hammering so loud, wouldn't stop. I said it to her, I said,
Cord, I love you more than any of them. You're my friend. "You're not my
friend," she said, she was crying. "You're a snake. You've slithered in &
poisoned us. We were fine before you. We were just the four of us. We were
happy." She was so pale I could see the blue veins on her forehead &
cheeks. Her big big grey eyes, her thick black lashes. Normally there's a
smile lurking deep down there no matter how sad she is. Not now, not any
more. She just kept saying it, there on the sofa in the beach hut, and I stood
at the door, shivering with the cold. "You poisoned us. Our family. You're
the bad thing. You're the bad thing."*

   *I see it all clearly now in the beach hut, everything hurtful & sharp
and real, like Cordy, or Tony, or Ben, or the smell and taste of my little
ones, and how awful it is loving someone that much, they all feel very
far away. As if I see them through thick, thick glass or plastic. Some
material. And it's easier that way, Book.*

   *Because when I think about what might happen to my girls. How they
might be hurt by horrible girls at school who tease them for their clothes
like I was teased. How nasty boys might use them and try and get them
to do things they don't want. How they might hate their bodies and stare
at themselves hour after hour in the mirror. How they might fall over &
tear their perfect soft skin or have accidents on bikes or skates or get into
unsafe cars or worse than anything be unloved, be sad and lonely and
broken by their upbringing like I have been . . . .*
*. . . . . Can't
think straight. It hurts so much to think of them hurt. I have hurt them
already. I am afraid I will make things much worse if I stay.*

   *I have to close the gaping hole. <u>I have to cover it over.</u> I am not a
good mother to them. I am not a good wife or sister, the pain of being*

like this comes in waves and at the moment I think the wave is too strong for me. It's crashing now.

2 pages left & I wanted to finish the whole book but it's not that neat, is it? That's all really. Thank you, Book.

One more list. To use the space.

Cord wore: A blue shantung silk halter-neck dress and cork-soled wedge heel shoes. Sunglasses. She bites her nails, they are chewed to bits. She has an expensive watch. She is reading <u>My Family and Other Animals</u>. She brought Althea a pile of Rosamunde Pilcher & Mary Wesley books. Althea is delighted. She bought Ben a neck thing to wear on flights that you blow up and it stops your neck hurting – a little thing but it has already helped as he gets a sore neck all the time, it cricks and freezes. She is thoughtful. And kind. But so different in her smart dress and sunglasses. Her passport is always in her handbag. She pinches her throat all the time when she's talking, she says it does her good. Pinches it really hard. She has left us behind and now I see why, I see why.

Keep on.

Tony: Yesterday he was wearing a navy polo shirt and some blue twill trousers. He had a red spotted handkerchief in his linen jacket, he wipes his face with it. He shakes a lot. I think he is ill. They all hated <u>Hamlet</u>, it knocked him for six. He has a book with all the reviews in. "Appallingly ill-judged". "Unbelievably offensive". He reads it every day I see him.

Althea is in a jersey silk dress from Jaeger in wine red / brown tiger print and she has sandals on, and her sunglasses, & her legs are slim and brown as ever, and all she does all day is lie on the porch reading her books, smoking and drinking camomile tea or gin. She grows the camomile here and collects it up and dries it and makes it into tea. She is totally oblivious to everything. I realised that long ago. She only wants to see what's nice. She will do anything for the babies. She will do anything for Ben.

Ben . . . Ben is in his old Kate Bush "Hounds of Love" T-shirt that we bought together one each from Kensington Market on that trip to London. We thought we were so cool, didn't we, so in love, oh my gosh, I loved him and his shorts from the market in Provence that summer after we were married. His chest is fuzzy with blonde hair. He picks the girls up and swings them over his head. He is reading Truffaut on Hitchcock and he is writing a screenplay about his childhood . . . I know this, they don't . . . Yesterday he cut his finger cleaning up a glass I smashed and has an elastoplast on it. I put it on him. It will still be there afterwards. His hair needs a cut but it suits him, so shaggy and ruffled. Help me, darling, help me, please. That's what she sings. Help me, darling, help me, please. I love him so much but he has to clean all the broken pieces up after me and he's tired. I'm tired. It will actually be a relief.

Chapter Thirty-One

Mads had few clothes; as a child she had been dressed in either school uniform or outfits cobbled together from charity shops and presents from Aunt Julia. Being a young girl concerned with science and experiments and not with her own appearance she had never acquired an interest in fashion herself, which Ben always thought was strange, as she'd always noticed what his mother and sister wore. Still, he told himself, clearing out her wardrobe would be straightforward.

The bedroom was at the front of the house; Ben could hear the faint noise of cars in the distance, and his daughters downstairs with Elsa, the nanny. Otherwise it was very quiet. He looked at his watch. Ten-thirty. In a couple of hours a group of friends were taking him out to lunch to say farewell – a table for ten at Le Caprice. Movie friends, whom he'd see in Los Angeles anyway. Movie friends who'd never known her and who didn't have children and who had no idea about his life but the gesture was kindly meant and one of them was a producer on the upcoming *Robot Master 3: Robots Attack*. Tragedy didn't spare you from work, nor would he have wanted it to, but it made everything harder to negotiate, made you a leper. He remembered this from when he'd run away and had his accident, with an ache of recognition, that people were terrified of you if you were different in some way. Sometimes over the previous six months he'd just wanted to give people a card, with a series of instructions on it.

1. *Please call my wife by her name. She was called Madeleine. Don't call her 'the tragic event'.*
2. *Please ask me about my children. Just because their mother killed herself doesn't mean they're dead or ill. Don't call them 'the poor children'.*
3. *Please look me in the eye. I'm not infectious. You can't catch what I've got.*
4. *Please return my calls. I need to work. I have two children. (See point 2.)*

The wardrobe was a vast mahogany thing that had come from Ben and Cord's old room in the Bosky. Ben squared his shoulders, and drew in his breath, slowly, as he had seen his father do sometimes, before he went on stage. Then he opened the great mahogany door and, feeling like Lucy Pevensie, leaned as far in as he could go.

The scent of his dead wife hung in the black air inside: sweet, musky, a faintly sour note at the edges. As his vision sharpened in the dark, so did the knot of pain around his heart and he blinked, his eyes sharp with tears at the smell of her again. It was chaos inside, clothes shoved in anyhow, jumpers rolled up inside out, T-shirts and plaid shirts balled up in crumpled heaps. Gently, he began dropping each item on to the floor in separate piles. Here was the Kate Bush T-shirt, which they had bought in duplicate, and those loose plaid shirts she liked, which drew no attention to her and her extraordinary, impish beauty, and the battered 501s, and shapeless maternity smocks and there was the baggy, faded blue sweater she used to hunch her entire body into, knees pulled up under her chin, until it became her favourite item to wear in the last stages of her pregnancy. All of it his Maddy's, uniquely hers. The task of going through her clothes had seemed like a chore; now he understood why he had avoided it. It was the closest to her he'd felt since she'd died. It was painful, so painful it actually hurt. He found the green silk shirt-dress she had worn to the girls' christening right at the back, shoved into a plastic bag; he pulled it out, and it was stiff with breast-milk and blood. She had bled for weeks after the birth. Methodically, Ben began sorting the clothes out, but the majority were either missing a button or dirty or torn beyond repair, and still the faint scent of her hung over them all and if he put the soft fleece of the inside of the sweater to his cheek it was like smelling her, touching her again.

So when his mother appeared, five minutes later, Ben was sitting on the floor, surrounded by Mads's clothes, his head in his hands, sobbing in wheezing gulps he could not control.

Althea sank to her knees. 'Oh, darling,' she said. She wrapped her arms around him. 'I know, darling. I know.'

Ben wiped his eyes. He didn't want to stop crying. When he was crying, keening, he was acknowledging how black and final it really was, facing up to it. It was getting on with living, day by day, that was what was so hard. 'They're all filthy,' he said. 'There's blood on most of the jeans and in the T-shirts.' Althea winced.

'Awful.'

'She was in so much pain. And I didn't know,' he whispered, for what must have been the hundredth time since he lost her. 'I knew it was tough for her but I had no idea. I didn't try hard enough to find out.'

'You did. You'd hired Elsa,' said Althea patiently. She sat back down on the floor carefully and, with a jolt, Ben noticed for the first time the stiffness of her movements.

Grief absorbed everything. It was like a blob of black ink, always there, wobbling slightly in front of him in his mind's eye, and then something would happen and it'd suddenly spread through him, as though on blotting paper, like tea leaves, colour swirling through the water. Emily and Iris would never know their mother, wouldn't see her grow old. He would never know her change; she was fixed as she had been the last time he'd seen her: a pale, hollow-eyed wraith, almost ghost-like already even before death, moving slowly about, crippled with some kind of pain that bent her forwards, almost double. The more the babies thrived, the older they became: the more it seemed to eat at her. He'd thought he'd understood her better than any of the other Wildes, but he'd been wrong.

Althea began putting the clothes into a plastic bag in forceful, punching movements. 'No,' he said, stopping her. 'They need to be washed, or mended.'

'I know,' she said, carrying on. 'That's why I'm here, isn't it? I said I'd help you sort her things out, and I will. I've got the car and I'll take them to the charity shop – is that all right?' She put her hand on his arm. 'Darling. It's best to do this, you know. You're leaving in three weeks. You must clear her things out.' She looked down at a soft cream silk shirt. 'Look at it. So small. She was just a little thing, wasn't she?'

Ben was just beginning to get used to the idea that Mads was gone for ever, though it sounded stupid when you said it like that, as if he couldn't understand she was dead. But she had been such a vital person, so alive and so very unlike anyone else, with her solemn face, half monkey-like, half beautiful, her quick movements and yet her great capacity for stillness. She had slept a great deal before she killed herself, sometimes with the babies, curled up in the bed when he was away, and her sleep was deeper than theirs – she did everything totally, utterly – when he had first found her that morning he hadn't believed she was dead, because so often before he had had to shake her awake from the deepest sleep.

That last time – the curled, hunched figure, the hands tightly clenched, the hair that spilled over the coverlet and almost to the floor . . . her soft, pale face, the dark gold lashes resting on the cheek . . .

She had been buried in her wedding dress. It was Cord's idea. She was quite insistent about it. 'She didn't have nice things for so long,' she'd said, standing in the doorway of the sitting room biting her nails. 'Her wedding dress was awfully expensive, for her. She paid for it herself.'

'Did she?' Ben hadn't really known, hadn't asked. He remembered it – a simple cream taffeta dress with a long skirt and a velvet bolero jacket, tightly tailored, in leaden silver. He remembered her shining hair around her face, her pink cheeks, her heart-stopping smile as she reached him at the front of the church . . . *It's just us*, she'd seemed to say, *just us now* . . .

'Yes, and she had three extra fittings at Liberty, because she kept losing weight.' Cord had torn off the corner of a nail and winced – Ben always remembered her, plunging the bleeding hand into her pocket again. 'She used all her savings to afford it. She'd want to be buried in that. I know she would.'

Now, looking into the wardrobe, Ben wished he still had the dress, something of Madeleine's to give to the girls, something that wasn't old and tatty and stained. There was nothing really left of her, other than them. What else could he give them, to remember her by?

The sound of one toddler crying floated up to them, and he closed his eyes, briefly overwhelmed as he sometimes was by the thought of both of them, needing him so much. He breathed in, smelling her scent one last time. It was already fainter than before and he shut the wardrobe door with a slam, that he might preserve what little of it there was. Perhaps before he left for LA he'd open it again.

Althea was tying a knot in the second bag. She stood up, dusting herself off, and a letter fell to the ground from her handbag. She picked it up, hastily. Ben glanced curiously at it.

'Downing Street?' he said, anxious to change the subject, to chase his misery away, for one second. She stuffed it into her bag. 'Why is John Major writing to you, Mumma? Is he asking you out on a date?'

She shook her head. 'He's not.'

'What on earth is that?' He scanned her face, touching her playfully on the arm. 'Come on. Tell me!'

Althea twisted away from him, staring into the wardrobe. 'Oh, it's nothing, darling. Let's talk about something else.'

'They're giving you a gong,' he said. 'That's it, isn't it? Which one?'

His mother shook her head again. 'I don't want to talk about it.' She patted the back of her head, where the perfectly lustrous hair was, as always, coiled up into a chignon, and then she picked up the bin bag. 'Let's put this in the car.'

Ben looked at her, curiously. He reached over, took the letter from her bag, and she didn't protest.

'A Dame?' he said, scanning the page. 'They want to make you a Dame? Oh, Mumma. That's wonderful. Dame Althea Wilde – oh, it does sound good. Dame Althea—' He took her hand. 'Can I cast you in my next film? You'd add some much-needed gravitas.'

She said, quickly, 'No, no. I've said no. I telephoned them this morning. Before I came. I've turned it down. Please, please don't mention it again.'

Her face was red. She took the letter, and folded it up, over and over again.

'Mumma. Why?' He squeezed her hand. 'Is it Daddy?'

'I told them maybe another time. They weren't very receptive.' She put the wedge of paper back into her handbag. 'I don't think you can ask to have it in two years' time because you're not in the mood at the moment. But I can't take it. I can't do that to him.' She rotated her head smartly around; Ben heard the clicking of her neck. 'He needs me.'

Ben stared at her thoughtfully. 'What you mean is he needs you to not be as good as him.'

'It's not like that. He's awfully proud of me. But at the moment, no. *Hamlet* was so bad for him. You know, we knew he was taking a risk, doing it like that, the council estate, the animal masks . . . but oh.' She put her hands over her face. 'I couldn't tell him I thought it was risible, that the audience wouldn't get it. I was too afraid to tell him the truth, and I should have done. Saved him from humiliation.'

'It's not your job to do that, Mumma.'

'But now he hasn't acted since apart from the peas advert, and that was a terrible mistake after *Hamlet*, it only made things worse. Why do they get at him like that, the papers?' she cried, the words tumbling out of her. 'As if things weren't bad enough with Mads, and all that. To mock him like that – he's not well . . . I've been away too much, with *Menagerie*. They want to do a Christmas special of *On the Edge* but I've said no . . .' She heaved the bag over her shoulder; she was as tall as him, and she faced him. 'He's not well. And he's so stubborn. He won't go out with his friends for dinner, or see anyone, won't call Cord to come and visit him, though he talks about her all the time – all he does is ask when she's coming and she never does, of course. I've pretty much given up with her.'

Ben lifted up the other bag. 'I don't know why she's being like this,' he said, bleakly. 'I know she cares. I know she does.'

The weight of the bag pulled at his arm; he felt as though it were Mads herself, dragging him down, and he stood up straight.

'Who knows what she's thinking,' said Althea, her eyes fixed on something far away, out through the window with its wintry sky. 'Go, darling.' She turned back to him, suddenly urgent. 'Go to LA. Take the girls. Get away from here. Don't come back. I'll come and visit you, often. I'll come out next month, after you've got there. But don't come back. Let them grow up there, give them sunshine, make them forget it, forget this.' She made a whirlpool gesture with her hands. 'All of this.'

'I wouldn't want them to,' Ben said, gently. 'I want them to know about us, where they came from.'

'No,' his mother said. 'You're wrong. Please don't ask me why, and please trust me. You're doing the right thing. I'll be with you. I'll come out often. But you must go. Daddy and Cord – they don't need you. They've shown that. But your children – your children need you.'

Ben kissed his mother's hand. 'Mumma, you're a wonderful wife to him. I'd have taken the gong, if I were you.' She clasped his fingers. 'I won't tell him about it, or Cord.' He hesitated, then picked up the second bag of clothes. 'Cordy'll come round, I'm sure. She's just stubborn as hell.'

Althea looked up at Ben. 'She's her father's daughter, my darling,' she said, almost sadly. 'You and I both know that.'

Chapter Thirty-Two

March 1993

'Well, that's very strange.' Althea had appeared in the doorway, the phone receiver still in her hand, the curling wire of the phone stretched out behind her. 'You'll never guess who that was, darling.'

Tony heard, but ignored, the odd note in her voice. He stretched out in his basket chair and nestled further into his rug, looking down the long thin garden. He could see a blackbird wrestling with a plump worm in the white-gold light of the spring afternoon. 'Don't know.'

'Guess.'

Tony's head pounded, as it did so often these days when he was crossed, or not given his way. He said, 'I don't want to guess.'

Althea's voice rose. 'Just guess, darling!' He turned to the doorway and she smiled at him, and there was something ghastly about her smile.

'I don't want to guess.'

'Cord. It's Cord.' Althea's voice shook. 'She's just got off the train at St Margaret's. She's coming here. She – she wants to see you.'

He started, and saw how pleased she was to have got a reaction out of him. He barely noticed her these days. Which was strange, she had screeched hysterically at him once, in a little showdown a few months after Mads had died. She was the only one left now, she'd pointed out, gleefully spiteful: wasn't it about time he paid her a little more attention? And she was right: they'd all gone, over time. Not just the critics who'd abandoned him after *Hamlet*, or the willing, soft, pliable girls who wouldn't go near an old, blistered, shaking man like him, or the jovial like-minded friends whom he'd pushed away for years now. Not just the parts, the offers, the ringing telephones and letters desperately offering astronomical fees for the tiniest of roles, no. The others had gone, those he loved.

Ben had gone, decamped to LA, to work on that imbecilic *Robot Master* franchise. He'd bought a house in Laurel Canyon. Said he might stay out there for a few years. He'd taken those wee girls with him.

Althea had been to visit him already, to look after the girls – Tony grimaced. She loved her granddaughters. An agonising, aching pain flowered in his chest, making him wince, groan under his breath. Althea had no idea – or did she? Lately, she was unknown to him, as mysterious as she had been at the beginning of their relationship, when he wanted her so desperately, pursued her with the ardour of a man possessed, thought only of her, dreamed only of her, her long slim legs, her cool, off-hand tone, her quirky, drawling conversation. He had lost her, he supposed, years ago, the first time she betrayed him, but he'd been too busy screwing everything else that moved to notice . . . and what it had unleashed . . .

He shifted in his chair, trying to trick the pain away. It came often to him now, sometimes waking him at night.

Cord he hadn't seen since Madeleine's memorial service: a grim affair at the Norman church in the village with the ashes scattered on the beach afterwards, the end of summer.

He knew what Mads had told him, that night they'd had together. He remembered her saying it as they lay together on the narrow divan bed, wrapped in that Indian silk-screen printed throw. Julia's empty urn lay on the floor by the door, which was ajar, banging very slightly in the breeze.

They had scattered Julia's carefree spirit and her honest, solid body, now reduced to ash, to the winds and the seas. They had walked in silence down to the beach, following the sunset, and at one point Tony gazed at the setting sun for a second too long, so that his irises became clouded, his vision blurred; he was acutely aware, suddenly, of her slim frame beside him, of the intensity of her presence, of how she reminded him of Julia –

Julia running through the grasses to the beach, Julia clambering over the dragon's teeth, Julia laughing as she sat on top of him, her white teeth glinting, her wild hair burnished to golden floss in the sun . . . her strong slim feet, running on ridged sand, the two of them on the porch steps, eating cherries, Dinah sitting on the wicker chair, listening to the radio, or reading aloud from her diaries, or watching them act together . . .

Althea had been an obsession, but Julia was his other half. And he saw it then, as the sun began to slip behind the land and they reached the beach hut, and the girl beside him turned, her hand on his arm, eyes full of tears, and said how much she loved him, how much it meant to her to have him there, how Julia had loved him . . . And he had kissed her, and she had pulled him towards her, and he had encircled her in his arms, and kissed her again . . .

And here she was looking up at him, gazing intently at him, and she was Julia and Madeleine but mostly, to him then, Julia.

It had been astonishing – intense, electric, her hair, her frantic, almost glazed expression – and he had felt, for the first time in years, like a real man again, as simple as that.

But afterwards, when he put his arm around her, as he tried to whisper in her ear, stroke her hair – no. It had been immediately wrong. He'd always been in control after any encounter like this, pacifying, soothing, comforting, flirting. But it was different. It was Mads. His daughter-in-law. He had screwed Ian's daughter, a girl he'd known since she was a child. The girl who'd married his son.

The old lines he normally used . . . he trembled, covered with a fine pelt of icy sweat.

Sitting up afterwards, that long pale silvery mane of hers tumbling down her moonlit naked back and the disgust and guilt flooding him. Like the first time. That very first time all those years ago. And she'd said, 'That's all I wanted.' Not adoringly, but matter-of-factly. Twisting the hair into a ponytail-thing again.

And he'd said, immediately, 'Darling, we shouldn't have done that. We mustn't – we mustn't do it again.'

She'd stood up and pulled on her underwear, hugged herself into her bra, winced as she rotated her shoulder blade, quite unselfconsciously. 'You squashed me a bit. It's jolly uncomfortable, that bed. I'd forgotten.'

'Do you hear me?' Tony felt sick. It was dark outside. The open door . . . the others back at the house . . .

She'd shaken her head, and pulled her sundress over her body. Her lips were pressed together when she emerged, and she was pale, her hair still tousled from where he had tangled it around his fingers, wrapped it over himself . . .

What have I done? Tony didn't know what to say. He stared at her and thought to himself, *But you're the same. You're the same as me and that's why you understand it. You're broken too.*

'Mads – when I saw you on the beach—' He wiped his forehead. He was shaking. 'I – I thought you were her. Julia. I shouldn't have . . .' He clutched her hands, as she stood in front of him. 'Oh, God. What have I done?'

But she had simply said, 'I wanted to. Don't think about it. We won't ever talk about it again.'

We won't ever talk about it again. He'd caught her gaze once when Iris had begun to walk. He'd looked over at Madeleine, standing in the corner biting her nails and they had stared at each other, for a split second that told him what he had long dreaded – or wanted, he wasn't sure. But she had looked away after a split second, begun wiping the table – she became obsessed with germs, after she had the girls.

Since they were born she had changed: even paler, even thinner than before, as though they had taken some life away from her. She was relentlessly, intensely concerned with them, and them alone. He knew it all came from this one night. It had driven her mad.

It was Ben who found his wife in the beach hut, curled up on the bed seemingly sleeping like a child. They all kept asking the same things: how had she got hold of the anti-emetic and the pentobarbital and why she would have done such a thing? But it was easy for her to get hold of, in her line of work, and he knew why, in fact Tony was the only one of them who wasn't surprised. He understood Madeleine better than any of them. Better than her oldest friend, better than her husband. She was lost.

Tony's eyes were heavy; he pulled the rug over himself as the pain shot viciously down his side. Through the open door he could hear Althea humming something in the kitchen. She was never in the kitchen, other than for the Cup-a-Soup or to make coffee. She never hummed, either. The house was quiet now, when once it had been full of lives, children, careers, visitors, friends.

'Tony? *Tony!*'

He must have been dozing when she arrived, for suddenly Tony opened his eyes and there was his daughter in front of him. He couldn't remember if she'd been there already – no, he thought.

'H-hello, darling,' he said, carefully. 'It's lovely to see you.'

Cord nodded. 'Hi.' Her hands were plunged into a long navy coat; her nose was pink with the spring cold – she had always had a pink nose in winter, he remembered suddenly. All his memories now were of summers. Her dark hair curled about her heart-shaped face. Love, and pride in her, made Tony's chest creak painfully. He felt nauseous; he was unused to company now. Suddenly he had a violent wish that she'd just go away: it was too much.

Althea stood behind them.

'Darling, would you like a cup of coffee?'

'No thanks, Mumma.'

'Something else to drink, something stronger? I suppose we could have a little gin if we've got any—' Althea looked at her watch.

'No. Nothing, thank you.' Cord perched herself on the edge of the table and cleared her throat. 'I'm not staying. I have a concert tonight. The *Messiah*.'

'*I know that my Redeemer liveth*,' Tony said, with an effort, and the arching opening chords of the aria sounded in his ears.

'That's your favourite, isn't it,' Althea said brightly, and Cord and Tony both nodded at the same time and he knew what she was thinking of: the old Huddersfield Choral Society recording, almost worn out through excess playing every Christmas in the big, airy sitting room upstairs. They never went in there now.

'*The trumpet shall sound*,' said Tony, raising his hands to imitate the action of the trumpet. 'Remember, Cordy?'

But his daughter looked away, and then she said, 'I can't stay. There's a rehearsal in South Ken—'

'Oh.' Althea glanced into the mirror. 'I see. Do you want anything to—'

'Mumma, could you leave us, please? I'll come and have a chat afterwards. But there's something I need to ask Daddy. And I don't have very long.' She cleared her throat again: her voice was hoarse. He saw her stand up, put her hand on her mother's arm. 'Please, Mumma.'

When they were alone, Cord did not look at him. She just said, 'Can we go for a walk? It's a nice day. We could go to the park.'

Walking was agony now, but he didn't want to say no to her. He shuffled to the coat rack and then down the steps, through the long garden and out on to the lane that led into Marble Hill Park. She walked behind him, in silence.

It was the Easter holidays; children were running and screaming in the playground at the bottom of the lane, overlooking the water. Tony looked at them with interest. 'Children make so much more noise than you imagine, don't they?' he said. 'I always forget that. Just playing, and it sounds like murder.' He glanced across the swollen banks of the river to where Ham House stood in the gentle sunlight, its dramatic purple-and-black bulk brooding at the edge of the riverbank. 'The foot ferry's running again, look,' he said, talking to fill her silence. 'And they've done something over there, cleaned up those boats. That tramp who lived up there – I say, he's gone.'

'When was the last time you left the house, Daddy?' she said, curiously.

'Oh. I – not for a while, to be honest. Not been very well.'

With no emotion she said, 'What's wrong with you?'

He said, casually, knowing how to hook the bait, 'They don't know. It's my side. I get these pains. They've scanned me. Nothing there but it lays me flat sometimes.'

'Oh.' Cord walked on, towards the park. He followed her, as fast as he could.

'Have you spoken to your brother lately?' he said, as she fell into step beside him.

'No. Not since he left.'

'He's been trying to get hold of you.'

'Well, he shouldn't have moved to LA.'

'He's all alone, Cordy.'

'I know . . .' Something caught in her throat; she clutched at it, rubbing her neck. 'I know that, Daddy.'

He was enjoying this almost, having her wriggle a little. Finally. 'He needs you. You're the stronger one than him. I thought you might have offered to go and see him, stay with him for a bit – your mother's gone out for a month, but she can't live there, can she?'

'I can't see them,' she said. 'Don't ask me to.'

'Can't see them?' Tony shook his head, in a bewildered fashion. 'I don't understand.'

Cord stared at him, her eyes narrowed. 'Oh, don't you? Really?' And then she backed down. 'In any case, I can't leave at the moment.'

'You could if you really wanted to.'

'No, Daddy. I have to have an operation. Next month when I'm back from the States.'

Fear scalded him. 'What? What – what kind of operation?'

'It's to remove some nodes in my throat. At least – it's not definite. I might have it. We haven't decided yet. The risk of permanent damage, you see.'

'Darling, I'm – that's awful.'

'Well, it might not happen. We're seeing the damage done next week. I just have to be careful.' She rubbed at her throat again. 'Listen, Daddy – I need to be there by four today—'

'I know.' She wasn't looking at him but he nodded as if he

397

knew her diary, the rhythms of her life, as if she wasn't a near-stranger to him, his lovely, talented, lonely daughter. It struck him that he couldn't even picture her home. *I've never been to her flat. I don't even know where she lives. My own daughter.*

'The thing is –' she was saying, as he turned back to look at her. 'The thing is, I woke up this morning and I was crying. And it keeps happening.' She stared at him frankly. 'Someone told me they loved me last week. A nice man, a good man, and I told him to go away, that he was mad. And I realised this morning, you know, these things, they're because of you. And 'cause I'm off tomorrow and then this operation . . . I realised something else. That I couldn't go another day without seeing you.'

He put out his hand. 'Oh, darling. I've missed you too.'

But Cord's face froze. 'I don't miss you. I mean I came to ask you to tell me the truth.' She was nodding furiously, and then she took her hands out of her pockets again and rubbed her cheeks with her knuckles. 'Are you the father?'

'The who?' For a moment, he honestly didn't understand.

'Ben's children. Well – Madeleine's children.'

Tony put his hand up to his eyes, shielding them from the light, from her gaze, as though he couldn't look at her. 'What are you talking about?' he said. 'Cordy, have you lost your mind?'

He stayed like that, not moving: they were facing each other on the brow of the gently sloping hill. After a few moments, Cord slid her hands back into her coat. 'So you are,' she said, after a while. 'Good. At least I know. You can't do it any more, can you?'

'Do what?'

She ignored him. 'Does Ben know?'

'Cord – I have no idea what you're talking about.' He clutched his back, more for support than anything, but she merely nodded. Her face was quite white now, her stormy grey eyes utterly still and Tony, blinking fast, was terrified. 'What on earth do you mean?'

'I saw you, Daddy. I saw you with her.'

'Cordy, darling—'

'It's so much worse if you lie, Daddy. Don't.' She said it so softly. 'Don't lie any more. We saw you with Belinda Beauchamp when we were children. That was our childhood, Daddy. I saw you and Helen O'Malley together once, when we came to the theatre, but I didn't understand. And then the night before the Proms, when I should have been . . . when Mads and Ben and Hamish and I were celebrating – I saw you in a pub with some girl and your hand was up her skirt and you were slobbering all over her and she was just staring into space, like she wished it was all over.' Tony wrinkled his brow, trying to remember . . . 'I grew up with you as a father. I know what you're like. They say you have to accept it or else go mad. So I did. I shut out everything else.' The wind whipped her hair around her face; she pushed it away. 'I forgot about what I'd seen, about what it's like, being in this family, and I entirely concentrated on singing. Only on my voice and myself. Because it's easier, much easier that way.'

'Helen, I don't understand, honestly—'

'Cordelia,' she said, putting her hand with a terrible gentleness on his arm. 'My name is Cordelia, Daddy. It's just . . . on the one hand, there's putting it about all over town and still being a good dad, because, oh, Daddy, you were!'

She broke off, biting her lip and staring at him, her face utterly white, her lips red with blood.

'There's all those things, and more, and then, then there's screwing your son's wife. Your daughter's best friend. Your daughter-in-law! Getting her pregnant. Letting your son believe those children are his. When they're his s-s-s—' Her voice cracked.

'They're his sisters. They're my sisters. You're foul. It's incest. You've – it's abuse, what you did to her. Abuse. And I wish I didn't know . . . but I do . . . And it wakes me up every morning.' Tears poured down her white face. 'Every morning it's like I forget and then I remember and it's – it's killing me. It killed her, I know it did. And I did that to her. Sometimes I can't think about anything else. All I think about is you. How you could do that.'

'They're not his sisters,' said Tony, hoarsely. 'I promise you, darling. I absolutely promise you. I swear it.'

She stamped her feet, with a growl of rage. 'Why? Why are you like this?'

'I swear to you, Cord. Cord! They're not Ben's sisters. You have to believe me, Cordy darling.' His voice cracked – how could he make her understand? Should he even bloody try? 'Listen, Mads was broken, trust me. She'd have killed herself at some point, I think. Honestly.'

'So that makes it OK, then? Doesn't matter if you were the one to break her, it'd have happened anyway?'

'Listen to me. I knew her family. I know where she came from, I know how hard it was for her . . .'

'She was my best friend, you vile, perverted idiot – she was my best friend!' Cord's voice rose. 'Are you trying to tell me you knew her better than me?'

'Yes!' he shouted, almost exhilarated at feeling again. He spread his arms out. 'Yes, I did, OK? I understood her. I knew her when she was little and I watched her growing up with you two and I could see it . . . some people are born to sadness, Cord, it's true!'

'No one knew her like I did,' said Cord, her low voice thrumming with fury. 'Not even Ben.'

It killed her, I'm sure it did. Suddenly Tony felt the chill of truth. 'What did you say to her, before she took the overdose?'

he said. 'You saw her that last night, didn't you? I heard you arguing in the beach hut, when I came back from my walk – I'm sure it was you.'

Cord stared at him. 'We went into the beach hut. I asked her about you. And she admitted it. I asked her how she could have, why on earth you . . . I told her—' She gave a sob, and rubbed at her neck again. 'Jesus. I told her what I thought of her, what we all thought. I made her cry. I left her there, crying.' Tears were pouring down her cheeks now; he moved towards her and she flung his arm away, pushing him backwards with a force so great he stumbled. 'I did that to her, and it was because of you. Not her, not her. You were older, you were like a father to her, and you—' She shook her head. 'You seduced her. You raped her. It is rape, when you coerce like that with persuasion and tricks and your old, old ways. I know you.'

'No, you don't.' He was sweating; he took out his handkerchief. 'It was her – oh, it was both of us – I – how can I make you understand?' He began to cough. 'Can we sit down? I don't feel well, Cord.'

'Why are you like this?' she said again. 'I don't understand. What happened to you, to make you like this? Not to be able to see what's so obviously wrong, Daddy – how could you not have seen it?'

Black sunlight flooded his vision. 'Listen to me, it wasn't like that, you understand?' He held out his hand. 'Let's find somewhere to sit. Just let me explain. I've only ever wanted you – all of you – to have a proper family. Give you a perfect life.'

He broke off. She was laughing, as if it were genuinely funny.

'You can't act any more, can you? Those reviews for *Hamlet*. I told everyone how unfair they all were but they were right. It's like a circus animal who knows which bit of the sawdust to creep around the ring to in time to the music but can't remember why he's there.'

'That's a horrible thing to say.'

'You're a joke.' She spat the words out. 'And it wouldn't matter but for what a bad joke you are. And you don't understand how serious it is. What you did. How happy we'd been . . .'

'I do,' Tony was shouting. 'I wanted the Bosky to be a golden place, like it was for me, only I wanted you all to feel safe, and secure, and loved, and never be abandoned, not like I was. I knew if I could give you all that, give you that childhood, that you'd be OK whatever else happened. Y-you and Ben and Mads too, yes, Mads too, even if you don't believe me. That's what she wanted too—' But she was laughing again, so loudly he couldn't hear himself over it. He clapped his hands, wishing the pain in his head would go away, it was stopping him seeing clearly. He clapped and clapped. A dog walker, a hundred metres away, stared at him. A couple on the brow of the hill looked over towards them.

'You've got an audience now,' Cord said, her mouth turned down with the effort of not crying. 'That's what you want, isn't it, Daddy? People looking at you. You made that house a little stage for you and your intrigues, and we were the audience for you. And none of it was real!' Her voice was hoarse. 'None of it!'

Tony said with difficulty, 'It was real to me. Always.'

'No! I used to believe it. But you've lost it, Daddy – I don't know what it was that you had but you've lost it. And I just want to know, what made you like this? What was it? Was it the war? You never talk about it. Was it Aunt Dinah? Listen to me.' He shook his head, and suddenly she shouted again. 'Listen to me! I tell you to listen to me! What made you like this? *Why are you like this?*'

He could hear a dog, barking in the distance. Tony looked around for it, wildly. Black shadows danced in front of his eyes. He stared ahead.

'Where are you?'

'I'm going,' she said, suddenly, and she straightened up. She was fainter with every second and he held his hand out towards her.

'I can't see you.'

But she was already walking away. 'I can't do this. I'm sorry. If you won't tell me anything, and you won't even admit it, say sorry, I can't stay. I have to go.'

'No,' said Tony, calling after her, but his voice was faint. His legs felt as though they'd turned to jelly. 'Don't go, Cordelia – come back here. Here.'

He could see the dog now, a black thing, a Labrador, perhaps – was it real? Could he really see it? Cord was further away from him now, ten metres or so.

'If she'd just come back – if she'd only told me why, if she'd come back just once, Cordy . . .' Tony sank to his knees, not caring any more, only wanting the violent, aching agony convulsing his side to stop. 'She saved me, and I loved her so much, and she left.' There was acid in his mouth; he opened his mouth and let it fall on to the grass, and he saw it was red, bright, dangerous, glossy red.

'Daddy—' Cord had come back, she had caught his arm. She sank to the ground, next to him, pushed his sparse hair away from his head. 'Oh, shit. Shit – Look, I'll run home and call an ambulance. Hey!' she screamed, into the chill air. 'Hey!! We need help! My father's not well! *Help!*'

Her arm was under his back, and he leaned on her knees; it was strangely comforting, this pose: he'd done it enough times on stage, dying like this.

I'm Antony, I'm on stage again, he thought, and it made him smile.

Unarm, Eros; the long day's task is done, and we must sleep.

Cord was still shouting, and he heard her voice crack. 'Hey! You! You there! Yes!! Thank you so much, please hurry. *Please—*'

Her voice broke off. Tony closed his eyes, and heard the planes again, saw the tape on the windows, the floral print of Julia's dress, smelled Daphne's perfume. Then he saw Aunt Dinah's face, peering over him in the hospital bed, for the first time in years.

'There you are, Ant dear,' she was saying. Her hair was exactly the same, her face, the little mole above her lip, her bright green eyes, the beauty of her, the faintest scent of sandalwood, of something exotic. 'Aha! There you are at last. I've come to collect you. I've come to take you home.'

And she had. He closed his eyes, as his daughter called out, but he couldn't hear what she was saying any more. He could hear her singing, her voice from long ago, the lilting purity of the age-old cadences:

I know that my Redeemer liveth
And that he shall stand at the latter day upon the earth—

The darkness was sliding over him again, as it had done when he was young, the soft settling of dust covering him after great noise and pain. Then it was quiet, no more voices. Just very quiet.

Chapter Thirty-Three

Dorset, 1943

For a while, everything continued as normal but it wasn't normal, he knew it. Strange things kept happening. Sweep vanished, never to be seen again. One day he was there, purring on the window seat in a contented ball, the next he was gone, and no trace of him was ever found. The weather was odd; sharp, cool, unpredictable. Dinah suddenly embarked upon a frenzied cleaning programme, clearing out the boxes everywhere and donating half her things to the church jumble sale. She had mended her bike, too: they were to go on their favourite ride up to St Aldhelm's Head the following day. She was due to travel to London next week; Ant didn't want her to go, even though the Blitz was over. He was afraid for her these days, for she seemed fragile, breakable: she who had won a bet to get on the last boat out of Basra, she who had survived desert storms and poisonous snakes, who had rescued him, borne him away from London.

At the beginning of the holiday, Ant had cycled into Swanage and found a chemist on Station Road who would sell him French letters. Depending on their plans for each day, either in the late afternoon or in the evening after dinner if she could manage to slip out, he and Julia met at the edge of the beach, and wandered together until they found an absolutely secluded spot, away from the dragon's teeth and the wire.

Though he would search ceaselessly for it Tony would never

get it back, the ecstasy and joy of those nights with Julia. He came to know her body better than his own, the crease between her groin and her leg, her round breasts, the freckles on her forearms and face, her long neck with the moles at the clavicle, her green eyes and the way she reacted when he stroked her and pushed inside her.

He would have more explosive sex, more illicit, more thrilling, more intense, but he would never find the same compatibility again, nor the secretive, joyous thrill of it that was, at the same time, entirely harmless. He would spend the rest of his life trying to recreate it, in dressing rooms and bedsits and hotel rooms.

'Look,' Ant said to Julia one night, as he lay in the crook of her arm, the soft sand cold beneath his shoulder blades. 'Up there?'

Her fingers stroked his hair, his ear. 'What's that?'

'The Milky Way. You can see it. It's the blackout, Dinah says it makes it much easier to see the stars.'

'She says a lot of things.' She moved down further against him. 'It's colder tonight, don't you think?'

'It's August. Always a little colder than you imagine, August nights. I remember, my first summer here, how chilly it was . . . Here, put your dress on.'

'How puritanical you are.' But she slipped the dress on over her head. 'We should get back soon.'

'Where does he think you are tonight?'

'Oh, the same as ever, that I'm with you at the Bosky and we're reading Shakespeare together . . . I'm not lying to him, I am with you. He thinks your aunt's house is one of study and intellectual retreat, so I'm in the clear. She wouldn't tell on us, would she?'

'It's not Aunt Dinah one needs to worry about,' Ant said heavily. 'It's Daphne. She's supposed to be coming back.'

'That awful old leech? How tedious. Why?'

'She wrote last week, and since then – Oh, I don't know.' How to explain the incessant tidying, the mysterious shuffling about at all hours of the day and night, the muttering, the opening of drawers and putting things away? He pulled her closer to him, wishing it was always them, just them, that she wouldn't ever break away from him. 'She has some hold over Aunt D and I'm just not sure what.'

'Is it like mistresses at school?' He looked blank. 'The kind that move in with each other and take up golf – like that?'

'No – well, not sure. Not Daphne, no.' He knew that much, at least. 'With Aunt D one never knows.'

'Yes,' said Julia. 'She's an enigma. She could be an Egyptian princess in disguise and it wouldn't be that much of a surprise, would it. I used to simply long to be like her, when you were both first here,' she said suddenly.

'Dinah? Really?' He was incredulous.

She knelt beside him, stroked his chest, ran her hands over his bare hips and bottom. 'Oh, yes. When I had crushes on girls, before you. Miss Bright. Terrific sex appeal. And Dinah.'

Ant was appalled. 'Aunt Dinah? I really don't think she has any sex appeal. I don't think she ever even *thinks* about . . . it . . . sex.'

She pulled lightly at his penis, stroked his thighs, then patted his cheek. 'My beautiful naked fool, how little you understand,' she said, in the way she sometimes still liked to mock him. 'She's repressed. Awfully repressed. You should read Freud.'

'I wish you wouldn't always go on about Freud,' Ant grumbled. 'I don't want to read him. Hey, don't go,' he said, as she picked up her shoes.

'I must,' she said, flinging out her hand, the thin nail-bitten fingers blowing him a kiss. 'Don't stay out here too long, naked and alone. You'll be arrested. And I'd miss you awfully.'

He could hear her whistling as she retreated, and he sat up and got dressed, thinking about Dinah, wondering when Daphne would appear, what she'd want this time. Julia's faint whistling stopped, and he heard her footsteps return. Just as he was putting on his plimsolls, she reappeared amongst the bracken, her face pale.

'Hello again,' he said. 'Everything all right?'

'Of course,' she said, quickly. 'It's just – often when I've left you, or you've gone, I wish I'd said it to you and I don't and I often think there might not be another time.'

'Said what?'

'Said that – well.' She cleared her throat. 'Well, the thing is, that I love you.'

'Oh.' Tony scrambled to his feet. 'Julia—'

'Let me finish. I want to say it. It's wonderful, being with you. I feel alive – I hadn't really ever felt that way before. Yes, ever. I liked acting, because it made things more dramatic when they were drab and awful. Well, now I've got this with you and suddenly I do care, and I wish everything wasn't dramatic. I'm afraid all the time – it's as though you've made me come alive. I don't want you to leave me. I don't want us to be killed by a bomb. I don't want my father to find out. I don't want to have a baby by accident.'

He caught her hands. 'I love you. I do. I love you too.' He stared at her, feeling her heart beating fast in her chest, her mouth, glowing a rose-red pink as it always did after he had been kissing her for a while. He kissed her now, pulling her as close to him as he could, and murmured into her neck, 'I want you to marry me. Will you marry me, when we're old enough?'

She gave a small cry, a moan in her throat, as his lips moved ver her skin.

'Ant – Tony – don't you see it? I won't be here, I won't. I'll have gone away. I can't stay here, not with Daddy . . . not with Ian.'

'Yes,' he said fiercely, gripping her shoulders. 'You can if I'm with you. You can.'

'We're fifteen,' she said, taking one hand and cupping it over her breast, and he squeezed it, aroused again, and then let his hand fall to his side. 'They don't let people our age do what we want.'

'There's boys a couple of years older than us fighting in the war. It doesn't matter.'

'Yes, it does, darling. I don't want to stay here for ever. The war will be over soon. I want to live, to get away from here, to do something afterwards to help. You want to go to drama school, your aunt is arranging the audition—'

'None of that matters,' he said, his voice cracking. 'We should be together, that's the most important thing—'

'Hell,' she said suddenly. 'Do you hear that?'

Over the sand dunes they could hear her name being called, faintly. *'Julia! Where are you?'*

Together, they ran quickly back past the barricades and the beach huts. He tried to take her hand but she brushed his fingers away. 'Not now, Ant, honestly.'

They went past the Bosky towards the lane, where Alastair Fletcher stood, hands on hips, and at the sight of both of them he took a step back. 'Oh,' he said. 'Hello, hello there, Ant.' He turned to his daughter. 'I went to look for you at the Bosky, Julia. Miss Wilde said you'd gone out walking together.'

'We were walking in the sand dunes,' said Ant, and he knew instantly how to play it, that it was easier to hide behind the truth than a lie. 'Sorry, we should have noticed the time, but it's such a lovely evening, we were looking at the stars come out.

And talking.' He took Julia's hand, and squeezed it, and smiled at her. She, eyes wide with terror, looked from him to her father.

'Sorry, Daddy,' she said. 'No harm in it.' But her voice was wooden, her hands that had been alive and playing with him hung limply by her side, shoulders drooping, and she was unconvincing; Tony knew he had to carry them both along, that he could do it.

'No harm, but you must have been worried. I'm sorry, sir.'

Alastair Fletcher stared at them both, his jaw clenched tightly shut. *Please believe me*, Ant found himself praying, willing that he could pull it off.

'Ah,' he said eventually. 'I suppose you're both sensible, aren't you? You're a good boy, Ant. Aren't you? I've always thought that you were.'

'Yes, sir,' said Ant, and suddenly he was terrified, of himself, of his ability to lie so easily.

'Come in now, Julia. There.' He pushed his daughter gently inside.

'Night night, Ant,' said Julia, patting her father's shoulder. 'See you tomorrow.'

'Goodnight,' he said, giving them both a casual wave, and he watched her go, mouthing, *I love you*.

When he arrived home, Aunt Dinah was already in her room and the lower floor was dark. 'Hello, Ant,' she called out as he came down the stairs.

'Hello. I was out walking, hope you don't mind.'

Her voice was muffled. 'Super. Looking forward to our trip tomorrow.'

'What trip?'

'The bike ride to St Aldhelm's,' she said. 'Do you remember? We said we'd do it weeks ago. If you don't want—'

'Absolutely, of course,' he called, and he was glad to be alone, in the dark, so that no one could see his flushing cheeks, his clammy hands.

He dreamed of camomile flowers, and of compasses and dandelion clocks, and of Julia's shoes growing huge, stamping across the beach and down the lane so loudly he had to beg her to walk on tiptoe, and when he awoke, the sun was not shining in rods through the holes in the blackout. Ant stared at his watch. It was ten o'clock. He couldn't remember the last time he'd slept that late: life with Dinah, and then boarding school, had reset his body clock and he was usually up hours earlier.

He washed his face and shaved, carefully – he was still not quite at home with the razor – and then dressed, humming to himself, though he wasn't sure why he felt so happy.

'Dinah?' he said, coming into the kitchen, but there was no sign of her, and then he heard her voice on the porch, and stepped out with relief.

'There you are!' he said. 'I'm so late I know I've probably missed breakfast, but do you want – Oh. Hello.'

There, sitting next to Dinah, as pristine and cool as ever, was Daphne, in a teal silk dress, a moth-eaten fox fur around her shoulders, smoking a cigarette, hand cupping her chin. Her other arm was stretched out along the back of the cane sofa, as though she'd always been there. The fox stared at Ant, unblinking. Daphne wiggled her fingers at him, then patted the sofa cushion.

'Come here, sit down, dear Ant,' she said. 'How nice to see you. You've slept well, haven't you!'

'I'm a little late, yes,' he said, rubbing his chin. 'Hello, Daphne.' He bent down to kiss her, feeling the sharp bones of her cheek, the pucker of the scar as it rubbed against his skin. Dinah had caused that. Dinah had dropped something on a glass table, had cut her . . .

Suddenly, she reached up, stroked his cheek. He started back, as if she'd pricked him.

'I see you're shaving now,' said Daphne, removing her hand and leaning back again. 'Quite grown up, isn't he, Dinah?'

'Absolutely,' said Dinah. Ant stared at his aunt, looking for any reaction, any sign that he might be able to interpret. But her face was immobile, the green eyes fixed on something in the distance.

Why's she here? he wanted to shout at her. *Why've you let her come back?*

Instead, she avoided his gaze and stood up. 'Poor Daphne's come all the way from London. She begged a lift with a chap from the museum but he dropped her at Corfe and she's had to walk from there.' She squeezed Ant's shoulder. 'We'll go for that bike ride later,' she said, brightly. 'I'll – well, yes, I'll go inside and get some tea. Ant dear, tell Daphne how you're getting on at school.'

'Oh, *do*,' said Daphne, stubbing out her cigarette as Dinah disappeared inside. 'Tell me all. French? Biology? Everything a young man needs to know all present and correct?'

She was glossier than ever, her white-blonde bob shaped and shiny, her fingernails perfect, glossy, coral-coloured ovals. She didn't look like someone who'd walked five miles over barrows and down dusty lanes. *I don't believe a word she says. Nothing about her.* She smiled at him. The gap in her teeth was like another eye, watching him.

'It's all right,' said Tony. He shrugged. 'I haven't thought about school much since I got back.'

'Oh, there must be some jolly japes you can tell me about, Tony.' Her gaze raked over him.

He considered telling her about the beatings, the bigger boys and what they did to the smaller boys, the feeling of ice water in the hip baths, the slicing pain of chilblained hands and feet, the sound of sobbing at night . . . the darkness that was as bad as it had been when he was first at Aunt Dinah's, and how at school he could never tell anyone about it. He hadn't told Dinah, because he knew there was no point. She wouldn't listen. So he'd just got used to compartmentalising it, this unhappiness. He *certainly* wouldn't tell Daphne. Ant smiled at her again.

'You keep staring at me,' she said, picking a piece of tobacco from her teeth. 'As though I have two heads or something.'

'No,' said Ant. 'You look different, and I can't quite tell how, forgive me.'

'Here.' Daphne beckoned him closer with one finger and, when he was inches away, said it again. 'Here, I'll tell you. Come closer. Here . . .'

He came as close as he could. The fresh morning air prickled his skin, deliciously tickling him. He could see the fine golden hairs on her cheek, smell the honeyed, musky scent which she always wore. Her silk shirt was thick, heavy, and he glanced down, and could see the lace edging of her brassiere, the swollen curve of her breast . . .

'Yes . . .?' he said, politely. 'What is it?'

'A secret, a secret you'll know about soon,' said Daphne softly and clearly into his ear, and she laughed, delightedly, and he drew back, trying not to show his disgust, and also his shame, for he was aroused by her.

Gulls cawed triumphantly overhead. Ant sat on the chair as far from her as he could, and looked out to sea. Already he was impatient – it was a treasured day out with his great-aunt, cycling to St Aldhelm's, talking and thinking, but now he resented it as time when he could be with Julia, could hold her, see her green-blue eyes like the sea, count the freckles that multiplied daily across her nose . . . He felt weak as always at the thought of a whole day to be got through before he could see her again. *She loves me. I love her and she loves me.*

So they sat in silence until Dinah kicked open the door with one leg and appeared with a tray. 'Tea! Breakfast is cake, if you want it, Ant dear.'

It was weak tea made from yesterday's tea leaves and some cake that Mrs Hill had brought over only the other day; she, like so many others, was fond of Dinah, bringing her little gifts of food, or help or encouragement, as though they knew she needed it. 'Isn't this nice!' Dinah said.

'Oh, just super,' said Daphne, and Ant saw the look of disdain she shot Dinah, covertly, as she set down the tray.

Dinah led the conversation, brightly telling Daphne about Ant and what they'd done that summer. In fact, she was more animated than he'd seen her in a long time, bright, and chirpy. He noticed she had done something to her hair, washed it perhaps, and it was fastened with clips at the side, instead of hanging around her face. And she was in a relatively clean navy cotton drop-waisted dress, and her lilac velvet kimono; she looked almost smart. She asked Daphne about the museum, about a colleague they'd recently lost fighting in Italy, and about Daphne's own work.

By contrast Daphne said very little.

'It's remarkable how they've managed to remove the lion, given the difficulties of the site,' Dinah was saying. 'I would love to return to Egypt, one day. And to Syria, if time allows. Do you know what plans for digs, if any, the museum has in that direction?'

Daphne was fiddling with her packet of matches. Ant thought she looked rather impatient. 'Don't be silly, Dinah. There's no digs in Egypt, or Ur, at the moment. Nothing at all.'

Dinah said quite calmly, 'Oh, but the British retook Baghdad last year. All is in order there now.'

'Hardly!'

'Nonetheless, I'm sure I'll find them.' Ant was gripped with fear, at her blank tone. 'That reminds me. There's something I must attend to.' She turned around and looked up at the porch door, but did not move, just stared at it.

'Let's face it, darling, you're not going to be allowed to leave—' Daphne was saying.

'What does that mean?' Ant began.

'And even if you did leave Blighty you'd never manage to make it out to Iraq, Dinah.' She held up her cup. 'I say, darling, get me another cup of tea, or whatever that stuff is. And some cake.'

'She's not your servant,' said Ant, furiously, and he felt something snap inside his head. He slammed his hand on the wall; the wooden timbers of the house shook. 'Honestly, Dinah, why on earth do you let her come down here and—'

Dinah was humming, her hands resting lightly on her knees, and didn't hear him.

'Oh, dear me, Ant. Dear, dear Ant,' said Daphne. 'You know nothing of the matter. Of *any* matters. Dinah, darling, keep your boy quiet, will you?'

Still Dinah said nothing.

Ant looked at her. Her eyes were calm, her hands weren't shaking. But she refilled Daphne's cup, still humming quietly, and handed her some more cake.

In her melodious voice she said, 'We must remember Jane Goudge is coming round to collect the last of the jumble for the Summer Bazaar, Ant – you will make sure she knows where the crates are if I'm not here.'

'Yes,' said Ant. 'You've told me before. Downstairs in the hall, bric-a-brac first box, toys second box, curios third box.'

'Wonderful. Now, I'll go and put my other shoes on, and we

can go off on our bike ride.' She reached over and took down the angel from her resting place above the door. She held it in her hand, looking at it. Daphne sat up a little straighter, and Ant thought she was about to reach out, as though she expected Dinah to hand it to her.

'Oh, Aunt D, she looks so comfortable there,' said Ant, impulsively. 'Don't take her down.'

'The truth is the lintel is rather wobbly,' said Dinah, ignoring Daphne, who was staring at the angel, and Ant heard the sharp intake of breath, like a hiss. 'And there's a little chip on the owl which needs looking at, because she fell off a couple of months ago when you were at school.' She turned to him and said, softly, 'She's yours, Ant, but I have to look after her. I've never told you this before, Ant: Daphne knows it, but she's rather valuable. And I'd hate, *hate* for her to be damaged or to be unloved or not appreciated . . . She's the heart of this house, isn't she? Don't you remember?'

Daphne was staring at her with a most curious expression on her face. A spot of red at the base of her throat was creeping slowly up her neck.

'Don't you remember, Ant?' Dinah repeated, holding the angel out towards him, and then she scratched her nose, pulling her hair away from her face, and her lovely eyes shone at him. 'I'll bring her back. Promise. I said she'd look after you, didn't I?' Ant was silent. 'Didn't I?' Dinah said, loudly, and he looked into her green eyes, saw her flushed cheeks. 'She has, hasn't she? Looked after you, and me? Do you believe me? Do you believe I'll bring her back?'

Ant nodded. 'Yes,' he said, smiling at her. 'Absolutely.'

He leaned forward and touched the proffered angel, stroked her downward-pointing wings. Dinah kissed his forehead, a brief, brushing kiss.

'That's good,' she said, and she wrapped the angel in her giant Liberty handkerchief and went back inside. At the doorway she paused. 'I'll just change my shoes, Ant, and we – we can go. Daphne, perhaps you'll have to stay here. In case Jane comes for the jumble.'

Her hand rested lightly on his shoulder, a small squeeze. Then she turned and went inside. Moments later the sound of the Home programme on the radio came on, very loud.

'Bit quieter, please, Dinah dearest,' Daphne called, but there was no answer. She looked at her watch. 'I did want to talk to her properly – you won't be too long on this bike ride, now, will you?'

'I'd like to be back this afternoon,' said Ant, thinking of Julia. 'Around teatime.'

'Terrific,' said Daphne, with satisfaction, and she pulled out her sunglasses, and leaned back against the sofa. 'I shall have a nap. That blasted racket. She's impossible, your aunt, worse and worse.'

'Where are you staying now, in London?' he asked, suddenly. 'Now Dinah's flat's gone.'

'Oh, different places. Awful bore. Having to beg, all the time.'

'I know,' said Ant. 'But I don't understand why you don't have anything of your own.'

'The truth is, Ant, I'm lazy, and I spend it on things I want. Life's so awful. I spend it on nice things, and nice meals, and nice clothes and drinks. And I persuade other people to pay for the rest. It's easy once you've worked out how to do it.' She slid the sunglasses over her eyes. 'That's the damned truth for once. Take that figure above the door. She lied to me – said it was a cheap plaster cast. But I'll have it, eventually. I *deserve* it.' She fluffed out her hair, gritting her sharp little teeth, and was silent. Then she said: 'Listen, I'm absolutely shattered. Do you mind if I close my eyes for forty winks?'

'Of course not,' said Ant politely.

He waited a few moments, looking out at the waves, and then he got up and went inside, with the teacups. He turned the radio down, and heard a car on the lane, a crying seagull, a distant conversation. He thought of the bicycle ride ahead, of the time in her company, of the endless blue sky, the promise of Julia's body that evening . . . Whistling, he changed his shoes too, and used the bathroom, and then sat on the stairs, and it wasn't until he had waited five minutes or more that he called his aunt's name, and only when there was no answer did he open her bedroom door.

There was no sign of her. Not in the bathroom, or anywhere in the house. He even looked in the huge wardrobe in his room, where she'd said once someone could simply get lost. And the final few boxes, too – where were they? Where were all her things? Nothing in her room . . . and when, with a sickening feeling of certain dread, Ant looked out on to the lane, her car had gone; only the tracks remained. He followed them up to Beeches, to the road, saw the faint skids as she had turned the corner, nothing more.

There was no note, no message. No sign of the angel, too. She was gone, just as she had whirled into his life three years before, like a sandstorm, conjured up out of nowhere.

Chapter Thirty-Four

'I have spoken to the school, in case Dinah had been in touch with them. Nothing,' the Reverend Goudge was saying, and Ant closed his eyes, listening for the comforting sound of the puffing at his newly lit pipe so it would catch. 'I'll be honest with you, Miss Hamilton—'

'Daphne, please, I've told you before, Vicar.'

'Daphne –' *puff, puff* – 'Yes, you see that while I have sometimes thought Dinah was a little – what's the word?'

'Eccentric? Unreliable?'

'Either of those.' Ant could hear the smile in his voice. 'But I did think she cared for the boy, and to simply *abandon him* like that, he of all people – I must confess one feels a little disappointed in her.'

There was a pause, and Daphne's clear voice floated out to Ant, sitting on the porch steps. 'Don't be. I know her, better than most. I should have acted earlier. I arrived too late to stop the pattern, you see.'

'The pattern?'

'Dinah's always been like this. She's fine for ages – it can be years – and then gradually she becomes extremely odd. She can't bear to be pinned down. She has to be free, I suppose is how she thinks of it. I'd heard of her before I first met her at the BM. Out in Babylon and Ur they used to call her the Rainmaker, simply because she'd always find the good pieces.

She had the knack and I think the other chaps found it infuriating, all that work and then Dinah would stride in and pluck out a board game that had been buried in soil for millennia that some king had probably played with, or a queen's gold death mask, or a Sumerian carving of a battle scene . . . But you couldn't hate her, no one could. They'd clap her on the back and give her her own special chair and cheer when she'd arrive and then one day she'd just . . . disappear.'

'Where would she go?' the vicar asked.

Daphne shrugged. 'On to the next place. I don't know. Search me. I didn't meet her till she was back in London. And she was there for a time, then she vanished, and then she resurfaced in Nineveh. She hates being shut in.' She glanced at Ant. 'The happiest I've seen her is in the desert travelling up to Mosul by camel with a scarf round her head and nothing for miles and miles ahead.' She lit another cigarette. 'She's cleared orf, or got herself into trouble somehow trying to clear orf. Mark my words.'

'Well,' said Mrs Goudge, firmly, 'the happiest I've seen her is here, with Anthony, being a jolly good guardian to him.'

'But you've only ever seen him here, dear Mrs Goudge,' said Daphne, sweetly.

'That's my point,' said Jane Goudge, rather crisply.

Daphne ignored her. 'When I arrived a few days ago she was already in one of her . . . "phases", I used to think of them.' She stopped. 'It culminates in a sort of breakdown, I suppose. It's been that way for a while. Her father shot himself here, can you imagine . . . I remember Dinah saying her mother had to sell a family brooch after the funeral to pay for the train fares back to London. They waited for two days, no food, nothing, while the man made up his mind on the piece. She'd have been about ten.'

It was early evening. A milky full moon had risen, huge

above the calm dove-grey sea and above it hung a single star, steady and still. Ant stared up at it. He wondered where Dinah's telescope was. All these things, these hanging threads that she'd left behind though there was no sign of her. The church bazaar had been a roaring success. Most of the sales had been Dinah's possessions that she'd donated. The stuffed monkey. Eunice the doll. Old marble dice. People who had nothing were queuing to get into the vicarage garden to buy a piece of Dinah Wilde's menagerie.

I miss you, he mouthed silently, into the air.

He could hear the vicar's confusion in his voice when he spoke. 'Thank you, Miss Hamilton. I suppose the first consideration must be to decide what we do with Anthony, as she was his legal guardian, and he is now left without one.'

Mrs Goudge, who had accompanied her husband, suddenly spoke. 'The best place for him is at school,' she said, firmly. 'I have had a letter back from them. Miss Wilde had already paid the fees in full for the rest of the upcoming year. Extraordinary. Term starts again on Thursday, wasn't that the day, Ambrose? He certainly can't stay here, at the Bosky.'

'I'd like it if he did,' said Daphne. 'He hates the school.'

'You're very kind,' said Mrs Goudge. 'But Miss Wilde was adamant about it. She wanted him to have a good education. Some order. After everything.'

'Perhaps she knew . . .' Reverend Goudge said, slowly. 'Oh, dear.'

She knew, Ant wanted to shout. *She knew she'd clear out, that's why all this school business happened. She was already planning to leave. She'd been planning it from the moment she arrived in the hospital. But why did she spend all that time teaching me things and helping me? Why did she make me love her?*

Mrs Goudge said, 'What should one do about the house?

One can't simply just *leave* it. Who knows when she'll be back?'

'I don't mind staying here,' said Daphne, and he almost believed the reluctance in her voice. 'I have to work on my book and since her old flat was bombed – I was renting it orf her, you see – I've had nowhere else to live.' She shrugged sadly. 'After all, who knows what she had in mind? Poor Dinah.'

'She gave the Bosky to Anthony,' said Mrs Goudge, rather sharply. 'So you'll have to ask him.'

Daphne tapped a cigarette on the table. 'I'm sorry. Gave what?'

'Signed it over to him. Earlier this summer. She told me, after church, the week before she left. Funny, she sought me out really, said it out of the blue. It was as if she wanted to tell me.' She gave Daphne a glance through narrowed eyes. 'Didn't you know?'

There was the tiniest, tiniest pause. 'No, but how wonderful. I'm awfully glad. Well, I shall ask Ant – or maybe if the house is his he'll have ideas of his own. Poor Dinah, it's hard to know what she wants us to do—'

'You know,' Ant said, his voice rising. 'You know why she left. Don't lie, tell the truth for once—'

Daphne put her hand on her heart, her blue eyes huge. 'Ant, that's terrible, of course I don't—'

Ant couldn't stand any more. He stood up, nodding at the vicar, and simply ran through the fading ragwort and vetch along the path towards Bill's Point, his heart thudding in his ears. There were pillboxes, newly built, and a couple of soldiers, strolling along the beach. He'd seen American soldiers when he and Julia had gone to Bournemouth for the day.

She was waiting – she was always waiting for him, always there.

'Hello,' Julia said, pulling him down on to his back so he lay up looking at her on the rug she had spread out. She moved on to his leg, and started taking off his shirt. He raised his knee, so she went up and down, as though riding a horse, and she slid to the side and laughed and he caught her. 'I've seen a couple of bats, flitting around. Beautiful.'

'Shh,' he said, and he began unbuttoning her blouse.

'How's things?' she said, as he fumbled with her suspenders and her woollen slip.

'I don't want to talk, do you mind?' he said. 'That woman – she's – she's the devil. I'm sure she made Dinah leave somehow, but I can't prove it. I don't know why . . .' He bent his head, kissing her neck. 'Please, let's not talk.'

She nodded, smiling, wriggling out of her skirt, their eyes on each other all the time. She helped him with the French letter and took off her own blouse, so they were naked and joined together. For the first time since Dinah had left, Ant felt free, his mind clear, his clothes shed. He put his hands on her hips and moved her up and down and she ground against him, smiling down at him.

'Oh, yes—' she said, 'I say, Ant, can you move a bit deeper so I – Hey! OI! YOU! Who's that?'

She leaped off him and they heard scurrying amongst the reeds. Pulling her blouse about her, and her skirt back on, Julia gave chase. Ant, his erection melting away like snow in July, scrambled into his trousers.

As he caught up with her, at the top of the lane that led down to the beach one way and along to the cliffs the other, they saw a lone figure in neutral colours running away.

'Bet it's a soldier,' he said, pushing her behind him. 'I saw two on the way here.'

'Urgh,' said Julia, fastening her blouse. She was panting. 'Oh, gosh. Filthy buggers. One of them tried to kiss Phoebe at the bus stop the other day, did you know that?'

'American?'

'One of our lot. There's hundreds of them about.'

They walked back to the rug. Julia flopped down again, defeated, and put her arms behind her head. 'What's that star?'

'What?' He was only half listening to her.

'There. One star, in the sky. You know all the stars.'

'Don't know this one.' He sat down beside her.

'Look at it properly.'

He shook his head, and she edged towards him, and shuffled her head on to his lap. He stroked her hair, looking down at her dear, round face. Upside down, it was unrecognisable, just features.

'I'm sure she'll come back,' she said, after a while, and she felt for his hand and squeezed his fingers.

'She took the angel,' said Ant. 'I don't think she's coming back. I think she had to leave.'

'Why?'

He shrugged, looking out at the lone star. 'It doesn't twinkle. It must be a planet. It's Venus. Dinah would know.' He was silent, Julia too, and he had never felt closer to her than then. Her kindness, her restlessness, her excitability, all were still when she needed them to be. 'I think she's gone back to Baghdad,' he said eventually.

'Don't be silly – how would she get back there?'

He shrugged. 'She's Dinah. She'd find a way. A war train, or smuggling herself on to a submarine, or something. She won a bet to get here . . .' He screwed up his face. 'Maybe she didn't. Maybe nothing she said is true at all. The point is, she's not coming back. She signed the house over to me.'

'But *why*?' said Julia.

'Why not?'

'I mean, why does it matter if you have the house or she does, if she's not there? She's your guardian, everything would be yours anyway. Why did you have to own it, and not her? Was she in trouble?'

'I don't know. She—' And Ant rubbed his face, and sucked his lips, in an effort not to cry. 'I miss her,' he said eventually. 'She made me go to school because it's what my father wanted, and she didn't have the money, I still don't know where she got it from. I hate it, and I've been thinking, I know she hates it too. But she's done it because she thinks it's for the best, even though she's wrong. She came back because I needed someone. She's left because she thinks it's for the best. And I can't help thinking she needs me now, and I'm not with her . . .' His face crumpled, and Julia sat up and hugged him.

'I know,' she said, over and over again. 'I know. I know.'

'There's no one else,' he said.

'There's me.' She kissed his wet cheek. 'I'm here. I'll always be here. We'll come to this beach when we're old, and you've got a limp, and you'll take me in your arms again and kiss me.' Her cheeks were red; her eyes shone, half-discs gleaming in the dusk. 'We'll be bored of peace, you know. Our children will climb on the dragon's teeth and they'll have sunk half into the sand and be covered in moss. And I'll have gone everywhere and seen everything and you'll be a famous actor . . .' She knelt up, and stroked his hair. 'Not now. Not yet. You've got to go to drama school. Be as good as possible. For her especially, but for me.' He laughed, and she laughed too, but then she said, quite seriously, 'If you're famous, and you're on stage, she'll always know where to find you, and if you keep coming back to the Bosky, then she'll always know where to find you.'

'I love you more than anything,' he said simply.

'Me too. I know.' And she took his hand, put it to her breast, then kissed him, moving on top of his crossed legs and rocking against him.

'Julia.'

The voice was near at hand, cold, light, and they both jumped again.

'It is you. Come here.' Ant's heart lurched sickeningly. Julia leaped to her feet and he got up after her, and there, in the clearing in front of them, was Alastair Fletcher, Julia's father, and, looking like the cat who'd got the cream, her brother, Ian. He was pointing.

'I said it was them, didn't I,' he said, and then stepped back, and crossed his arms.

And Alastair didn't even look at either of them, but away across the sea. He said, quietly, 'Julia, get your shoes and come now.'

'Daddy – we weren't—'

His voice was like ice. 'You will come now.'

She began picking up her gas mask, the rug, her skirt which she had just removed. But she was clumsy and dropped them all, and Ant tried to help her, and the used condom and its packet fell out of the rug on to the ground, and one of Ant's shoes.

'Just a minute,' said Julia, perfectly calm, but her face was white. 'I'll – I need to gather it all up, and Daddy, we weren't doing anything wrong.'

'You're a whore, you know that, don't you,' said Alastair, conversationally. 'A whore is a wanton, and you are that. So I'm glad your mother's dead. So she can't see she has a whore for a daughter.'

426

Even Ian stopped smiling and looked rather taken aback. Julia slipped into her shoes, with a sob. 'Daddy, please don't say that.'

His voice cracked. 'How you could – nope, we'll not discuss it. You'll go back tomorrow to school, a week early. I'll not have you in the house again. Not until you're married. As for you,' he said, turning to Ant, 'I see why Dinah's gone. You're perverted and dangerous, and she'd had enough of selling things that weren't hers, putting up with you and your nancy-boy fear of the dark and complaints about school . . . Oh, she pandered to you for all those years and you showed her no gratitude. You're a bad lot, Anthony. Bad to the core of you.'

He grabbed his daughter's arm and with the other hand pointed at Ant. 'You. Stay there. Wait till we've gone back down.'

'Sir, please listen—' Ant began, but they made to leave, Alastair tapping his daughter's arm, and he pointed at Ant.

'I mean it. I'll hurt her unless you stay here.' So Ant stood still, stunned as though Alastair had actually hit him, and he watched her go, and his failure to help Julia stained him forever.

As Alastair, Ian and Julia went back up towards the lane, Julia stumbled in her unfastened shoes. Ant saw Ian sharply pushing her along to be quicker and she stumbled again. Her father walked beside his son, head down, hands in his worn tweed jacket.

Ant watched them go and, after a minute or two, followed behind, as quietly as he could. He watched as she went into the house with them, but she didn't turn round.

Now it was almost dark and the moon was higher. Venus shone steadily, as Ant, more tired than he had ever thought he could be, climbed the steps up to the porch. The scent of rosemary was heady in the night air.

There's rosemary, that's for remembrance. Pray you love, remember.

Dinah had said it, that first day here, when he had placed the angel above the lintel and she had told him he'd be tall one day.

Chapter Thirty-Five

He pushed open the door, and there was Daphne, on the window seat with the blackout blind pulled down, reading and smoking. Her soft head glowed in the low light but otherwise she was cast into shadow and he had the fanciful thought for a second or two that she was like a malevolent spider, waiting for him in the corner of the room.

'Hello,' he said. He thought she jumped when she saw him.

'Oh, hello, Ant. Come in.'

Ant sat down heavily at the kitchen table. He was very tired. He felt old, suddenly, much older than fifteen, and he couldn't imagine what it must feel like to live to be seventy, or eighty. Getting up every morning, carrying all this – this – with him, for ever, all the time, the only escape when he was with Julia, or if he was on stage, pretending to be someone else.

In the glow from the oil lamp Daphne's features were exaggerated: her round cheeks and protruding cheekbones more pronounced than ever. Her crown of blonde hair seemed to be a dirty kind of yellow. She patted the seat next to her. 'Come and sit next to me.'

'M'all right here, thanks,' he mumbled. 'I might go to bed soon.'

'They found you with Julia, did they?' she asked, almost conversationally. 'I heard that nasty little boy shouting to his father after he'd seen you. Have you been up to no good? Did you ask her permission?'

He looked up. 'Course I did.'

Daphne laughed. 'I only wondered. Some girls like it, you see.' She stood up, and came towards him, leaning her thin white hands on the back of the chair beside him. 'They like to pretend they don't want you to, but really, they do.' She scratched his chin with her nail. 'You'll see.'

'I wouldn't – it's not like that,' said Ant, hotly, and then he stood up, backing away from her. There was a pain at the front of his temples, as though his head were being squeezed in a vice. 'I'm going to bed and I think you'd – when I go back to school I think you'd better leave. If that suits you,' he added weakly.

She laughed, wildly. 'If it suits me. Very polite, Dinah would like that.'

'I don't understand why you were friends,' he said, and his head hurt so much now he wasn't sure what he was saying and what was silence.

'No, well,' said Daphne airily, 'you wouldn't. I didn't, for a long time.' She stubbed her cigarette out on a saucer on the table, the china service Dinah's father had bought when he kitted out the Bosky as the grand surprise for his wife and daughters. Ant wanted to slap the fingers that squeezed the cigarette viciously into the gleaming porcelain. 'Actually, I used to think Dinah was queer, but now I'm not so sure. I simply think that side of her didn't exist. Poor old bean.'

'Please—' said Ant, resisting the urge to clap his hands over his ears. 'Please don't talk about her in that way.'

'Of course.' Her eyes danced in the dim light. 'So innocent, aren't you, for all that dirty business in the sand dunes! But we had something in common, you see – bad with money. And I like money, Ant, in fact I rather love it. It's awfully boring, having none, when you've grown up with it. War is awfully boring, when you want to be able to buy things and eat what you want and drink what you want and go dancing . . .'

Ant thought she might be mad. 'No one can. We're all in the same boat. Come on, Daphne.'

'But I want to do what I want, I have to.' The eyes stared at him, huge, blue, utterly expressionless. 'And your aunt was awfully useful for that.'

'She's kind, and you're a bloodsucker,' Ant said, his mouth trembling. He was so angry with her, so excited, he thought he might punch a hole through the wall. 'A nasty bloodsucker—'

'Ah, you think so, don't you? But here's the thing you don't know about your darling auntie. She's a thief. A rotten bloody thief. When she came back to London ten years ago or so she was broke, of course. She sold a little statue she shouldn't have taken from Ur. From the temple, the ziggurat.'

'No, she didn't.'

'Darling, she did. You see, the dealer contacted me – we had a little arrangement that he'd call me if people tried to sell him things that weren't theirs to sell. Someone more competent than Dinah would have gone through an intermediary, maybe sold it in Baghdad instead, but she was a fool. It's my job to stop precisely that kind of thing happening with people we send out from the BM. Gives us rather a bad name to have archaeologists running around all over ancient sites pinching whatever their grubby little fingers dig up.' Her hands moved against the rough blackout material. 'I thought I was on to rather a good thing with her, because of course she was absolutely desperate not to be exposed. She said it was just once . . . The usual rubbish.'

'Why would she do it? You're lying. That's not her, she wouldn't . . .' Ant trailed off.

Don't gamble, Ant. It gets into the blood.

'Wouldn't she? I don't think you knew her very well, dear.

431

Don't we all want to gamble, to risk everything, at some point? Have you found an ancient lion's paw in the sand, or the golden headdress of a queen that's thousands of years old? Do you know what it's like to hold them in your hand, to think . . .' She moved her face towards him, and hissed, suddenly, '"It could be mine, I could just take it and nobody would know!"'

She laughed, wildly.

'She's a thief, darling. She'd squirrelled away lots of odds and ends she should have reported to the museum and I knew it . . . So we came to an arrangement – she'd let me have her flat, and she went back to Baghdad, and she wasn't supposed to come back, not ever. I really did like living in her flat, you know – so handy for Harrods, and the park – only you came along and ruined it all.'

'You've ruined it,' he said, in throbbing tones. 'You've ruined everything, you've driven her away—'

But she ignored him. 'So I don't have a flat, and I don't have this house, and she's kippered me, gone off with the rest of the loot and that angel. If she's real, she's worth a huge amount. I'd be set up for *life* if I could find the right chap to sell it for me. But she's left me with nothing at all. So I have to take what I want,' she said, coming towards him so she was facing him.

He was against the wall, and she was in front of him, and she took his hand and shoved it abruptly inside her silk shirt. His fingers automatically closed over her small, plump breast; he felt the nipple tighten, and his mouth opened very slightly, the unfinished business earlier with Julia making him more eager than he might otherwise have been. She saw this, and he saw the flash of triumph in her blue eyes, and moved closer towards him, holding her hand over the shirt, over his hand under the shirt, on her cool, naked breast.

'Your aunt, darling, is a bad woman,' Daphne said, and she

put one leg between Ant's, pressing on to his crotch, and instantly, he felt himself starting to harden. 'Oh,' she said in a low, pleased voice. 'I thought you were just a little boy. Well, you are really, aren't you? Say you are.'

Ant said, through gritted teeth, 'No. No, I'm not.'

'Oh, you are to me. Still a kid.'

Yet he didn't move away from her firm, hard leg, the pressure it exerted on him, and she saw the shame in his eyes and her own eyes glowed.

'Listen,' she said. 'That angel's mine.' She moved her knee, nudging him, very slowly, so that he hardened even further. 'It's not even an angel. Isn't that a riot. It's the goddess Ishtar. It's Mesopotamian, three thousand five hundred years old . . . almost priceless. I don't know where it came from, but I don't believe she bought it at some market which is what she always claims. It's an extremely valuable piece, unlike anything else – it shouldn't be hanging up above some draughty wooden cabin by the sea. It's a joke. If you were the one who found it . . . your place in history would be assured . . .' Her eyes were gleaming, she took small, rapid breaths and there was something about the intensity of her expression, her rigid body, that was fascinating and repellent at the same time . . . She turned her catlike stare upon him. 'It should be in a museum, not with Dinah.'

'She bought it, paid for it, she believes it has some kind of special powers, that it'll keep her safe.' Ant blinked away the memories, tried not to look at her, tried not to show how much he wanted her. 'Sh-she doesn't have to give it to a museum.'

'Rubbish, it's unique. It's been around longer than most things in the world – it'll outlast Hitler, that's for sure . . .' Her hand replaced her knee, and she was rubbing him and he thought he might be sick, the desire was so strong, the way she rubbed him was almost too intense, her pillowy, soft pink lips caught in her

433

white teeth and yet he couldn't make himself ask her to stop . . . he simply couldn't. Ant closed his eyes. 'You like that, don't you. Just a boy, a young boy, and you like it already. Well, it's not what it seems, never is. Your school fees, for example. She couldn't afford them so I helped her sell a nice seal she'd found in Nimrud.' He felt hotter than ever, and her fingers, her skin, were both so cool, and he moved against her, helplessly. 'She got desperate, you see, wanting you to have this silly education – wanting you to grow up to be a proper man, brought up in the nice British public-school tradition – she got afraid too much time with her would bend you the wrong way, make you like her – isn't that funny . . .'

Her face was mocking him, her pink lips softly saying these things, the sweep of hair falling into her face. She shook it out of the way, then leaned forward, letting her silk slip fall from her shoulders, and kissed him, and he kissed her back.

'You're not really a man yet, are you?' she said, and so he kissed her again, more forcefully, hands squeezing both her breasts, and then the siren went, loud and clear, echoing across the empty beach, and he stepped back, breathing hard. Surely this would end it . . . surely it would end now. But Daphne rubbed him again, harder, until he sagged against her, and then she broke off abruptly, and took his hand.

'Downstairs,' she said. 'Your room.'

She led him in and shut the door, and he saw the sparkle in her eyes, the gritted teeth, her square, set jaw, and he was almost crazed with wanting her by now, wanting to prove himself to her, to blot out what had gone before, to simply finish it.

She removed her clothes, her pale smooth body glowing like bone in moonlight. He made to undress and she put a hand on his shirt.

'Keep the clothes on, little one. The shorts, keep them on.

Let's play a game, shall we?' Tony nodded, urgently. Daphne gripped his wrists, her jaw hard, eyes set. 'I'm your teacher, you see? I'm your favourite teacher. And you – you're a bad pupil. I'm very upset. You need to calm me down.'

She made him take his shorts down.

'Round the ankles, don't take them off.'

'Yes—'

'Yes, miss. Say, yes, miss, Tony, otherwise . . . You don't want to know what I'll do.'

She pulled at his penis all the while, making sure he was still erect, and he was so sensitised he nearly came as he mounted her, and then it was over, very, very quickly, so quickly that he passed out and then woke up twenty minutes later as she tapped him on the shoulder, this time wearing her silk dressing gown, burgundy lipstick on her mouth, ever so slightly smeared at one corner, as though applied in haste. And she used a high-pitched voice, so she was an airy-headed teacher and he was a young boy.

'Naughty,' she kept saying, in a soft, cloying voice. 'Naughty boy. You said sorry, didn't you? You like touching Miss Hamilton there, don't you? She's not cross any more, she likes you touching her, and you like it when I touch your little thing, don't you?' Her curved mouth was slack as she fumbled hungrily with his shorts.

And there was more in that vein, things she said that he tried to block out for the rest of his life, and the memory of her sinewy body, her staring eyes, so unlike Julia in all ways, and as he was saying to himself that he'd have to just break away from her and run out of the room, she was bringing him to ecstasy again and he ejaculated over her and himself, and she patted herself down, and him, pretending he was a child who'd had an accident in the playground as he stood there with his shorts around his ankles, dripping, and she smiled and said, 'He likes it, doesn't he?' and so really, he was complicit in it all.

Afterwards, when Ant turned away from her, eyes stinging with tears, and laid his head on the pillow, and began to silently weep, Daphne saw this in the mirror and she laughed. She told him to grow up, and then she did more things to him that she told him he should have enjoyed, but which he thought demeaned her, and himself. It hurt, it should have hurt her, to have it there, but she liked it. Tony understood some of what they talked about at school and realised they knew nothing, those strutting, silly boys, playing at being men, knew nothing of how disgusting and brutal and ugly it could be, amongst the ecstasy.

She fell asleep, her face utterly still in repose, as though she were dead, and as he stared at her he wondered what would happen if he were to kill her, put a pillow over her head . . . He crept out of the room, up on to the porch, and spent the night there, shivering in the cold, under an old blanket, waiting for the sun, the day to come.

Daphne laughed at him in the morning when he offered her some dried egg and burned toast, when he said hesitatingly that she should leave.

'Of course I'm leaving. What's here for me now? Nothing.'

'Where will you go?'

'Back to London, to the museum. Find someone else who can help make life more bearable.'

'You – I'm going to write to them, tell them what you've done to Dinah.'

'No, you're not,' she said, amused. They were standing outside in the lane. 'You know I'll get the museum to report her to the police. I'm the one they trust, she's seen as a liability. She'll be on every list, won't ever be able to come back after that. You're weak. You're a scared little boy, you always will be, it's in your eyes,' she said, as she prepared to cycle off on Dinah's bike which he had, in an act of rashness, said she could take, just so she would go.

He couldn't bear to watch her cycle speedily away, on the bike Dinah had haphazardly pedalled around the bay, her knock-kneed posture and wild hair making her instantly recognisable.

Where are you now? Where have you gone? Why did you leave me?

He would go to Reverend Goudge's later, ask if he could stay with them. They would make sure he didn't starve, would see him safely back to school. They would do right by him, though they had many other obligations, everyone did. Looking around the empty, dark room with the crumpled pink candlewick bedspread, Tony knew that he was entirely alone now.

He grew up that night, entirely the wrong way, and he spent the rest of his life trying to atone for it, to make up for what he had done. He told no one about it so there was no one to tell him that he was not at fault, that he was a good person, deserving of happiness.

Chapter Thirty-Six

Fifteen years later
1958

She didn't like driving too fast, she said – but he saw the way that when he took the corners really fast, she drew her breath in with a gasp and he knew it was excitement, not fear. Her little hands in their coral kid gloves clutched the cream interior of his new Austin as he took the lanes past Wareham at a lick, occasionally reaching over to touch her thigh, or turning to smile at her.

'I want you to love it,' he said. 'As much as I do.'

He'd said it before, but he thought this time he might mean it.

Althea Moray was nineteen – ten years or so younger than him. He liked her youth. She had been a child in the war, barely remembering it beyond being cold all the time and National Banana Day in 1946, when every child in Britain was given a banana. Her first clear memories dated from the Festival of Britain, seven years ago. She'd come down to London for it, with her family. She mentioned it often, as though to back up her credentials as a woman of the world; he found it rather touching.

She was Scottish – she'd been in London for six months, studying at Central School of Speech and Drama, and she lived in a hostel with several other girls in Marylebone. She'd never been to Dorset. And she'd never heard of Anthony Wilde, wasn't impressed by him, hadn't heard about *Hamlet*.

'It was eight years ago, rather well-received, you see, sort of

438

right-place right-time jobby,' he'd explained to her over dinner, with the blend of self-deprecation and awkwardness that he knew he could pull off without being nauseating and which oh-so-modestly drew a veil over the rhapsodic attention he had received.

'Why would I have heard anything about it, squirrelled away in Dumfriesshire?' she'd said, laughing at him. 'Who came to see you, then? Marilyn Monroe? Mario Lanza?'

He couldn't tell her she should have heard of it, that a critic had written an entire book about his performance and the production, which was stripped back and all the actors dressed in black, the only item on stage a vast rusting, half-gilded and lopsided metal carapace to represent Elsinore: part prison, part birdcage. Mario Lanza *had* come, and Olivier with Danny Kaye and Vivien Leigh and she'd written him an utterly sweet note afterwards. That they'd had to draft policemen in on the last night to control the crowds. It had made the front page of the *Evening News*. One policeman had told Tony the crowds hadn't been this hysterical since Ivor Novello's funeral.

'Because it was a huge – oh, never mind, I sound ghastly, explaining it like that,' he'd said, giving up, and taking her hand to kiss it. 'Princess Margaret came one night. There. You're a child.'

'I was a child when you were Hamlet, yes.' Her eyes twinkled. 'Tell me, was she very beautiful?'

She was self-absorbed, but could laugh at herself, and he liked that, because he recognised a little of himself in her.

Bertie Hoare, that awful mischief-maker, had introduced them one night at the Phoenix club. 'Tony darling,' he'd said, in his drawling voice, stopping in front of his table. 'Here's a new prize for you. Meet Althea Moray. She's desperate to know you.'

Tony of course had fallen for it, had stood up, hand

outstretched, polite but showing just a little of the boredom he aped in front of his friends now to demonstrate that it was awfully tedious, being hounded like this . . . he had held her hand and then looked into the face of this ravishing Titian-haired girl and murmured, 'Awfully nice to meet you, Althea,' and then been astonished when she had replied, in a soft, Scottish burr, 'Bertie, forgive me, but I've already told you I don't know who this gentleman is at all.'

Tony had sat back, to general shouts of mirth from his friends, and gleeful pats on the back. He'd stared up at Bertie, furious, realising this was a stunt to take him down a peg or two, and then once again gazed at this girl, at her green eyes, her white skin set off by the black polo neck and the heavy eyeliner.

'Anthony Wilde. He's a dangerous man, darling,' his friend Guy had said to this impassive young beauty.

'Oh.' But still his name appeared to mean nothing to her, and as she shook hands with Guy and Dougie Betteridge, he'd said to Bertie, 'Can I buy you both a drink? Please, join us.'

Before Bertie could answer she'd said, 'Champagne, please,' and settled herself into the booth, folding the voluminous netting of her skirts against her legs, like the petals of a flower.

'I say,' Bertie had said, not sitting down. 'Weren't we going to catch that show?'

'Some bored girls wiggling in wee frilly knickers and taking ten minutes to remove a glove really isn't my idea of a grand way to end the night, Bertie,' she'd said, shaking her head ruefully. 'I'd rather stop here with these gentlemen, especially since one of them is apparently famous.' She smiled at him. 'You're not cross, are you?'

Bertie had rolled his eyes and Tony watched his friends oppo-site him at the booth as Guy and Dougie had stared at her, open-mouthed, at the fresh-faced charm of her words, and at her staggering beauty, which simply kept rolling over you again and again in waves, the more you looked at her. But it was her manner, her smile, her sense of humour, the twinkle in her eye, that was so immediately attractive to him. He wanted to laugh, and he didn't know why.

'I have to go, need to see a man about a dog there,' said Bertie, huffily. 'But this means your card is marked. You owe me dinner, darling. Ditching me for these three reprobates.'

For the first time her eyes widened and she looked uncertain. 'Yes—' And Tony could see her wondering whether she ought to stay here alone with three men about whom she had claimed with pride to know nothing. Bertie, the bounder, didn't help but, spotting someone he knew, called their name and simply melted into the throng. He saw her fingers clutch at her black-and-gold silk evening bag.

'Miss Moray, I'm Tony Wilde, and I'm a gentleman, not a scoundrel, I promise you. And these fellows are my friends, Guy de Quetteville and Douglas Betteridge.' They shook hands with her, formally. She nodded, lips pressed together, as though she were trying not to laugh. 'If you agree I'd like to escort you home. We'll take the night bus too, with other people, so you can see I don't want to try to murder you.'

'You aren't putting your life in danger, are you? What if we're accosted by hysterical fans wanting a piece of your jacket?'

He frowned, then saw her irrepressible smile, and grinned, unable to stop himself. 'We'll risk it.'

Outside her hostel in Dorset Square, he'd taken her key and unlocked her door, then removed his hat, and said, without thinking, 'I say, would you like to come to the seaside with me some time? I've a place there. It's awfully jolly.'

She'd paused, her gloved hand on the door knob, calmly

looking him over. And then she said, 'I'm working on Saturday. I could go next Sunday. Yes, I'd like to.'

'Sunday it is, then,' he'd said.

When he told Guy, with whom he shared a dilapidated flat in Onslow Square, South Kensington, Guy had said, 'You're crazy. Taking a girl you've never met before tonight down to the Bosky? I thought that was for sure things only?'

'Oh, come on, Guy,' Simon Chalmers, his other flatmate, who had turned up later in the night at the club and met Althea, chimed in. 'She's worth it, old boy. And she's a terrific actress.'

'She's an actress?'

'Well, she's at Central. But she's doing the Open Air Theatre this summer. Viola. She's got special dispensation.'

'And she'd never heard of you?' said Guy, in mock tones of outrage, and then he'd laughed.

'Leave him alone,' said Simon, taking a cigarette from Tony's packet, and Tony smiled at him with gratitude, and not a little surprise, Simon being well known for stealing a girl from under one's nose if he could. Privately, they had christened him the Waltzing Snake after he had literally waltzed off with Guy's first great love, a willowy blonde deb called Candida.

'Thanks, Simon old man,' said Tony.

Simon said, with a straight face, 'Well, you know how difficult it is for Tony. He can't rest until he's personally deflowered every virgin in London. Poor old chap. I say, bring her to the flat some time, let me have another look at her, will you?'

'Do shut up, Simon,' said Tony, staring out of the window on to the garden square, where the first blossom of spring was emerging. 'Not this one.'

And now they were almost there and as ever, his heart sang with joy at the swallows darting out from the hedgerows across

442

the fields, the vast barrow rising behind them, the curving lanes thick with flowers, and eventually they turned down the small track and Tony switched the engine off.

'Here it is. The Bosky,' he said.

Her hands were clenched in her lap. She smiled at him, thinly, and he realised she was nervous.

'Come on,' he said. 'I won't bite. Let's go inside, get a drink.'

He would have her, of course, but not yet, not until she was quite relaxed and sure it was what she wanted, perhaps even that it was her idea. Of course not.

It was all part of the game and he had to keep playing. He was always busy, either working, or out with his friends, or down here having fun. He worked especially hard to avoid thinking about Daphne. Once, he thought he saw her in Coptic Street, by the British Museum, and simply turned and walked the other way. He dreamed of her, and that night, terrible, churning, sickening dreams. But he told himself he'd locked it away. That it was old news now, just as Dinah was. He barely thought about Dinah.

He hadn't been here alone with a girl since the Easter weekend – a plump, funny little receptionist at his agent's office named Ann who was from Dover and whose father was, somewhat improbably, a clown: she was a limerick waiting to be made up, he told her. She was fun; he'd taken her into Swanage to see the amusements. As they bowled through Staines on the way back into town, he'd done his bit about 'entanglements', where he explained about his dead parents and usually made them cry and agree they mustn't bother him ever again. Ann had taken out a powder compact and started making herself up.

When he'd finished she'd said, 'Tony, I've got a fella already. He's doing National Service. He's out next month. It wouldn't do for me to see you again anyway.'

'Oh – well, I didn't know that.'

'Yes. We'll get married when he's set himself up. He's very into shoes. Wants to open a shop. So you don't need to give me your sob story, honest.'

'I just wanted you to understand that I—'

'I know your sort, Tony. We're the same, you and me. It was fun, wasn't it? Thanks ever so. Don't you worry, I won't blab, but I can't do it again, much as I'd like.'

It was the clear, breezy assumption that they *were* the same – both in it for sex, fun, uncomplicated companionship – that stung. It was the truth, that's what he loathed. In that instant he wanted to hurt her, or say something cutting, for he hated her for understanding what it was. Who he was. He had dropped her at Richmond, almost frostily. When the May Bank Holiday came around, he took a group from the play down, and achieved a successful result with both the Winslow Boy himself (in reality a young-looking actor of twenty playing a thirteen-year-old boy) and the actress playing his sister. He didn't care that they were both annoyed and upset at the discovery of the other's presence in his bed during the weekend. He gave them both the orphan speech and was richly rewarded both times. The less he seemed to care, the greater those rewards. It was a weekend of pure debauchery, the high-water mark for the Bosky, and at one point he came across Simon having his way with the Winslow Boy's mother on the porch – which Tony thought a little unnecessary, but didn't comment on. He never liked to seem a prude in front of Simon.

No trace of any of this existed in the Bosky – he had Mrs Proudfoot's newly married daughter, Eliza, coming in to keep the place shipshape while he was away and getting everything ready, and though the new Mrs Gage was a deeply conservative soul she never seemed to question any of his demands, nor the endless stream of bright young people who thronged the Bosky at Bank Holidays, leaving bottles of champagne stuck on to branches of the rose bush, or sheets filthy with scrambled eggs, gramophone records out of their cases and piled high for her to put away.

You'd never have known that on his previous visit someone had been sick on the porch seat, or that ten people had crammed into the wooden house that previous Bank Holiday . . . Tony passed a hand across his forehead. He was glad Althea hadn't met Simon yet.

The honeysuckle was beginning to open, and scented lavender and rosemary sprang from the cracks by the house. Inside, a small vase of tiny sun-yellow roses, from the rose bush that had begun to climb up the side of the house after years of inactivity, had been placed on the wooden table. A cold chicken salad stood on the dresser, the table was set for lunch, the cushion on the window seat where someone had accidentally dropped a glass of red wine miraculously clean once more. Althea walked about the place, taking it all in. She didn't exclaim breathlessly, nor flutter round him while he was opening the shutters and windows, she just stared. At herself in the mirror, out of the window, in drawers – not nosily, but calmly, with intense interest in everything but still revealing nothing of what she was thinking. He liked that about her. Oh, he liked her so very much and he hadn't realised before that one ought to like someone, as well as wanting them. Not since . . . a long time ago.

He made them both gimlets – not too strong, it wasn't done to get a girl tight. They sat on the porch together, for the first time, the only sound the wind and the chink of her swizzle stick against the crystal.

'So it's your place, then?' she asked, after a moment or two.

'All mine.'

'No family?'

'My parents are dead.'

'Yes. Bertie told me.' So Bertie had been filling her in. 'I'm sorry. I meant any other family.'

'Nope.'

Her stick clanked against the glass, mechanically. 'Really no one at all?'

'Dammit!' He said, much louder than he'd meant. 'No. I said no one.' There was an awkward silence. 'I'm so sorry. Would you like a refill?'

'Not just yet.' She stood up and looked over the balustrade. 'When I was little, my sister and I used to catch trout off the jetty at the end of our garden, even though our father absolutely forbade it.'

'Your garden?'

She turned round to face him, leaning against the railings, her hair blowing about her face. 'The house I grew up in Kirkcudbright. It had a long garden that led down to the River Dee. My father's an artist. He had a studio at the bottom of the garden, and he sang all day long while he was painting.'

He nodded, liking the feel of the prickling breeze on his neck, and the chink of metal on the wet glass.

'There's a castle just along the way, and a wee harbour. It's a beautiful place. The sky's bigger than here. I don't know why. Anyway, one day my sister had a catch but she lost her footing and fell into the river, and I had to dive in to rescue her, and she's bigger than me and I was only about nine. It was quite a job. But when we got back, absolutely drenched and stinking, Father dashed out of his studio and asked us why we were dripping wet and Isla said, 'It's best we don't remember why.'

Father thought it was the funniest thing he'd ever heard. He gave her a toffee.

'The point is, sometimes one has to forget.' She held on to the railings, and leaned towards him. 'Just forget it ever happened.'

'Mrs Gallagher, our neighbour in London,' said Tony thoughtfully. 'She lost her son in the Great War. She never mentioned him ever again. Her daughter told me. It was as though he'd never existed.'

'I think it's for the best, that course of action,' said Althea, frankly, and she held out her glass. 'I've changed my mind about the refill, if you're offering.'

He stood up and took the glasses inside, thoughtfully, and mixed more cocktails. The idea that one might simply never think of it again, of Mummy and how much he still missed her, of Dad and how he'd died, of Dinah and whether she was alive, safe, happy (but he knew she couldn't be happy, because she wasn't here) – of Daphne's face as she left the house the morning afterwards. When he went back into his bedroom she had left her underthings behind, and he knew it was deliberate, so that he would have to get rid of them, so that he would think about her with no underwear on for the rest of the day.

He never went back into that room again. Not once. Over fifteen years later, a grown man by then, in the darkness of the kitchen-diner, it seemed to Tony that it was the solution he had been searching for ever since that morning in wartime when he'd realised he was totally alone, for better, for worse.

It became the metaphor in his head, the shut door of that bedroom where he and Daphne had sex, the same night he lost Julia. What if you simply pushed this all out of your mind, like shutting the door on that room? What if you pretended it had never happened, instead of enduring these periodic bouts of misery that led one to drink and treat people so badly, that meant one sometimes dried on stage, or couldn't concentrate because of the shakes. What if one simply . . . tamped it down, like tobacco into a pipe, set fire to it, let it burn away?

He poured the gimlet mixture into Althea's and his glasses, reflecting that this was another thing it was best not to think about.

'*It's best we don't remember why.*' He gave a small smile, and went back out on to the porch with the drinks. Althea was talking to someone, and he paused in the doorway, watching her, how gracefully she turned round on the balustrade, how she left one white hand holding on to the railing, as though she belonged to this place, as though it was hers. He peered forwards to see who it was. Reverend Goudge, who had taken him in and made sure he got to Central, had died a couple of years ago, his kind wife had moved away, and there weren't many others in the village now that he knew. The war had scattered people – some simply hadn't come back. A hotel had been built further along the beach. People were starting to come here on holiday, not to live here all year round. Tony stared, and realised he recognised the stranger.

Althea was talking to Ian Fletcher. He looked much older; the shock of unruly black hair that stuck up on his head was greying and his curling, untidy eyebrows were flecked with white. His face already showed signs of dissipation, a redness that he hadn't had as a boy. Tony was used to him hanging around whenever he had visitors, literally an uninvited guest, but he never spoke to him. He'd walk past ostensibly on his way down to the beach and raise his eyebrows, as though wanting to come in, but he never did. He never said hello, just stared at Tony. It must have been well over a decade since Tony had actually looked at him properly, much less spoken to him.

'Where in Scotland?' Althea was asking him, politely.

'Stirling, but we moved down to Bristol when I was eight, after my mother died, and we bought our place just along the way from here.'

'So you boys must have played together then,' said Althea, catching sight of Tony, as he advanced towards them with the drinks.

'Me and Tony, yes, and my sister, Julia, though of course it was the war, and we were all away at school, and various other happenings,' said Ian, and he didn't look at Tony. 'I had a letter from Julia, only yesterday.'

Tony handed Althea her drink and she took it, and lightly touched his hand, and her calm certainty and self-assurance was like a raft in a churning sea, something to cling to, as black spots fizzed around the edges of his vision.

'Oh? How is she?'

Ian rocked on his feet. Tony wished he'd just scarper, clear off. But he seemed to be gearing up to say something.

'She's well enough,' he said.

'That's good. Where's she living these days?' said Tony.

Ian looked directly at him. 'She lives in Melbourne now, she's married, she's got a dog called Buster, after Mottram.'

'Ah,' said Tony politely, his heart hammering. Something was in his throat, closing it up, a ball of something.

'Her husband's English, tennis mad. They have it as their little joke against the Aussies, you know. And she's working for an animal wildlife place. She likes bats,' said Ian, to Althea, who was looking a little bored. 'She's running a campaign to get them protected. Bats, of all things.'

'She always did,' said Tony. 'Used to look out for them in the evenings when we were walking back from rehearsals and so on . . .' He trailed off.

'It's not been easy for her,' said Ian, suddenly. 'You knew her, didn't you, Tony? They were friends in the war, he and Julia.'

'Oh,' said Althea slowly. 'I see.'

'She wasn't a *bad* girl, was she?' Ian said innocently. 'She wasn't . . . you know, one of those girls. Just misguided and it was a jolly hard time, jolly hard . . .' He shrugged.

'I never heard back from her,' Tony managed to say. 'I did write to her, here, but she never answered. I don't know if she got the letters—'

'Father sent her to school in Scotland, and then of course she stayed there till the war was over. She wasn't well for a while after that summer, the air in Scotland did her good. And then, then . . .' His face clouded. 'She was first to leave for Australia after the war, you know, they were looking for teachers. She went as soon as she could and she's never been back. I don't know if she ever will . . .'

Althea had wandered to the other end of the porch, looking out over to Bill's Point and the calm, grey sea.

Tony said quietly to Ian, 'I'm sorry to hear she wasn't well. I trust she recovered.'

Ian faced Tony, and his shoulders hunched, and he smiled, slowly; it was an extraordinary expression, a ghastly rictus.

'She had an abortion,' he said. 'She nearly died. A nice place it was supposed to be, a wee house in Shepherd's Market in London. Father took her. But they did it badly, I suppose – she was very ill, an infection. She nearly died, yes, and Father wouldn't have her in the house afterwards. She stayed at school. They taught her alone, didn't want her with the other girls, so she failed her School Cert. I saw her once before she left . . .' He had lowered his voice, so Althea wouldn't hear, or to draw Tony closer, Tony didn't know. 'My father died, soon afterwards. She never saw him again.'

'She never answered my letters . . .' Tony felt his heart pounding, hands sweating.

'Funny, she wrote to you at school, and at the Bosky, but she wasn't ever sure the address of the school was right because you never replied . . .' He shrugged, and Ant knew Ian had had a part in it, whatever had happened. Maybe he'd given her the wrong address, or torn up the letters . . . 'She was rather upset, especially when she was so ill . . . I suppose you were off and out to drama school afterwards. We've heard all about you down here.'

'I went a year early . . . they let me in because . . .' Tony rubbed his eyes. 'I should have let her know where I was . . . I didn't know why she wouldn't reply and of course she wasn't here any more . . .'

Ian's frightful sing-song voice carried on. 'It's all in the past, isn't it? She's awfully glad to be out of Britain. Says it's a dead country and perhaps she's right. She got as far away as she could.'

It's all in the past, isn't it?

Tony nodded, using every ounce of self-possession and acting ability to keep control of his emotions. Althea wandered back over, looking from one to the other.

A car sounded its horn in the distance, and Ian looked up. 'I must go. That's my wife.' He shook hands with Althea. 'We'll have you round, if you come back here,' he said, almost jovial now. 'My wife loves to entertain. She'd be pleased to meet you.' He nodded at Tony, and he saw the twisted pain on his face. 'G'bye, then, *Anthony*,' he said.

'What a curious man,' Althea said, after he'd gone.

Tony shook his head. He pushed it all down, as far down as it could go, took a great gulp of his drink. 'I never knew him that well.'

'But you knew his sister,' she said, wryly. 'That much was clear.'

I abandoned you, Julia. You never wrote back and I never wrote again and I was too busy surviving to carry on. I abandoned you.

'I hope she's happy,' he said.

She looked at him intently for a moment. 'I hope so too.'

Push it down, push it all down . . . Tony briefly closed his eyes, and then he opened them, focusing on the seam of Althea's stockings, the auburn curls on the nape of her neck where her hair was swept up into a chignon. 'Come inside,' he said, with difficulty. 'Forget about him. I want to show you the rest of the house.'

She smiled over her shoulder at him and he drank in the sight of her. Her knowing smile, her great beauty, her seriousness, her gentle Scottish accent. She was new, and strange, and didn't know him yet, and he could be himself, or a version of himself that he liked, and didn't have to edit. She might even take it all away for a while.

'I'm jolly lucky you trusted me to come down here,' he said, trying to affect a jovial tone, but inside he felt sick, shaking, as they went downstairs towards the bedrooms. He had seduced scores of women, many of them here, this being his preferred line, but this was the first time he'd felt sick. He clutched on to the railing.

Althea was ahead of him – she said, in her carefree, calm way, 'I like you. I liked you the moment I saw you. That's all.'

She shrugged, as though it was as simple as that, and as she turned to him Tony stumbled on the last step, holding on to the bannister.

'Goodness,' she said, as he righted himself. 'You look awfully green. Are you ill? Here.' She took his arm. 'Let's – oh, gosh, the lights are off. Where's the switch?'

He could hardly hear her. It was safer to just stay holding on to the bannister, gently swaying, letting darkness and waves of nausea wash over him. 'Here,' she said, taking his arm. 'Perhaps you ate something. Come in. Come and lie down.'

'No.' He pulled away from her, tears starting in his eyes. 'No!'

'Here,' she said, firmly, and she almost tried to push him into the room. 'You really need to sit down, or lie down, Tony—'

'No.' Tony actually shoved her, so that she rocked back against the corridor wall. 'I won't go in there. Don't. I won't go into that room. Please.' He cleared his throat – this was terrible, all of it, and he'd absolutely ruined everything now, if he could only stop the black wavy lines that ran up and down his vision, and the feeling that he was going to pass out . . . 'Sorry,' he said, reaching out and clutching Althea's hand. 'I'm so sorry . . .'

And everything went mercifully black.

When he woke up, he was lying on the bed in his old room. The nodes of the pink candlewick bedspread rubbed his neck; it was comforting, like fingers. He sat up, shaking his head, and a wave of dizziness overtook him again.

Althea was at the end of the bed, playing with something. She looked over at him, and swallowed.

'Sorry. I found some marrons glacés in the cupboard upstairs. Delicious. I'm afraid I attacked them. Here. Have one. Do you good.' She pressed the moist, caramel-coloured sweetmeat between his lips. 'And here's some water.'

'Thanks.' He raised his head and drank, then lay back, watching her.

'What's that you've got there?'

She passed it over towards him. 'An old game.'

'Oh.' Heart thudding, he sat up. 'Where'd you find it?'

'Under the bed. I'm sorry if I shouldn't have meddled. It's beautiful. The tiles, and these metal flowers. What is it?'

Carefully, Tony put the tiles and the flowers back into the mahogany case and shut it, smoothing his hand over the mother-of-pearl dragon. 'It's a mah-jong set. It belonged to my great-aunt. We used to play it while the bombing raids were on.'

He put it under the bed again and smiled up at her. There was no point in being embarrassed, or acting his usual part. He'd shoved her, he'd cried, and he'd passed out. 'I'm really sorry about all this. I – I don't like this room.'

'I guessed as much.' She ate another chestnut. 'My father used to get the sweats whenever he got the train back to Glasgow. Right at the train station. Nowhere else. But his father once beat him there, in front of everyone. He'd forgotten all about it till his brother reminded him. Isn't it strange, what the mind can do?'

Tony nodded. It was late afternoon; very still. The smell of mothballs and mildew, of old books and comforting wood, wrapped around him. He felt peaceful.

'So what happened in here, or don't you want to tell me?'

He screwed up his mouth, and said nothing. Eventually, he shook his head. 'I was a boy . . . I . . . Sorry.'

'That's no problem, and it's none of my business.' She stood up, brushing down her long blue skirt, and a beam of light caught in her auburn hair. 'You can be two things, Tony. You can be the boy in the bedroom, for the rest of your life, or you can leave him in there, and come out. Jolly depressing to be the former, though.'

'Yes.' He stared at her. 'Yes, it is.'

She ate another marron glacé, and then shut the box firmly. He watched her, and felt calm for the first time since they'd arrived.

Somehow, haltingly, he managed to tell her what had happened in that room, about Daphne, about Julia, and of course about Dinah. Later, when it was dark, he brought her back down there, and in the darkness he removed her clothing, her suspenders, her bodice, the silk shirt and the full skirt. She was large-breasted, large-thighed, tall like a goddess – she was magnificent, all of her. He took her there, frenzied, vengeful, and then again, more tenderly. She was impassive at first, as though she understood, and then fiery, passionate, catching his wrists above his head and biting his lip with her sharp white teeth, climbing on top of him so that he could hold her milky-white thighs, see her hair fall about her face, watch her ride him, take her pleasure – it was the first time, since Julia, that he had been with a woman who could with such unalloyed enjoyment, who wanted it as much as he did.

They stayed that night in Ant's old room, and then, the next morning, crept into the master bedroom. And for many years neither of them went back into that room unless they had to. For a long while, it stopped mattering. For a long while, they both thought they'd beaten the ghosts back.

Chapter Thirty-Seven

London, 2014

'The house is painted. They did it in a week. It looks great. And I got them to put some furniture in. I just had a coffee, looking out to sea. That view of the bay – man, it's beautiful here, Ben. I get it, I really do.'

'I can't wait to see it. Thank you so much, darling.'

He could hear his wife crossing something off a list. She loved lists. 'OK. Ben – honey, you still need to tell me what you want to do with the beach hut. It's just there, rotting into the sand.'

Ben, used to commanding entire movie sets, to silencing a room with one raised hand, was, in the home, as low-key as ever. He rubbed at the bridge of his nose. 'Yep. Well, I don't know.'

'We'd get a good price for it,' said Lauren, ever practical. 'I made a few calls. The land is worth more than the building. '

The first time Ben met Lauren, at a charity dinner in New York years earlier, she had outbid an American baseball player for a signed David Hockney print which she promptly resold to an ageing movie producer she knew who collected Hockneys. He'd watched her long fingers alternately tapping on her BlackBerry to do the deal and tucking her bob behind her ears. She'd donated the extra money back to the charity. The whole thing had been sewn up by the time the green-tea panna cottas were served, and Ben had watched throughout, transfixed by her, this force of energy, quite unlike anyone he'd met before.

She added, ruthlessly, 'You want my opinion? We should just tear the thing down.'

'It's Cord's. She's the one who'll have to decide.'

'Sure.' He could hear her scribbling something. 'So, no news?'

'None. She was here again last week, you know. But that was to see the girls. It's the third time.'

'What do they say about it?'

'They say it's great. She tells them about Mads when we were little, what they used to get up to together. Funny things.' He thanked his lucky stars once again that Lauren wasn't the jealous or awkward kind and he could always mention Mads in front of her. 'She remembers it all, stuff I'd totally forgotten. And of course she knows about staging so she's been a great help to Emily with her dissertation. But she won't ever stay for a meal, or even a glass of wine. Iris thinks she has a melancholy heart.'

'What a sad expression.'

'Well, but it's true.'

'When can I meet her, Ben? It's totally crazy I've never met her.'

He shrugged. 'Listen, I haven't seen her for ten years and she's my sister.'

'When was the last time?'

'Would you believe it, I bumped into her on the street, outside an all-night pharmacy in Wigmore Street, do you remember? She had toothache, and I was picking up a prescription for Emily's eczema. And we chatted, and she was perfectly friendly, but she hurried off the moment I mentioned meeting up. Just said, "I'm so sorry," and she was off.'

'I don't get it.'

Ben gave a deep, shuddering sigh. He still found it upsetting.

'You know, I think she just didn't want to be close to us any more. I've thought about it a lot. Where's it written that you have to stick like glue to your family for the rest of your life? She always was a loner.'

He trailed off, shaking his head, because while that was the version he'd chosen to believe and the one he'd repeated to their mother over and over through the years, and the one he used to explain things away to curious friends and relations, he didn't actually believe it. As a child, Cord had loved company, loved bringing people together and organising things. He didn't believe she enjoyed her solitude. He didn't believe she didn't want love, and rejected intimacy. *I know you, little sister*, he thought now. *I still know you, I always will, and I know you're not happy.*

'Well, next time, you tell them to tell her I wanna meet her.'

His phone buzzed with a message and Ben jumped slightly. 'She won't stay at the house if she thinks I'm going to be there. She's told them she needs time to get used to it all. She has some operation coming up on her throat again, too, they're going to try and repair the damage. Apparently what they can do, how precise they're able to be, has moved on an awful lot in ten years.'

'That's incredible. I mean – if it worked – What are the chances?'

'The girls say she thinks it's pretty even fifty-fifty. So it might be a disaster but it's a good thing she's trying. Right? I mean, all of this is good. It's amazing she's even in touch with the girls. I wonder what made her change her mind all of a sudden.'

'Honey. I don't know. Your mother, presumably.'

'Yep – but she's so stubborn.' He paused. 'God, Lauren. I hope we're doing the right thing. Bringing the Bosky back to life – it's for her. I hope she doesn't just – freak out.'

Lauren said nothing; the crackle of the line whirred between them. 'I wish I knew what to say to make it better.'

He laughed. 'You can't always make it better, my dear.'

She said, 'You want to bet? Now – decide about the beach hut. Tell me what you think we should do.'

'I don't know,' Ben said, bleakly. There was another silence and he wished he knew her more, this kindly, beautiful woman who was his wife. Who decorated houses in weeks, organised parties at the drop of a hat, made life smoother and more comfortable than it had ever been and yet with whom he still sometimes felt uneasy, like wearing a warm woollen jumper that's just a little scratchy. A woman who was nothing at all like brave, haunted, indomitable Mads. Nothing at all.

Then she said, 'I know you have happy memories of it but you know, honey, it's the place she killed herself. I think you should—' She paused; the static silence crackled down the line. 'Start again.'

'I have.' Ben rubbed the stump of his fingers against his knee.

'Not really. You need to take practical steps, Ben. If Cordelia is too. It's time to give it a new lease of life, the whole house, and it seems kinda weird to leave the hut where Madeleine killed herself just standing there.'

He wanted to say, *But I have so many happy memories there too. I remember her letting me kiss her, I remember the feel of her, I remember the three of us, Cord, Mads, and me, sitting on the steps talking or sleeping the night there as a special treat. We were always together.*

The time we lit a fire inside the hut because Cord insisted it'd be OK and we toasted marshmallows and nearly burned the place down. Or when Mads removed the curtains because she said they were dirty and they just fell to pieces in her hands, they were so ancient. Or when we did that play that was a rip-off of Peter Pan on the Bosky steps and made Mumma and Daddy watch it with Mrs Gage, and Daddy fell asleep and his head kept falling on to Mrs Gage's shoulder and she was horrified . . . The rules for Flowers and Stones, they're still up there, they've been up there since the day Cord pinned them to the wall. These things matter.

I remember how my wife looked in death. Not peaceful – that's what they always want you to say. Her arms were above her head, her eyes wide open . . . The hair flooding the bed like a Victorian bride . . .

'Tear it down,' he said, suddenly. 'Do it.' There was a knock at his door.

'Dad?' came a voice from outside. 'You in there? The car's here for you.'

'What did you say? Keep it?' said Lauren, quickly.

'Absolutely,' Ben said. 'Look, I have to go, darling, I'll call you later—'

'Ben, I just want you to love the place—'

'Yes,' said Ben, not really listening again. 'Me too. Bye, darling.'

He heard, but did not process, the little sigh she gave as he ended the call and swung the phone back into his pocket with his remaining finger and thumb hooked together. He stared at the smooth stump, remembering for a moment, until the noise of the waiting car in the driveway recalled him to the present.

But it wasn't until he'd put on his jacket and had his hand on the door of the study that Ben remembered to check his phone for the message that had buzzed while he'd been speaking to Lauren.

OK OK. You are annoying. I've been doing a lot of thinking. I will come to the Bosky with you. Just once, to see Mumma. Don't go to any trouble, please. It'll be lovely to see you, Flash Gordon. Cord x P.S. This is a stupid question but is Hamish living in your basement and is he an accountant?

460

Ben smiled, and stared at the photo he always kept on his desk of him and his sister, kneeling on the sand, plump arms flung tightly round each other, grins as wide as their faces. He heard the car outside revving its engine a tiny amount, a respectful reminder and, slinging his phone and wallet into his pocket, he picked up his satchel and left the room. On the way out, he bumped almost straight into Emily, who was leaning against the hallway looking at her phone, her long bronze hair falling about her face.

'Oh, Dad,' she said, vaguely, staring at the back-lit screen. 'Hello. Listen, have you got any cash on you?'

'Cord,' he said, pinching her cheek. 'Cord's coming. She's coming.'

'What on earth do you mean?'

'She's coming back. She's coming to see Mumma. Oh, Emily. You and your sister are geniuses. Well done, darling. She's finally going to come back.'

Emily didn't look up. 'Of course she is. She always would have. You two are both crazy for that place.' And she carried on tapping at her phone.

Chapter Thirty-Eight

Lauren's enormous Mercedes 4×4, like a giant black truck with its blue-tinted blacked-out windows, collected Cord and Ben from Wareham station. As they bowled along the lane towards Worth Bay Cord sat stiffly upright in the back, as Lauren smilingly made small talk. The blackout glass, viewed from the inside, gave the autumn countryside a strangely dappled, filtered look as if it weren't quite real. She had to keep telling herself that it *was* all real. That she was here again, and in a few minutes she would see the house once more, see her mother.

Like so many Americans, Lauren had beautiful manners. She talked politely about the area, asking questions about the Isle of Purbeck, their holidays there, telling Cord she loved her shoes. Cord, glancing at the sturdy old biker boots where the sole was coming away from the base, chose to believe her and, after a while, chatted back. She liked Lauren. She wanted to like her: perhaps that was even more important.

She felt very calm. That morning, she had put on her deep pink cardigan and black jeans, wrapped her throat in a big floral-patterned scarf, and had looked at herself in the full-length mirror in the hall, pushing a pile of old books out of the way and inadvertently knocking over a half-dead trailing spider plant. She had become flustered, trying to pick up the dry soil with her fingers, the scarf getting in her way. Tears had sprung to her eyes and then she'd stopped, stood up and looked at herself again.

It can't be as bad as it's already been, she told herself. *Don't get upset. Stay calm. The worst has already happened, hasn't it? And you're OK these days, aren't you?*

And her reflection had nodded back at her. *I'm OK.*

In her bag was Mads's book, and the angel. She didn't know what to do with either of them. She couldn't tell anyone else about the book – she knew that. She had vowed years ago that she must be the one who carried the burden of knowledge alone. So she couldn't ever tell her darling nieces what she knew. *I'm your sister.* And yet she couldn't bear for them not to know about their mother, because rereading the diaries had made her remember things she had pushed away for so long. How she had loved Mads, how terrible her childhood had been but for the Wildes. It made more sense of what had happened, and it reminded her of something: how happy they were. And she kept coming back to that.

Those girls were her family, no matter what kind, they were family. And what a difference it made, having people who cared about you. Iris had helped her immeasurably with her upcoming operation; she'd come to the consultant's meeting with her and asked lots of sensible questions Cord hadn't thought of. Cord had taken Emily around Covent Garden – a tour arranged by Professor Mazzi. Halfway round, in one of the old dressing rooms she had once used, she had bumped into Jay Washington, older, grizzled around the temples, but the same. His hand had crushed hers as he gripped it and pulled her towards him.

'Man, but I wouldn't have known you, Cordelia,' he said, and she felt stung, and smiled, and pretended not to care as he ogled Emily.

The gap between them – she, a drab, plimsoll-wearing wraith in black dress, black leggings, shrugged-on cardi, poking around the scene of her former glories, and he, sleek with years of success. And yet after that he had been so kind, and treated her as if she were still someone worthy of notice, and Emily was impressed, tapping her shoulder as they moved on.

'Gorgeous, Auntie Cord. Well done.' And she had texted Iris immediately, informing her of their aunt's hot ex, and they had teased her mercilessly about him, and she had absolutely loved it.

They had both been for tea at the flat, and she had shown them photographs of their mother, and Iris had told Cord she should wear patterns more. 'Florals and prints. They suit you. Not all this grey and black.'

'Oh, well, thank you so much for the feedback.'

'Trust me.' She'd gone back to her phone. 'Emily, this is hilarious, come and look at it. It's this stick insect, and it's like dancing to Carly Rae Jepsen?'

There was one more surprise, one more thing she wanted to tell Ben. But how to do it without revealing the existence of the book?

Now Cord looked around at the fields sloping away towards Brownsea Island, at the barrow that led over towards Bill's Point and Swanage: in summer harebells nodded in its long grasses and blue butterflies danced, but by now in late autumn it was covered in the blood red and green of the gorse, the wind whistling through the bare, bent trees and one could already see how different it would be in winter. *I only know it in summer*, she thought. *Isn't that strange.*

And there was the first glimpse of the sea, over the flame-and-peach-coloured treetops, a dark blue line that grew larger, turned into a diamond, then disappeared again.

They went through the village. 'It's exactly the same,' said Cord, hoping fake gaiety would see her through for she could not remain silent; she thought she might be sick otherwise.

'Even in winter. Look, there's the vicarage. There's Mrs Gage's house. Oh, here's the lane.' She had gripped Ben's hand and he held it tightly. 'Oh, my goodness, there's Beeches. Is Mumma there? I'd love to see inside it.'

'She'll come over later. She wants to come to the house.'

'My, my,' said Cord, feeling sick with nerves. She looked from her large black padded coat which kept out the cold brilliantly to Lauren's elegant, simply cut navy jacket. She flexed her hands, feeling trapped in the people carrier, the weight of the angel and the book on her knee; suddenly she was desperate to get out. 'Oh, the bumpy lane – it always was like this, I'm so glad it hasn't changed—'

'I'd love to tarmac it, but even I couldn't get that through,' said Lauren. 'It's the only change I wasn't allowed, Cordelia. I hope you can live with it.'

'Change?' said Cord, smiling politely. 'I don't know what you mean.' She glanced at her brother.

'Well, Cordy . . . Listen, we've something to tell you. Lauren's been down here working on the house,' said Ben, now releasing his hand from Cord's grasp and squeezing his wife's shoulder. 'She's had the bathroom done and the wood's been treated and varnished, and she's sorted out the damp, redone the storage heaters, put some furniture in, a kettle, that kind of thing. We did it for Mumma, and for you.' He looked at Cord, as the taxi jolted and then was still. 'We want it to be habitable again, in case Mumma wants to sleep here for a night or two before – while she can. And we – we wanted you to like being back here, you see.'

'And maybe invite us down some day,' said Lauren, smiling as the car stopped and the door slid open, as if by an invisible hand. Cord thought she was nervous now. Ben handed his sister down and she stood on the gravelled pathway, looking up at the back of the house.

'Daddy always said the first time he saw it was covered in wild flowers, do you remember? Honeysuckle and brambles and those roses. Yes, look, Ben, they're still flowering. Isn't it extraordinary . . .

They passed around to the front of the house, up the tiny side path, and oh, the exquisite strangeness of the familiarity, the same shrubby sea nettles and messy brambles in the sand, the little stretch of yellow before the beach huts below and, as you climbed the steps to the porch, the view of the sea and the bay below, opening up to you.

Cord bit her lip.

A voice behind her spoke.

'Hello, Cordy.'

Lauren yelped. 'Oh! My gosh, you gave me a shock, Althea.'

Cord turned around slowly. There, alone on the porch, sat her mother.

'Mumma, you're early! I thought they were going to bring you here for lunch,' said Ben, going over to his mother, who sat on a new wicker sofa covered with bright pastel cushions. He kissed her, and stood back, and Cord stared at her.

'I wanted to be early.' She looked at her daughter. 'Cordy darling. Well, here we are.'

The bags that Althea had under her eyes when Cord had last seen her – on TV, arriving at an actor's memorial service at Westminster Abbey – now rested somewhere below her cheekbones, like little smiles of paunchy skin. The bottom eyelids drooped so that her eyes watered constantly. Her hands were so thin her gold wedding ring hung loose. But Althea pushed her still-glossy, pale Titian bob out of her face and said again to her silent daughter in that delicious voice, 'Well? Have you come to apologise, or to shout at me?'

Cord bent over, and kissed her soft papery cheek. 'Hello,

466

Mumma.' She stroked her hair. 'How – how are you today?'

'I am well. I had a seizure two days ago, and fell down.' She lifted her long watered grey silk skirt, printed all over with huge blue and cream hydrangeas, to reveal a bandaged knee. 'They think another one might kill me and they want me to stay quietly in the home but I won't have it. There's worse ways to die than a seizure. And it's best to go before you start wanting to die.'

'Now, Althea, you mustn't talk like that!' Lauren said, mock-impatiently.

'Thank you for your concern.' Althea raised her eyebrows imperiously at her. Cord wanted to smile. 'Cordelia, would you go and put on the kettle? I have been inside. I must say, Lauren, you've done a wonderful job.'

Cord stepped over the threshold, steeling herself for the old familiarity of the place, for the smell – of pine needles, dust, sea, people – but it never came. The wood panelling that made the place feel so warm and cosy was still on some walls, but on others the damp had meant the panelling had been removed, and replaced with freshly painted plaster, primrose yellow in the kitchen, cream and warm grey in the sitting room. Cord filled the kettle and turned it on, admiring the blinds in the kitchen-diner and the window seat, covered in a Duncan Grant print. The old skirting boards and door knobs and the damp were all gone – everything was clean, fresh and new. Gone were the photos lining the staircase – just a few remained, four or five at most.

It was the house it had always been, but the weight of memory on the place had vanished. Cord took a deep breath and closed her eyes, as the autumn tide roared outside. She opened the French window, admiring its smooth new action, to thank Lauren, to tell her how wonderful she was, but only her mother was there.

'They've gone for a walk on the beach,' Althea said, and she patted the back of her own head, then ran her fingertips over her pursed, lined mouth. 'Come and sit down.'

Cord sank on to the wicker seat next to her mother. She wanted to stare at her ruined face, to ask her if she minded: it was the thing she had always feared most. She wanted to ask her so many things, she didn't know where to begin.

Eventually Althea said, 'First things first. The Bosky is yours after I die, that's what you need to know. It's in my will – but briefly, so you hear about it before I'm dead, you will also receive a share of the money we raised from the sale of the Twickenham house, not as much as Ben, to make reparation for your being given the Bosky. But it was your father's most fervent wish that the house be yours. So there it is. Now, as to the other assets—'

Cord put her hand on her mother's arm. 'Mumma, I don't care about the assets. Why did he leave it to me? Why not Ben?'

'Ah.' Althea blinked. 'Well, Ben had money. You don't.'

'But – when Daddy died I was doing OK,' said Cord, after a moment's thought. 'I was still performing, my voice hadn't gone. He wasn't to know I'd – he didn't know I'd need the cash more than Ben. That doesn't make sense.'

Her mother shrugged. 'Things don't always make sense.'

'Anyway,' Cord said eventually. 'I don't need the house. I don't need anything from you. I just wanted to see you again.' Her voice sounded very thin. 'I'm sorry, Mumma.'

'For what?'

'For – not seeing you, all these years.' Cord bowed her head; a tear fell into her coat, staining the hatched texture a darker black.

'You had your reasons. And Daddy had his. That's why he left you the house, you see. He wanted you to remember . . . to remember that you'd been happy here.'

'But—' Cord opened her mouth to say something, and stopped. 'Thanks, Mumma. Now, tell me how you are.'

'Boring.' Althea shook her head. 'Not me. I want you to understand, my darling. You have to understand why he did it. He knew, you see. He knew it was all his fault. That Ben ran away, and lost his fingers. It was his fault you rejected us, long before the business with him and poor Mads, his fault Mads killed herself – he knew.'

The clouds on the horizon swelled and retracted; Cord blinked. '*You* knew that?' Althea nodded. Gently, she pressed her fingers to each side of her head. 'Mumma, you never said anything.'

'But it was so long ago,' said Althea, almost impatiently. 'Moons ago, Cordelia. We were all different then. *Golden lads and girls all must, / As chimney sweepers, come to dust.* You remember that? You sang that song, darling. He was the golden lad, do you understand? I long ago stopped holding your father to the same standards as other people.'

'Why?' Cord pressed her hands to her burning cheeks. 'Didn't you care?' She swallowed. 'You must have known, Mumma. About the affairs. Those younger women. *We* knew.'

Althea looked out to sea and shrugged.

'You are funny. And you're not at all like me, are you. I never realised before. Look at this jacket, for example.' She fingered the black nylon, and Cord blinked, then found herself laughing.

'Mumma. What on earth are you talking about?'

'I simply mean I'd never embark on a day out wearing a coat like this. One of the ways in which we are entirely different.'

'Thanks ever so much,' said Cord, laughing again.

'You've always been like this, darling. You see it your way – you understand? You can't conceive of how it could be any other. You consider that you are Right. You only see your father, an adulterer, lying to all of us, responsible for your relationship breaking up, Ben's accident, Mads's death, all these other terrible things too. But I see him as the young man he was when I met him. I still see the man I fell in love with.' She nodded at something imaginary, as if it were in front of her, and then blinked heavily. 'Gosh.'

'Are you all right?'

'Yes. It gives me strange sensations, this object growing inside my head. It makes me forget some things and then quite suddenly remember others. And I like sitting by my window, at the home, just up from the Bosky. I like thinking. I see the past quite clearly.'

She fiddled with her skirt, the too-large wedding ring swinging on her scrawny finger. Cord watched her, then swallowed down the ball of whatever it was at the back of her throat. 'Do you, Mumma?'

'I do, Cordy. People don't consider there might be another side to the story, another way of viewing the action, do you understand me?' Cord nodded. 'Exactly. The first time we came here, for example. And he found out about Julia's abortion and her illness. He told me about Daphne. And the war. And his parents.'

'Julia? Mads's aunt, you mean?' Cord thought her mother was a little confused. 'Who's Daphne, Mumma?'

Althea blinked again. 'Did you know, Cordy, Daddy saw his mother die? He was next to her in the cupboard under the stairs when they were hit, and he saw her. One side was completely torn away.' She was speaking faster and faster, gabbling to let the words out as if she didn't have enough time. 'Did you know he was in a hospital in Camden for a month, and no one came to visit him, because his parents were dead and everyone else had either been evacuated or killed or they didn't know where he was? Did he ever tell you that? Not one person, till his aunt came for him.' Cord shook her head, mesmerised by the low, musical voice. 'Did you know the last time he saw his father he said he'd got him a place at Downham Hall, which was his old school. And Daddy had a blazing row with him about how he wasn't going to go to some stuffy, stuck-up boarding school, especially not in the middle of a war. His father left in a terrible rage. He was killed a few days later. Dinah did everything to get him to that school, she felt she had to. She was wrong, of course, but that's why Daddy was so keen for Benny to go to school, and why he couldn't see how stupid it was to force him. People repeat mistakes.

'And did you know he was in love with Julia, they used to meet in the sand dunes and make love – all very innocent, he told me all about her. And she was caught by Ian and her father and she had an abortion. She lost two pints of blood, then she got an infection, and she nearly died. She was in hospital for weeks. She couldn't ever have children. She wrote to tell him but her father and her school never posted the letters. They said she was – oh, they told her she was a whore, a slut, a prostitute. He managed to get a letter to her years afterwards, in Australia, but she didn't really want to know. It was just before our wedding, I remember how upset he was when she wrote back and said they couldn't be friends, they couldn't be anything any more. Poor Julia. And he blamed himself, your father did, and it wasn't his fault, wasn't at all, just a condom that didn't work properly. All they were doing was loving each other.

'And his greatest love was maybe Aunt Dinah. I often think she's the woman he was looking for all his life, and he never found her again. He told me everything. He *used* to tell me everything, that is.

'Now. Tell me why you think what he did with Madeleine was so wrong.'

Cord said, quietly, 'So you knew? About Daddy – and Mads? And you – you don't *mind*?'

'I wish he hadn't been unfaithful. Her too. But I don't *mind*. Look, look at what the result was.'

'She killed herself, Mumma.' Cord lowered her voice, her throat hurting so much now she could hardly speak. 'Her children are my half-sisters, they're their *father's half-sisters*, for God's sake. How can you possibly not see it? It's like a Greek tragedy. It's – it was abuse. It's incest, I told him it was. It's disgusting.'

'You don't know that.' Althea pushed her hand over her hair, blinking fast.

Cord moved away from her. 'Oh, Mumma. For God's sake. You sound like him.'

What had Daddy said to her on that dreadful last day? *They're not his sisters . . . I absolutely promise you. I swear it.*

'He had his reasons.'

'That's absolute bull—' Cord took a deep breath and stopped, remembering the promise she'd made to herself that morning in the flat. Don't get upset. Stay calm.

Althea said, again, 'You aren't listening to me, I know. He had his reasons to do what he did. You see, it goes back to what I was saying. You see it your way. I see it from his point of view. Yes, it was wrong in lots of ways, but he gave Mads children. That's all she wanted. He made her happy before she died.'

'She killed herself, Mumma!' Cord wanted to laugh.

'She was fragile. Too fragile for this life, Cordy. Couldn't you see that?'

Cord thought of the diary, safe in her bag, which she had now read five or six times. She would bury it under the porch at some point, where it had always been. Remember Mads in the right way, say sorry. She thought of the girl in the pages of that diary, who fought and struggled and tried to make it all better, but who couldn't.

'She wasn't always fragile—'

'Maybe she wasn't, but she became like that. Life wore her out. It wasn't you, darling, it wasn't even Tony. I saw the effect her childhood had on her. That awful father. How desperate she was to be part of us. She got what she wanted but the wave of all of that pain, well, darling, it simply crashed over her at times – she couldn't stop it. And she did do wrong, of course I know that. Of course she shouldn't have slept with him.' Tears swam in her watery, drooping eyes; she put her hands out towards her daughter. 'Forgive me. It makes me rather unhappy. I loved the girl, I loved her almost as much as you two. Those grandchildren might not be my flesh and blood, or they might – they're still mine, and I love them to pieces. I can't condemn her. It was what she had to do.' Althea wiped her nose on a cotton handkerchief; her fragile shoulders hunched over, and Cord felt great tenderness towards her. 'There's one thing I wish she'd known. She never knew the whole truth. If she'd known, maybe she wouldn't have blamed herself so much.' She sat back again and patted at her neck, unconsciously.

'The truth? About what?'

'About Ben, darling.' Althea moved a little on the cushion and peered out at the beach, and the sky. 'Look, it's going to rain soon. Fix me a drink, will you, dearest? A gimlet, perhaps? I want a drink.'

Cord couldn't quite believe it. 'Oh, honestly. Afterwards, Mumma. Tell me.'

'Well.' Althea's thin fingers plucked at the wicker of the seat. 'Darling. Ben – Ben isn't really Tony's son. I'd have thought you'd have worked that out as well, with all that time to think about it.'

Cord's eyes widened. 'What?"

Althea shrugged. 'Really, when you think about it, they're nothing like each other.'

'Ben – Ben isn't Daddy's?' Cord blinked. 'So – who's his father?'

'Doesn't really matter. That's not the point, darling—'

But Cord wasn't letting her get away with that. 'Come on, Mumma. You can't not tell me, not after all this. Does Ben know?'

Althea exhaled. 'Yes, yes. Ben knows. OK. An old actor friend of ours. Simon Chalmers. He was Daddy's flatmate. We used to see rather a lot of him, in the early days. Then . . . Well, we saw rather less of him,' Althea said. She spoke quite calmly. 'You know, it wasn't that uncommon then. There were a lot of parties, all sorts of things went on . . . I remember once at a house party of a friend of the Armstrong-Joneses, near Bath it was, where—' She stopped. 'Anyway. Those early years of our marriage, they weren't easy. Daddy was – oh, he was difficult! And I was young, and used to having my own way . . .' She folded her hands on her lap, looking out to sea.

'Simon and I had a very brief affair. Daddy found out, he was furious, it ended, I had Ben, he looked like Simon, we never spoke of it, and—' She made a little gesture, brushing her hands together. 'There you go. He used to come and stay in the early days, do you remember him?'

'Yes, of course. He'd come with Bertie.' Cord shook her head, utterly bewildered, as memories surfaced in her mind's eye, new slides on a carousel. 'He had blonde hair. Oh, oh, my goodness. He was fun. And he loved spy novels.'

'That's him. You liked him.'

474

'What happened to him?'

'Well, Daddy liked to think he was hip and fine with it, that we were all just humans and should get along, and he didn't have a leg to stand on when it came to fidelity. But Simon did used to wind him up. Popping down here when Daddy was away, always trying to persuade me to . . . Anyway, I didn't mind, isn't that awful? But Daddy got sick of it, of him and Bertie too, he banned them from coming. I suppose it was fair enough. Simon married some girl and I didn't see him much after that. He died a few years ago. He was a lovely man. Troublemaker, but awfully good fun.'

'So Ben's met him?'

'Absolutely.' She nodded, and Cord saw the years of intimacy her mother had had with her son, years she, Cord, had missed out on. 'Of course. Simon gave Ben a job after university, actually, working on a film. He was a great help. And when Daddy died Ben came to me and told me he'd always known and said he wanted to meet him properly.'

'No.' All this time, the secrets she'd been holding on to, and there were Ben and their mother carrying one of their own, quietly dealing with it.

'He went to see Simon, several times after Daddy died. He went to his funeral, darling.'

'I can't believe it.'

'You do, though.' Althea drummed her fingers on the chair. 'My point is, darling, that the girls might have been fathered by Tony, but your brother wasn't. I made one mistake. One. Sleeping with Simon a few times when your father was away, but I was furious with your father and darling, I was attractive then, and awfully lonely. You might say what they did was much worse—'

'Of course it was!' Cord interjected.

'They were damaged children, Tony and Mads, both of them.'

Althea shifted carefully on the seat, adjusting her voluminous skirts, and then she rubbed slowly at her temple with one pointed finger. 'I've learned nothing over the years, apart from lines from terrible plays I did fifty years ago that I can't seem to forget – and one other thing, that damage done in childhood stays with you for ever.'

Cord could see a kite, a Disney princess of some description bobbing about on the beach, being lifted up and then diving dramatically out of view before popping up again. She could feel the anger ebbing away from her, the loss of something on to which she had been holding so tightly, as though she had been holding her breath for a long time. She nodded.

'Oh, when I first knew him, Cordy. He was utterly beautiful. He'd been this huge sensation in *Hamlet* and he was so vain, so pleased with himself, so terrible at being falsely modest. And it was charming, utterly beguiling. They'd all had him, he'd been with hundreds of women and Uncle Bertie warned me off him. But I saw straight through it. It wasn't the handsome tousle-haired star I wanted, it was this little lost boy underneath, who was frozen in time, who couldn't get out. Frozen exactly at the point that aunt of his left him . . . It was him I fell for, him I wanted to look after.' She looked up, with a smile. 'We were really happy, you know. I loved the bad boy and I loved the little lost boy, and I let the bad boy do what he wanted and I looked after the lost boy. And, Cordy, for years I thought he was cured of it, that we'd packed these demons away and then something happened to change it.' She blinked, trying to remember. 'He became much worse. Selfish. Cruel. He wasn't ever cruel. Then Ben ran away after the row about the school, and perhaps we all grew older, and less tolerant . . . I didn't have the appetite for it in the later years, I grew angrier with him . . . I regret it.' She was silent then, and pointed at the kite, now fluttering higher than ever before. 'But it's very important you understand, that you remember that for years, until Ben ran away and still for a time after that, we gave you a proper childhood, it was everything, we were in love, we were happiest when it was the four of us together and yes – it was glorious.'

Cord took her mother's hands. 'Yes,' she said simply. 'Yes, it was.'

She leaned forward and touched her forehead to Althea's, and they stayed like that for a long while. Cord could hear her mother's breathing, feel her skull hard and warm against her temple, the ticking time bomb.

'Do you know what happened to Great-Aunt Dinah?' she said, eventually. 'Did you ever find out?'

'She came back, because she brought the angel back.'

'What do you mean?'

'Well, she took it with her when she left. So she must have brought it back at some point. So there's that. But we have no idea how or when it reappeared. I never knew, anyway. It was just hanging up there one year, and it hadn't been before and it wasn't till your father was getting old that he started saying things . . . I don't know where she went.'

Cord propped the little square stone up against the cushions, and stared into the angel's huge eyes. 'Perhaps we never will.' She turned to her mother, and said quietly, 'I'm so sorry. All those years I lost.'

Althea said softly, 'Darling. You did what you thought you had to. I couldn't have done what you did. So you mustn't look back at those years now without remembering it was the right thing to do. It won't help Ben, or the girls, to know what we know. You are a brave, good girl, darling, and I'm so sorry everything else has been so hard for you – there – ah, don't cry, Cordy. Cordy, don't cry.' She was smiling, though her eyes were swimming with tears. 'There, there.'

And Cord rested her head on her mother's thin, frail shoulder, and cried for all of them and when she had finished crying, she sat up, eyes and nose swollen with weeping, and cleared her throat.

'The kettle's boiled but I think I'll make you that gimlet.'

'Strong, please. I'm absolutely not supposed to drink, and I don't bloody care. What does it matter?'

'Mumma, you look well, you know,' Cord said in the doorway. 'You don't look as though . . .'

'Don't.' Althea shook her head violently. 'Don't talk about it. We don't bring it up. I'll conk out one day and that'll be that, but the point is we don't talk about dying, we live while we can.' She turned, slowly, pointing into the sitting room. 'All those photographs. That American girl's taken most of them down, hasn't she? Ah well. I didn't realise till it was almost too late what matters. It's the real life in between those photographs, that's what's important. That's what you remember. The little moments. How happy we were. We *were* happy, weren't we?'

Cord paused, for a long time, her throat aching. Eventually: 'Yes,' she nodded, smiling at her mother, eyes full of tears. 'We were. We were happy.'

'So, darling. Fetch me that drink.'

And Cord, walking slowly, her head spinning, went into the kitchen of the house that would be hers and mixed an extra strong gimlet for herself and her mother, and when Ben and Lauren arrived back half an hour later, and it was drizzling, the view across the bay obscured by mist, Althea was asleep with the angel next to her on the sofa and Cord beside her, dried tears on her cheeks, an empty glass in her hand as the rain pattered softly down.

'Oh, Cordy,' said Ben, as he came up the steps, dripping wet. 'Sis – is everything all right?'

Cord smiled at him, smoothed her skirts down, and stood up. She took his hand, clutched the finger and thumb. 'No. But it will be. Lovely, lovely Ben.' She held his hand tightly and he looked at her, astonished. She smiled over his shoulder at Lauren, then at her brother. 'It will be, I promise.'

Epilogue

I

Summer 2015

The wake for Althea Wilde at the Bosky was quite something; Olivia de Quetteville, long a widow since Guy had died ten years previously, declared that Althea and Tony would have been immensely pleased at the amount of champagne consumed, the number of guests, the lateness of the hour at which the party concluded. 'Just like the old days,' she said. 'No bad behaviour, sadly, but you can't have everything.'

Althea died in July, having enjoyed several months when her condition did not worsen and only at the very end was she beset by seizures and pain, and it was controlled with morphine. She was only seventy-five, still young, but she seemed happy to be going, as Ben said, slightly mystified, to Cord, and Cord could only smile and agree. Althea had remained in control, she had died with the Bosky rejuvenated, with her children by her side, and those beautiful girls whom she called her grandchildren too. She hated the idea of a long decline, she'd run out of books to read, and her admirers were getting thin on the ground as time went on, or dreadfully bald – in short, the thing was as within her control as one could hope for, given the circumstances.

The funeral was at the Norman church in the village and Althea was buried next to Tony in the uneven ancient graveyard that gave way to the orchard where the boughs of the apple trees were bent with fruit, fringing the garden where Tony had first acted in *A Midsummer Night's Dream* all those years ago.

From the graveyard you could see the sea, a fine blue ribbon with the white of Bill's Point in the distance. It was a private service, just the immediate family, although Uncle Bertie, now eighty-five, was dusted off and allowed to come, and he read: *'I am a spirit of no common rate; The summer still doth tend upon my state.'* For, as he said, Althea was like a Fairy Queen, surrounded by admirers, never happier than in the warmth of approval and admiration.

On the Sunday of the August Bank Holiday, Ben and Cord held a wake for her – in reality, Lauren organised it all. Cord, arriving on the Saturday to help, was astonished to find, as she came up the steps, three stacks of chairs on the porch, two trestle tables on the sand nearby, and a young man up a ladder attaching strings of Chinese lanterns to the gables and the roof. Above the door in pride of place, the angel, hanging on a new hook and smiling down at them once more.

'The pub down the lane is doing the food,' said Lauren. 'Big plates of sandwiches and salads and I have a guy bringing some local bread and crab for crab rolls, and these –' She pointed at three rolled-up rugs in a canvas bag. 'I thought people could go sit on the sand in front of the house, or maybe we could all go to the beach or even the beach hut now we're finally getting around to having it knocked down, we could say a few words or whatever . . .' She trailed off, smiling at Ben. 'Why are you laughing?'

'Mumma wouldn't like people standing around being solemn, I don't think,' he said, putting his arm around her and kissing his wife's ash-blonde head. 'Or talking about their *feelings*.'

'Besides, she never went to the beach unless she could help it,' Cord added. 'She was always just up here, on the porch, with a drink and her sunglasses on.'

'Feet up on the table, reading a script.'

'Or *The Thornbirds* or a P. D. James or something. She really was fantastically lazy. It was Daddy who was usually down there with us.'

'He taught us how to swim, how to play rounders, and how to properly hide in hide-and-seek. Cordy, remember that time he told us all the story about the ghost of the young lady who lost her young man to smuggling and wanders the lanes looking for him, and Mads wrapped her hair entirely round her head because she was so terrified and it got so tangled we nearly had to cut it all off?'

'Mads's hair, honestly, it used to cause her so many problems,' said Cord.

'How so?' said Lauren, rolling up the rug again.

'It was very, very long, and she used it as a sort of safety blanket. She chewed it, she covered herself up in it, she twisted it . . . She used to sleep with it around her, didn't she, like a cloak.'

He nodded. 'Just like Emily, isn't it strange?'

'I hadn't noticed before,' said Cord, 'but you're right. Of course, she does it too.'

Lauren added, 'And Iris twists her hair into tiny points, like Ben. It's cute.'

'Oh—' Cord began, and then she stopped. Perhaps she did. Perhaps – so many perhapses, and they'd never really know the truth other than that they were here together again.

'It'll be OK, this party, won't it?' said Cord.

'Of course it will,' Lauren said. 'Your mom was so well loved. Everyone who's invited is coming.'

Cord turned to her brother. 'But won't people want to know what happened . . . Why we didn't come here for so long . . .'

Ben didn't answer.

'You know what,' said Lauren. 'I think you just tell the truth. Say you weren't so close, all of you, for a few years there, but that before Lady Wilde died you were all reconciled. People aren't as interested as you think they are. They just wanna hear an explanation that makes sense so they can get on with eating and drinking. Tell them the truth.'

'The truth,' Cord said, and she turned away from them both so they wouldn't see her smile, for how could she explain to them? 'A version of the truth.'

Four of Althea's carers from Driftwood popped down the lane to drink to her memory, and added considerably to the party as two of them were Polish and brought vodka. Jan from the village, Mrs Gage's daughter, brought her three children, and the vicar and his wife came too.

'It's lovely to be here,' said the vicar, Reverend James. He was an ex-trader from the City, a rangy, rather intense man who'd found God, retired early and been ordained a few years ago. 'I used to run along the beach and wonder who this house belonged to. Then I'd hear stories from the older villagers about the Bosky and the famous Wildflowers and I'd feel rather sad no one was using it.'

Cord offered him a sausage roll. 'We didn't come here for years. Things were rather difficult after my father died, for various reasons.'

'I heard something like that,' said the vicar, and his long ascetic face grew thoughtful. 'Here's a thing I keep meaning to tell you and your brother since your mother's funeral. Your father's first acting job was at the vicarage. Did you know that?'

'I didn't,' said Cord. 'What was it?'

'*A Midsummer Night's Dream*, funnily enough. He was Bottom. The comedic role, rather unusual to give it to a fourteen-year-old, wouldn't you say? But I suppose it was during the war. The vicar then was a remarkable man. He took your father in after his aunt left from what I understand, and sponsored him through drama school. He took lots of photographs, of the plays and life in the village – there's one of your father with the girl who played Titania, lovely thing she is . . . And a terrific one where they're all flat on the ground and a Messerschmitt is flying over during a rehearsal.'

'Good God. Sorry – good grief. How fascinating.'

He smiled. 'His name was Reverend Goudge. I have the diary and the photographs together, you and your brother must come up some time and look through them. In fact – here. I brought one with me.' He patted his pockets. 'A lovely shot of him and his mother, too, I think?' He pulled out a shiny photograph, a young, unbearably handsome boy, tanned and wearing an old-fashioned costume, with his arm around a woman. Her dark hair was pinned up wildly, falling down around her face, and her mouth was wide open as she laughed, showing her fine cheekbones, her clear eyes, fringed with dark lashes. She had a paisley shawl tied in a careless knot around her neck, and she was gripping him proudly. Both of them were smiling at the camera: he with lowered head, slightly embarrassed, but beaming, she looking at him with a huge grin.

'That was his aunt,' said Cord. 'She's beautiful – I never realised. She's young, too—' She peered at the photograph. 'She was young. I always thought she was old when she looked after him. Fifties, sixties.' And something began scratching away at her again, something that troubled her whenever she thought of Dinah, though she couldn't have isolated it and understood it as such.

'His aunt. I see. They're very alike.'

'Aren't they?'

487

'Yes,' said this nice vicar. He took the photo and turned it over. 'Look. He's written on the back, "The Wildflowers, Ant and Dinah, 1942." Isn't that interesting.'

'Dinah Wilde, that's her. Actually, she was his great-aunt,' added Cord, but at the same time she found herself thinking, *What does it matter?* Family titles, what did they actually mean, as long as one loved and was loved in return?

'Well, come up soon and have a look.'

'Yes, please. I plan to come down here for weekends and so on, and my brother and my nieces too. It's all of ours, really. These days I'm more likely to be away for . . .' She trailed off. 'For work,' she added, and it sounded so strange to say it again.

'Ah, well, yes,' he said, rather eagerly. 'I didn't want to mention it . . . My wife and I saw you as Dido last month at the Bath Festival. You were quite wonderful.'

'Oh, gosh—' she began, still hardwired over the past twenty years to feel a mortification when confronted with someone who'd heard her sing. And then she stopped, and remembered. *It worked. It works again.* For it wasn't as romantic or dramatically satisfying as saying she'd Found her Voice, despite the narrative of numerous newspaper articles about her return to performing. It was that a part of her had been fixed, by an operation in which two men in blue scrubs talked to her and cut open her throat and three days afterwards she could sing again and a month later her voice was better than it had been for years. It was scientific. One could fix this problem, but not others.

'It was sublime,' the Reverend James was saying. 'Quite the best version we've heard. We came up from Dorset especially for it. I was there at the Proms that night, you see, all those years ago – I've often felt rather privileged to have been there at the beginning of your career. Yes, it's something we've often remarked on, Allison and I. A great privilege.'

The tip of his nose was rather pink. He smiled at her, awkwardly.

'Gosh. Well, thank you. But the operation was only four months ago – I'm still not quite back to where I'd like to be.'

'My dear, it was a great honour, to hear you sing again,' Reverend James said. 'Come up to the vicarage soon.' Then, touching her arm lightly and, in that abstract way of vicars and the Royal Family, giving a small nod, he moved seamlessly on to another guest.

Cord turned away, to catch the sun just beginning to fade, amber and silvery gold ripples threading through the sky. An elderly guest, one of Althea's cast mates on *Hartman Hall*, begged her attention, wanting to ask about her singing too, and so Cord answered her questions politely, settling her into a chair and fetching her a glass of wine.

As she returned with the glass she saw Iris, at the bottom of the porch steps, chatting to someone, an older man. She put her hand on her niece's shoulder.

'How are you, Iris dear?' she asked, tenderly, and her niece smiled at her with a look of familiarity that took Cord's breath away. 'This is such a lovely party, isn't it?'

Iris was looking at her a little strangely. 'Yes, of course – Aunt Cord, can I introduce you to someone? He's an old friend of Dad's – he's the one who lives in the basement at the moment – I can't remember if you know him or not. Hamish? Hamish Lowther?'

Oh, come on, Cord thought, as she glanced around for her brother, so she could give him a hard stare. But he was nowhere to be seen and so she shook the proffered hand of the man before her.

'Hamish Lowther. Well, hello,' she said.

'Well. Hello to you too.'

Hamish folded her small hand inside both of his, and looked at her. He was older – of course, the blonde beauty of his youth grizzled to grey, his willowy figure gone, more thickset, his shoulders broad, his face lined. He suited middle age, in fact. His dark grey eyes smiled at her as he carried on holding her hand.

'Cordelia,' he said, in his low, tremendous voice. 'It's wonderful to see you.'

Her skin prickled, the old instinct kicking in, telling her danger was near. But she ignored it, with great effort. She smiled at him; she found she couldn't stop smiling. 'What on earth—'

He interrupted, and leaned towards her. 'Listen, before you get cross with me – your mother wanted me to be here. Was quite insistent. She gave Ben a list of people, apparently – I wouldn't have come otherwise, promise—'

Cord was torn between amusement at his obvious fear of her displeasure and sadness. *I really did do a great job of pushing him away, didn't I?*

She thought of the men over the years with whom she'd managed to escape becoming too entangled. That was how she'd always thought of it – an enmeshing, becoming trapped in some net from which there was no escape. She looked at him, her fingers still clasping his.

'But it's lovely to see you. Mumma loved you. Thank you. I'm glad you're here.'

'I'm glad to be here. It's very strange, being back.'

'I know. But you get used to it,' she told him. She looked around. The soft light from the lanterns glowed as the sun slipped behind the molten silver sea. 'You have a daughter, don't you? How is she doing?'

'Amabel's very well, thanks. She's training to be an optician.'

'An *optician*?'

'I know,' said Hamish. 'An actual job. I'm so proud of her.'

'Good for her – but Hamish, how old is she? Isn't she about twelve?'

'She's twenty-five, Cordy.'

'Jesus,' said Cord, automatically. 'Sorry. So she didn't want to be an actor then.'

He was still holding her hand. He shook his head, solemnly. 'No. I think it's a pretty stupid occupation, if you ask me. No job security. Sends you mad.'

'You gave it up, didn't you? I assume you're the Charles Trenet-loving accountant who lives in Ben's basement?'

'Yes, I am,' he said, smiling. 'I'm actually being interviewed on the radio next week. I'm the only actor-turned-accountant alive, apparently. They want to know what's wrong with me and why you'd give it up.'

'You were successful, though, that's why they're interested.'

'I didn't want that life. I was changing.' His jaw was tight. 'It's hard to explain.'

'I can understand why you'd leave it behind.' She looked down at their entwined fingers. 'I really can.'

'You need to understand something else, too – I'm moving into a flat of my own, next month. I'm not a permanent house guest there. Just – you need to know that.'

She pulled her fingers away from his. 'OK.'

'It's awfully good to see you again, Cord,' he said, and she gave a soft, broken laugh.

'You too. Oh – oh, dear, you too.' Already she ached for the warmth of his hands again. Oh, the comfort of him, someone who knew her, who'd known them all for years, who wouldn't, couldn't, be shocked by the Wildes and their stories . . . someone who understood her absolutely, knew what she was like – it was lovely. It wasn't something to be feared. It was immensely comforting. She said, with an effort at hostessing, 'How's — how's Sunita?'

'I hear she's fine. We divorced about five years ago. I brought her here once, you know, to visit your parents. Your father was very keen on her.'

'Well, that applies to many people. Many people here, in fact,' said Cord, waving her hand across the assembled gathering, and he exhaled, with a shout of laughter.

'I can believe it. Dear old Tony.'

She smiled at him again, joy bubbling up inside her, and Hamish gave a short, sharp intake of breath.

'Oh, Cordelia. So, Ben says you've seen a bit more of him lately.'

'Oh, yes. And my nieces. And I've been down here more. Spending time with Mumma.'

'I'm so glad. I know it hurt him.' He said it without reproach. 'It must have been awfully hard for you. What changed, do you think?'

She shook her head slowly. 'It's a long story. For another time.'

'I'm sure. Of course.'

There was a silence, comfortable, sad. Cord took a deep breath.

'Do you think one evening we could go for a drink? Catch up, see — see each other again?'

Hamish stared at her, seriously. 'Maybe,' he said, and shrugged his shoulders, though he was smiling. 'Maybe that'd be a good idea. Are you sure?'

'I think it'd be a good idea,' she said and he moved against her, so that he covered her, so that he blocked out the rest of the party, so that they were enclosed in their own space, and she didn't move.

He said, under his breath, '*I* think it'd be a good idea.'

'I'm busy, though,' she said, age-old instinct kicking in, and she ducked out, away from his shadow. 'I – I've got lots of work on. I'm in Italy next week, Turin, Milan, Florence, and then I have to go to Salzburg in August . . . You see, I had this operation, earlier in the year and I – I have to sing now. It's been years since I could and I've got lots of work, Hamish—'

Hamish nodded. 'I heard. Darling, I heard all about it. Of course I did. Ben tells me everything.'

Darling. The word, on his lips, was like a caress, not like the *darling*s that cluttered her parents' conversations. *Darling.*

He said, slowly, 'I read the *Observer* interview. I saw a thing on Facebook that someone put up about your first concert. I saw that review in *The Times*. I check in with Ben most days about you. I really have very little to do at the moment, you know, out of tax return season, apart from follow you and what you're up to. In a non-sinister way,' he added, laconically. 'Very important you understand that, Cord.'

She gave a small laugh.

'I know you've got lots going on. The thing is, I'll be here. When you want that drink. Or – anything else.'

'Anything else?'

'Oh, I'm sure there's a plethora of burly baritones in opera houses around the world hopeful for your favours.' He shook with laughter. 'But be very clear, I'm in my mid-fifties, I have one dodgy knee, my eyesight's terrible, but I will track all of them down and fight them for your hand. Whilst wearing a large curly moustache and a cloak.'

She laughed. Out of the corner of her eye she saw her brother appear. 'How can I say no?'

'Hi, Ben,' said Hamish.

'Hamish,' said Ben, and they clasped hands. 'I'll catch up with you in a bit. Cord—' He touched her arm, and she turned to her brother, still smiling. Her face froze at his expression. 'What's up?'

'Come with me,' he said, nodding at Hamish, but almost tugging at her arm. 'The beach hut. I was in there—' He drew her away, and they went down the steps together. 'I was in there just having one last look round before they take it all down and I pulled off the Flowers and Stones rules, and I found – I found something.'

They were alone on the grassy, sandy expanse between the house and the huts. He handed her a well-known piece of paper, the rules so carefully written out by Cord all those years ago for herself and Mads. The letters were faded to brown, the paper cracking with age. 'Turn it over,' he said. 'Turn it over, look.' He gripped her hands. 'Don't you remember her, coming back? Do you remember her giving it to you? Did he ever see it?' He rubbed his face.

Cord held the rules with the note scrawled on the back, scanning the fine, looping black characters that had faded almost to nothing. 'Good grief. This—' Every hair on her neck seemed to prickle. 'The angel – that's what Mumma was trying to remember. So she did come back.' She blinked, trying to think.

'Do you remember her?'

'I don't know . . . She had wide patterned trousers on. Flowers, they were covered in flowers.' She laid a hand on her brother's arm. 'Ben, she told me to sing.' She was nodding. 'She said we were the Wildflowers. It was her. Do you remember?' She winced, the tiny slivers of memory glinting in her mind's eye – patterned trousers, messy hair, her father's hands white at the knuckles as he clutched the angel again and . . . and Mads – a small girl who must have been Mads – laughing . . . laughing till she hiccupped as they staggered in and out of the grasses and flowers as the sun moved across the sky, towards the sea. But Ben was there, or was he ill? Or was it another time? For they had played Flowers and Stones so often it was impossible to remember . . . They had played games all summer, every summer, so how to recall one hour among so many golden days?

Cord shook her head. 'I'm sorry, darling. But I'm glad we found it. It explains something, doesn't it?'

Ben nodded, and he scratched his chin. 'Some things. Not everything.'

'What do we do? Do we leave the angel there?'

The stiff, crackling old paper felt as though it might crumble at any moment, like ancient texts exposed to the air after years sealed in a tomb. She looked down at the childish writing, turned it over.

Ben said, 'I don't know. Probably not.'

'We can't just leave her there. She's not ours.'

'She is ours, in a way.'

'Ben – if what's in this letter is true . . . We have to tell someone we have the angel. The British Museum, or something. Oh, gosh, Mumma would like this, though, drama at the wake.' Cord smiled. 'And we don't know. There's so much we still don't know.'

'That's it. That's it exactly. We know some of it, not all of it.' Ben took the letter, and folded it up. 'Let's not think about it now, let's worry about it tomorrow.'

'We have to give her back, Ben,' said Cord, firmly.

'Maybe. Yes.' He nodded, their eyes meeting. 'Yes, Cordy. Listen, before I forget – I keep meaning to tell you Mumma wanted Hamish here. She said he had to come, it was the one thing she really insisted on. I hope you don't mind—'

'She knew exactly what she was doing,' said Cord, trying to keep a bubble of joy from making her laugh. 'I don't mind. I'm very glad, in fact.'

'That's almost a declaration of love, coming from you, Cordy.'

She nudged him affectionately. Ben shut the door on the beach hut and put his arm around his sister, and together they walked back up the winding path to the house, Cord plucking flowers and leaves as she went: poppies, little red knotgrass, lavender, honeysuckle. The Bosky rose up in front of them as they came to the top of the path. The coloured lights hanging from the roof swayed with the gentlest motion in the summer breeze. Behind them, the sea licked the shore. It would do so all night, and in the morning it would still be there, water gently lapping at the land. Nothing would change.

'It's your house,' Ben said in her ear.

'It's ours,' Cord said, hugging him firmly. She was here, with them all. She looked up at Venus, firmly shining, a pinprick of platinum in the pale blue night sky.

'Goodbye, my loves,' she said, quietly, and she scattered the flowers she had picked, letting them fall around her feet, and Ben's. The scent of them hung for the briefest moment in the air, and then was gone.

II

1972

Miss Cordelia Wilde, six years old, sat gloomily in the window seat staring out at the cloudless sky. Laid neatly next to her on the floor were her shrimping net, her new blue spade with the wooden handle, and a jar with the little crab that she and Daddy had caught the previous day when they'd arrived, hot and sweaty after the long car journey from London. The crab was not moving. It had not moved since she'd brought it back.

'It's not *fair*,' she said again, for the tenth time. 'Why can't I go for a swim yet?'

'Life isn't fair,' said her father, not looking up from his paper. 'It's utterly unfair, as you'll discover. However, as I have said to you now about fifty times, old girl, the moment I've finished me coffee and me paper I'll have a shave and we can go out.'

'I can go swimming on my own.'

'You're six years old,' said Daddy. 'You haven't been in the sea for a year. You can't go on your own. Even someone as intrepid as you, my sweet girl.'

Cord picked up her square of toast from the cushion, and chewed on it. 'It's not fair.'

'Look, ' said her mother, turning the page of her book. 'While Ben's got his temperature he's staying in bed and you can go to the beach with Daddy. He's nearly finished his cornflakes, look, darling.' Tony didn't move. 'Haven't you, darling?' She shoved her husband's chair with one slender foot.

497

'What? Oh. Yes.' Tony's head appeared above the paper, and he looked at his wife, and then patted her calf. He leaped out of his chair. 'My dearest, you are ravishing this morning,' he told her, spreading his arms wide and then, with a quick glance in the mirror at the top of the stairs, tightening his cravat. 'You make me the happiest of men.'

'Stop talking like you're in a play,' said Cord, disgusted, but her mother was laughing.

'Oh, your highness,' she said, putting down her coffee. 'You flatter me, and I am not worthy of your affection.' She stood up, and he caught her in his arms, and they waltzed for a little. Cord watched, half appalled, half entranced, at their figures whirling in the darkness of the kitchen-diner, Mumma's bright green silk dressing gown swinging behind her, a second after their steps.

'Shall we take a turn upon the verandah, fair maiden? The moon glows tonight, soft silver like your burnished tresses.'

'Which I never understood,' said Althea, sitting back down again and picking up her novel. 'He's saying her hair is grey, isn't he? Jolly rude. She's only nineteen.'

'Well, you were only nineteen when you played her,' he said.

'Still, she's not an aged crone, is my point, darling. Now, off you go. Please, remove that crab from my sight.'

'Absolutely,' said Tony, and he drained the last dregs of coffee and disappeared for a few minutes, and when he came back, shaved and rubbing his palms together with excitement, he held out his hand to his daughter, who scrambled off the window seat with a huge grin, gripping her father's fingers. So they left, Tony tutting at the soft rumbling of the porch as Cord thundered down the steps.

'There's a loose board somewhere there,' he said, and he picked her up and swung her around and she screamed with

498

delight. 'Come on, love. Let's open the beach hut and put our swimmers on.'

It happened like this. Her father and she had swum in the sea, drying quickly in the scorching heat of the mid-morning sun, and Tony was having 'forty winks – don't tell your mother' in the chair on the porch, handkerchief over his face. Cord had found a nice boy called Tom to play with who had an engaging mongrel called Tugie with fluffy brown ears who kept digging himself into holes and had to be rescued. They were making a complicated castle with a vast moat, ignoring the encroaching tide and the still-lifeless crab, which she had placed in a home-made pool. She was absorbed in what she was doing, singing softly to herself, when a shadow covered her, and she looked up.

A woman was standing in front of her, holding a little girl by the hand. The little girl's face was stained with tears, and she wore a mulish expression.

'Well, good morning. And may I say you have a beautiful voice,' said the lady.

Cord scratched her face, embarrassed, as though caught doing something naughty.

'My friend would like to play with you, Cordelia,' the old lady went on. 'Would you let her?'

Cord stared at the girl. 'All right then, but you can't touch my castle. You'll have to build something else, please, if you don't mind. Thank you so much.'

'I don't want to play with you,' said the girl, her small face creasing into a furious snarl. 'I want to play on my own.' But she looked hungrily at the marvellous new wooden-handled spade.

'There you go,' said the old lady, and she smiled at Cord. 'Thank you, dear. Very kind. What's your name, little one?' she said to the other girl, who was twisting her long, silvery hair into a spiral.

'It's Madeleine,' said the girl.

'Where do you live, where's your mummy and daddy?'

'My mummy's in the ground because she died and my daddy's still asleep and I don't have anyone to play with. There.'

She pointed at the large old house with turrets that stood behind the Bosky. Cordelia, at six not yet entirely confident with distances and neighbourly relations, stared at it.

'Our house is there,' she said, jabbing a figure in the direction of the Bosky. 'That's my daddy there. He's asleep too.' She stared at the little girl. 'How old are you? *I* am six.'

'I'm actually seven,' said the girl. 'Seven,' she repeated for emphasis, swinging her hair about.

'Your hair is silvery,' said Cord, surprised. 'Not grey at all.'

'What does that mean?'

'Nothing,' she said. 'It's funny, but I can't explain it.'

The old woman loomed high over them, watching them, then she crouched down. Cord noticed her knees creaked and clicked. She was old, but not as old as Bethan in the village's granny, who didn't move, not even to speak, and who had a face like an apple left too long in the fruit bowl, yellow and wrinkly. This old lady had something about her still, and her tanned, weather-beaten face was watchful and alert. She had long, brown fingers and she clasped Cord's shoulder. She knelt on the sand, in her rather loud floral trousers. She had a pointy face, and her hair was short and shingled. Her eyes were green, and danced. She looked, in short, like a witch, only a rather nice sort of witch. Cord smiled involuntarily at her.

'What's your name?' she said.

'Oh, I'm too old to have a name now,' she said. 'You're Cordelia, aren't you?'

'Yes,' Cord said again.

'Look after Madeleine, won't you?' said the old lady. 'Be her friend, now I've introduced you two. She doesn't have many friends, and she's not like you. You'll be all right, I can tell.'

'Yes, OK then,' said Cord, not understanding much of this.

'It was lovely to see you, Cordelia. You should sing more. Sing and sing till your throat hurts, then carry on singing. It's the only way. Will you remember that?'

'Yes.' Cord thought for a moment. 'How do you know who I am?'

'I've always known about you.' The woman shifted the bag on her shoulder. 'You're the Wildflowers and that's your house and it's a place to be happy and be kind. Don't forget that.'

'We're the Wildflowers,' Cord said, nodding in agreement. 'It *is* our house.'

And they stared at each other for a moment, in perfect understanding, though one was dying and would be gone by the end of the year, and the other would forget the meeting in a few short hours.

'Listen, Cord, dear,' the old lady said. She put her hand on Cord's shoulder. 'Can you – will you do something for me?'

Cord shrugged. 'Course.'

'Can you give this package to your father? It's for him.'

'He's over there—' Cord pointed with her finger. 'He's asleep.'

'I know, I saw. I – I don't want to wake him. So will you give this to him? It's very important.'

'What is it?'

'It's for the house. You tell him, I took it away but it didn't belong there, so I brought it back. It's to look after him. I always said it was. Now, don't forget.'

She handed her the parcel, with a note wrapped around it, tied in string.

'Yes, of course,' said Cord politely, but already a little bored. 'Thank you,' she added automatically because that seemed to make grown-ups shut up or go away. 'Thank you very much for the delicious – thanks.'

The old woman chuckled to herself, then heaved herself to her feet, shaking the sand from her wide trousers. 'Thank you, dear Cord. Now, I will be off and away.'

'Where are you going?'

'I am going back to my home. I wanted to see this place one last time. Thank you again, dear. Don't forget, now, will you?'

Then she was gone, walking slowly towards the beach hut, and Cord turned to the mutinous little girl beside her, suddenly feeling wild and carefree and absurdly happy, not sure why. 'Come on,' she said with a gurgle of pleasure in her voice. 'Let's make up a new game.'

The girl's dirty face was suspicious. 'A new game?'

'Yes,' said Cord, decisively patting the heavy little parcel on her lap. 'Let's call it – hmmm . . . Let's call it Flowers and Stones. Yes, and we'll have scores, for the different flowers and stones. Can you write? Sorry, what's your name again?'

'Madeleine.' The girl shook her head. 'I sort of can spell words but I hate writing them out. I hate practising letters, too.'

'You can do the spelling then.' Cord jumped up, and the old lady's parcel fell out of her lap on to the ground, the twine and the note sliding off the package, the old lady already forgotten. 'Oh, yes. I need to give this to . . . Now, let's go to the beach hut. Here, come with me. I'll write out the rules, I'm really good at three things, hula-hooping, handwriting and blowing bubbles with bubblegum. And singing. That old lady's right, I'm really good at singing!'

They didn't see the old lady climbing the path back up from the beach, and the arthritic salute she gave the old house as she passed by. They didn't see her gingerly ascend the steps of the porch one more time to stare at the man fast asleep there. Nor that she touched him, very gently, long thin fingers grazing his forehead so that he shifted slightly, swatting the hand away as though it were a fly.

They didn't see her bowed head, her puckered mouth, and the way she vanished past the profusion of wild flowers beside the house, nor the same hands picking ragwort, knapweed, dried grasses, lavender. She got into a waiting cab, wrapping the flowers up in her handkerchief as the car drove away down the uneven lane, drove her far away from them.

She was a long way away by the time the rules for Flower and Stones were being finalised, scrawled on to the back of a piece of paper Cord had found and fixed to the wall of the beach hut by piercing the paper on a rusting nail.

FLAWRS AND STONES
THESE ARE THE ROWLES

Blue flawRs: 5 POyNts
Red flawrs: 8 PoyNts
Pink Flawrs: 10 poynts

Gold/yllow flAwrs: 100 Poynts
GRAy Stohne: 5 poynts
Yellow stonhe: 8 poynts
Dark red stoneh: 10 Poynts
Black STOnhe witH Veyns: 100 poynts

Shells: No POYNTS At ALL
You Lose ALL Your PoYNTS

They spent the rest of the morning playing Flowers and Stones – a surprisingly easy and hilarious game where you put Daddy's old sunhat from the beach hut over your eyes and ran into the wild-flower meadow below the house, gathering as many flowers and stones as you could while the other person counted to ten. Madeleine's hair was covered in leaves and petals, and Cord was breathless with laughing and yelling instructions, and it wasn't until Madeleine's father appeared, curt, bad-tempered, that she abruptly vanished back to her house without even saying goodbye.

Cord closed the beach hut and walked back to the house, very pleased with herself but rather exhausted. At the foot of the steps to the porch she saw her father, rubbing his chin and stretching his arms into fists and she paused – what was it she had to tell him? The old lady – that strange old lady. She'd told her to sing. And wild flowers. They were good.

'Hello, Cordy, did you have fun on the beach?'

The parcel. The figure. Cord stood stock-still. 'Yes – oh, Daddy, wait a minute.'

She scrambled back down through the flowers and the gorse towards the beach huts and, hunting desperately, crawled around outside the beach hut, looking for it. Oh, dear – oh, dear, the trouble she'd get into—

But the figure was not to be found, and her knees ached, and her arm hurt where she'd scraped it along the side of the beach hut, sprinkling it with splinters like iron filings. She stood up and stubbed her toe, exclaiming, and just as tears formed in her eyes she looked down and saw the little angel with its huge wings and big bird eyes and the owls on either side of it. Cord scooped her up and stared at her. The stone was warm though the sand under the hut was cool. She carried her carefully back to the house.

'Here – Daddy.' She put the angel in his lap. Her father looked at it, casually, and then froze.

'Where did you get this?' A vein throbbed in his tanned cheek. He turned towards her, his eyes huge.

'At the beach.'

'Who gave it to you at the beach?'

'A lady. Can I go inside, I'm really hungry.'

'Cord – little one?' He took her hands. 'Can you remember about the lady? And about this angel? It's very important.' He stroked her cheek.

'Of course,' she said, standing up straight. Though her stomach was grumbling, she tried her best to please her darling daddy. 'An old lady gave it to me by the beach hut. I was playing with that girl from the house down the way. The one whose daddy you don't like. She appeared, anyway. She had big feet, and the pattern on her trousers was flowers in brown and orange and green and yellow – it was quite nice actually.' Cord scrunched up her eyes, trying to remember. 'She said she wanted me to give this to you. I said, you should give it to him, and she said you were asleep and she wanted me to. And something about Wildflowers. She said this was for the house.' The smell of chicken pie drifted out through the kitchen window and her mouth watered – actually watered, so it was right, what Ben said, that had never happened before. 'We played a game . . . Daddy, I'm really hungry. Is lunch—'

'Darling . . . please, can you finish telling?'

'About singing too. She said I should sing and sing till my throat hurts, then sing some more.'

He was clutching the angel so tightly his hands were white. 'Cord – well done, darling. What else? Can you remember what else?'

'She said it was to look after us or something.' Cord stood on one foot. 'Daddy – please, I'm so hungry.'

Daddy was smiling. 'Yes, of course. There – there wasn't anything else?'

Cord thought for a moment. 'Well, yes, I'm trying to tell you. We invented a game called Flowers and Stones,' she said eventually, because that was what she'd been wanting to tell him, she was sure. 'I wrote the rules, I put them up on the beach-hut wall. I wrote them out myself, all the spelling and everything. That's what I was going to say. I want you to come and look at them.'

Her father kissed her gently on the forehead. 'That's wonderful. Flowers and Stones, eh?'

'Yep.' Cord drew herself up. 'Maybe we can play it after lunch. I wrote the rules. I stuck them up on the nail,' she repeated, not quite sure why but she thought it was important. 'Can I go and see Ben, can I tell him about the game, can I?'

But her father wasn't really listening; he was turning the angel over and over in his hands. So Cord, tired already of his strange mood, ran inside to find Ben, to tell him she'd met the strange girl from next door and she was all right really, and they'd invented a game and Ben was going to love it, love it, only she had to go first when they played it.

Her father watched her go, heard her thundering steps rattle the stairs. He sat on the porch looking up at the rose climbing along the side of the house, and inside to the warm honey-coloured wooden walls. He looked at the angel again.

'It must have been,' he said, and, pulling away at the Virginia creeper that sneaked under the roof and along the guttering, he hung the angel above the front door on the hook that was still there even after all these years. He said nothing to anyone about it, though after lunch he went to lie down, and the sounds of bombs screaming, louder than hell, began in his ears, and when he closed his eyes all he could see were faces from the past, and he didn't know how to stop them, how to stop the noises or the people from leaving, from going, though you cried out and begged them to stay . . .

It began that day, his slow decline, and he battled it for twenty and more years, trying to stay ahead of it, always looking over his shoulder for the moment it would overwhelm him, until at last it did. As he held the angel in his hands that windy, bright morning and hung her back up above the house, he knew she must have returned to him, that this was her way of saying, I am alive, I am OK. He saw then, that he had what she hadn't been able to have – security, stability, success, a measure of sanity. He had given his own children a childhood both he and she would have dreamed of having.

Later, as he watched Cord drag Ben, blinking in the sunlight, down to the beach hut to play this new game, and as he heard their screams as they ran helplessly around in circles, falling blind into the flowers and crying with laughter, he felt that for that one afternoon at least he was doing all right.

The letter she wrote him hung in the beach hut, words facing the wall, as the rules of the game grew ever fainter with the passing of the years. No one read it, no one saw what she had written, until many years later that little girl and her brother, all grown up, took it down from the wall.

Dearest, dear Ant,

Years ago I left you. I took the angel and promised I would bring her back.

Here she is – hang her up above the house again in her rightful place. The Assyrians believed we should bury little figures around the threshold and the throne. To protect the house, to guard from evil. I say hang her high.

I am sorry for everything. I stole things, to get money. To survive. I didn't steal the angel, though Daphne always thought I did. I told you the truth all those years ago which is that I bought her honestly for once though I knew her real worth and I suspect if you knew how old and valuable she really is you'd feel obliged to return her to the museum, where she'd be locked behind glass and stared at all day. No. I want her to protect you, instead.

I found her on a wayside stall, coming back from a dig, just before I got the telegram calling me back to you. I bought her from an old man who had a lizard in a jar. He gave me pomegranate juice to drink. She had been in his house for years. His sons were tall and strong, his family was safe, he said.

I knew the moment I saw her that she was old — much older than Nineveh, probably four thousand years or so. She would have been the greatest archaeological find of my career. Maybe they'd have named her after me. The Wilde Panel. But I kept her, I liked her, I wanted her to keep us safe. And she did.

Let those children be free. Let them make mistakes, let them be themselves, do not try to train them to bend one way or another. Wildflowers must be allowed to grow how and where they like. If you give them a childhood full of love and warmth, then they will weather whatever comes.

I decided when I went that a clean break would be better and so it must be. I knew I was dragging you down with me, filling your life with lies — I missed you so much when you went to school, it quite undid me, but it was for the right reasons, the same reasons that I left you. I find being normal rather hard. I'm not suited to family life.

But oh, Ant, to sit out there with you once more. To point out the stars, to talk about Julia and the war and the chickens and the bicycle and dear Reverend Goudge and the wild flowers and the times we had — if I could have had one more evening with you . . . For you were my dearest delight, my dear boy. In that terrible time we were safe, and happy for a while, were we not?

Dear boy, try to be happy. What endures after you are gone is not the striving, but the happy memories, the moments of sunshine, the warmth and the feeling of safety and joy in a loved one's company.

I am sorry, dear Ant. I loved you very much. You did know that, didn't you? And looking after you really was the greatest privilege of my life.

Hang her up high.

Your loving great-aunt,

Dinah Alexandra Wilde

The stone goddess made as an amulet for an ancient, long-forgotten king was hung back up in its place, above the door, by Tony that very afternoon. She remained there for forty years, becoming more and more tangled in with the wild flowers that slowly smothered the house until, one summer's day, she fell to the ground. Someone picked her up, and so was set in motion the train of events which the goddess needed to finally, after all those years, help her mend the house, and its family.

Acknowledgements

Thanks to everyone at Headline for the joy of knowing I am in such safe hands. Especial thanks to Sara Adams, Viviane Basset, Katie Brown, Yeti Lambregts, Frances Doyle, Georgina Moore, Becky Bader and most of all, in every way, Mari Evans, who continues to make me feel every day like I am the luckiest author in the world and for whom no thanks are adequate.

Thank you to everyone at Curtis Brown, especially Lucia Rae, Emma Bailey and Melissa Pimentel, with a big thank you to Jonathan Lloyd who buoys me up and was an enormous help in the early stages of this book.

Thank you to Mary Nelson for all her information and advice about singers and singing; to Simon Mulligan and Nicole Wilson, and to Jo Roberts-Miller, for her help and general greatness. I love you Jo-Jo. Thanks to Rebecca Folland for being a reassuring early reader. And thank you to Katie Cousins for accompanying me to Studland Beach, days out forever.

I'd like to say a big thanks to all the amazing readers and book bloggers who have supported my last few books and have let me know you liked them. Thank you for being so generous and kind.

Thanks to my mum for her support and to my magic brilliant dad for being my hero over this last awful year, and my lovely sister Caroline to whom this book is dedicated. And to Prêt à Manger for feeding us.

Most of all thanks to my two precious girls, Cora and Martha, for giving me joy I never thought I could have and finally to my Chris, because no matter how hard I lean on you, you stay strong.